The King's Son

Teresa Ann Winton

The King's Son

Scripture taken from the Holy Bible, King James Version, Cambridge, 1769. Poetry also inspired by the King James Bible.

ISBN: 978-1-7344627-0-8

Cover design and illustrations by Valentina Burimenko
Interior design and layout by Ian Winton
Editing by Ian Winton
Author photograph by Craft Photographic Gallery

Dedication

Ian, the time I've had with you—chatting about the plot, revising scenes, and all the crazy stuff in between—was by far the greatest part of publishing this book. We've had a grand time haven't we, especially the hysterical laughter over the original ice monster's descriptions. Even as I write this I'm still laughing! This book is for you! I love you!

Table of Contents

N
W
E
S
Brightonvale
Romanague
Scarlet's Peak
La' Fleure'
Lorlea Mar
Abbystone
The Village of Greyflow
Set me as a seal upon thine heart, for love is strong as death.
- Song of Songs -
Londonmere

Isle of Wisteria
rdens of Fairnesse
Evernora
Perldore Castle
Fairdell Manor
Kaishore Ocean
Tin Island
Firegate Castle
Oakmoor Manor
Oakhollow Forest
rblemist Chapel
Larkfair Gardens
Crystalhaven Lighthouse
Summergate Meadow
Beauport

The Kingdom of Evernora

Jonathan Geoffrey Sainesbury founded the Kingdom of Evernora in 927 and was the first established king. Evernora is a country bordering five other kingdoms, Brightonvale, Romanague, Abbystone, Londonmere, and Beauport. The country of La' Fleuré lies to the West of Evernora. Kaishore Ocean flows East of Evernora with Oakhollow Forest close to the shoreline.

The terrain of Evernora is chiefly valleys, hills, and mountains. Scarlet's Peak can be seen for miles showcasing red poppies dancing delightfully all summer. Evernora's land is rich with fields of grain and livestock. Whales, otters, seals, and puffins can be spotted in Kaishore Ocean. The sandy white shoreline enchants many when the sun's golden rays beam across the ocean's waves.

Oakhollow Forest is vast, luminous, and thriving. Its canopy is overshadowed by oak, redbud, and pine. Twinkling lights bursting through their crowns allow for a mosaic of plants to rule the moist and fertile bottom layer. A few of the trees, ferns, and potpourri of flowers

—growing in a sprinkled and disorderly fashion—are embraced by curling vines. A medley of animal noises, predominantly those of foraging animals, brighten up the forest and form a chaotic orchestra with the occasional sounds of birds gliding in the air. An ancient tree tunnel is the centerpiece of the spacious forest; a serene seclusion where the people of Evernora share secrets, joys, sorrows, and prayer.

The people of Evernora experience four seasons with plenty of rainfall all year round. The winter season is especially cold, however, and snow can blanket the land unexpectedly overnight. Blizzards are rare, but when they occur, the people of Evernora do not venture into Oakhollow Forest or even get near Kaishore Ocean. The legend of Havís, the ice creature, terrifies even the bravest knight.

Havís is a small core with spikes all over his body. When he rises up out of the ocean during a blizzard, snow and ice coalesce around his body, increasing his size. Once on land, few can escape his detection. His lofty height enables him to peer over tree tops and dash swiftly toward prey with his long legs and wide feet. He snatches his victims with his hands or injures them with his spikes.

Gregory Roland Sainesbury was crowned king on November 16, 1380 after his father passed away from a brief illness. King Sainesbury is revered as the most noble, discerning king in all of the land. He is a faithful friend and protector of the destitute, outcast, misunderstood, and orphaned in the community. His generosity, compassion, and deep spiritual values govern all that he does and are the foundation of his rule as king.

The king's castle, Firegate, is on a hill surrounded by luscious green grass and statuesque evergreens. Massive displays of red, ivory, and pink scented rose blossoms grow over the wide arched doors and windows of the castle's exterior. The majestic structure stands forty feet tall with several turrets showcasing the red bricks. The walls inside the spacious rooms are painted with red rose blossoms and dual hearts are carved at the top of each crest in the vaulted ceilings.

The opulent architecture portrays the king's love for spirituality, beauty, and art. Its esteemed interiors echo the sorrows, defeats, the victories, and the memories of all those whose feet walked the halls of the king's lavishly arrayed interiors.

The Taviks are barbaric people known for plundering and raiding. They originated in the country of Romanague, but are a nomadic people. In the fall of 1035, the raiders made their first attack. Elgrist, a town in the country of Abbystone, was invaded by the pillagers while the people were worshiping. The believers looked on, terrified as the thieves took treasured offerings and a few captives. The vast majority of the Taviks earned a meager living by fishing. They created longships, a type of narrow, open vessel with oars and a square sail. The swift boat allowed the predators to navigate coastal and inland waters and land on beaches.

In the Isle of Wisteria lives Princess Pearlensia, a captivating unicorn princess. Her kingdom is a floral meadow centered on Kaishore Ocean. Princess Pearlensia's castle, Perldore, is a turreted white pearled structure with scrolled spiraled steps reaching far into the sky. On the Isle of Wisteria there are no Autumn or Winter seasons; only zephyrs of Spring and Summer caress the luscious land and its ever blooming petals.

Prodigy

Evernora
Firegate Castle
In the reign of Gregory Roland Sainesbury
Early morning on April 4, 1411

A young flute prodigy was orphaned when his parents were killed in a dispute erupting in the Village of Greyflower on April 3, 1411. He was discovered by one of King Sainesbury's revered knights, Hayden Cheswick. Hayden brought the boy of seven back to the king's palace.

Three stone steps led to the king's solid oaken throne. The red velvet seating boasted an eagle head carving on the front of each arm. A black wool rug decorated the stone floor in front of the steps. Matter root roses, with gold painted leaves, trailed gracefully along the outer edges of the kneeling rug.

Hayden approached the king who was adorned in a scarlet velvet robe. Two stoic guards stood on each side of the king. Hayden bowed with the orphan standing a few feet away.

"Your Majesty, the battle was fierce with casualties on both sides," Hayden said. "We were not able to locate any of the child's family. His parents were the only ones living with him in his home; they are dead. His mother was with child, but the baby girl died. The stress of the attack was the cause of the premature birth. Seabert Gaines tried to revive the infant but his attempts failed. This boy is the only survivor of his family's massacre."

The king set his gaze on the orphan. The child's arms hung heavy at his sides, he sniffled softly, casting his swollen eyes downward. His pale, blotchy cheeks bore the chafe of salty tears.

The king sighed, his inner eyebrows raising. "Who were his parents?" he said.

"Kenley and Seren Westbrook. According to a man living nearby, his father was a traveling merchant and his mother a weaver of cloth. We had a difficult time pulling the boy away from his father's body; he was covered in blood, screaming. He kept crying out for his missing dog. One of the other knights saw the greyhound pup dash under a nearby tree. He wanted to rescue the animal, but attending to the human casualties was more urgent."

The boy could be heard whimpering, but he did not move, keeping his head tucked to his chest. His grief penetrated through to the guard's reserved hearts; their faces were etched with pity for the abandoned boy.

"To appease the child, we searched for the missing pet, but were unable to locate him. Lady Genevie had a difficult time settling him and getting him bathed. He would not let us touch him unless we promised we would not take away his locket. He has not let go of it.

"Our son walked into the room and wanted to know what was going on. He had heard the orphan crying and was worried. We told Landon very little, seeking only to introduce the boys. Landon offered to allow him to sleep in his room, but the boy wanted to be left alone. We took him to his room. He sat on the bed and sobbed, refusing our comfort. I believe we can help the orphan and would like to raise him if you do not object."

"The impressionable boy deserves a proper home," King Sainesbury said. "I cannot think of anyone more qualified to care for the youngster than you and your kindhearted wife. Were you able to find the ones responsible for killing the boy's family?"

"Two men were seen invading the child's home, according to a reclusive man living nearby. We captured one of the murderers, but the other one got away. The witness said the man fleeing had a badly injured hand with missing fingers. We followed the blood trail, but never caught him. Those killers were at the center of why the land dispute took place. The old man further confirmed the two men killed some of the other people living close to his home."

"I see," the king said. "I'd like to talk with the boy before you leave with him."

"Of course."

"Very well, please have a seat," King Sainesbury said, indicating a chair.

Hayden sat down and waited while King Sainesbury talked with the troubled boy.

King Sainesbury knelt beside the weeping child, placed his hand on the boy's shoulder and said in a tender tone, "What is your name young lad?"

"Chanson Westbrook," the pecan brown-eyed boy said.

Noticing the locket clenched tightly in the child's hand, the king further inquired, "May I see the locket in your hand?"

Reluctantly, Chanson opened his hand and surrendered the engraved locket to the king. The frightened boy continued to tremble and cry more profusely as King Sainesbury opened the locket revealing a cameo carving of a young couple. Upon seeing the carved image he closed the locket and took Chanson's hand into his and said, "This locket means a great deal to you, I see."

The orphaned child wept; his tears gushed out like a raging waterfall plunging over a jagged cliff. He shouted in a fiery tone, "That's my mother's locket! *I tried to save her . . . I tried—"* the boy wailed, collapsing on the hem of King Sainesbury's velvet robe.

The king—stirred deeply and moved to compassion—bent down and scooped the distraught child into his arms and said, "If it were within my power, I would restore your home and return you to your parents. Even though today you cannot imagine ever feeling safe or happy again, I assure you, God in Heaven knows how you suffer and it is *He* who will help you.

"I know your parents would want you to be brave—to discover your strength—strength that will help you through the difficult days ahead. Look inside your heart now, Chanson, do you see the loving faces of your parents? Can you recall tender moments shared with them?" the king said thoughtfully, looking compassionately at the distraught orphan's forlorn eyes.

"Yes, a-and Jade, he's romping around the tree where I sat and played my flute," Chanson said, tears flowing down his pale cheeks.

"Is Jade your dog?" King Sainesbury said.

"Yes," Chanson said timidly, his shoulders wilting in discouragement.

"Remember, child, no one can take your family or your dog from your heart," King Sainesbury said, placing the locket back into Chanson's hand. He put the orphan down. "It is there in your heart you can revisit your parents and find comfort. Chanson, were you ever sad before losing your family?"

"Yes."

"What did your parents do to help you feel better?"

"My mother hugged me and my father prayed with me."

"I'm happy to hear your father prayed with you; now you can emulate your father's example. When you are alone, tell God how you feel. He wants to be your friend as well as your healer. Young Chanson, whenever you feel alone, scared or upset, I want you to *remember* what your parents did to help you feel better. Then I want you to close your eyes and imagine they are still with you. In doing so, you will keep them with you in your heart. Will you do that?"

"Yes, but it would be easier to do if I had my flute," he said, wiping his tears away with the sleeve of his cotton shirt.

"Your flute, of course. Was it not recovered?"

"No. It was broken by the man who threw our things out. He kept shouting to my mother, 'This house is not yours! Out with this rubbish—I say—out with it!' I was holding my flute and he grabbed it and broke it in two pieces. They tried to force my mother to move out. But when she did not do as he said, he k-killed—"

Chanson was once again overcome with anxiety. His chest tightened and his tremors worsened. The grip of terror had his wicked hands around the orphan's throat. He could no longer speak nor could his desperate cries be heard raging within the farthest reaches of his heart.

King Sainesbury sighed.

"I'm sorry you suffer as you do. Come, young Chanson, I want to show you something," the king said, taking the orphan's hand and leading him to his exclusive prayer chapel.

King Sainesbury's personal chambers housed a private sanctuary where he knelt in prayer and allowed the Holy Scriptures to nourish his soul before the start of each day.

Chanson and the king entered the sanctuary. The altar was arrayed with white calla lilies; their fragrance lingered in the air.

"See that oak prayer bench near the window?" King Sainesbury said, gesturing with his hand.

"Yes."

"That's where I go to pray about problems weighing heavy on my mind. Would you like to kneel beside me as I pray for you?"

"Yes."

The king and Chanson knelt in front of the bench. Chanson had been accustomed to praying with his parents as evidenced when he placed his hands together and closed his eyes. King Sainesbury prayed.

Almighty God,

Please soothe Chanson's pierced heart and heal his ravaged life. Extend your hand, take hold of his ache, soothe his mind. Please show him your mighty fortress of love, understanding, and unsearchable wisdom. In the Lord Jesus Christ, we pray, amen.

King Sainesbury rose to his feet, Chanson followed.

"Chanson, did you have a Bible in your home?"

"No, but we read it during worship in the Village of Greyflower where I lived."

"Very good. I'd like to show you a very special Scripture that may help you today. Come," the king said, leading Chanson to a table with a large Bible laying on it. "Please, Chanson, have a seat in the chair beside me and we'll read God's Word together." King Sainesbury picked up the Bible and placed it on his lap. He reverently opened it, turning to the book of John. "*Please,* look on the page, Chanson, and listen as I read."

Chanson obeyed the king's request, sitting up straight and attempting to shift his focus away from the grief incising his soul.

Jesus wept.

King Sainesbury took Chanson's hand and said, "Young Chanson, do you know why Jesus wept?"

"No."

"Jesus was touched by the death of his friend Lazarus; he loved him like you love your family. Jesus is your friend too and he weeps with you now at the deaths of your parents and baby sister."

"And for Jade?" he said, his shoulders lifting and eyes glimmering with hope.

"Yes, and for Jade. God knows all you've been through. The book of Psalms affirms God knows you've been shifted from your home to a new place and He has put all your tears in a bottle. In other words, God knows all that troubles you. He has seen every tear that has fallen from your eyes, he even knows their number.

"Whenever you feel alone or forgotten, remember God cherished you before you were born. Along with God's compassion and love, you have mine and the Cheswicks'."

Chanson looked back at the words on the pages of the Bible. He cried again.

"Many years ago, Chanson, I cried too," the king said, placing his arm around the boy.

"You did?" Chanson said while tears puddled on his cheeks.

"Yes, when my wife, Queen Chloette, died. She caught a fever and died the next morning. There was nothing the doctor could do to revive her. I held her in my arms and cried hard. My little girl no longer had her mother . . . our home was a tomb that night."

Chanson relaxed beside the king's warm side. He stared at the king's eyes, examining his wrinkles and envisioning the king wiping away tears too. "Were you ever sad when you were little like me?" Chanson said. His eyes softened and his body relaxed.

"Not so much when I was young, but before my queen died, there was another night . . . when I wept . . . like Jesus."

"Does it still make you sad?" Chanson said, focusing intently on the king's moistened red eyes.

"It does not consume me like it once did, but on occasion, I reflect and wish it had turned out differently. Perhaps one day when you are older I will share the loss that wounded me deeply, causing me to question my reign. Know today, we understand your grief and are going to do whatever we can to help you through it. And go through it you must—healing will come later."

Chanson continued listening respectfully to the king's sentimental expressions.

"I enjoy reading the Bible because I need God's help too; His words remind me of His promises. In the book of Psalm we are told God even made a home for the sun. Imagine, young Chanson, the huge sun in the sky having a home too. Did you know that?"

"No. My parents won't be back for me, will they?" he sobbed, his hands perspiring and his shoulders slumping again.

"No . . . I am very sorry. God has made a new home for you, I believe it is with us now. Will you try to accept that?"

"I don't want to, I only want *my family—*" Chanson wailed, staring at the floor.

"It's to be expected that you are afraid now of what lies ahead. But the absence of fear isn't necessarily a sign of not being brave. I'm a king with thousands of men at my command, and yet, at times I experience reluctance in stepping into the unknown."

"You do?" Chanson said as his tears ceased rolling down his cheeks.

"Yes. At times when war is upon us. It's then that I have to pray and turn my fears over to God and ask for His strength to lead me."

"I didn't think Kings got scared."

"Oh yes, we all get scared. Your mind is a powerful force, young Chanson. Let it help you get through the rough times and you will grow into a mighty man of valor.

"A sword can inflict a mortal wound on our body, but it cannot destroy love; it is permanent like your parents now in Heaven. Be assured, young one, in time the happy memories will remain as the gloomy recollections fade. Trust and believe. Will you do that?"

"I can try," Chanson said, his teary eyes glancing down as he clenched the locket tighter in his hand.

"Very good. You have inner strength. I believe you have a warrior's heart, my little friend."

Chanson smiled through the tears, straightened his shoulders and sighed deeply.

"Let's go back to where Sir Cheswick waits," the king said, placing the Bible on the table.

King Sainesbury took the boy's hand and led him to where Hayden Cheswick waited. Only a few minutes ago, the orphan held his head down with pronounced grief, but was now walking beside the king with hope beginning to bloom in his spirit.

"Chanson, you will find the Cheswick's son, Landon, will be a fine friend. Now I want you to go with Hayden. He and Lady Genevie will take care of you, providing a home for you. I will see to it no further harm befalls you. You will be safe in their care."

With sorrow-dimmed eyes, Chanson smiled at the king. Hayden took his hand and led him away. While holding to Hayden's hand, Chanson remembered a day his parents took him to the chapel in the village.

'Chanson, after our picnic this afternoon, how about we take you to the chapel and read the Bible?'

'I would like that very much! What story will you read to me today?'

'Your father and I would like to read a story about a little boy who grew and anointed the first king. Hannah, his mother, prayed for a baby and God blessed her with a son. She named him Samuel, which means *God has heard*. She promised God she would give her son to Eli, the high priest, to serve in the house of the Lord all of his life. Samuel grew in wisdom and favor with God, becoming a prophet then later a judge. He was granted amazing strength to fight for God's people.'

'Son, are you ready to hear that great story now?' Chanson's father said, taking hold of Chanson's hand.

'I am!'

'You're going to love this story,' Chanson's mother said, taking hold of Chanson's other hand.

God is love
I in Him, He in me.

Sacred Scrolls

Firegate Castle
Late morning on April 4, 1411

Before Hayden and Chanson returned home to Oakmoor Manor, Chanson said, "The king read the Bible to me, will you read it to me tonight?"

Hayden bent down in front of Chanson, looked into his placid eyes and said, "I'm pleased King Sainesbury has enticed you with desire for the Holy Scriptures. The king has another prayer sanctuary, Marblemist Chapel. We'll go there now and not wait until tonight."

"I would like that. In the village, my father and mother took me for prayer when Father was not away gathering food for us. My father cried when he read the words to us. I asked him why the Bible made him sad, he said it was because he loved us and wanted God to help us."

"And now *you cry* . . . in time your heart will mend and those tears cascading down your cheeks will dry," Hayden said, looking into the orphan's vulnerable eyes and patting him on the back.

They walked hand in hand toward the turreted chapel and could see the three white glass windows; a white marble dove, bearing an olive branch, was carved at the crest of each arch.

"It's so big," Chanson said delightedly, staring intently at the tall dome-shaped structure.

"Yes, a massive safe haven. King Sainesbury's father, the reigning king at the time, had it built for his son. On his father's death bed he summoned his son. After King Sainesbury arrived at his father's bed chambers, he instructed his son to open the oriel window next to his bed and take notice of Marblemist Chapel. His cherished son beheld the chapel his father had designed for his heir to the throne.

"The sun's rays lit the father and son's faces; tears shimmered in their eyes. They folded into each other's arms and wept. Shortly after the king endowed his son with the brick-laid architecture, the king's father passed away. The magnificent sanctuary was the last thing King Sainesbury's father saw before his eyes closed in death.

"And like you cry now, King Sainesbury also wept for a father who died."

"He told me he cried too, but not when he was little like me," Chanson said, tilting his head and furrowing his brow.

"That is correct. King Sainesbury had a happy childhood, but was a young man when his father died and left him the throne."

“Did the king have a sister too?”

“Yes, there were two, but King Sainesbury was the only boy in his family.”

“Oh,” Chanson said softly with interest.

“Well, are you ready to go in now?” Hayden said, letting go of Chanson's hand and taking hold of the chapel’s gold door knob.

“Yes. The stories help me to feel better.”

Hayden and Chanson ascended the stone steps, entering the house of prayer. Chanson stood mesmerized by the windows of the chapel. He found solace in having some elements of his former life still intact even though the king’s house of worship was more elaborate than what he had been accustom to.

“Like those diamond pane windows, I see,” Hayden said, observing the child’s eyes focused intently on the Gothic glass.

“The chapel where I prayed with my mother and father didn’t have windows, only a tall door. I like the sunlight . . . me and Jade played in the sun. He liked chasing me around the tree.”

Chanson wiped his eyes, attempting to conceal the unrelenting tears.

“This is now your new place to worship and find serenity for your troubled heart. The king allows everyone access to this one. He was bestowing you with honor when he invited you into his personal prayer room. He does not allow others access to it like he gave you. Chanson, I think you’ve made a new friend in the king’s heart,” Hayden chuckled.

Chanson smiled and said, “I like him. He’s a lot like my Father; he loved God and cried too.”

Chanson wailed again, missing his father. His shoulders slumped, his face fell, grief froze his steps. He stood still and trembled.

Hayden bent down, put his hands on Chanson's shoulders and said, "I'm sorry grief consumes you. Let's open the Bible on the altar and allow God to soothe your heart." Hayden's eyes moistened with tears.

"Are you sad like me?" Chanson said.

"I am sad for you—with you. Your losses have touched me and they also touch the heart of our Father in Heaven."

"King Sainesbury said that too when he told me about a man named Lazarus."

"I'm impressed with your memory, Chanson. As you've already done, continue to keep God's words stored in your heart. This will please Him greatly while helping you to feel better."

"The king's Bible is older than this one," Chanson said after glancing over at the altar. He was captivated by white lilies near the Sacred Word. "This Bible is a lot like the one in the village. The altar also had these flowers on it."

"Those are calla lilies. The king likes flowers and has them growing in a special garden."

"My mother liked the flowers . . . she would often touch them and smile," Chanson said, glancing at the blossoms and remembering their scent from times past.

"In the Bible we are told of a righteous man named Job who lived in the land of Uz. Satan came and took all his possessions, his children, and struck him with painful boils from the soles of his feet to the crown of his head. He sat in ashes and cried while scraping his wounds."

The words touched Chanson. His eyes brightened and he leaned in closer to the Bible.

"Job was alone because his friends blamed him for his troubles. He prayed for his friends, despite how they treated him. Job's wife was also overcome with sorrow after losing her children. Job never cursed God, he actually worshiped and loved him more, never turning his back on His creator.

"The LORD blessed the latter end of Job's life more than the beginning; he had more livestock, children, and kind friends. Job went on to live to the old age of one hundred and forty years.

"Did you like this story, Chanson?"

"Yes. Will you tell me more?"

"All right. I'll read a few scriptures," Hayden said.

Chanson wiped away his tears, placed his hands on his lap and continued listening.

Hayden opened the pages of the Bible, turning to the book of Job. "I believe you'll be inspired by these descriptions of God's mighty power."

Hayden read:

> *God thundereth marvelously with His voice; great things doeth He, which we cannot comprehend. For He saith to the snow, be thou on the earth; likewise to the small rain, and to the great rain of His strength. By the breath of God frost is given: and the breadth of the waters is straitened. He hangeth the earth upon nothing. He divideth the sea with His power. By His spirit He hath garnished the heavens.*

After reading the Scripture Hayden smiled and said, "What did you think about those descriptions of God?"

"Can God bring my family back to me?"

"With merely His voice, He could make it so. Your parents cannot come back to earth, but one day you will see them again. I believe the story of Job has been written so that we can find hope when our lives are in ruins and our hearts are crushed like yours is today. Neither the king nor myself can repair the damage or heal your heart, but God can. He will give you courage to face the future without your parents. And we will be right beside you, encouraging, and loving you as you go.

"Reflect upon these Scriptures when you are alone and feeling bewildered. Remember, if God can blanket the earth with snow on command and cause ice crystals to form with only His breath, He most certainly has the power to secure all areas of your life.

"You have the protective power of God with you. Imagine God's enormous hand reaching and taking hold of yours, leading you to happier days and richer blessings."

Enthralled, Chanson envisioned the descriptions. He was transported in the gloved hand of God. They flew over the mountains and hovered over the rippling waters of the Kaishore Ocean. They even encountered a hawk and a few other birds; they perched themselves on God's shoulders and joined the miraculous ride in the sky. Away they went, soaring around the moon, leaping over castle tops, and speeding mightily through Oakhollow Forest.

"I see you've cheered. The smile on your face tells me you were lost in thought."

"Yes."

"Do you think you could try allowing me, Lady Genevie, and Landon to be your new family?"

"But I don't want another family! I don't want to be here without Father and Mother. They said they would always love me—they promised to—" the orphan sobbed, covering his face with his hands.

"Chanson, they love you still. Death does not change the heart's devotion. If they could, they'd come to this room right now and take you in their arms and never let you go. It was not their choice to die. The men who killed them sealed their earthly existence. But that does not, for one moment, negate what you meant to them. No, not at all."

The orphan continued to wail. His thin body shook with each excruciating sob. He was consumed by grief's devastating hold. Hayden picked him up and held him tightly to his chest. He patted Chanson's back like a child held in the consoling arms of his mother.

"I know, Chanson, I know it hurts . . . go ahead, cry and let it all out . . . "

Hayden said nothing more as the boy continued to release raging sorrow. After a few minutes Chanson settled. Hayden's green shirt was stained with the orphan's tears, but he did not mind. He welcomed the boy's expressions, knowing releasing the pain was necessary for Chanson's healing. Even though Chanson's face was swollen and wet with tears, he was content to hear more of the Bible.

"So, I see you're feeling better now," Hayden said, wiping away his own tears with a handkerchief.

"I think so. Will you tell me more about Jesus?"

"Of course. May I wipe your face and nose before we read again?"

"Yes."

After wiping Chanson's face, Hayden resumed reading from the book of Isaiah.

> *He is despised and rejected of men; a man of sorrows, and acquainted with grief.*

"Chanson, this Scripture is talking about Jesus Christ. He was sad too and his grief was profound. So, He does understand, better than any one, your loss. God's kindness and compassion is as gentle as a baby's breath."

"In the same way he understood when Lazarus died and the people were crying?" Chanson piped.

"That's right! He was able to see past, present, and future deaths and even his own on the cross. I believe that's why he cried when Lazarus died even though he knew He could raise him back to life.

"So whenever you feel depressed, do what you're doing now, ask me, Lady Genevie or the king to read the Scriptures to you. Even though you are unhappy, do you at least feel someone understands and that you do not cry alone?"

"Yes. I wish I could sit in Heaven with God like Jesus does. I'm sure my mother would want to make Him special food like she made for me."

"When you get to Heaven you will spend forever in the lap of God and with Jesus. In spirit, Jesus is here with you now and with me. We can't see him until we get spiritual eyes and behold His face in Heaven. This should inspire you to live a good life so that you will spend all of Eternity with God, Jesus, and those you love. It inspires me."

Chanson's tears ceased tumbling down his cheeks. He cast his eyes on his locket and reflected quietly. He envisioned sitting on the enormous lap of God with his parents, baby sister, and dog with him. He imagined Jade's tail wagging rambunctiously as he licked God's face.

"I will behave and do my best. I hope Jade will be found. I would not feel as sad if he were with me, especially at night. If I could have his paw to hold onto while sleeping I would not feel as bad. He's my friend . . . I miss him . . . "

"I know, Chanson, I know. I can't promise your pet will be found, but I assure you, we are doing everything we can to find him."

"Thank you," Chanson said. He smiled with his lips pressed together trying to regain some measure of hope. In the gathering of tears in his eyes there did appear to be a slight sparkle of joy returning.

"There's a comforting Scripture in the book of John," Hayden said, proceeding to read.

I will not leave you as orphans; I will come to you.

"This is a promise Jesus made to those He loved and it's a promise to you and me. When Jesus died on the cross and was resurrected, He left his friends behind. In His place we now have the Holy Spirit, the part of God who lives in us and is unseen. We are never alone even when those we love die and leave us, like your parents and sister.

"You are an orphan without your parents, but not an orphan in the spiritual sense. There are seasons of life—moments, changes, transitions, tragedies—that can leave us feeling as orphans. The Holy Spirit never sleeps and never goes from us. When you feel alone, afraid or bereaved, ask the Holy Spirit to comfort you.

"A very long time ago. I was downcast and hurt. I laid on my bed, distraught, begging God to hold my hand. While I could not see God's hand over mine, I was made better from envisioning it. And I knew God was there consoling me because I began to feel better. Do you think you could do that when pain overwhelms you?"

"Yes. One time I heard my father praying in his room. I did not tell him I was there, but I heard him tell Jesus 'I know you understand my grief and you are here with me in this very room. Please, Holy Spirit, help my bewildered soul!'"

"You're getting it, Chanson. That's a good memory for you to focus on. Use your father's example of faith and devotion to help you find strength as you move forward in your pain."

"I will," Chanson said, sitting up confidently, determined to be the best boy he could be.

"I take it from the smile perched on your face these stories have enchanted your spirit?" Hayden said.

"I like reading the Bible and knowing you respect my father. King Sainesbury also likes my father; he wants me to remember him too. Will you tell me more stories?"

"I would be happy to. The Bible also tells us there are angels among us. They watch over us and console us with divine messages."

"I've never seen an angel, where do they hide?" Chanson said.

Hayden chuckled again and said, "Inquisitive child, they are not always seen, but often remain invisible to the naked eye; although at times, we may come in contact with one and not even be aware of it. The book of Hebrews commands us to share our bread with strangers because they may be angels.

"How about we talk more about it later. You need something to eat."

"No, I'm not hungry!" Chanson said. "I want to hear more about angels."

"It delights me to see you feeling happier, and I'm glad the stories have brought a smile to your face. We'll come back and read more later. Will that be all right?"

"Yes," Chanson said, looking down at the Bible's pages.

"Would you like to put the Bible back on the altar, then we'll pray and go home?"

"Yes," Chanson said, taking the book in his hand and placing it back on the stone table. He glanced longingly at the Holy Bible remembering when his father read Scripture with him in the Village of Greyflower. He found himself not wanting to leave, as if to not let the Sacred memories of his past slip away. Hayden prayed.

Merciful God,

Thank you for your inspired Word, your heart, that has calmed our souls today. Please help Chanson to uncover gems of strength and resiliency from the shattered places in his heart. Protect his impressionable spirit; mold and shape it for your glory and his good. Even though his life has changed, your mercies remain unchangeable. In our Savior, we pray, amen.

Hayden and Chanson returned to Oakmoor Manor after praying. Chanson was only a few hours away from meeting a new friend. The poignant encounter would send his heart into a cathartic slumber.

Brayleigh

Firegate Castle
King Sainesbury's throne
Late afternoon on April 4, 1411

Hayden Cheswick approached King Sainesbury. He bowed and said, "Your Majesty, you summoned?"

"Thank you for coming so quickly. *Please,* sit," the king said, indicating a chair. "We need to discuss Chanson Westbrook's situation while there's nothing more urgent going on. How is Chanson?"

"Lady Genevie is trying to encourage him to eat the victuals she prepared. He shrugs his shoulders and says he's not hungry. He tries to be brave, but weeps unceasingly over the loss of his family. Chanson begged me to take him back to his home. He's convinced his dog wandered off when his home was invaded.

"His wound is deep. The memories of that day will likely haunt him for years. To see a child collapsed over his father's dead body while lying in a pool of blood is an image I will not forget. The puppy was seen meandering with blood on her paws, a few feet from where the father lay dead."

The king tilted his head, as if in deep thought. "I see clearly that your concern for the child is deep," he said. "I, too, have great empathy for the boy.

"I've given more thought to the orphan's unfortunate circumstances. I want you and the other knights to return to the child's former home and search for the dog one more time. While there, look for any document in the home that could give us clues about his heritage. I would advise we do not tell him of our plans to search his former home. I'd hate to disappoint him further if we do not find his pet."

"Of course, My King, as you wish."

"After prayer, I was enlightened of a way I may be able to help the orphan," King Sainesbury said. "Since Chanson had such a strong attachment to his pup, I'd like for you to bring the lad by and allow him to visit with my mastiff dog. Brayleigh is a gentle girl, allowing him a few minutes each day with my dog could help him in a way we cannot. It's a pity a boy has to grow up without his family."

"That's a kind gesture given how protective you've been with Brayleigh. I am honored—impressed by your wisdom on this matter. I will bring Chanson by after the evening meal with hopes the mastiff will calm him. The evening, as you've recommended, is best given the wee hours seem to escalate Chanson's fear and grief."

"Hayden, then it's settled! Bring the boy to me after sunset this evening!"

"As you wish, My King," Hayden said, exiting to carry out the king's instructions.

The king's quarters

Hayden returned with the orphan for his scheduled play time with King Sainesbury's dog. The guard ushered Hayden and Chanson into the king's private chambers. Hayden bowed before the king and left to spend nurturing time with Landon and Lady Genevie.

The king approached Chanson, who was looking around with a slight grin on his face. The king bent down and smiled into his curious eyes.

"Come Chanson," the king said, motioning with outstretched hand to follow him, "I want you to meet someone who's very special to me."

Chanson eagerly followed the king to his ornately scrolled balcony that overlooked a small flowing brook. He saw Brayleigh standing next to the balcony's tall stone rail. The spacious ivy-arrayed platform, and its floral-adorned structure, did not seem of interest to Chanson. His eyes connected with the dog's gentle, expressive eyes.

"Meet your new friend, young Chanson. Her name is Brayleigh."

"Why is Brayleigh wearing a black mask?" He giggled.

King Sainesbury roared, "She's not wearing a mask, that's Brayleigh's furry face!"

"Oh," he said timidly. "She's so tall—I've never seen a dog like this one!"

"*Go on*, you may pet her," the king said after noticing Chanson stretching out his hand to pet the dog, but quickly folding it back to his side as if needing permission to touch the dog.

Chanson was totally captivated by the mastiff's colossal frame. He smoothed the dog's broad forehead, comforted by her warm, welcoming eyes. With each tender touch of his hand, Brayleigh wagged her tail in approval, hunching down on her hind legs for more affection. Chanson knelt beside her, continuing to stroke the dog's striped, apricot fur.

With a smile beaming like a ray of the morning sun, Chanson giggled again. He glanced at the king who was pleasantly observing the new-found friendship.

The king folded his arms across his waist and tilted his head in fatherly approval. With a jovial smile, he said, "So, you *like her*, I see."

"Yes, and she likes me too!" Chanson beamed.

"Indeed she does! It pleases me to see the two of you getting along so splendidly. You know, young Chanson, Brayleigh lost her parents too."

"She did?" Chanson said, continuing to look at the king's welcoming face that was lit like a room full of candles.

"Yes, it happened last Fall. Her mother was injured during one of our battles. Having pity for the puppies, two of my knights gathered the fragile newborns in their arms and brought them back to me. I gave the other three to some of my servants, but Brayleigh never left my side. I couldn't let her go, something about those huge, golden brown eyes melted my heart. She's been my best friend since!" King Sainesbury chuckled. "And now, she can be your friend too."

"I'd like that very much!"

"Then it's settled, come by every day and you may visit with her. For now, I'll leave so that the two of you can get better acquainted."

The king stepped away gingerly, his long robe sweeping slightly over the floor behind him.

Chanson and the dog were alone, both relaxed on the stone floor. Brayleigh's dancing eyes gave Chanson permission to share his most reserved thoughts.

"Brayleigh, you would like my dog," he said, stroking the dog's ear and muzzle. "His name is Jade. He's a puppy . . . my friend. If he were here, I'd let him be your friend too. Some bad men killed my family. They scared me and Jade. He ran away and I can't find him.

"I have to live somewhere else now, but I don't want to. At night the shadows on my walls scare me. They look like big hands coming to snatch me from my bed. Have you ever been scared, Brayleigh? I hope the killer doesn't come back and kill me too.

"My mother used to talk to me before I went to sleep; she kissed my head before leaving the room. I used to be happy. I don't think I'll be happy again. Papa loved me too. When he came home from getting us food, he picked me up, tickled me, and hugged me tightly. Sometimes he cried. He said it was because he missed me and loved me . . . *I love him too—*"

Chanson could no longer speak, his throat choked with sobs. Brayleigh's tail ceased wagging; her eyes drooped as if sensing Chanson's sorrow. She tilted her large, square head, and put her muzzle up to Chanson's face; she licked away the tears from his cheeks.

Touched by the dog's sympathetic affections, Chanson wrapped his arms around Brayleigh and continued to wail. Brayleigh remained faithfully snuggled in Chanson's arms, not budging from the boy's cathartic embrace.

The orphan's cries could be heard by the king, but he did not interfere. Even though the boy needed rest, King Sainesbury knew Brayleigh could help Chanson sort out his raw feelings better than anyone. King Sainesbury allowed Chanson to play with the dog until late in the evening.

When the king could no longer hear Chanson or the dog stirring, he stepped back onto the balcony and found a scene that touched him deeply. Chanson and Brayleigh were asleep on the stone floor; Chanson's head was lying on Brayleigh's warm side. His locket was in one hand and the dog's paw in the other. The locket's chain fell lightly over the curves of his small fingers.

King Sainesbury stood with his hands crossed in front of him, pondering the two sprawled out on the stone floor. He looked on as if he were a father coming in the night to make sure his children were snuggled safely in their beds. He smiled, pleased the orphan had found solace in his dog. The king gently folded the sleepy orphan in his arms and took him back to his new home with the Cheswicks.

After the king brought Chanson back to his bed, he felt alone and was afraid to close his eyes. He pulled the cover up over his face, keeping only his eyes uncovered. Chanson peered around the room. He worried, *Will the killer come back tonight or will he wait until no one remembers—and then slay him? Will he awake tomorrow in a shallow grave?*

Princess Pearlensia

Evernora
Oakmoor Manor
Late evening on April 4, 1411

Chanson lay in a spacious room, suffocating as if entombed in a sepulcher. He knew he was alive—his heart beating within his chest affirmed—but the room was gray, silent, and deathly cold. He was stripped of all those he once held dear; the cloak of loneliness was his attire. The world had gone on living without him.

He sat in his bed watching the distant tree limbs sway effortlessly outside his window, manifesting their silhouette on the vaulted ceiling in his room. The cool spring air brushed over his sorrowful cheeks. He clutched his locket tightly in his hand, hoping that one day Jade would be found. The moon's glow sent beams of light over his wet cheeks. As he peered out the slender Gothic window, he remembered cherished moments shared with his family and Jade.

'Chanson, your mother and I have a special gift for you,' Chanson's father said, motioning for his son to follow him to the front yard. 'Come, Son, see what I brought home from my travels abroad.'

Chanson took hold of his father's outstretched hand and followed him outside. He saw a puppy laying on the grass; he was like a live shadow in the sunshine.

'A puppy, Papa—for me?' Chanson said, his eyes bright and dancing.

'Yes, your very own playmate.'

'Papa, he will be the best friend ever!' Chanson said, taking the greyhound pup in his arms. 'I will take good care of him.'

'I'm glad you like him. Let's decide on a name fitting for a breed as rare and royal as he, shall we?'

'His eyes are so big—how about we name him Jade?' Chanson said.

'That's a delightful name for a dog with eyes as green as the stone itself!' Chanson's mother piped as she sashayed out the door to join them in the yard.

'Jade, we are going to be the best of friends,' Chanson said, dancing around in a circle, barefooted with the puppy snuggled tightly in his arms.

'And you'll be getting a brother or sister soon,' his mother said, smiling.

'I will?' His eyes glistened and cheeks flushed with color.

'Yes, we're going to have a baby!' she said, circling her hand over her growing belly while peering into Chanson's colossal eyes.

'Does that make you happy, my son?' his father said, moving close to his wife's side and wrapping his arms around her thickened waist.

'I can hardly wait for a brother or sister! We can play together, the three of us!' Chanson said, continuing to swirl on the verdent lawn with the puppy in his arms.

'You and Jade may play for a few minutes before I call you in for supper,' Chanson's mother said, taking the hand of her husband and leaving the boy and dog to play.

The winter of suffering had slipped away momentarily by Chanson's sentimental recollections, but the reality he would no longer hear his mother's comforting voice, or enjoy more happy family moments, overwhelmed him. He sobbed into his pillow barely able to breathe. Not only had the claws of fear come for him, but the suffocating grip of sorrow had left him paralyzed and unable to move.

"Now, now, sweet one . . . " a female voice whispered thoughtfully, "I know your wound seems incurable, but your sorrow will soften with the passage of time. You will come to accept your new home, even like it."

Chanson sat up in his bed and searched for the female, but he could not see anyone. He cried out, "Who are you? Why can't I see you?"

A white feathered unicorn appeared beside his bed. A bright halo of light resembling the sun illuminated her breast and a circlet headband of ivory pearl adorned her head. The white horn was also illuminated. Dangling between her eyes was a ruby gem with pearls. She also wore a pearl and ruby necklace. Strands of pearl were also weaved through the unicorn's mane and tail. Tendrils of hair framed her rosy cheeks and striking features.

She batted her colossal sapphire eyes, setting her gaze on Chanson's small frame. Her lustrous, long, purple lashes swept elegantly over each sparkling-jeweled eye.

"Do not fear my child, I am Princess Pearlensia, and I have come to help you," the unicorn whispered with a soft melodious sound echoing gracefully with each word.

"My mother told me about unicorns. She said they live deep in the forest and are able to heal sick people. Is that true?" Chanson said, touching the unicorn to assess she was real. He withdrew his hand back to his side.

"It is God who heals, not me or any other created being. In the land where I live there are blossoms, petals, and trees. If used with prayer, the flora can bring about healing if one has the faith to believe. There are times, however, when even the greatest faith cannot stop death. Those are questions and decisions best left with God. Do you understand what I have expressed?"

"I think so, but why are you here in my room? Am I dying too? Have you come to take me to your kingdom where I'll be healed with petals?"

"No, no sweet child, you are not ill. It is your spirit that needs healing for it has been crushed by sorrow. I am here as your friend of hope, love, and comfort."

"Oh," Chanson said, examining Pearlensia from her crown to her hooves.

"Go ahead—it is all right—touch my feathers."

Chanson reached out and touched Pearlensia's white feathers. "They are very warm, like a summer day," he said.

Princess Pearlensia giggled with delight, her wings lit from within.

"It is the light that brings forth healing, my little friend. I am here to bring you God's warm rays of hope."

"Is the bright light in your breast God's light?" Chanson said, perking with curiosity.

"He has created me, but has not told me why my body is lit within. I do believe God has given me some essence of His breath, but I cannot presume to know His mind. His mind, heart, and breath cannot be grasped nor are they measured. I choose to believe God has given me life and I am to honor Him with it," Pearlensia smiled, batting her eyes again.

"This you can be sure of, my little friend, whenever you are in the presence of my lambent light, you are near to God and He is near to you. His Majesty is revealed in all of creation, even in the animals stirring about and the birds soaring in the skies. Their intricate designs behold an artist of vast creativity. I feel safe knowing God has created me and you should feel safe too. You are safe in the heart of God tonight."

Chanson examined his body, smoothed his hands over his chest. "But I don't see His light in me and my body isn't warm like yours," he piped, the corners of his mouth turning downward in disappointment.

"Even though you cannot see God dwelling in you, He is there, an abiding friend who is touched by your pain and suffering. He is able to experience our sorrow from endless directions—past, present, and future. Just as He gathered the little lambs in His arms, so will He carry you."

"That's what Father Hayden said!"

"He is a man who studies God's Word and does his best to impart wisdom to others as I seek to do. I am happy knowing he is teaching you those astonishing pearls of wisdom, my little friend."

Chanson noticed a pearly powder on his hand that glistened like diamonds.

"What is this on my hand?" Chanson said, stretching out his hand for Princess Pearlensia to see.

"It is sumptuous jewel dust. God designed me this way. For as long as I can remember my wings have been iridescent. The strands of pearl weaved in my mane and tail have also been with me. The roses you see adorning my mane and tail were of my doing. I plucked them from the rose bushes where I live; their scent makes me happy! Would you agree that I am an intricate creation?"

"Yes. I wish my mother could see you, I know she would like you as I do!" Chanson said, his eyes widening with delight. "Mother liked flowers and her hair was long too. I often picked daisies for her and whenever I did, she kissed and hugged me. She even cried. At first I thought she didn't like daisies. I asked her why she cried and she told me it was because I had touched her with my affections. She said the tears meant she was very happy being my mother. I want my mother to hold my hand and tell me she loves me . . . I miss giving her flowers and seeing her smile at me."

"Your mother was a loving woman. Dear child, I am here to help ease your troubled heart. Do not worry about your parents and baby sister. They are in a world where the street is paved with pure gold; gold so lovely its sheen is like that of glass. The cottages are made of beautiful jewels—spectacular jewels—nothing like the ones you humans gaze upon. The homes have ornate pearl glass windows. It is a world where no one gets sick, lonely or dies; only beauty and love abide there and always will."

"Do my parents and sister live in a cottage with pearl windows?"

"Yes, they live with God and are safe in His tender care. No one will ever hurt them again. And though their bodies have perished here on earth, their souls went back to God who gave it. The soul is incorruptible. Your father, mother, and infant sister have new bodies and a new home where they are waiting for you," Pearlensia reassured.

"So, have you come to take me home to them?" Chanson sobbed, opening the locket and showing Pearlensia the etched carving of his parents.

"Little one, I cannot bring them back to you nor am I able to take you to where they are. Even though you saw them die at your former home, they have not left you. Between the heavenly world and the earthly is a great divide. You have not received your new spiritual body like they have and are not ready to see them yet, but one day you will. When God is ready for you, He will send an angel back to carry you home to them."

"But why can't I go now? I'm ready—please ask God to send an angel for me—I miss Father and Mother. I don't want to live here . . . I don't!" Chanson sobbed gently in an abundant fall of tears.

"Now, now, dear child, it is not your time yet. God has not finished writing the final chapter of your life. He is the great author of all His children. Until He puts down His pen and finishes your script, you must follow in God's light and make the best of your grievous circumstances. Your parents would want you to do that. Will you, sweet child—will you try?"

"Yes, but what about Jade? Can you bring him back? Will the angel bring him to me? Jade's my friend—he's scared and alone without his food—*please,* find him, *please ask God to find Him.*"

"Sweet Chanson, it is getting very late, please close your eyes and rest."

"But I cannot sleep. I'm scared and sad here without my family and dog." His eyes swam with tears as he shook his head.

"Do you like watching the stars twinkle at night?"

"Yes. Me and Jade used to lay on the grass and watch them before I was called inside to go to bed. And Papa would hold me on his lap by my window and we'd watch the stars before he tucked me in bed. He told me I was a good boy and that he loved me. *Please*, ask God to send the angel for me—tonight—"

Chanson wailed louder and was having trouble swallowing.

"Ahhh, darling one. I know you are deeply pained," she said, wiping tears away from his face with her wing. She locked her misty eyes with Chanson's and continued, "When you are frightened and cannot put your head to rest on your pillow, look out your window and watch as the morning stars begin to sing. God painted the stars for us to enjoy. His creation brings solace to our troubled hearts. Look into the never-ending horizons and talk to God. He hears everything you say even if you cannot hear him speaking to you. Your tears affect Him, He weeps for you because He loves you so. Try to imagine His tender hands reaching down from the heavens and wiping away those tears from your cheeks."

"Does the book of Job talk about the morning stars?" he said, reminiscing about the Scriptures Hayden read to him.

"Yes. God is reminding Job that he does not have the power to make the morning stars sing. But he does have an amazing Father who has given him the world to enjoy and sing about. So, why not turn to God's tapestries in the sky and allow the blankets to soothe the aches when you are lonely at night?"

"I'd like to watch them, but Papa and Jade aren't here," Chanson said, casting his teary eyes toward the lonely window ledge.

Touched by Chanson's words, Pearlensia enfolded him in her warm feathered wings as he wept. The melodious sound heard from her soft voice cooing comforted and settled Chanson's troubled spirit.

"Now, now sweet child, everything is going to be all right, you will see," she said. "God's devotion to you is timeless, dear one. Trust and know that Jesus is as close as a sigh. And though you cannot see Him, God is in this very room, His face is turned toward you. He sees those tears, He hears you cry and He knows that you look out the window and see a lonely sky. Close your eyes and imagine God snuggling you close to His breast."

"But it's hard to imagine because I feel so sad."

"Then we can imagine together—will it help you to feel better if I stay until you are asleep?"

"Yes." Chanson's eyelids were heavy as he yawned.

Princess Pearlensia caressed Chanson's head with her wing and whispered a scripture over him as his eyelids closed for rest.

> *How precious also are thy thoughts unto me, O God! How great is the sum of them! If I should count them, they are more in number than the sand: when I awake, I am still with thee.*

Soon after those words Chanson fell asleep. He did not speak of Princess Pearlensia to anyone, but took to heart all she shared. Even though he did not comprehend all that she had spoken, he did recall his parents telling him about the beautiful world, Heaven.

Early Morning on April 5, 1411

Chanson had rested for several hours before awakening to the reality of his shattered family. He was still convinced Jade was wondering alone, sad, and hungry. He took hold of the locket and left the manor, determined to venture out on his own in search of Jade. He sprinted toward the forest as soon as his feet were on the dew-dampened grass.

"Jade, where are you? Please come back to me! Jade!" Chanson cried, while looking under trees and around the forest woods. "If you're hurt, bark and I'll help you! Jade—JADE—my friend, please, p-please, come home!"

A tumult of beastly sounds filled the air with the sounds of twigs breaking beneath the feet of larger animals. Chanson's eyes filled with tears. He was seized with fear as he heard the crackling noises around him. He imagined bears and other animals coming to hurt him. He wondered if his dog had been killed by them or if the man who had murdered his father was hiding in the woods where he stood. He jerked his head around at every movement and sound, checking to see what was lurking.

Chanson's body shivered with fright. His slender legs quivered as he circled around trying to find the path back to the Cheswicks. Even if he could turn around and go back to Oakmoor Manor, he wasn't sure which path would lead him there. He was confused and lost in the forest. His breathing labored; he could see his breath in the cool morning air.

He closed his eyes, trying to imagine God's hands reaching down to pick him up and carry him to safety. But when he did not feel God's hands around him, fear took an even greater hold on him. He opened his eyes and paced in a circle, searching all corners of the forest concerned the killer would reappear. The sounds of the ghoulish forest hummed in eerie cadences in his ears. He crouched low to the ground, slumping forward while pulling his knees close to his chest in an attempt to appear undetected.

Chanson's world was hollow. Those he once loved could no longer be seen, heard or felt; their faces only images passing through time. With the locket in his hand, he opened it and cried softly, "Papa—*Papa . . .* please come get me—*please Papa . . . Papa—*"

Soul Ties

Oakmoor Manor
Mid morning on April 5, 1411

Lady Genevie called Chanson to breakfast, but when he did not come, she went into his room to check on him. After opening the door she observed he was not in his room and his bed had not been made. She also noticed the locket, containing the treasured carving of his parents, was also missing. She searched around the manor for the child, but he had vanished from the premises. She ran out the doors to alert Hayden about the missing orphan.

"Hayden, please, come back, I believe Chanson's run away!" Lady Genevie cried, trying to catch Hayden before he left for an early game of jousting with his fellow knights.

"Whoa, easy Ole Gal, my lady's calling me!" Hayden said, pulling the reins on his horse to stop her from galloping any further. Hayden turned around, got off his horse and said, "He has to be in the forest. He's bewildered over the missing dog. I can only conclude he left in search of the lost pet. I'll look for him. Don't worry, he'll be all right," Hayden said, cupping his wife's cheeks in his hand. "Wait inside until I return." He kissed his wife's forehead and left.

Hayden tore through Oakhollow Forest. After riding for a while, he saw the distraught orphan sitting on the ground under an ancient tree tunnel. Trying not to startle the boy, Hayden tied his horse to a tree and crept to where Chanson was sobbing. He knelt beside him and said, "Chanson, are you all right?"

"I'll never be all right—h-h-how can I be when I've lost everyone I've loved?" Chanson said, his eyes flooding with tears while staring at the moss covered ground.

"I believe you will always love and miss your family, but in time the pain will get easier. You will find better days ahead—you will. I know Lady Genevie and I cannot replace your mother and father, but we can be the soul ties to help you build a new home."

"But I don't want another home! I love *my family!*" he said, his bottom lip jutting out. He crossed his arms, unwilling to accept anyone else as his kinsfolk.

"Do you believe it to be mere coincidence I found you after your parents died?"

Chanson responded by shaking his head, but still staring down at the ground as tears fell from his eyes.

The tears were heard pattering lightly on the moistened path.

"God is precisely why you're not out here wandering around alone and forsaken. The Bible tells us in the book of Psalms we are fearfully and wonderfully made. Those words affirm God cherishes you, all of you—your body and your wounded heart.

"I wish I could lift this tragedy from your crushed heart, but only God has that power. He will help you find your way in this world. My home and my heart are open to you, you need only to accept it as your own."

Chanson's anxiety increased; his chest tightened and his face grew red. He lashed out, "I don't want to be here without them! Why didn't God take me with them?"

"I don't know, but it was not God's sword that killed your family. I believe God will work all of this for your good. He will use this tragedy to build greatness in you. Will you trust that, Chanson?" Hayden said, placing his hand on Chanson's shoulder.

"I will try . . . like I promised *her*," Chanson said, while gripping the locket in his hand and brushing away the tears with the sleeve of his shirt.

"Her? Who are you speaking of?"

"Uhhh, never mind. I will try," Chanson said, attempting to conceal his encounter with the unicorn.

"Fair enough," Hayden said in a hopeful tone. "Why don't we ride further into Oakhollow Forest and look for your dog—would you like that?"

"Yes!" Chanson said, jumping as if he had found hope once again. The sun shone on his wet face; the tear drops sparkled like raindrops lit by a fleeting ray of sunlight.

"Come, let me hoist you," Hayden said as he picked up Chanson and placed him on his horse. They rode away in search of the dog. However, after several hours looking for the puppy, Hayden and Chanson were forced to return home without Jade.

Oakmoor Manor

When they arrived at Oakmoor Manor, Lady Genevie and her son, Landon, were waiting at the door, eager to hear whether Chanson had been safely found.

It was apparent Chanson was physically fine, but emotionally he was profoundly defeated. Moving to comfort the grieving child, Lady Genevie took him gently by the shoulders and said, "I know you've been disappointed about your broken flute. Would you like for us to buy you a new one?"

"Would you do that for me?" Chanson said. A smile took captive his tears and stars dazzled in his eyes.

"Of course, sweet boy," Lady Genevie continued, smiling, "Music would be a welcome delight for us all!"

"My Lady, that's a splendid idea! I'll buy one from Kian Emerson. His instruments are the best in Evernora! How about it, Chanson, would you like another flute similar to the one you had?"

"Yes, I would like one! I used to play for my parents and Jade. We often sat under the big oak tree in my backyard as I played. Jade would sit beside me with his paw on my thigh while my parents danced around in the yard. We were so happy then," Chanson continued, hope vanishing as his thoughts took him back to the forsaken hills and valleys of his former home.

"I have a puppy!" Landon piped. "Sometimes Father takes me and my dog horseback riding. Would you like to ride with us too?"

"Yes," Chanson said, engaging Landon's receptive eyes, making an attempt at accepting his new life.

"It's settled then, we'll get you a flute," Hayden said, taking Chanson by the hand and leading him inside the manor. "It's been a very long day. You must be getting hungry Chanson, having not eaten much since coming here."

Late evening on April 5, 1411

After the family shared a meal together, Hayden gathered the boys around him announcing he wanted to talk with them.

"I think it's time you both know about the ice monster, Havís, known to rise out of the ocean's floor in past winters."

"A monster?" Chanson gasped.

"Yes, that's right, an ice monster has been known to kill people who wandered too far into the forest during Winter.

"Legend tells of the monster sleeping on the ocean's floor during Spring, Summer, and Autumn, never reappearing on land until the Winter. It is believed the dormant time allows the beast to gather ferocious strength during those seasons.

"The monster only appeared on land during severe snow storms, particularly blizzards that brought massive ice. It was said when the freezing temperatures were just right, the creature whirled out of the Kaishore Ocean onto the snow-covered land. The ocean's salted water froze immediately, forming large ice blades on his gargantuan body."

"I'm never going back to that forest!" Landon piped.

Chanson covered his mouth, shocked to hear about the ice creature.

"You shouldn't ever go there in severe weather, but in the other seasons, you'll be fine. Never go alone. Take someone with you and stay clear of the forest when the weather is bad."

"Did you know the people who were killed by the monster?" Chanson said, sitting up straight, his eyes enlarged like marbles.

"No, but I have talked with a few men who say the monster killed one of their friends when they were caught in the bad storm of 1398. While on Kaishore's beach they witnessed their friend being attacked by the creature. The man's injuries were substantial; he later died. They narrowly escaped being the monster's next meal by fleeing swiftly into the forest."

Chanson and Landon sat on the edges of their seats, terrified.

"I know you're both scared by hearing this news, but there's nothing to worry about if you take precautions and do as I've instructed. Now that you'll want to take Dulcie along with you to the beach, I had to warn you of potential danger that lurks in Oakhollow Forest. Until you're a little older, it would be best if I or one of the other knights rides along with you. Aston de Sille enjoys the sunsets as does Seabert Gaines. They will take you if I'm unable. Promise me boys you will do as I've asked and be careful of your surroundings?"

"Yes, Father," Landon said.

"Me too," Chanson agreed.

Oakmoor Manor
Evening on April 7, 1411

The Cheswicks were gathered around their oak wood table and had finished eating when Hayden excused himself.

"Dear family, all of you remain where you are," Hayden said, "I'll return momentarily." With a spring in his step and a big smile on his face, he left the room.

Hayden returned with a linen bag full of items. He stood beside Chanson and said, "Here, consider this gift as our pledge in supporting your God-given talents. Open it, our son."

Chanson took hold of the bag and said, "Is this for me, you're giving me a gift?"

"Yes! Go on, open it!" Hayden said, while placing his hand on Chanson's shoulder and grinning with a sparkle in his eyes.

Chanson untied the burlap string and took the items out of the bag.

"A new flute! I've missed my old one so much! Thank you, Father Hayden . . . thank you!" Chanson beamed and continued to remove the rest of the items from the bag. Landon looked on with kindred eyes. Chanson and Landon's eyes connected.

"Look, Landon, sheets of parchment paper, a quill, and a bottle of ink for me to write poetry and music!" They smiled, forming a bond.

"I've wanted a big brother for a long time, Chanson! I'm glad Papa brought you to us! I'd like to hear you play!"

"Me too!" Lady Genevie piped. "We are happy to have you with us and would love for you to play a tune when you feel up to it."

"I can't wait to play for you, all of you," Chanson said, making eye contact with each one. He popped out of his chair and put his arms around Hayden's neck and said, "I will try very hard to make you proud of me . . . and I will try to accept you as my new father . . . " He turned toward the others and continued tearfully, "I will try to accept all of you as my family. Thank you, thank you!"

Landon's eyes brightened and his smile was as wide as the sea. He stood up with excitement and Lady Genevie clapped with delight. Her infectious bliss rubbed off on the others. The Cheswicks stood around Chanson, smiling and hugging him. Hayden and Lady Genevie's eyes moistened with tears as they glanced toward one another; love and cherishing poured from their eyes in a stream of radiance.

Since the gifting of the flute, Chanson sought solace in his melodies. He often sat in the flower garden and played for hours. The locket was never too far away either.

Chanson also found comfort in having the Cheswick's dog to love and play with. Dulcie was a black and white spaniel with a long silky coat and white drooping ears. She was a gentle and friendly dog who often traipsed alongside Landon and Hayden as they rode through Oakhollow Forest. The dog endeared herself to the Cheswick's heart as well as to Chanson's.

It was nearly a week before Chanson's appetite for food returned. He refused most foods, only accepting fruit and small bites of fresh cheese. Even though Chanson grieved greatly over the loss of his family and Jade, the impressionable orphan soon found tremendous courage and strength from the love and support of his new family.

Oakhollow Forest
Early morning on April 8, 1411

Hayden, like the king, often sought prayer when he needed guidance and wisdom. With the orphan's emotional trauma weighing on his mind, Hayden retreated to a peaceful brook in Oakhollow Forest. Nestled on its bank, with birds chirping melodiously, Hayden prayed to his God.

> *Father God,*
>
> *I dedicate this child to you; grant me discernment in raising Chanson alongside Landon. Please, Holy Spirit, enlighten my soul with compassion and wisdom. Search me, my whole being, and remove any false way in me. Forgive when I've stumbled unaware. Praise and glory, most Holy God, in the cross of Jesus, I plead mercy for our souls, amen.*

Firegate Castle
King Sainesbury's throne
Morning on April 8, 1411

"Hayden, I'm so glad you've arrived on such short notice," the king said.

"Of course, My King. How may I assist you?"

"Chanson spoke of his flute, expressing it was broken by one of the killers. Have you considered buying a new one?"

"Yes. Kian Emerson had one for sale. I've already purchased it and presented it to Chanson. He hugged my neck and kept thanking me. Lady Genevie and Landon smiled, clapping over having Chanson with us and attempting to accept us as his family. It made me happy to see Chanson taken by the finely crafted instrument."

"Very good. It pleases me to hear how well all of you are accepting the boy. Your teary eyes tell me you've taken this boy's heart as your own."

"Yes, Your Majesty, I have. From the moment these eyes set gaze on that tragic scene in Greyflower, I have not been able to separate him from my heart. I already love him as a son, despite having only known him for a mere five days. I will stand by him no matter what!"

"And that too, I have noticed. You're a good man, Hayden. I am blessed to have you as my commanding knight. None other could be what you are to me."

"I, too, feel these strong bonds of friendship with you. I not only want to please God and serve you, but I desire to leave a legacy of love for my family. If being the orphan's father, both in soul and spirit, allows me do that, then I will open my heart fully to him as I have to Lady Genevie and Landon."

"I was planning to send my chief adviser, Esmond Scott, to Kian's shop later today to purchase a flute. But since you've already done so, I'll inform Esmond that Kian's services won't be needed."

"Thank you."

"Of course. Hayden, I'd like to have Chanson perform in Chloette's theater. I'm sure that if Chloette were still with me, she would encourage the boy to pursue his talents. I'd like to think my queen is elated by the theater I've had built in her memory."

"I believe he would benefit greatly by this request. Even though he still suffers, Lady Genevie and I have noticed Chanson is soothed by his musical expressions. A few times he has awakened us by his violent screams, so I gave him permission to play his flute until he's settled.

"Kian Emerson also suggested I purchase other supplies to help with his writing. He expressed Chanson would find solace in penning melodies and poetry on paper."

"Wise words from Kian. He impresses me, with not only his craft, but also his wisdom concerning those having poetic souls like Chanson. I believe the Almighty has guided you and is allowing us to see the boy's intended path. I'm pleased to hear you have purchased the papers and ink."

"Thank you for you're words. I am honored you see it as I do. I know Chanson's spirits will lift when he receives your request."

"Very well then. I will arrange it."

"Thank you."

"Oh, and Hayden," the king said as Hayden was about to leave, "I'd like for you and Landon to attend Chanson's recital. Having his new family around him will provide Chanson with increased support and help to ease his nerves."

"Of course, Your Majesty," Hayden said and left.

King Sainesbury sent the orphan an invitation to perform at the theater.

To Chanson Westbrook, flute virtuoso,

I request your presence at Chloette's Theater on April 16, 1411 wherein to serenade our spirits with your exquisite talent. Please arrive late afternoon to perform for my daughter and the ladies of the court.

Sovereign King,
Gregory Roland Sainesbury of Evernora

Chanson's stomach swirled with butterflies because it was the first time he would play his flute without the faces of his parents cheering him. His anxiety would be eased, however, by meeting a new friend. She will inspire his heart and he will no longer feel alone.

I've eaten ashes and feasted on the bread of sorrow;
While drinking goblets of tears in the night.

Chloette's Theater

Firegate Castle
Late afternoon on April 16, 1411

King Sainesbury allowed Chanson to entertain the women of the court because the young flutist was able to take orders well and respected the code of chivalry.

Even at a young age, Chanson's musical accomplishments were exceptional. The king insisted, as did Hayden and Lady Genevie, that encouraging Chanson's musical talent could be a bridge to soothing the child's heart.

Unless there was an urgent crisis to solve, King Sainesbury could be found enjoying music in the theater with his daughter, Parisina. Spring was an especially delightful time because freshly cut rose blossoms perfumed the air with their captivating scent.

"Father, who's the new boy?" Parisina said, her eyes twinkling with curiosity.

"That's Chanson, dear one. He's our newest virtuoso," the king beamed.

"How old is he?"

"He's seven, only a year older than you. Quiet, Parisina, Chanson's about to begin."

Chanson stepped onto the grand stage after being introduced. He was dressed in an ivory ruffled shirt and black silk pants. He bowed gently and paused, struggling to maintain his courage. The crowd was enormous and he was small on the elaborate stage. His longing eyes peered out hoping to see his parents' faces, though he knew it was futile to expect it. As he scanned every face in the crowd, his anxiety increased in knowing his family was not there. A thousand tears pooled in his eyes, but none fell down his cheeks.

The audience waited, reassuring him with smiles and refraining from any abrupt movement that would further distract him. He made eye contact with Hayden who was beaming at him and nodding as if to affirm an uncommon strength and certainty in his capabilities. It was Hayden's smile that gave him the courage to overcome his fears. Chanson smiled in return, took a deep breath and banished fear from his heart. He straightened his shoulders, raised his chin and said, "My prelude piece is for my baby sister." He put the flute to his mouth and played.

The melody was high tempo, lively, and joyful. Chanson captured the hearts of his audience. It was as though they were in the room sharing in the debut of

Chanson's sister. Spring had arrived; her sweet innocence kissed the vernal buds, awakening nature to sing in the chorus of life. The infant was swaddled in a white blanket and placed in her mother's arms. She wept as she held her daughter for the first time. The baby had only a few strands of hair, ginger like those of her mother. Her emerald eyes and light lashes were also shared with her mother.

Chanson sat beside his mother on her bed. He took his sister's tiny fingers into his hand, comparing their size to his own. Taken by her fragility, he kissed her forehead and pressed his cheek against hers and smiled.

Chanson's father soon joined them on the bed and he prayed, thanking God for his family. His father's eyes filled with tears; they rolled down his cheeks while he smiled. Chanson hugged his parents' necks refusing to let them go.

He concluded the piece and bowed again. Applause could be heard as Chanson stood before the exclusive gathering, mesmerizing all with his extraordinary talent. As soon as the audience quieted, Chanson said, "The next melody is about my family loss."

As he played the tender piece, the listeners envisioned Chanson having a picnic with his family. It was a warm March day; a hummingbird flitted from flower to flower while nature joined the grand overture. He held his baby sister on his lap with both arms secured around her. His mother and father leaned in closer, pressing their cheeks to Chanson's. They cooed to the baby; their laughter was heard echoing over the meadow and whistling through the tree tops. Jade laid beside them, his eyes darting back and fourth at every word spoken. Robins sang as the butterflies sipped nectar from the pink phlox swaying in the balmy breezes. They were happy, all five of them, nestled on a blanket in the golden sun. Chanson giggled as the puppy licked his face. He pet and squeezed the greyhound pup while serene feelings stirred within him.

Suddenly the spirited tone shifted, the promising picnic halted. The wind increased and the sky grew savage with black clouds forming a ferocious funnel. An unexpected tornado rolled through the village. It ripped off roofs, yanked trees out of the ground, and picked up the houses, leveling them. The storm's claw hurled Chanson's family onto rubble of splintered wood, shattered glass, and crushed stone. He was the only survivor, his family and neighbors had been killed. The crescendo of suffering was unimaginable as he stood swallowed in a plethora of nothingness.

As the concluding note passed away, the listeners were moved with cathartic expression; their sobs were heartfelt.

"Father, you're crying . . . the ladies . . . they're wiping their eyes too. Why are you sad today?" Parisina whispered, leaning in closer to her father's side.

"No no, Parisina, do not let your heart be troubled. The boy impresses me with his ability to play so flawlessly on the cusp of enormous grief," the king reassured, taking hold of his daughter's hand.

"But he's not crying, Papa," Parisina said, not understanding that her father was referencing the orphan's recent losses.

"Some day you will understand better, but for now listen and enjoy Chanson's music. Don't forget my promise to allow you time with the ladies for cheesecake if you have behaved."

"I remember! Will there be strawberries too, Father?" Parisina said. A rush of joy came across her face.

"Of course, my girl," the king chuckled, and then patting her knee affectionately. "Let's be quiet and listen to the music."

Parisina sat erect, obeying her father's wishes. She anticipated eating the strawberry cheesecake following Chanson's performance.

"The next melody was written the night I received my new flute and is for my dog, Jade," Chanson said. "This piece will conclude my performance today."

Chanson paused, as if in deep thought. The theater was silenced. He took a deep breath and resumed playing. Within moments, the crowd could be heard sniffling again. It was evident that neither the ladies nor the king had ever heard music like this before. Chanson's third piece erupted reservoirs of thought, hypnotizing their spirits. Their minds were held captive by the child's cherished affection for his dog. They wept too—crushed over losing the dearest friend they'd ever had—a friend in whom all secrets were shared and confidently kept.

With each metaphoric note, the audience was inspired to help Chanson find his dog. News of the dog's disappearance spread through the village; a community of people came together to search for Jade. They scoured the hills, mountains, and forest. From dawn until sunset, they thought of nothing more than to find Jade and return him to Chanson's outstretched arms. They envisioned the greyhound pup and the orphan inseparable, like bookends; the one leaning on the other.

Chanson had managed, with mere melody, to evoke pathos with each listener.

King Sainesbury took notice of the ladies' radiant smiles and their delighted faces as they sat wiping tears from their eyes with lace handkerchiefs. Even his energetic daughter sat captivated by the orphan's rare gift.

The Majesty was moved to tears again by the child's exquisite gift; fond affection was beginning to blossom for the grief-stricken orphan. King Sainesbury was humbled—touched by the boy's ability to stand before them, calmed and poised while raging sorrow warred in his soul.

"Father, the cheesecake!" Parisina whispered, taking notice that the king was engaged in thought and not aware Chanson had concluded his performance.

"Yes, of course, my sweet daughter," the king said, quickly turning his attention to Parisina.

"Give me your hand," the king said as he proceeded toward the stage where Chanson stood at the reception, greeting all in attendance.

"Father, but the cheesecake!" Parisina said, envisioning the delectable dish covered with ripe berries.

"Yes, yes I have not forgotten—how could I—cheesecake is all you've talked about since I announced I'd bring you along today," he chuckled.

"You may go with Lady Genevie after we've spoken with Chanson. Don't you want to meet the little boy?"

"Yes and he can be my new friend, Papa," Parisina said in a hushed whisper. A trusting smile graced her delicate face as she walked snuggled close to the king's side, holding her father's hand.

The king and Parisina approached Chanson. Chanson's unassuming eyes took notice of the king's daughter. He stood, gazing at her childlike wonder, and smiled as if he was no longer alone.

King Sainesbury observed the unexpected connection and grinned with delight.

"Young Chanson, I've never seen you look so happy," the king said with a boasting smile. "I'm pleased your spirit has been revived with joy."

Chanson bowed, surprising the king with his respectful courtesies.

"I see that Sir Cheswick has taught you manners and respect for those in rule."

Chanson nodded slightly to affirm the king's perceptions.

"I'm impressed with your capabilities, young Chanson. It is apparent to me that this is not the first time you've entertained."

"My Father and mother gave me a flute when I was three years old. A musician in the Village of Greyflower taught me to play. My parents wanted me to practice on the floor of my home. They clapped their hands whenever I played for them," Chanson said, struggling to hold back tears.

"I believe God has blessed you with these memories and has bestowed this grand talent to help soften the pain of losing your former home. Look around, Chanson, many are gathered and they have been enriched by your gift and strengthened by the bravery you've demonstrated with your impeccable performance."

Chanson again nodded his head slightly, seeking to respect the king's gracious words, but unable to speak because of sorrow erupting within.

"Chanson, I think it's time we enjoy some food and have some merriment," the king said after noticing Parisina beginning to tap her feet, anxiously awaiting the strawberry cheesecake. "So, brush away your tears and let's celebrate this jolly occasion."

The king and Parisina engaged Chanson with smiles. Parisina asked inquisitively, "Do you like cheesecake too, Chanson?"

"I've never tried it. My mother was not fond of me eating sweets. I heard one of the ladies say earlier that your father's girth was enlarging because of the cheesecake. What is a girth?"

"Haha, haha!" the king roared, "All right, Parisina, you may join Lady Genevie now for dessert. Take Chanson with you, I won't have one of our own deprived of cheesecake!"

The king's jovial laughter was heard throughout the luxurious theater.

Hayden and Landon walked up to Parisina and Chanson before they left to have cheesecake. The king remained.

"Chanson, I'm so proud of you and the way you've carried yourself," Hayden said. "If I had not known differently, I'd say you were a grown man with several performances to your credit."

"Thank you. I only wish my family had been here. This was the first one they've missed." Chanson's eyes welled with tears again.

"Oh, but they were, Chanson. In spirit they have never left you nor will they ever," Hayden reassured, placing his hand on his shoulder and smiling gently.

"Let me be your brother," Landon piped. "I've wanted a brother for so long, but Mother can't give me one."

"Landon," Hayden said, "your mother would not want us telling others those personal details."

"I'm sorry, Father."

"It is all right, but from now on those matters need not be discussed at social events." Hayden turned toward Chanson and said, "Chanson, we've wanted another child for a few years now, but God has not blessed us with one until you."

"We'll be your new family and will come to all your performances," Landon reassured with a sunny afternoon smile.

"All right," Chanson said, "I'll try to be happy in your family."

"Well, I believe it's time for cheesecake now," the king interrupted. "Parisina's been nudging me to have the dessert ever since we arrived. Why don't we all go and dine together in the rose garden?"

Before the king or anyone else had time to say another word, Parisina had skipped over to Lady Genevie for the cake. The others followed behind as the king chuckled all the way. They sat outside on stone benches in the rose garden enjoying cheesecake while listening to water flowing from the fountain.

After Chanson, Parisina, and Landon finished eating cheesecake, they skipped around the stone fountain, chasing one another. They splashed the water with their hands, getting each other's faces wet. The children continued frolicking around the fountain and darting around ornamental shrubs while their parents were engrossed in conversation and laughter. The king had been too preoccupied to notice his daughter's silk dress was dripping with water and the ribbons in her hair pressed against her soaked locks.

"Let's dip our heads in the water fountain," Chanson said proceeding to dunk his head into the cool water.

Landon dunked his head too, but when Parisina didn't go along, Chanson said, "I'll dunk mine again if you'll do it with me."

"All right," she said.

"Ready, Parisina?" Chanson said.

"I think so," she said, hesitating.

They took hold of the large basin and waited for the other to take the dive.

"All right, ready now!" Chanson said.

They dipped their heads and just as they came up out of the water, King Sainesbury walked over.

"Parisina! What are you doing? Boys, what is the meaning of these shenanigans?" the king said, observing the children soaked from head to toe. There they stood with water running off their heads and their hair wet, covering their eyes and faces.

Before they could answer, Hayden, Lady Genevie, and a few of the other ladies rushed over to see why the king left so abruptly from the conversation.

"Parisina, you've never behaved so unbecoming of a little girl," the king scolded. "Why, look at you, you've ruined your dress."

"But Papa—"

"It's my fault!" Chanson interrupted, his satin pants also soaked and his ivory shirt wet and clinging to his skin. "I asked her to. Punish me!"

Hayden was seen, grinning, but trying to keep his composure.

"I don't mind you frolicking around the lawn, but please keep your heads out of the fountain!" he said, shaking his head and looking at the three children standing side by side sopping wet.

"I'm sorry, Father, I won't do it ever again," Parisina said, casting her head downward is if to hide from spectators.

"I'm sorry too," Chanson said.

"Me too," Landon piped.

"Come child," the king said, taking the hand of his daughter and escorting her inside, "little ladies don't carry on in such forward ways."

Before the king had whisked Parisina inside the castle, he was heard laughing about the incident.

"Boys," Hayden said, "I think it's time to go home and get into dry clothes. I suppose a soaking was a good way for you to relieve your stress, Chanson. I know you were only having fun so you won't be a punished."

"Thank you, Father," Landon said.

"I never meant to cause the king to be upset by my behavior," Chanson piped.

"Don't worry. He's not accustomed to his daughter playing with young boys. I believe the three of you could be good friends as long as you have more respect for the king's wishes. Let's go home now."

Chanson had been calmed by the lighthearted frolic with his new friends. He enjoyed his first full night's rest without haunting memories and nightmares waking him.

King Sainesbury's throne
Early morning on April 17, 1411

King Sainesbury ruled with respect and honor. Those who served under him were carefully chosen, exemplary men who revered God. Hayden was King Sainesbury's finest. Like the king, Hayden sought the Holy Scriptures when looking for guidance and wisdom. The two were inseparable in matters concerning spiritual integrity and foresight.

Hayden Cheswick was summoned by the king. He bowed and said, "Your Majesty, is there a threat?"

"No, no Hayden. I only wanted to speak with you about Chanson. I know how fond you are of reading the Bible in the chapel. I'd like for you to take Chanson back again today. The meditations will help the orphan to form a stronger bond with you, and at the same time, settle and nourish his spirit. I'm relieving you of a few of your duties this afternoon so that you can spend more time with Chanson. We both know how much comfort and wisdom is gained by reading God's word every day."

"Yes, of course, My King. I know it will take some time before Chanson is settled, but I believe we're doing everything we can to help him feel safe and loved."

"Hayden, you've been an extraordinary father to your own son. Both those young lads are sure to grow into mighty men of valor under yours and Lady Genevie's care."

"My King, in allowing Chanson time with your dog, I believe it goes without saying the orphan could not be in better care. While Chanson is with you and Brayleigh, that will afford me some time alone with Landon. He's been moping around since yesterday and clinging to his mother more than usual. Perhaps he's feeling replaced by Chanson's arrival. I reassured him I'd take him for a ride while Chanson plays with Brayleigh tonight."

"I was afraid that would happen. I don't want you to neglect your own son's needs. But if the orphan is to discover his destiny, these first few years are crucial to that end. Perhaps helping them to strengthen their bonds as brothers will smooth over any tension that could arise between them."

"Fitly said, My King. I'll take Landon along with me to the chapel. With a son on each side of me, we will allow the Holy Scriptures to draw our hearts closer to one another and closer to the very heart of God."

"Very well, why don't you take the boys now and then bring Chanson back here later to play with Brayleigh?"

"Of course, as you wish My King."

Diamond Belle

Firegate Castle
King Sainesbury's throne
Early morning on April 20, 1411

Hayden Cheswick approached the king. He bowed and said, "My King, I came as soon as you summoned. How may I serve you?"

"It's about the orphan. Have you considered training him to become a knight? I don't favor forcing him into knighthood, but it does seem logical to begin introducing him as a page. As he matures we can then assess if he desires further training."

"Yes, I have pondered it. One of my mares is due to give birth any day now. I considered allowing the boys to witness the foal coming into the world. And depending on the outcome, bestowing the foal to Chanson. Having a horse to care for would further help to heal his scarred heart."

"That's a splendid plan, splendid indeed, Hayden! The foal and the boy could grow together. When Chanson's fully trained he could remain under your command as a knight."

"So, you would not object to me encouraging this direction?" Hayden said.

"Not at all. Do you think Chanson is ready to begin training now?"

"He's still fearful of the dark and troubled, but I believe having a goal and something to do will keep him from being idle."

"Ahh, yes. Too much time to ponder and relive those horrifying scenes could cause more harm."

"That's what Lady Genevie said as well. She further expressed the Scriptures are soothing him greatly. She reminded me of Landon and how the colt we gave him a year ago has brightened his spirit. The horse has taught him responsibility, and at the same time, given him a pet to love and cherish. Landon and the horse have formed a loyal friendship! I've learned that my lady has maternal wisdom and is worth considering."

"I agree. A good wife's wisdom should indeed be heeded."

"I'm honored you see it as I do!" Hayden said, his eyes glistening with pride.

"Of course—I trust your judgment."

"Chanson hasn't learned how to ride a horse, but with the foal arriving soon, I can begin training him to handle one. And if he takes to it, I'll begin teaching him to shoot an arrow. I've already begun training Landon.

It would perhaps bond the two boys more if I take them out together to practice. Lady Genevie agrees that allowing him to continue his study of music will further enhance his talents in the plans God has for his life."

"I agree. We have already seen the boy is a musician at heart. In time we will know if he has a warrior's heart as well. A few of the ladies have requested the orphan play exclusively for them. They've raved about not only his talent, but his charm and the courage it takes to put aside his sorrow and play flawlessly.

"Send word immediately when the mare delivers. It'll lift my spirit too in seeing a vibrant young destrier around here."

"Of course . . . the stable hand indicated she could deliver tonight, expressing she was restless and walking around in circles."

"That's delightful news for you and the boy."

"And for Landon! He's asked me to take him out to the stable every morning and night to see Silver Belle."

"Well, sure sounds like a very good time for a birth to help lighten the mood around here!"

Hayden chuckled and left.

Oakmoor Manor
Before dusk on April 20, 1411

The Cheswicks received a knock on their door. It was a servant sending news the mare was giving birth.

"Sir Cheswick," the stable servant said, "I believe Silver Belle's in the first stage of labor. She's doing well, soon I believe she'll have a healthy foal."

"That's wonderful news!" Hayden said. "I'll get the boys and meet you there. Hurry back and assist however you can!"

"Of course," the servant said.

Landon had heard the news and came bursting toward his father before he had time to tell him.

"Father, is Silver Belle having her baby now?" he said. His cheeks flushed with color and his eyes enlarged with excitement.

"Yes, Son, tonight! We're going to have a new horse soon! Go tell Chanson and get dressed!"

"Yes Father!"

They arrived at the stables. The boys walked toward the mare. Silver Belle was laying on a bed of clean straw. Her water had already broken and one hoof was partially birthed.

"It smells like hay in here!" Chanson said, leaping toward the birthing horse.

"Careful boys, don't get too close," Hayden said, noticing the boys attempting to sit beside the mare. "Mares are usually uncomfortable with others around them as they give birth. Her instincts are to protect her baby, so we could upset her if we get too close. Stay back here with us and she won't feel threatened. Let the servant help Silver Belle now."

The boys stood in front of Lady Genevie, their eyes glistening with wonder and faces lit with joy, anticipating the foal's arrival.

"Birth is painful," Lady Genevie said, "we need be respectful and not move suddenly or do anything that could scare her."

"Why is her tail wrapped with cloth?" Chanson said.

"It protects both the mare and the foal from dirt, keeping the mother and baby clean," Genevie said.

Chanson smiled, keeping his eyes on the mare.

"Have you ever seen a baby horse being born?" Landon said, whispering in Chanson's ear.

"I've seen mice, but never a horse. Father had a horse, but she never had babies."

"Papa, another hoof, another hoof!" Landon squealed.

"That's right, Son! The baby's on his way! The hooves are pointing downward; a sure sign the birth is proceeding very well. Soon the head will emerge!" Hayden said, putting both his arms around Landon.

"This is a beautiful event for us to share," Lady Genevie said, putting her arms around Hayden and Chanson, "a blessing bestowed by our lovely Creator. Birth is beyond expression! Even the greatest artist among us could never capture such majestic expression!"

Silver Belle snorted, breathing heavy. She was distressed and appeared anxious, glancing at the foal trying to emerge.

"There he comes . . . look boys, the head! Watch carefully, he'll come out fast now!" Hayden said.

"What's that white bag?" Chanson said, turning toward Hayden.

"It's a sac that has protected the developing foal. Keep watching, the baby's coming!"

"Look, his head!" Chanson squealed. "The baby's out!"

"And breaking out of the white sac!" Landon piped.

The servant and the stable hand examined the foal carefully while the mare rested on her side.

"It's a girl!" the stable hand said. "Sir Hayden, you've a healthy foal!"

The foal held up her head, looking around. She let out a soft grunt, trying to chew. The boys were entertained and laughed. The foal tried to stand, but was too weak to do so.

"Don't worry about how wobbly the foal is. She'll need some time to gather her strength," Hayden said.

Silver Belle stood and groomed her baby.

Hayden knelt in front of Chanson, taking his hands into his and said, "Chanson, would you like the foal as your very own horse to raise and take care of?"

"You would give her to me?"

"Yes. As soon as she can walk and is nursing you may begin spending time with her. Even give her a name of your choosing. She's all yours, if you want her!" Hayden smiled, patting Chanson on the back.

Chanson's colossal eyes welled in tears. An enormous smile, like a jewel kissed by the sun stretched across his face. "I would love to have her!" he said.

Hayden's benevolent actions ignited a sense of trust between them. Chanson wrapped his arms around Hayden's neck and wailed. The knight embraced him tightly, seeking to confirm his devotion to him.

Chanson's feelings were still tender, and it was evident suffering would consume his spirit for a long while. However, witnessing the splendor of birth and sharing it with a loving family helped to endear Chanson's heart to the Cheswicks.

Landon and Lady Genevie soon joined in their embrace. The family remained in the stable with Silver Belle until the foal suckled and walked around, curiously checking out her surroundings.

The next morning on April 21, 1411

Chanson and Landon woke up early, begging their father to take them to the stables to see Silver Belle and her foal. After convincing the boys they needed to eat breakfast first they were allowed to go with Hayden.

Upon arriving at the door of the Cheswicks' stables, they saw the mare and her baby getting better acquainted. Silver Belle had recovered and was standing close to her baby while grooming her coat. The foal was still weak, as evidenced by her mother's gentle touches knocking her off balance. The foal's legs never buckled; she was determined to remain strong and stately for her attentive mother.

"Boys, looks like Mama and baby are fairing well! In no time the foal will be leaping over hills and valleys like the rest of them!"

"May I get closer to the baby?" Chanson said.

"Of course! But remember what I said about being cautious. Go on, you may walk over to her."

Chanson tiptoed on the strewn hay.

"That's it, Chanson," Hayden said, "easy does it."

The foal peeped at Chanson. The orphan smiled while admiring the newborn. Silver Belle kept her eyes on him, as if giving permission to admire, but not to touch.

Hayden stood behind, smiling with a satisfactory grin. He prayed within himself that this newfound friendship would inspire healing and hope for the orphan.

"Have you thought of a name for her?" Hayden said.

"Diamond Belle—I want to name her Diamond Belle!"

"I like that name!" Hayden said.

"Me too!" Landon piped.

"I picked it because of the silver patch between her eyes!"

"The silver design also bears a likeness to her mother's silver coat," Hayden said. "Diamond Belle it will be then! In a few days you can begin walking her, but for now why don't we leave and finish our chores for the day?"

"All right," Chanson said. As he walked away, he looked over his shoulders to have one more glimpse of his new friend.

The Bassinet

Firegate Castle
The banquet hall
April 4, 1412

A year had passed since Chanson was orphaned and brought to live with the Cheswicks. King Sainesbury chose to celebrate the one year anniversary of Chanson's arrival by hosting a feast in his honor. He called on his servants to fill the table with the tastiest food found in Evernora. The honorary guests included the Cheswicks, Esmond Scott, Seabert Gaines, and Ashton de Sille, one of the king's knights. Landon and Parisina were also among those gathered.

Since the King was adamant that Chanson be surprised by the celebration, he arranged for all the guests to arrive before Chanson and Hayden. When everyone was sitting at the banquet table and all the food prepared, Hayden entered the banquet hall holding Chanson's hand. Hayden wore a smile as wide as the ocean.

The king stood and said, "Chanson, this feast is in honor of you being with us for a year now."

Chanson's eyes enlarged to the size of the moon when all the those gathered stood up and clapped. He bowed gently before them, his eyes meeting King Sainesbury.

"Come, young Chanson," the king said, indicating two empty chairs, "sit and let us enjoy this momentous occasion."

Chanson took a seat beside the king and Hayden sat down beside Chanson and Lady Genevie. Landon and Parisina sat across from Chanson; they exchanged smiles.

"My dear friends, let us eat and be merry for today we count ourselves richly blessed in having Chanson as part of our family," the king said, raising his goblet. The others raised their goblets too and said, "Amen."

"So, Chanson, are you happy for what the king has done for you?" Hayden said.

"Yes, Father Hayden. I did not expect it, but I am glad to be here with everyone, especially Parisina."

"Of course," Hayden chuckled. "It seems you and Landon have grown quite fond of her, haven't you?"

"Yes. I like having her as a friend. She's fun and generous. Will I be able to play with her after we've eaten?"

"Oh, I'm sure that can be arranged. But for now, let's enjoy this delicious food."

"All right."

"Look Parisina," Chanson said, "cheesecake, your favorite food! And strawberries on top too!"

"That's right, young Chanson," the king piped, "I made sure the two of you had that delectable dish since you have come to enjoy it as much as my little girl. Go on, have some. The strawberries were picked fresh off the vines just yesterday. April's a fine time for plump juicy berries like these."

"Thank you," Chanson said, scooping a piece of the cheesecake into his bowl. As he ate the cheesecake he and Parisina giggled back and fourth.

"Papa," Parisina said, "may I play with Chanson and Landon after we've eaten?"

"That will be fine as long their parents permit it."

Hayden and Lady Genevie nodded in agreement.

After the guests had finished their meal, many of them departed to their homes. The Cheswicks, Esmond, Seabert, and Ashton remained at the banquet table talking.

"Father, may I be excused to play with Chanson and Landon now?"

"I suppose, but stay in the castle. Perhaps you would want to play with Brayleigh for awhile. Here, take her with you as you leave." The king stood and nudged Brayleigh out from under the table. "Go on girl, go with Parisina." With her tail wagging, Brayleigh zipped alongside the three children and out of the room.

"This is a big castle, how about we explore it and see how many rooms it has?" Chanson said.

“Father told me not to ever do that,” Parisina said. “He said he didn’t want me playing alone in the older rooms.”

“But you're not alone, Parisina,” Landon said.

“That’s right, we’re with you and can protect you!” Chanson said, petting Brayleigh.

“Well, all right. I suppose Papa won’t mind then.”

“I’ll lead us,” Chanson said, “and that way I’ll protect both of you.”

They followed behind Chanson as he and Brayleigh led them through the castle.

The children had seen nearly every room of the castle, except the basement. Their curiosity led them to the lower level of the castle.

“Be careful,” Chanson said, “these steps are steep.”

Parisina took hold of Chanson’s hand and he continued to guide her and Landon down to the basement. The walls were moldy with cobwebs, but they were careful not to touch them.

“I’m getting scared,” Parisina said, looking up and seeing the cobwebs dangling above her head.

“Yeah, me too,” Landon piped. “Maybe we shouldn’t go down there.”

They huddled closer and continued, descending the long winding steps.

“Look, only a few more steps to go,” Chanson said, descending cautiously.

“All right,” Landon said. “We might find hidden treasures down here.”

The children arrived at the bottom of the steps and were surprised to find a tall granite door.

“Should we go in?” Chanson said, taking hold of the dirty knob.

“I don’t know,” Landon said, peering around and seeing a large spider on the ceiling.

"The king has guards around the castle," Chanson said, "I believe it's safe to enter. Besides, we have Brayleigh with us, she'll protect us."

"I'll go in if *you do*," Landon said.

Parisina squeezed Chanson's hand and snuggled closer to the boys.

Chanson turned the knob and opened the door.

They saw a dusty cobweb-filled room with a bassinet in the center of the room.

"Look, a bassinet," Chanson said. "Parisina, was this yours when you were a baby?"

"No. I've never seen it before."

The children examined the bassinet. They found several gold pieces.

"See, I thought we'd find treasure!" Landon said.

"But it's not ours to take!" Chanson said. "Shhh, I hear footsteps. Quickly, hide!"

The children ducked behind the door as the footsteps grew louder and closer. They imagined intruders coming to snatch them for entering the room.

"Parisina," the king yelled, "are you down here?"

Hayden and Seabert followed behind the king.

"Yes, Papa," she said, stepping out from behind the door, relieved it was her father.

"My girl, what are you doing down here?" he said while Chanson and Landon inched out from behind the door. "I searched every room in this castle and was worried about you. I'm shocked the three of you came all the way down here without telling me."

"We were exploring," Chanson piped.

"Papa, whose bassinet is that over there with coins inside?" Parisina said, pointing to the infant bed.

The king glanced over and saw the bassinet. A cloud settled over his spirit, dimming his enthusiasm. His heart rate increased and his hands trembled. He turned toward the children, shaking his finger, and snapped,

“Parisina—boys, all of you get back upstairs this minute and don’t you ever come back down here!”

The king hung his head as if in great turmoil.

“Of course,” Hayden said, leaving with the children. Brayleigh refused to leave his master. She took her place beside the king, standing with her tail down and her muzzle pressed to his thigh.

“My King,” Seabert said, placing his hand on King Sainesbury’s shoulder, “are you all right? Would you like for me to take the bassinet out now?”

“I don’t know, Seabert, I don’t know,” he sobbed. “No matter where it is, I’ll never be able to forget. It’s going to haunt me for the rest of my days. Please, Seabert, just leave me.”

“Pardon, my intrusion, Your Majesty, but is it wise for you to be all alone down here dealing with this shock? Shall I stay with you . . . I won’t say a word . . . please allow me to help you through this again.”

“Seabert, *please* . . . ”

“As you wish.”

“You’ve been a good friend to me, Seabert, but you can’t change what has happened.”

“I only wish I could, My King. If only I could have prevented the children from coming down here, then you would not have had to face this nightmare again. I wish now I had defied your instructions to keep the bassinet and destroyed it myself. I thought I was sparing you more hurt by not telling you they didn’t want the gold returned. So I did the only thing I knew to do, just put them in the bassinet, out sight, and hoped that one day you would find the strength to do with it as you desired.”

“Seabert, it’s not your fault, I’m the one who told you to put it here. I just didn't expect to see it after all these years and I didn’t know the gold wasn’t returned . . . but what difference does it make now anyhow, he’s gone . . .

they're both gone. I need to be alone. Now, please, leave me to my thoughts."

"I'll check on you later. Will that be all right?"

"Very well."

Seabert placed his hand on the king's shoulder again and then left him in the deserted room.

King Sainesbury stooped over the bassinet and sobbed, "Why God, why am I to be reminded of this now? Why have you forsaken me? I've been faithful and I've served you with my entire soul and yet, you leave me with such desperate longing. Why my Lord, why this sorrow?"

The king took the coins in his hands and hurled them against the wall. His cries competed with the piercing sounds as they fell to the floor. He then picked up the bassinet as if it were a bolder and smashed it against the moldy wall, hitting it several times. It was broken in pieces while he screamed, releasing his rage. Brayleigh hunched down, lowering her head, but keeping her eyes on the king's actions. The king yanked the crown off his head and threw it on the stone floor, shattering the garnet stones.

Brayleigh hunkered lower to the floor, curling her tail closer to her body and lacing her paws over the top of her head. Her eyes remained focused on the king. He stood in the wreckage—shattered garnet, broken wood, and a dented crown—weeping, paralyzed by events he had desperately tried to bury long ago. Brayleigh inched closer to the king and licked his hand as it hung at his side.

Meanwhile, the others arrived back at the banquet hall where Lady Genevie, Esmond, and Ashton sat.

"Are you all right, children?" Lady Genevie said, popping out of her chair and leaping to embrace them.

"They are fine, but have upset the king over discovering an unoccupied room in the basement."

Hayden looked at the children's droopy faces and continued, "Boys, you must not do that again. I don't know why that upset the king so badly, but I believe an apology will help to smooth it over."

Even though they waited for the king to return, he did not. The guards ushered the guests out and a maid took Parisina to her room where she stayed the rest of the day. Concerned about the king, Seabert summoned one of the guards to go with him to check on him. When they arrived at the room, they saw the king sitting on the floor balled up and sobbing while Brayleigh stood clinging to his side.

Seabert approached the king and knelt beside him. "My King, let me help you . . . please," he said, taking hold of the king's hand.

The king struggled through the tears and rose to his feet with the help of Seabert. He wiped his eyes with the sleeve of his robe and wailed, "I've lost him, I've lost him again. When will this suffering end . . . when?"

"I don't know. I only wish I could take it from you, once and for all," Seabert said, drawing closer to the king and peering into his swollen eyes.

"I'll be all right, don't worry. I just need to close this door and bar anyone from ever entering it again. Look at the mess I've made of his bassinet."

"Perhaps you will heal now. I believe we should rid the castle of these reminders for your own good. What would you like for me to do with the gold?"

"Yes, you are right," the king said. "Take the gold and give it to the poor."

"As you wish," Seabert said. "Let's get you back to your chamber for now and let me and the guard handle cleaning this up."

"Very well. Thank you, Seabert."

Seabert smiled at the king and took hold of his arm and led him out of the room as Brayleigh clung close to the king's side. The guard went ahead of them, protecting the king from being seen in his frail state. After making sure the king was settled safely in his chambers, the guard rid the room of the shattered bassinet. He also gathered the gold and gave it to Seabert.

Seabert stayed with the king until he had drifted off to sleep. He gave instructions that the king was not to be disturbed for the rest of the evening or the next day, unless it was urgent. Neither Seabert nor King Sainesbury ever explained the incident to the guests, but it was evident that Seabert knew why the bassinet was in the room and who it belonged to.

Gold of Honor

Evernora
Two years later on May 1414

Chanson Westbrook had completed his training as a page boy. He was elevated to squire after desiring to become a knight. His mare, Diamond Belle, was also promoted; she was three years old and ready to be trained as a war horse.

The morning of Chanson's first jousting competition had arrived. King Sainesbury, his advisers, and their ladies were sitting in the arena, awaiting the much-anticipated event. The king's daughter, Parisina was also among the cheering crowd. Parisina was dressed in blue gloves and a white embellished gown. Her tresses were braided and wrapped in a chignon atop her head. The knight's ladies were dressed in their best attire; hair swept up and adorned with jewels struck by the sunlight. The morning dew had lifted, leaving the air waft in the scent of the king's blooming roses.

The field was bedecked with flags. Hayden's flag waved victoriously; the commanding knight's emblems proudly honored his accomplishments. The four fields on Hayden's flag were, red denoting warrior knight with a bull of bravery, black denoting knowledge with a bear of strength, blue denoting loyalty with a boar of ferocity, and maroon denoting victory in battle with a two-headed eagle indicating protector of vast realms. The emblems and fields were set against a scarlet background with gold tassels on the lower scalloped edge.

King Sainesbury's knights and their ladies paraded in view of the audience. The king's trumpeters marched, their melodies intensifying the occasion. The Herald was in place, ready to judge the squire's abilities against a mock knight.

The excitement was high and the faces of the attendees glowed with pride for the orphan's decision to become a knight for the kingdom of Evernora.

The gate opened in the arena. Chanson walked out with Diamond Belle by his side. She wore her costume with ease. The blanket was reminiscent of Hayden's flag, scarlet with gold tassels swaying elegantly on the edges.

He took in the huge gathering and beamed. He whispered a few words to Diamond Belle, "Well girl, this is it, the day we shine for our king." He kissed her head and mounted on the horse. He proceeded to ride toward Hayden and Landon.

The crowd cheered louder. They chanted, "Chanson-Chanson-Chanson . . . "

King Sainesbury and Parisina were among his greatest fans. Smiles, grins, and cheers inspired Chanson to do his best. He wanted the Cheswicks to be proud of him, to please the king, and to strengthen his skills for knighthood.

Hayden approached Chanson. None was more proud of the orphan than Sir Cheswick. He gave Chanson his shield and armor. He put them on with the help of Hayden. Landon placed his flag in his gloved hand after he was suited.

"Show the crowd how powerful you are, big brother!"

"I will, Landon, I will," he said as they exchanged smiles.

"You're going to do great today, Chanson," Hayden said. "Remember all you've learned and keep your focus. And know that no matter how you score, if you've done you're best, you still come out a winner."

"Thank you, Father, I will do my best!"

"I love you, Chanson—now go. Let the joust begin, Son!"

The trumpeter paraded across the field, signaling the contest was ready to begin.

The Marshall read out the rules of the jousting loudly over the roaring crowd:

"The mounted Squire, Chanson Westbrook, will attack the mock opponent, aiming his lance at the shield secured on the front of Ashton de Sille's horse. The knight will guide the horse but will not be a participant in the joust.

"If the opponent is injured and falls off the horse, he will gain three points. If the squire hits the target and the mock falls off the knight's horse, uninjured, not torn and not pierced, he will gain two points. If the opponent is torn or pierced, and not unhorsed, that will count as a one point.

"The squire is allowed to charge at the mock opponent eight times with lances. Only three lances will be allowed. The squire will be awarded one of King Sainesbury's coins if he has unhorsed the mock opponent four times within the allowed eight charges. If the squire has not unhorsed the mock opponent four times at the end of the contest, the winning prize will be awarded to the knight, Ashton de Sille. Warriors, ready yourselves. When the flag is raised you may begin the first charge."

Chanson studied Ashton on his horse with the mock warrior; a torso and head made of hollow wood wrapped in cloth. The mock opponent was fastened around the waist and secured loosely to the knight's belt.

The flag was raised. Chanson and Ashton's horses galloped down the dirt track. The feathering on Diamond Belle's hooves caressed the air like fresh blossoms swaying by the winds of Spring. The crowd cheered louder and their faces beamed with enthusiasm.

As Ashton and Chanson sped past each other, Chanson struck the opponent, but it did not fall nor was it torn or injured. They charged toward each other for a second time. Chanson struck the mock. It was pierced in the shoulder, but not unhorsed.

They charged a third time. This time the opponent was injured, but not unhorsed.

The crowd chanted again.

"Chanson-Chanson-Chanson . . . "

Chanson and the opponent were now in the fourth charge. Chanson struck the opponent, breaking his lance when he pierced through the opponent's wooden torso. He gained another point. Hayden and Landon rode out to where Chanson waited for another lance.

"You're showing yourself a mighty warrior today Chanson!" Hayden said. "I could not be more pleased of your skill and spirit!" Hayden patted Chanson on the back and winked at Diamond Belle.

"Here's another lance," Landon said. "You're going to win that coin, I just know it!"

"I hope so!" Chanson said, taking the lance in his hand and raising it high for all to see. He was focused; the fire of determination lit his spirit.

"And now the fifth charge," the Marshall said.

Seeking victory, Chanson charged again. With power in his hand, he struck the opponent and knocked the torso off Ashton's horse. The cloth was still intact, suffering no further injury. The crowd was mad with excitement. Their cheers could be heard echoing in the valleys and up the hills along Evernora's terrain. Parisina could be seen standing and clapping for Chanson. The king nodded as if pleased by Chanson's desire to succeed as a warrior knight. The orphan's tenacious spirit impressed him. Lady Genevie's eyes filled with tears of elation.

Diamond Belle and Chanson rested for a moment. Landon ran across the field and gave him and the mare some water. Chanson wiped the perspiration from his brow. He kissed Diamond Belle's head, whispering, "You've done well my diamond girl. Let's go now and get that prize!" He mounted to resume the joust.

The spectators cheered and clapped. They were touched by the squire's affectionate expressions for his horse. The chants grew louder.

"Chanson-Chanson-Chanson . . . "

He and Diamond Belle charged toward Ashton with a fresh mock. He mustered as much strength as he possibly could. He hit the opponent with such force the mock flew several feet from Ashton's horse. The mock was torn upon impact with part of the wood exposed.

The audience chanted, "Two more-two more-two more . . . "

A new mock was secured to Aston's horse. The knight and Chanson charged again. Chanson struck the opponent, tearing the cloth and unhorsing the mock.

The crowd kept chanting Chanson's name over and over.

"Chanson-Chanson-Chanson . . . "

Ashton secured the last mock, attaching it to his horse. Chanson's adrenaline was high. Before his final charge, he stared straight ahead at his opponent and envisioned himself a grown man, suited in steel and girded with strength. He took a deep breath and he and Diamond Belle charged ahead speedily. Chanson not only unhorsed the opponent, but the mock's cloth was ripped in half by the force of the lance.

"Chanson Westbrook has successfully unseated his opponent four times," the Marshall said. He will be awarded the prize later by Our Majesty."

Chanson stood before the supportive crowd looking out at the people assembled to support him. He got off his horse and bowed before all who were standing in a resounding ovation. He hugged Diamond Belle, kissing her head all over. "My girl, we did it—you're my star, a true star!" Chanson whispered.

The banquet hall
Before sunset on May 1414

King Sainesbury, his knights and their ladies, advisers, along with Parisina, Landon, and Chanson were assembled at the banquet table. They feasted on delicious food and delectable cherry juice celebrating Chanson's victory at the joust competition.

"Stupendous work, Chanson! You're skills are coming along," the king said. "I'm impressed!"

"Your Majesty, I am honored, but I have to give much of the credit to Father Hayden for patiently helping me to perfect my speed and agility with my mare. Without Diamond Belle's strength, I would not have been able to race down the long track eight times."

"Well, Ashton sure set the standard high!" the king chuckled.

"Chanson, I had to challenge you!" Ashton piped. "You've got a fire in that heart of yours, I was convinced you'd unleash it's power and win the coin today!"

"And speaking of the coin," the king piped, glancing at Esmond Scott, "would you retrieve the prize now?"

"Of course, Your Majesty." Esmond reached in his pouch and presented a cloth bag to King Sainesbury.

Parisina and Chanson exchanged smiles. Parisina had seen her father's coins before and was privy to the value the rare coins held. She knew Chanson was about to be given a royal gift few are bestowed.

"Chanson, please accept this gift as a token of appreciation for how far you've progressed in such a short period of time."

Chanson took the cloth bag from the king's outstretched hand. He untied the red ribbon and removed the gold coin.

"It's the finest piece I've ever seen!" Chanson said. "Who's the king pictured in this bust?"

"Chanson, that's my grandfather, William Edric Sainesbury. When he was king he had that coin designed. An artist, the best in Evernora, sketched his face and shoulders. Grandfather had the etching set in gold.

"Before my father died, he gave me my Grandfather's estate. My father instructed me to give the coins to warriors who had exemplary skills and who had the greatest potential when training for knighthood. You could say, they were to be given as rewards to strengthen the Sainesbury legacy while inspiring Evernora's warriors. So I give the gold piece to you now,

Chanson. May you continue to perfect yourself so that one day you will serve close to my side. It is my desire you will become a commanding knight like Hayden."

Chanson smiled, his eyes glistening with tears. Hayden was seen beaming, his eyes moistening with tears too.

"My King, I am blessed far beyond what I ever imagined. Be assured, I will remain loyal to the Sainesbury legacy and to those who are training me. I want nothing more than to stand before you one day, a knight willing to die for his king, if called upon to do so. Though perhaps I do want to live a while longer before dying for you, My King."

The king roared with laughter as did the others assembled at the huge banquet table.

"No more talk of death tonight!" the king said, lifting his gold goblet in the air. "Let us enjoy ourselves and use this time to strengthen our bonds!"

The men shouted Amen, while enjoying the food and fine friendship. Chanson continued perfecting his skills, setting high standards for his personal achievement. His bonds with the Cheswicks strengthened. As time passed, his troubled heart settled. The years ahead, however, would inevitably bring more sorrow and personal triumph.

Bonds of the Heart

Oakmoor Manor
Summer of 1417

Six years have passed since Chanson was orphaned. He was thirteen years old and stood taller than his peers. His colossal eyes were a nice complement to the blond curls touching the collar on his crisp cotton shirt. He was warm, sensitive, and pleasant with an engaging smile.

Even though Chanson did not have chestnut hair and khaki green eyes like that of Landon and those of his father, the two boys had bonded as if they were true blood brothers. Landon admired his older brother, often looking to Chanson for support and comradeship.

After sunrise, Chanson and Landon awoke, eager to have breakfast and then to take a ride through Oakhollow Forest. They mounted their horses and left with Dulcie chasing alongside.

"It looks like we're going to have to slow down, the fog's heavy this morning," Chanson said after having difficulty in seeing the path ahead of him.

"I've never seen fog this thick!" Landon said.

They slowed down, but Dulcie had disappeared.

"Where's Dulcie?" Landon said.

"Don't worry, Landon, we'll find her! Let's have a look around."

They got off their horses and proceeded to search the forest, even backtracking, but she was not to be found.

"Where could she be?" Landon said, his face wilting and his arms hanging hopelessly at his side.

"I don't know, perhaps she ran ahead of us. I think we need to keep going and see if she's found something of interest."

"Okay," Landon said as they continued riding through the forest.

The thick fog was beginning to lift, but there was still no sign of Dulcie.

"We've been riding for a while now—why haven't we found her?" Landon said.

"I don't know, but she'll show up one way or the other."

"You mean she could be dead or we'll make it to the shore and find she has drowned, don't you?"

"I didn't mean to imply the worst. I only meant I won't give up on trying to find her. Let's not jump to any conclusions yet, she will—"

"Be careful, my friends!" a female voice warned.

"Shhh," Landon said, "did you hear that too?"

"Yes. That sounds like Princess Pearlensia. We must do as she says or we'll regret it," Chanson said.

"Princess Pearlensia? Have you seen her? 'We must do as she says' . . . why are you so willing to obey a voice?"

"That doesn't matter right now. Be on alert—something's about to be revealed. Slow down, Landon, take it easy," Chanson continued, pulling the reins on Diamond Belle.

Chanson and Landon advanced into the forest while trying to heed Pearlensia's warning.

Oakmoor Manor
Before nightfall

Hayden arrived at the manor and was met by his distraught wife. As soon as he entered the door, Lady Genevie ran to Hayden, threw her arms around his neck and cried.

"Genevie, what's the matter?" Hayden said, pulling Lady Genevie's arms away from his neck and taking them into his own.

"It's the boys, they never came home after riding in the forest this morning with Dulcie! Ashton de Sille reported earlier that neither of them were seen at jousting this afternoon."

"All right. We'll go look for them. Please don't trouble your heart over this. This is not the first time they've explored the forest and lost track of time. I'm sure they are fine."

"But nightfall will soon be here! What if they're—"

"Shhh," Hayden said, placing his fingers gently on her lips, "we'll find them . . . don't worry, my Lady. I'll ask Ashton to ride with me."

Hayden took Lady Genevie's face into his hands and kissed her. "I must go, Genevie." Hayden touched her face with feather-like caresses and left.

Nightfall would soon arrive and the men had not found the boys.

"I've warned those boys about being out late in this forest. I don't know why they have chosen to defy me," Hayden said. His brow wrinkled with worry lines.

"They could be hurt in some way, Ashton said. "It's certainly not like Chanson to miss his jousting lessons. And well, Landon, he's still young, you know?"

"Yes. I have to keep reminding myself to not have the same expectations of Landon as I do Chanson."

The men sped away because they feared the boys would get lost in the forest when night fell.

The boys saw something unusual ahead. They rode closer to what appeared to be a patch of cattails. The boys got off their horses and walked cautiously toward the marshy soil. As they drew closer they saw Dulcie trying to get out of thick muddy water.

"Hang on Dulcie, we'll get you out," Landon said, watching in horror as Dulcie was about to sink to the bottom of the grimy pit. Landon walked closer to Dulcie. He reached, trying to grab her, but slipped in with her.

"No, Landon, don't go any further! It's quicksand! Don't move or it will swallow you both."

Dulcie kept trying to resist the liquefied soil, only to sink further. Landon attempted to move toward the dog, trying to grab her so that she would not sink further.

"No, Landon, stay still! You'll both drown if you keep moving. I'll go find a limb or stick for you to grab onto."

"All right."

Chanson searched the area and found a large tree limb. When he returned Dulcie had sank further with the sludgy debris hovering around her neck.

"Here," Chanson said, extending the stick out to Landon, "take hold and I'll pull you out."

"But I can't leave her here . . . Dulcie's almost completely under, she'll drown!" Landon cried.

"But you have to! Perhaps Father Hayden will be here soon. Someone's bound to have missed us by now. Please, Landon, grab the limb—do it now!"

With teary eyes, Landon took hold of the stick. Chanson pulled with every fiber of his being, but he could not get Landon out of the quicksand. Each move only sank them further into the watery pit. Chanson stood helpless in trying to save Landon and Dulcie. He prayed.

> *Please God, help us! Don't let them die—please God—save them!*

"Be still, Landon, help is on the way!" Princess Pearlensia assured.

"It's her again, Landon. You must heed what she says!"

A peaceful breeze brushed over Landon's face, he calmed.

The sound of Hayden and Ashton's horses were heard rushing toward them.

"Landon, that may be Father coming to save you. Hang on, don't give up. Be still a little longer!"

Hayden and Ashton jumped off their horses and hiked to where Chanson was standing. Hayden brushed away fear and anxiety in seeing his son about to drown. He prayed within himself for God's hand of mercy on them.

"Father! Help us!" Landon said.

"Don't talk Landon, don't move. Trust me, we'll get you out, we will," Hayden said, stiffening his upper lip. He quickly took a rope out of his leather bag. "Son, I'm going to throw the rope out to you, grab it and we'll pull you out."

"But what about Dulcie . . . we can't leave her here!" Landon cried.

"Son, please do as I say! We'll have to get her later. Please, Landon! There's no time to argue this, I'm going to throw the rope now."

He threw the rope out and Landon took hold of the end. Ashton, Hayden, and Chanson pulled Landon to safety, but Dulcie sank further with the rippling movement.

"No! Dulcie can't die!" Landon sobbed, dashing to the edge.

"Landon get back from the edge! Let me try to get her. Stay back boys!"

They stepped back and Ashton leaped out to help.

"I'm going to tie the rope around my waist and swim back out to her. Ashton, you and the boys can pull me back out when I've got a good hold of her."

"All right," Ashton said, getting as close as he safely could to the edge of the quicksand.

"Hurry Father, Dulcie's head just went under!" Landon said.

Hayden had the rope tied securely around his waist. He stepped in, sinking quickly. He felt around the area where Dulcie was seen and grabbed onto her slimy body, lifting her into his arms. Her body was limp and she was barely breathing. As he held her in his arms, she sank further.

"Hurry Ashton!" Hayden said, fearing Dulcie was about to die.

Ashton and the boys pulled hard on the rope, bringing Hayden back to level ground.

Hayden laid Dulcie down and proceeded to smooth away the debris from her mouth. "Come on Dulcie, wake up. It's all over." Despite Hayden's pleadings, the dog's breath was labored.

"Father, may I hold her?" Landon said.

"Of course," he said, placing Dulcie gingerly into Landon's outstretched arms. Landon sat down on the muddy ground.

"She's dying, isn't she Father?" Landon cried, observing Dulcie's shallow breathing.

"I believe so, Son. She seems to have swallowed some of the muddy water and can't cough it up."

Landon ran his fingers through her long wavy coat. Her breathing ceased. He whispered, "Dulcie, *please, Dulcie*, don't leave me."

Chanson knelt beside Landon. "I'm sorry, Landon. Dulcie's gone . . . s-she's gone," Chanson said, his voice breaking with empathy.

Landon continued petting the dog. A whirlwind of memories swirled with each cautious smoothing.

Hayden knelt beside his distraught son, placed his arms around his shoulders and whispered, "I'm sorry,

Son, there's nothing we can do for her. Let's go home now. We'll bury her in the morning. I know a fitting place."

Landon took off his shirt and wrapped it around Dulcie. They got on their horses and rode home.

Oakmoor Manor

Hayden and the boys arrived home, meeting Lady Genevie on the lawn. She gasped at seeing mud all over Landon and Dulcie's body wrapped in his shirt. "What happened?" she said.

"Dulcie drowned!" Landon cried.

"Oh no," Lady Genevie said, her eyes welling in tears. "Our sweet Dulcie can't be gone, she can't—"

Landon collapsed into his mother's arms.

"I know it hurts," she said, kissing her son's cheek. "Dulcie's been a loyal friend, we'll miss her. Our yard won't be the same without our Dulcie chasing the butterflies."

"We need to get cleaned up now, Landon," Hayden said. "I'll take her to the gatehouse, there's a cool place there. We'll bury her at Summergate Meadow in the morning."

"I'll take my flute . . . Dulcie loved it when I played for her!" Chanson said, smiling as tears shimmered in his eyes.

"That's a fine idea," Hayden said, "I'll secure her body now."

The next morning

Chanson and the Cheswicks arrived at Summergate Meadow, a grassy hillside outside Oakhollow Forest.

"Look, Landon, Summergate is in full bloom with violets and pansies," Hayden said, pointing to a sunny hillside with butterflies fluttering among masses of blooming yellow, white, and purple petals. "That's a splendid spot to bury Dulcie, don't you think? Lying here is sure to satisfy her insatiable curiosity with butterflies and allow her to scurry through thickets and wild flowers for all of Eternity."

Landon chuckled as tears continued to flow. He remembered times in the past when Dulcie's fur had to be combed after it became matted with leaves, twigs, and other debris from the wooded areas where she frolicked.

With a serene glance, Landon responded, "Yes, she will be happy here."

"Very well. Please wait here with your mother, there's quite a few briers and brambles, let me clear them first then you can follow the cleared path behind me."

Hayden cleared a way into the violet, pansy-arrayed meadow and walked back to where Lady Genevie, Landon, and Chanson were waiting. He scooped Dulcie into his arms and walked back to the lavishly blossomed flowering field. After digging a suitable grave, Hayden placed Dulcie's body into the ground and covered her with dirt. Chanson played wistful tunes for Dulcie after she was sufficiently covered.

Landon and Lady Genevie picked a few violets and placed them on her grave. The family sat on the warm grass, holding hands, while Chanson continued playing his flute. They shared favorite memories as they laughed and cried, reminiscing about the past with Dulcie.

Late evening

Hayden announced he wanted to talk with the boys after the family had finished their dinner. They gathered around Hayden and Lady Genevie, regretting ever riding through the forest during heavy fog. They sat quietly to hear what Hayden had to say. Their eyes were misty with tears.

"Boys, I understand you could not have known about the quicksand," Hayden said, "but from now on, you cannot ride into the forest again when there is severe fog. Further, there's the potential for a stranger to come along and hurt you. If you can't see the path clearly as you ride along, then you may not see someone hiding in the bushes who would want to harm you. Is that understood, boys?"

"Yes," Landon said. Chanson also agreed by nodding his head.

The family spent the rest of the evening comforting one another in memories of their beloved pet. Chanson enjoyed a reprieve from sorrow and trouble following Dulcie's death. Soon, however, an expected turn of events would shift Chanson back into the jaws of helplessness.

The Killer

Oakmoor Manor
Late Morning in Autumn of 1417

Chanson and Landon had finished breakfast when Hayden announced plans to take the family for a ride on the beach of Kaishore Ocean. Having a day to enjoy, without chores and training, was news both Chanson and Landon were delighted to hear. They quickly dressed and prepared for the promising day ahead. The family mounted their horses and were on their way, riding peacefully through Oakhollow Forest.

"Autumn is a particularly good time to ride our horses along the beach," Lady Genevie said, smiling at her husband. “The white sand, lit by the fiery sky, inspires the senses.”

“I see you remember our rides along the beach when we courted,” Hayden piped. “I recall your gilded locks flowing behind as we rode along side by side. Your topaz eyes drew me in right away.”

“Those are cherished memories, my darling Hayden.”

“It’s been awhile since we’ve taken the boys to the beach, I thought today would be the perfect time to do so. We’ve all worked hard and are deserving of an afternoon of rest and play.”

“How long will we stay, Father?” Landon said.

“Your mother packed raisin cakes, nuts, and water to enjoy so we could watch the sun set before returning home. Would you like that?”

“Yes!” Landon said.

“I've had some ideas on a new piece of music I’d like to explore while there.” Chanson said.

“I also brought some blankets so that we can lie on the beach and watch the puffins and otters play,” Lady Genevie said. “Chanson, you’re sure to be inspired by the marvelous birds as they soar above your head.”

“Boys, in a little while we’ll come to the shoreline and then we’ll have all afternoon to be refreshed in the breezes of this new day.”

The family arrived at the beach. They got off their horses and tied them to trees along the wooded section of Oakhollow Forest. With the blankets and other supplies, they skipped along kicking up sand while singing an old folk song.

Chanson spotted an old piece of driftwood floating along a cliff near the ocean. Intrigued by the wood, he left the others to explore the nooks and crannies of the beach.

"Don't be too long, Chanson, we'll be eating soon," Lady Genevie said.

"I won't." He proceeded to sprint toward the driftwood with his writing supplies in his hand.

Chanson secured the perfect place to release his creative energy; an ancient willow tree. He spread the blanket under the swaying branches and sat down to compose a new melody.

With the tree's trunk behind him, Chanson had not noticed a man walking toward him. As the man drew closer, Chanson sensed an uneasiness erupting within him. He could hear slight creaking noises. He carefully placed his writing supplies on the blanket. *Perhaps it's only an animal . . . an animal isn't anything to be scared of*, he reasoned.

Chanson stood and turned sharply to see who or what was creeping upon him.

He saw a dirty, long haired man. The man appeared to have been homeless. His clothes were too large for his thin frame. His pants drug the ground and were tattered on the hems. Feeling pity for the stranger, Chanson said, "Do you need help?"

"I need some food and water," he said, keeping his hands in his pockets and not making eye contact.

"Come with me and I'll take you to where my family is. There's food and water; we will be glad to share with you."

The man followed Chanson to where the others were seen riding their horses along the beach. Chanson put down his blanket and writing materials and raced after Hayden.

"Father Hayden, Father Hayden, please stop!" Chanson yelled.

Hayden and the others turned around and rode back to Chanson.

"This man needs some food and water," Chanson said. "May I share what we have with him?"

"Yes, we've plenty," Hayden said. He opened the bag containing the food and water.

"Here, have it," Hayden said.

The man reached out with only one hand to take the food and water. He kept his head low and did not make eye contact with Hayden. But when he kept his right hand in his pocket, Hayden grew suspicious of the man. To ease his mind, Hayden said, "Is something wrong with your hand?"

The man refused to answer and turned his back proceeding to walk away. In his haste, the water canteen dropped onto the sand. Chanson sprinted toward him, picked up the water and handed it back to the stranger. He was not prepared for what he saw. The man's other hand was out of his pocket revealing four missing fingers.

Fear took over Chanson and memories he thought long hushed away rose from his suppressed mind. It was all clear now; the stranger was his father's killer. Flashbacks to his youth paralyzed him. He recalled his mother screaming for the man not to hurt her husband. His father sliced off the man's four fingers before the blade was turned on him by the killer.

"YOU! IT WAS YOU WHO KILLED MY FATHER!" Chanson screamed. The man dropped the food and tried to flee before getting caught. Hayden dropped the bag and sprinted after the man. He secured the man after grabbing onto his long hair flying behind.

Hayden was furious, his jaw clenching. He put his sword to the man's chest and yelled, "Get on the ground, NOW and don't you move! Landon bring me two ropes."

The man laid down on the ground, but was reluctant to do so.

Landon retrieved the ropes quickly and took them to Hayden. "Tie his ankles and wrists while I hold him down."

Landon secured the ropes like his father had taught him to do in his training.

Hayden's eyes darkened and his temper sparked. He pointed his sword at the man's neck, and yelled, "You're about to meet your fate! GET UP!" Hayden shouted.

The man stood with a sneer on his face. "I've never killed anyone. I don't know why the boy said that!" the man yelled, his dark, eerie eyes settling on Chanson as if they were peering into his soul.

Chanson stood, his eyes glazed and his feet frozen in the sand. Shock drained his face of color as he gaped at the killer, remembering his mother's fingernails clawing at the man's face before she was stabbed to death. Lady Genevie put her arms around him.

"Landon," Hayden blurted, "get that old cloth out of my bag and let's cover this man's disgraceful eyes—I don't want those murderous eyes looking at anyone!"

Hayden threw the man over his horse and secured him further. When he had the killer bound, he turned his attention toward Chanson.

"Chanson, are you all right?" Hayden said.

"My legs are weak and I have a sick churning in my stomach. It's been a dreadful day. I can't begin to tell you how scared I was when I saw the man kill Papa," Chanson said, tears welling in his eyes. His hands trembled and his face was pale and clammy.

"Chanson, it's over. Now you can put this revolting man out of your mind. As I've done before, I will do now and help you through this upheaval. Let's get you back home and I'll deal with the killer. I'll take him to King Sainesbury while you and the others rest at home. Everything's going to be all right."

"Thank you, Father Hayden. This is not something I expected to happen today. I wanted to write music and enjoy this day with my family."

"Family—yes, we are family. I'm happy you have come to accept our love."

"I love you, Father Hayden."

"I love you too, Son," Hayden reassured, taking Chanson into his arms. Landon and Lady Genevie also reassured Chanson of their unfailing love for him.

They mounted their horses and left in haste for home.

Firegate Castle
Late afternoon

King Sainesbury was alerted there was urgent news regarding Chanson Westbrook. Hayden Cheswick was allowed to speak with the king privately regarding the information.

"Hayden, what's troubling you, those beads of perspiration on your brow tell me you are vexed greatly."

"Yes, Your Majesty, to the depths of my soul. It's Chanson."

"Has he been hurt?"

"He's shaken, but not hurt. The killer, I have him bound on my horse."

"Killer, what killer?"

"The man who murdered Chanson's father! I captured him on the beach."

"What! How were you able to find him?"

"I didn't. He was on the beach while I was there with my family. Chanson recognized him."

"Well now, that's some news. Please understand me when I say this, we need to be certain of this man's crime before he's punished. We should return to Chanson's former home and inquire about the men who had been seen killing his family."

"You mean the old man who had witnessed the murders six years ago?"

"Indeed I do. I'll put the man in confinement until we knew more details. I believe you should go home and comfort your family and let me deal with this man in the morning. We can both head out fresh and rested to the Village of Greyflower tomorrow."

"All right, Your Majesty."

"Hayden, don't let this trouble you. I realize your much needed day of rest was interrupted, and in the cruelest way imaginable. But I believe all of this will turn for his good. Chanson will once and for all be able to let this tragic past go and allow it to remain in the past."

"Yes. that's what I told him after we walked in the door. He was weak in the knees and ghostly pale, but I believe he will be all right once he's had time to let it settle."

"Hayden, it's very likely he has suffered nightmares and worried the killer would one day find him. Perhaps coming face to face with him is what he needed to finally let it rest in the past."

"Yes, of course. You are right. I value your wisdom. I will go home now and try to console him."

"Very well. Be back here in the morning and we'll finalize this matter."

"Good night, My King."

"Good night to you and your family."

I will carry you even when you are old and silver-haired.

Auden Willoughby

Firegate Castle
King Sainesbury's chamber
The next morning in Autumn 1417

The king awoke early with yesterday's events heavy on his mind. He yawned and stretched while peering out his window at the gray-clouded sky. He was consumed with a foreboding about the man believed to be the killer of Chanson's father. The king prayed, ate, and left with Hayden to visit the old man who had witnessed the murders six years ago.

After riding for a while, they arrived at the Village of Greyflower.

"Look at these ruins, My King," Hayden said, "the blood stains have been washed away, but not the wreckage. I had hoped I'd never have a reason to return to this eerie place."

"It's a wretched scene," the king said, as he surveyed the area and saw houses vacant with shattered windows. "I'm glad Chanson isn't with us to see what has become of the house he once lived in. I fear we may not find the reclusive man still living among this destruction."

"That's his house on the hill," Hayden said, pointing to a small stone house.

"In that bleak place with moss and mold covering it?" the king said, surprised.

"Yes, that's his home, and only one window in the place. I begged the man to let us take him back with us, but he refused to leave, saying he liked his privacy and preferred to be left to himself."

"That explains why the men did not invade his home; it must have appeared to be as desolate as it does today."

"That's right, My King. His life may have been spared because of his miserly ways."

"Well, I think it's time we knock on the rickety door," the king said.

"Watch your step, My King, the broken rocks on these winding steps seem unsteady."

"I see. I pity the man if indeed he still lives here."

Hayden knocked.

"Hello, you in there," Hayden said.

They waited, but no reply from the man. Hayden knocked again, louder.

"He must be in there, his horse is still here," the king said, noticing the horse tied to a nearby tree.

"Perhaps he's scared and doesn't remember us," Hayden said. "It has been a while since someone lived near to him as evidenced by the way this village looks.

I'll knock once more and if he does not answer we'll go in and make sure he isn't ill or worse."

Hayden knocked again, and said, "Hello, we mean you no harm, we only need your help—*Please*. We believe the killer is back!" Hayden yelled.

They heard glass breaking.

"Did you hear that Hayden?" the king said.

"It sounded like a bowl shattered on the floor."

"Please, we know you're in there. We only need your help and then we'll leave you alone. I'm Hayden Cheswick and I have King Sainesbury with me. It's about the murderers who killed Chanson Westbrook's family.

Upon those words, the man opened immediately. He had aged considerably since Hayden had last seen him; deep lines on his sunken face were overshadowed by a silver beard. His long, sable hair laid flat against his nape, covering his ears. His shoulders slumped forward as he moped cautiously out the door. His tattered black robe was held closed with his hand, revealing severely chewed fingernails.

"What do you want?" the scraggly elderly man said, his eyes twitching. "What about the orphan?"

"A man was captured on the beach yesterday," the king piped. "My instincts tell me he is the murderer who escaped six years ago right after the Village of Greyflower dispute took place."

"I'm an old man, and don't want to get involved with this again. I'm sorry for the boy, I am, but I can't see the killer's face again; his heart is cold iron . . . cold iron, I tell you. Do you have any idea the nightmares I've suffered from seeing those dead bodies? I still don't sleep well. The killer's face hovers over me in the pitch blackness in my room, stealing my rest. Maybe now that everyone's abandoned the area, I will be left alone!"

"Imagine the nightmares Chanson has had," Hayden blurted. "I spent many a night trying to console him over the massacre he witnessed, and now when he's beginning to settle down, this dangerous man comes to slash open his wounds. Are you willing to turn your back on the boy, refusing to help him to put his fears to rest?"

The old man peered over their shoulders, taking inventory of the village's destruction. Memory took him to the day of the killings. He could hear the screams of his neighbors' final cries; they resounded like cannons firing off in his head. His wrecked nerves led him to chew on what was left of his fingernails.

"If you come with us to identify the man, he won't get the chance to haunt you or kill another person," the king interrupted. "You have my word, I will protect you. We will smuggle you in through a secret passage and no one will know nor will anyone pester you."

"Well, if you are certain of what you promised then I will go. Wait here and I'll change into clothes more suitable for traveling on a horse."

"Very well," the king said.

The man soon returned, dressed in torn, faded clothes and ready to leave.

The king did as he had promised the peculiar man and slipped him in through one of the secret passages in the gatehouse. He was also promised a festive meal after the stranger's identity was made.

King Sainesbury and one of his guards led the frail witness to a secluded alcove in the castle's gatehouse.

The doorway into the alcove was concealed by an opaque black drape. The king pulled back the drape and they entered the granite-floored room. Soon after, the shackled man was ushered in with two guards holding each arm. King Sainesbury summoned the other guard to stand beside the man to reassure him he would be safe and protected. But before King Sainesbury had the chance to ask the witness to identify the killer, the insecure man screamed, "It's him, he killed the father and others! I saw him do it from my window. The father fought hard, slicing the killer's hand with his knife. But the killer overpowered him and killed Kenley with his own blade. It was him—he killed the boy's father then fled, holding his bloody hand!" The witnessed glared at the man and screamed, "Murderer-MURDERER—"

The frightened man shuddered in fear. His knees gave way and he fell on the floor. Beads of perspiration broke out on his forehead. He pulled his knees up to his chest and sat with his arms secured around them.

"Guards, get the killer out of here! Summon Desmond Pierce to force the rest of the truth from this prisoner."

"Of course, Your Majesty," one of the guards said. The two guards took hold of the killer's arms and returned him to the dungeon.

King Sainesbury and Hayden came to the aid of the witness and reminded the angst-ridden man of the delicious feast awaiting him. The man soon regained his strength and rose to his feet, still weak and visibly shaken.

"What is your name?" the king said.

"I'm Auden, Auden Willoughby, Your Majesty."

"Well, Auden, I have some fine food prepared for you. I'll have it brought down to you and you can enjoy eating it here, away from people and anyone you fear could hurt you."

"No, no, I believe I'd prefer to have some company. May I be permitted that, kind king?"

The king was surprised at the man's request after he had informed him he would allow him to eat his food in solitude if he wished.

"Absolutely, whatever you desire, it will be done for you. Come, join me and my knights in the banquet hall," the king said, stretching out his hand to invite the man to follow him to the banquet already prepared.

Auden wept after seeing the enormous display of food and the welcoming faces of the king's knights and advisers sitting at the banquet table. He cowed in embarrassment over allowing others to see him vulnerable.

"What's the matter, Auden?" the king said, leaning toward the man.

"Well, I-I'm overwhelmed by your kindness—and this food, well, I've never had food like this before. I've been accustomed to living alone and eating meager meals for years now. I didn't know how rich life could be when shared with benevolent men."

"Please sit and enjoy!" the king said with a welcoming smile.

Auden Willoughby sat and continued to sob. He could not hold back what appeared to be years of pent up loneliness and disappointments of life. His body shook in sorrow as he held his head down.

"You have demonstrated great courage to come here and face the man who murdered Chanson's family," the king reassured.

"And because of you, the killer won't run loose hurting anyone else," Hayden piped. "It is I who feels honored by you. So have plenty of food. Be of great cheer and let us be your friends."

"I'd like that very much. Now that I've had a taste of true friendship, I don't know how I'll go back to a desolate dwelling."

"Well, Auden, you don't have to," the king reassured. "I'm happy to have you come live here with us. I'll see to it that you have a quiet place that should suit you well. That way, if you wish to have our company, we're here and if not, you may enjoy your solitude. Of course the scrumptious food is always available to you, as much as you wish."

"Auden, would you like for us to help you move?" Ashton de Sille piped.

"You have been cordial to me. I would like that very much, kind friends."

"Well gentlemen, we've a new friend at the table," the king said, raising his cherry juice-filled goblet and all the men joining the king's welcoming toast.

Soon Auden's tears ceased and he was no longer a lonely recluse without friends; his eyes gleamed and the hollows of his face lifted. The king and his loyal friends sat for the rest of the evening being entertained by the man's funny tales and interesting experiences.

The knights took Auden back to his dilapidated house the next day and helped him pack. They moved him into the castle. King Sainesbury gave him private quarters with a window that overlooked a small creek running along the outer edge of the castle grounds.

The man had lived all of his adult life hidden away and scared of society. King Sainesbury's hand of friendship transformed him. He lived surrounded by loyal friends and decadent food.

Upon interrogating the murderer, Desmond Pierce found the man had only lived in Oakhollow Forest for a few weeks. He kept a low profile by moving around periodically to avoid detection. The man also confessed to killing five other people in the Village of Greyflower. The killer was executed shortly after his confessions.

Chanson had lived in fear of the murderer of his father since that fateful day on April 3, 1411. Because of Auden Willoughby and Chanson's encounter with the killer, the orphan was finally set free from the haunted past. Chanson's life will now explode with refreshing seasons of love and family.

Accolade

Firegate Castle
King Sainesbury's throne
Sunrise on July 7, 1420

Chanson Westbrook was summoned to the king's throne.

"Your Majesty, Chanson Westbrook is here, should I send him in?" the king's guard said.

"Yes."

Chanson saw the king sitting on his throne with his mastiff dog, Brayleigh, standing on the right side. Brayleigh wagged her tail when Chanson approached the dog who had been his devoted friend since first being orphaned nine years ago. It was apparent to the king that the two shared a significant bond when Chanson reached out to Brayleigh.

"You've secured a lifelong friendship with my Brayleigh. It pleases me know how you've bonded over the years," the king said.

Chanson soon took his focus away from Brayleigh. He approached the king and knelt. "Your Majesty, you called for me?"

"Yes, Chanson, please, sit."

Chanson sat in a red brocade chair to the left of King Sainesbury.

"It cheers my heart to see you smiling more," the king continued. "Those first few years were difficult for you, I know. I can see that allowing you to bond with my pet has indeed proven to be of benefit to you. Brayleigh, too, has been helped by the time you've spent with her, as evidenced by her reaction to you.

"Hayden Cheswick has informed me you are ready to take on the position of knighthood, expressing your skills as a swordsman are noteworthy. When considering warriors in my kingdom, I seek out those who are loyal like you. You are controlled and sure of yourself—confident, but not arrogant. You would be my youngest knight, only sixteen years old. You have earned the title, not only in your strengths and skills, but also in your character.

"It takes time to find loyal men. I need men whose word is their seal of honor and whose lives exemplify chivalry and integrity of heart. You have the qualities this kingdom needs to maintain a strong army. I am appointing you as my next knight. Can I count on you, Chanson, to protect the kingdom at all costs by accepting this noble position?"

"I would consider it an honor, Your Majesty," Chanson said, bowing again in respect for the king.

"Very well. It will be done. Leave now and I'll send Hayden to prepare you for the knighting ceremony. Oh, and Chanson—"

"Yes, Your Majesty."

"Pack your flute. I should think I'll still be in need of the melodies you play so flawlessly. I wouldn't want to disappoint the ladies in the inner court either, especially my daughter," King Sainesbury chuckled.

"As you wish, My King." Chanson smiled as if smitten by the beautiful daughter. He bowed and left the king's presence.

In preparation for the knighting ceremony Chanson was dressed in a white vesture, black wool hose, and soft black leather shoes with a crimson robe overlaid. The Order of Knighthood ceremony started with a night vigil in Marblemist Chapel. He fasted and prayed at the altar for ten hours.

The following day the king gathered his knights, his advisers, and the families together inside the court to begin the knighting ceremony.

Landon and three other squires led Chanson to the king's presence. He knelt.

Hayden Cheswick stepped forward with Chanson's new sword. King Sainesbury said:

"The sword has two sides, to slay and wound and a point to stab. You must be willing to defend the destitute and the weak, your fellow men, and the king, sacrificing your own life if necessary. You are to wear your sword with chastity at all times. Chanson

Westbrook, for what purpose do you wish to join the order?" the king continued.

"I desire to be a knight so that I might serve God and my King. I promise to uphold the sacred virtues—loyalty, generosity, and truthfulness—protecting the kingdom while defending the weak, widowed, and orphaned to the best of my ability."

Lady Genevie removed Chanson's crimson robe, placing a velvet blue houppelande on him. Hayden Cheswick, Ashton de Sille, and the king's other knights stepped forward with the regalia. Chanson bowed before King Sainesbury after his belt, chain, spurs, and sword were placed on him.

The king tapped him on the shoulders with the flat of his sword and said:

"In the presence of God I dub you Sir Knight—be valiant, fearless, and loyal. You may now rise and greet the members of the order."

Chanson rose and greeted the members.

Landon Cheswick and the rest of King Sainesbury's squires returned with baskets of gold and silver and distributed them among the family and guests.

The king showered the knights and his members with a festival of fine food, music, and dance.

Chanson played his flute, catching the eye of Parisina. They shared smiles. She walked toward him, her gown sweeping over white lilac petals behind each graceful step.

"My father's told me a great deal about your bravery, Chanson," Parisina said with engaging eyes.

Chanson put down his flute, stood, and bowed in front of the dainty woman.

"Lady Parisina. Please, allow me to be a gentleman—take my seat."

Parisina raised the lower edge of her silk gown and sat on the bench Chanson had offered. The stone bench had large claw feet and grape leaf motifs trailing on the back.

Chanson inquired further, raising his eyes with a hopeful sparkle, "Your father has spoken of me?"

"Often. I am not allowed to hear my father discuss the strategies concerning this kingdom and its political affairs, but he expressed that he trusted you with his very life. Father has a noble heart and would only choose men of the highest esteem to serve close to him. He is the sincerest, wisest man in all of Evernora and would not bestow honor on any who had even one trace of guile in their souls.

"When you played your flute, Father was often moved to tears by your touching melodies. I cherished those times with my father and could easily see the deep respect he had for you. It was as if you were more of a son to him than an orphaned boy. He cherishes you—surely you must know how he favors you."

"It is me who feels honored to defend such a man as your father, a king of the highest integrity. He could have chosen to send me away to live elsewhere after my parents were murdered. Instead, he has endowed me with the blessing of serving close by his side."

"You are a grateful and humble man. I see why my father loves you so. I admire the way you have risen out of a tragic past becoming a great warrior. You are someone my father can count on. When we frolicked on the lawn as carefree children, your heart impressed me even then. I saw your soul—open and beautiful—reflecting in your kind, generous eyes."

"I, too, cherish those days of innocence. Without knowing, you were an elixir for my wounded spirit. Somehow I wasn't as lonely when you were near me."

"It was because I understood it. I, too, suffered significantly while in youth. My dear mother died when I was a wee child. Of course I was never left without my father's love and protection like you, Chanson. When I missed my mother's soft kisses at night, only hearing her tender voice in the echo of memory, Father stayed with me until I fell asleep."

"Beautiful Parisina, we are not so different after all. I am touched in my soul that you have spoken of those tender sentiments with me," Chanson said, reaching out for Parisina's hand.

Parisina allowed Chanson to hold her supple hand. A strand of her long waved hair floated over her shoulder as she leaned closer to Chanson. Radiance lit her face. She smiled and said, "I will also cherish our conversation today. The principles ruling your spirit are trustworthy. I know of none other more suited to protect my father."

"I owe all that I am, first to our God then to all those who had a hand in raising me, namely the Cheswicks and King Sainesbury. Your father has been gracious to me since being orphaned. I will defend him until my dying day. That is a promise you can count on."

"You say it as if you are certain you will die," Parisina said, her voice whispering with melancholy.

"I hope I do not die, but defending the king is all that matters."

"It can't be a secret to any of how vast my love and devotion is for my father. I am pleased to hear you say you will defend him until your dying day!"

"Be assured, I do mean it."

Parisina smiled again and whispered, "Please Chanson, would you play your flute for me? I'd love to hear one of the touching melodies you performed in the theater."

"Of course. I would be honored to do so."

Chanson serenaded King Sainesbury's daughter, with not one memorable tune, but several. It became apparent to the other knights, and to the king, that his daughter was taken by the flute player's chivalrous manners. Taking notice of his daughter's blushing face, King Sainesbury approached Chanson and Parisina.

"Your Majesty," Chanson said, bowing.

"Please, do not stop playing, Chanson," King Sainesbury said. "If my daughter enjoys listening this much, then, by all means, play on—play on, even dance with her if you wish!"

"Oh Father, he is sublime; his melodies have touched me deeply over the years. His bravery and courage inspire me."

"So I noticed," the king said, chuckling robustly. "He will be one of my finest knights. Enjoy yourselves and have some of the berries and cakes prepared."

"Father, may I take Chanson to the Gardens of Fairnesse tomorrow? The fragrant blossoms are in full bloom. Spending tomorrow morning with the birds flirting around the petals would delight our souls immensely. That is, if Chanson would like to promenade through the gardens," Parisina said, looking at Chanson as if to invite him for a summer stroll.

"Of course," the king said.

"I am honored you have asked me," Chanson said. "When should I come for you?"

"Late morning will be wonderful as the sun begins to dabble over the petals."

"Remember Chanson, we ride out when nightfall approaches. We can't break tradition," King Sainesbury interrupted.

"Of course, Your Majesty—as you wish."

"Very well."

King Sainesbury kissed his daughter's cheeks and went back to join his most trusted adviser, Esmond Scott. Chanson and Parisina danced around the garland-laid ground.

The king and Esmond sat on a raised platform, their eyes taking in the exultant festivities. The king's chief adviser towered over the king by a few inches. He was a pearl-haired man with a peppered beard. While well groomed, his curly hair was often unruly. Esmond's sterling gray eyes were lined with wrinkles. The kind of wrinkles that were welcoming and calming, garnering respect.

As was King Sainesbury's custom, whether in his private quarters or out on the castle grounds, his mastiff dog, Brayleigh was ever by his side.

"It appears Chanson and your daughter have become more than friends, Your Majesty!" Esmond said, peering over at Parisina's love-struck eyes.

"Well, if that's what pleases my little girl then let her have what makes her happy," King Sainesbury said, petting his dog as if he and the canine had formed an agreement concerning Parisina's happiness.

"Chanson's been faithful," the king continued. "I cannot think of anyone better for her. I've noticed how her eyes light up when Chanson's name is mentioned. I had suspected for some time she found him desirable.

"If her mother had lived to raise her she would be so pleased at how she has blossomed. Parisina has a pure soul—she's more valuable to me than a kingdom of boys."

"I know you wanted a son as heir to the throne," Esmond said.

"Yes, but it wasn't meant to be, despite how much I pleaded with God to grant me another son. Perhaps Landon or Chanson will desire the throne when my reign is over. In time Landon will be ready to take his place with Chanson."

"As a knight, Your Majesty?" Esmond said.

"Yes. I've kept him in mind over the years. Though he's not as even tempered or self-controlled as Chanson."

"Your Majesty, wouldn't Landon be your number one choice? I've seen how loyal he is. He never hesitates during training."

"Well, there has been something about Chanson that I've not seen in one so young. He's conscientious, compassionate, and yet, strong willed. These traits have also resided in the hearts of other mighty warriors I've known.

"When Chanson stood before me, broken by the unfortunate death of his family, I knew we were all the youngster had. To see how brave and tall he is now, makes me beam with pride. He's one of us. How does a man get this blessed, Esmond—how?"

"You've allowed God to be your guide and He has blessed your faithfulness, My King."

"It pleases me to hear you say that. It's been difficult since Chloette died. On the night she left my side, I asked God *why?*—why did He leave me with a kingdom to rule and an impressionable little girl to look after?"

"Your faith has seen you through this."

"By the sheer grace of God, Esmond," King Sainesbury sighed.

"Parisina's a lovely young woman now, a virtuous one at that," Esmond said.

"Yes, she is. If she loves Chanson I'll permit the marriage."

"Well, from the looks of how close they've gotten while we've been sitting here, you might be doing just that!"

"Yes, I see," the king said, noticing his daughter's rapturous smile and girlish laughter. "If she loves Chanson then I will grant her whatever she desires. It does my heart good to know she's found someone who treats her with respect and gentleness like Chanson does. I haven't seen her smile like that before. Her eyes sparkle like her mother's when she was her age. Oh, so tender and young she still is—but, Chanson's a good man. I knew early on he had a kind soul with the potential of maturing into a loyal warrior. At the end of the day, it only matters that we stood for the right, defended the weak and helpless while keeping ourselves untainted by corruption and conceit."

"Indeed," Esmond said.

"Esmond, we'd better gather the knights for the initiation ride. It appears the sun's beginning to set on Scarlet's Peak," the king said, standing beside his dog and petting her as if to bid farewell to a successful and joyous occasion.

Esmond bowed before the king and left to take Brayleigh back to his quarters. He then gathered the knights for the traditional forest ride.

Chanson mounted Diamond Belle and led the other knights through Oakhollow Forest. The scent of fresh pine lingered in the air.

"It's a full moon, Chanson," the king said, pointing to the clear moonlit sky. "Would you look at that crystal halo around the moon. It appears to be dazzling with jewels. Take it in Chanson, I believe the heavens have favored you tonight."

"I will do just that!" Chanson said. "Your Majesty, I hope to never disappoint you, my God or the very ones I've taken an oath to uphold."

"Chanson, your mother must be looking down from the heavens with a heart beaming with joy at how well her son has turned out," Hayden said with a slight mist in his star-gazed eyes.

"I count myself honored to now be shoulder to shoulder with one as mighty and loyal as you, Father Hayden," Chanson said in humble tone. "You've been a heroic light—led me through the thickest of dark despair while instilling a desire for the Holy Scriptures. I'll be grateful for the rest of my life for how you and Lady Genevie cared for me."

King Sainesbury piped, "Chanson, on behalf of myself and all these men here tonight, welcome to the heroic brotherhood."

"I'm honored. Thank you, My King," Chanson said as he, King Sainesbury, and the rest of the knights rode further into Oakhollow Forest.

Marblemist Chapel

The day following his accolade ceremony, Chanson rose before daybreak to pray and read the Bible before taking on his new role as Sir Knight. He was interrupted by Hayden and Lady Genevie.

"I thought we'd find you here," Hayden said.

Chanson stood and said, "I did not expect to see you this early. Is all well?"

"Oh yes," Lady Genevie said, "very well in fact. We've come with a gift for you—here—take it, it is yours." She handed him a wrapped linen parcel tied with string.

"Thank you," Chanson said, accepting the package. He placed the parcel on his lap and opened the gift.

"A Bible! Is this mine to take with me?"

"Of course, Chanson," Hayden said. "God's Word is your spiritual sword, it will protect your soul against the enemy of God's people."

"You've grown greatly since coming to live with us," Lady Genevie said. "We've seen how reading the Bible has transformed you; instilling peace in your soul and healing the wounds of your past. Now that you are one of King Sainesbury's warriors, Hayden and I wanted you to have your very own Bible to inspire you in this new season."

He opened the leather cover and gingerly turned the pages.

"It's exquisite, the gold leaves on these drawings are beautifully etched," Chanson said, caressing the papyrus page.

"It was about a year ago I commissioned the manuscript to be made for you," Hayden said. "I was confident you were going to be chosen to be one of King Sainesbury's knights. Let God's Word guide and give you strength, for there will surely be hardships to come against you, as you've already found."

"I am so honored. I will remember this day for as long as I live and will cherish God's words, hiding them in my heart," Chanson affirmed.

"We love you, Chanson, and are so happy you are one of our sons," Lady Genevie said.

"Please don't cry, Mother Genevie," Chanson said.

Hayden put his arms around his wife and Chanson. They embraced.

Chanson was beginning to form stronger family ties with the Cheswicks as well as finding his place in King Sainesbury's realm. The friendship between him and the king's daughter had also grown with deeper trust and loyalty. Their stroll in her father's garden would enlighten Chanson's heart with revelations about King Sainesbury's past.

He that walketh with wise men shall be wise.

Gardens of Fairnesse

The Gardens of Fairnesse
Late morning on July 8, 1420

Chanson and Parisina arrived at the king's royal garden. The sun kissed the earth beneath their feet, promising the couple a beautiful, sentimental Summer day.

"Parisina, may I hold your hand as we walk along?" Chanson said.

"I would love for you to!" she said, her eyes bright and fresh like a sunrise.

Chanson wrapped his hand around hers. They continued to walk, approaching two myrtle trees that were at the entrance of the massive floral garden. Parisina's white satin gown swept delicately over the white petal-covered ground.

"The myrtle trees were planted soon after my mother died. Father said he planted them to symbolize her beauty and their fidelity in marriage. Of my father's gardens, this one is his favorite."

"Impressive! It's nearly overflowing with flowers," Chanson said, while glancing over the stately garden beds.

"Father created this white petal garden to symbolize the pure and unending love they shared. The white azalea is for the first awakening of his love for my mother and then the white gillyflower to symbolize their love would continue to grow eternally. The white carnation is a promise of his undying devotion to their love."

As they walked further along, birds sang sweetly. They set their gaze upon a lush floral display of blue and purple flowers.

"The blue irises were my mother's favorite."

"That must be why there are so many." Chanson touched a blue petal and smiled at Parisina as if longing to hear more of her heart's affections.

"Yes, and she liked other blue flowers. Father put in the blue hyacinth too and these pink carnations to affirm she would never be forgotten."

"The white azalea with the pink center is a nice complement," Chanson said.

"I love the beautiful hues too. Do you see the white and pink peonies growing in a circular pattern?" she said, shifting her attention to another flower bed.

"Yes," Chanson said as they continued through the vibrant garden.

"Father planted the bulbs in the late autumn after Mother died. They came up the following year in early summer and have returned every year as if promised to do so. Father said their generous blooms were poignant reminders of how grand and beautiful their love was, and yet, how fleeting their time together when the blossoms faded early."

"So I would assume the circle is symbolic of the wedding ring?" Chanson said.

"Yes. My father is a thoughtful man. I believe that's why he and my mother got along so well; he was attentive and sensitive to her needs and desires.

"Father spent many an early morning in these gardens, praying and missing Mother. He often brought me with him. We reflected while sitting on that bench," Parisina said, referencing a stone bench bearing a carving of a heart with two wedding rings on each side, joined together in the heart's center. "I sat on his lap and we talked about her, sharing how much she meant to us."

"Would you like to sit with me?" Chanson said.

"I would love to."

They sat down and leaned against the heart motif.

"Your father cherished your mother deeply."

"Yes, more than his life. And that has surprised many because their marriage was arranged when they were children. They did not know each other before marriage, but fell deeply in love despite the forced political union between the two kingdoms. Father had the stone bench placed here to portray their unbroken souls inseparable for all of Eternity."

"Where was your mother from?"

"She was from the country of La' Fleuré and had to learn to speak Father's language. He said he loved everything about her except the language barrier. When they quarreled, tears of frustration filled her eyes. Father took her in his arms and reassured her they would understand one another in time. He said she smiled after that and every time since when they had miscommunications. Somehow the smile became her way of telling him she did not understand."

"Your mother sounds like a patient woman and one with a gracious disposition."

"She was and so much more. To help them further communicate, Father commissioned one of the noble's wives to come every day to teach her the language of Evernora."

"Was your mother spiritual too?"

"That's another reason why Father chose the heart carving, the joining of the two rings depicted their spiritual union in the Lord's spirit."

"As I listen to your tender expressions, I am inspired by your father's undying devotion."

"I'm so happy you are. Love like theirs is rare and should be held onto."

"I agree, Parisina. That's exactly what your father has done! So, like all the other flowers growing here, I suppose those red tulips and red carnations also have some significance to their love," Chanson said, noticing the flowers interleaved along the back and sides of the bench.

"Yes, all the flowers in this garden do. Father loves red flowers and he always kept Mother's chamber filled with them. He had them planted so she could have them throughout Spring and Summer. Now, when he sees the red tulips and carnations, he reflects, finding solace in remembering how her eyes filled with tears of delight when he gave them to her. It is the red flowers that touch him the most with her memories."

"She was treated with high esteem by your father," Chanson said, looking at the scarlet petals.

"Father is not aggrieved over her death as he once was, but on occasion he misses her and retreats to this garden to refresh his mind. He says it allows him to be close to her and that helps the ache in his heart."

"I've noticed those zephyranthes placed in the middle of this array of flowers. Are they symbolic in some way?" Chanson said while glancing at the huge gathering of white petals dancing playfully in the dreamy breeze. "Did your mother like those flowers too?"

"They were the first flower to appear in this garden. The white petals sprung to life after my baby brother died at birth."

Chanson gasped with surprise to hear of the king's loss. He continued to listen, not wanting to interrupt Parisina's expressions.

"Father told me it rained heavily the night Ambrose died and then the next day the flower was seen with an abundance of blooms. That was the inspiration for this garden. He later added all these others to help him recapture serenity."

"I did not know your father had lost a son. He told me when I was first orphaned that something hurt him deeply, but did not want to talk about it then. Wait, I remember now . . . the bassinet we found in the basement . . . did it belong to Ambrose?"

"Yes. Father stayed in his room for two days following the day we discovered the baby's bassinet. Later he told me he was sorry he had treated us poorly and it was only then that I knew of my lost brother. He sobbed saying Seabert Gaines had been told to take the items out of his and my mother's sight. Seabert took them down there and that room had been untouched before we went in there."

Chanson leaned closer to Parisina and took hold of her hand, caressing it.

"I did not know. Father Hayden told us to apologize for upsetting him, but it was several days later. The king smiled and said it was all right, but to never go back down there or to speak of it. His eyes were teary despite telling us he was all right. I wish I had known not to go in that room. I feel terrible about it now."

"No, please don't. We were only being children, Father knows that. This is his wound and we can't heal it or stop it from hurting him. Father still won't talk about Ambrose. As soon as I mention his name, his eyes well in tears and he walks away. And no one in the castle was allowed to speak his name or discuss his death. Father was respected and so no one even dares to talk of the baby in his presence. He will mention my mother often, but not Ambrose. It was as if he buried my brother and dismissed his birth."

"I won't mention it to anyone."

"Thank you. That might be best. Perhaps one day he will have the courage to share it with you."

"I hope so. Your father impresses me. He and Hayden are strong, yet compassionate men. He's always been my spiritual guide and pillar of support. I hope we can talk like this again," Chanson said, his eyes dreamy, clinging to Parisina's face.

"I would love that!"

"I have enjoyed your company very much, Parisina. I suppose I'd better get back to my responsibilities. Now that I'm a knight, I have a king to defend."

They shared smiles and made their way back to their respective places.

Chanson and Parisina's friendship remained faithful; the bond between them helped to assuage his grief over the loss of his family. Jade was never found, but with Parisina's friendship, Chanson was able to find peace and fulfillment. Soon his peace would be disrupted, however, when a letter reveals secrets from his past.

From His chambers the hills drink from the brook.

Prince of Brightonvale

Firegate Castle
Late afternoon in Autumn of 1422

King Sainesbury was interrupted while enjoying a goblet of juice.

"Your Majesty," a guard said, "a man from the Empire of Beauport insisted he must speak with you about an urgent matter. Shall I send him in?"

"Yes."

The king put his goblet of cherry juice down and waited for the guard to usher the man to the throne.

"I'm Eurig Symons," he said. "I have been searching for a baby who was taken from his dying mother's arms."

"I do not know of such a boy," the king said.

"With all due respect, I believe this belongs to one of your knights," he said, handing King Sainesbury a wax-sealed parchment. "The princess instructed you were to open the document first before presenting it to Sir Chanson Westbrook."

The emblem of wax bore a princess riding a crowned horse.

"This is an official notice from Aderyn Crystin Wynne, Princess of the Kingdom of Beauport," Eurig said. "I am an ambassador sent on her behalf."

The king broke the seal. As he read the long letter, his heart thumped in his chest, his brow perspired and his hands trembled.

"Are you sure of these facts, Eurig?" the king said, holding the letter tightly in his hand.

"So, you do verify then that the knight is here?"

"Well, yes, but until I have more information I will not disclose this to him."

"Here, this should be all the proof you need," the man said, pulling out a certificate of birth, "this verifies his identity. Look for yourself and see that this is an entitlement that should be granted to the young man."

The king read the document. Before he was finished reading the letter, he gasped, shocked at the contents. He slouched, as if in a fog. The letter was barely within the grasp of his hand.

"Your Majesty, Your Majesty," Eurig said, noticing the king was distracted by the news.

"Forgive me," the king said. "Go on . . . as you were saying?"

"I was able to confirm the facts of this letter a few years ago by relatives of Tesni. Before Chanson's parents fled Beauport they told their family of their intentions. I tracked the Westbrooks to their home in the Village of Greyflower and they affirmed my suspicions regarding the child's true identity. Seren and Kenley felt Chanson was too young and pleaded with me to wait a few more years before telling him the truth about his heritage. I granted their request. I expect you to have the boy ready to leave this evening."

"As to taking him, I cannot allow that either. I will need some time to discuss these revelations with him—first with the man who has raised him."

"All right. I will await his decision tomorrow evening," Eurig said, exiting.

"Guard, summon Hayden Cheswick immediately," the king said.

"Of course."

King Sainesbury sat and re-read the letter. He pondered how he'd break the news to Hayden.

Hayden approached King Sainesbury's throne. It was evident to Hayden that whatever was in the king's hand was of monumental importance. He observed lines of anguish on his forehead and the corners of his mouth turned downward. The king held the letter close to his side as if attempting to prepare his words and to delay the inevitable cyclone of confusion the letter's content was about to unleash.

"My King, what's wrong?"

"Please, be at ease Hayden. Sit . . . we'll talk."

Hayden sat down and waited for the king to speak, but he seemed reluctant to talk about the letter's contents. The king tried to speak, but the words would not come.

"Take your time, My King."

"An ambassador from the Empire of Beauport arrived a few minutes ago. He delivered this letter and the certificate. I d-don't . . . I d-don't know how—here, read it for yourself," King Sainesbury said, handing the paper to Hayden as his hands continued to tremble.

King Sainesbury folded his hands on his lap and reflected.

Hayden proceeded to read the letter.

Elgan Telor Rees,

In the spring when Beauport rebels fought for their independence, Ceri Rees and his wife, Tesni, fled their home with their infant son, Elgan, seeking refuge. Along with the family, a friend, Seren Frost, left with them. The father was killed while trying to escape with his family. Tesni and Seren continued to travel by foot with the baby, but Tesni took ill shortly after leaving. Ravaged by fever, the mother was unable to continue the journey with Seren and her son.

Tesni did the only thing she knew she could do and instructed Seren to take the baby to safety, without her. Seren did not want to leave Tesni behind. Tesni convinced Seren to raise Elgan as her own because she knew death was upon her. Tesni further instructed Seren to teach the child about God's love, making sure he grew into an honest and kind man. The dying mother made one last request of Seren; to teach the boy to pen poetry and learn to play music. Upon those words, Tesni died.

Seren was able to enlist some help from Kenley Westbrook, a man she met in Londonmere. The two traveled by horse and arrived at Evernora. The man and woman fell in love, married and raised the boy as their own. The child was later renamed Chanson Westbrook. When the child was seven years old his parents were killed in the Village of Greyflower by men who sought to steal the land from the boy's parents.

Before the war ended, King Arthfael Kidwell was killed. His son, Ifan Kidwell, took the rein after his father's untimely death. However, King Kidwell does not have children as an heir for prince. The king wishes to appoint a monarch to govern the Kingdom of Brightonvale, which has recently agreed to join Beauport. The prince would establish laws of government while selecting members of his court.

It was later discovered that the Rees family is a pertinent relative to the late King Arthfael Kidwell. Because Elgan Telor Rees is blood family to King Arthfael, a nephew to his youngest brother, it has been decided Sir Chanson Westbrook is to become King Kidwell's reigning prince. His exceptional loyalty to King Sainesbury and the integrity he has demonstrated has impressed King Kidwell. Elgan Telor Rees is under no obligation to accept the position, but he is a candidate among two others.

To accept this title, Sir Chanson Westbrook must take his former name, Elgan Telor Rees. If he declines, another will be chosen by the younger brother, who does not desire the position.

I beg thee to consider carefully my request. If I have not received a response by the seventh day after receiving this notification, I will assume the endowment has been declined dismissing Elgan Telor Rees as the Prince of Brightonvale.

Aderyn Crystin Wynne,
Princess of Beauport

Hayden folded the letter and said, "My King, I must tell Chanson, but I do not want to lose my son. How will he accept this? Will he understand why his parents kept his family's lineage from him?"

"Hayden, I know this news will disrupt all of us. But Chanson deserves to know the truth even if we lose our knight, and are forced to have our hearts ripped out by seeing him go," the sober king said. "Take the rest of the day and pray over it, then you'll gain strength in being able to present this news to him."

"Yes, of course, you are right. But no matter how fervently I pray, I know he will feel betrayed and forced into a decision that did not warrant him any preparation. I'll leave now and hope that God will help Chanson make the best decision for his life and one I can accept."

"Very well," the king said, "may the Lord Almighty bring a peaceful resolution to the matter."

Hayden parted. The king instructed the guard to not disturb him unless it was urgent. King Sainesbury spent the rest of the day sitting on the balcony with his dog by his side.

"Brayleigh, what will I do if Chanson accepts this title? How can I be woeful about losing him when he has an opportunity to becoming a distinguished man of God, serving beyond our borders? How will we deny an orphan his entitlements and ask him not to leave us?" the king sobbed, petting Brayleigh.

After deep prayer, Hayden was convinced it was time to apprise Chanson of the news. He knew where to find him; without fail he usually resided under an oak tree in the forest, playing his flute. He often went to the forest after his chores were completed for the day.

Hayden mounted Silver Belle and left the castle. He eased the horse's reins as if galloping through thick, blinding fog, attempting to delay the inevitable. The autumn wind whipped his wet cheeks, lacerating them with welts. With an unrelenting gnawing in his gut, he feared the bonds made with the orphan would soon be severed by the letter's revelations. Hayden recalled a battle where Chanson, fifteen years old, trained by his side as a squire.

'Sir Cheswick, I think you should consider making him a knight. Look at him go with your flag waving behind him!' Ashton de Sille said, noticing Chanson riding confidently ahead of his trainer, Hayden Cheswick.

'He seems born for this doesn't he?' Hayden said, smiling.

'He sure doesn't bear the wounds of an orphan,' Ashton said. 'Does it not astonish you how an elegant flute player could be so brave and forthright in battle?'

'Every day, my friend.'

'If you ask me, Hayden, I would not be surprised if he rises to become a leader in the land, defending those who cannot speak for themselves.'

'Yes, well for today he has certainly proven he has that potential!'

Hayden could hear Chanson's flute. He secured Silver Belle and walked toward where Chanson was sitting.

Home

Oakhollow Forest
Before sunset in Autumn of 1422

Hayden approached Chanson, dragging his feet. His eyes cast downward as he stood before the teen with the letter and certificate in his hand.

"Father Hayden, what's in your hand—what's happened?" Chanson said, "You've been crying." He stood with the flute at his side, sensing tears were about to unleash their fury.

"It's a nice autumn day, don't you think?" Hayden said, forcing a smile on his face. "I don't think they'll be many more like this. You know it rains a lot, have you noticed that?"

"Uhh, yes I-I have, but—"

"Here . . . read it!" Hayden said angrily, his mouth beginning to quiver as he tried to resist tears from flowing.

"All right," Chanson said, cautiously taking the letter out of Hayden's outstretched hand.

They sat down under the oak tree. Hayden lifted his head to the heavens as if listening for the voice of God to tell him everything would be all right. He prayed silently, forcing sorrow inward. Chanson read Princess Wynne's letter.

As he read, he tried to maintain his composure, but was unable to hold back the tides of sorrow. The dam broke loose; the surging waters flooded his eyes. His tears fell onto the parchment, smearing the words.

"Lies! All lies! It's not possible . . . they wouldn't lie to me, my parents loved me . . . I know they did! Why is she doing this to me—why is the princess fabricating these lies? Why Hayden?" Chanson yelled. He grasped his head with his hands and then covered his eyes, desperate for some form of relief from the pain within. His eyes darted all over, desperately searching for a way to relieve his mind of the miserable revelation.

With quivering lips Hayden said, "Her letter is authentic." He handed Chanson the birth certificate. "This validates her words."

Chanson snatched the certificate from his hand and read.

Herein is recorded the birth of Elgan Telor Rees. The infant, a son, was born to his parents: Father, Ceri Rees, and Mother, Tesni Rees. On the twenty-first day of the month of March, in the year of our Lord, one thousand, four hundred and four.

"Did you know?" Chanson said, stifling internal confusion.

"I just found out today," Hayden said, tilting his head and drawing closer to Chanson.

"What am I to believe when I've been told my whole life I was someone else—when my identity has been a lie?"

"I can help you through this if you will let me," Hayden said, reaching out to take hold of Chanson's arm. Hayden's compassionate gesture was rejected, however. All Chanson could focus on was the piercing words and the betrayal he felt.

"Was I ever loved . . . loved enough to have been told the truth about where I came from? I trusted them . . . I trusted you—but can I trust anyone now?" Chanson cried, circling around and putting his hands on his ears as if to escape Hayden's penetrating words.

"These revelations do not change who you are nor do they change how I feel about you,"

"Please go . . . *Please*," Chanson sobbed.

"Chanson, I can't leave you out here in this shape, please let—"

"Maybe you only cared for me because you felt sorry for me," Chanson interrupted sharply.

"Chanson, I've loved you from the moment I picked you up and held you close to my breast," Hayden said, his face becoming contorted, his voice choking, and his eyes welling with tears. "In carrying you away from that bloody scene, I felt a precious son had been given to me. And I desired only to love you earnestly, without reservation of any kind. Because I wanted to be your father . . . to stay with you through the sorrowful nights and to help ease your suffering. I wanted you to feel whole again, nurtured in our family. I stayed by your side because I love you as I love my own soul. Nothing will ever change that . . . not the letter—nothing!"

Chanson's cries were audible and more desperate. Tears gushed down his cheeks while he remembered his former parents' deaths and Hayden carrying him away in his arms.

"I've never lied to you nor will I ever. If I could have spared these truths from you I would have chosen to. Because deep in my heart I didn't want to tell you . . . I feared y-you'd . . . leave—"

"*Please . . .* " Chanson said, crossing his arms in front of him and turning his back to Hayden.

"All right, I'll leave you to your thoughts. Will you let us hear from you before morning so that we won't worry?"

Chanson did not answer. Hayden's words were muffled by the shrills of shock spinning though his head.

With great reluctance, Hayden got on his horse, proceeding back to the castle. He stopped, glanced over his shoulders, hoping Chanson had changed his mind, but Chanson had not moved. Hayden left to discuss the matter with the king.

Firegate Castle
The King's quarters

"I must speak with the king," Hayden said to the guard.

"Of course. Proceed, he's on the balcony."

"My King," Hayden said, "Chanson has the letter and certificate and now he insists on being alone. I fear he'll not come home. Chanson shut me out; he won't speak to me about it. In all the time I've spent with Chanson, he has never raised his voice cruelly as he did today. I fear we've unleashed a storm that will undo all the good we've done for him. What can I do?"

"You will have to let him work this out in his own time. I should take Brayleigh to him for protection in case its warranted."

"That's a good idea, may I take her now?" Hayden said, turning toward Brayleigh as if preparing to leave with her. She wagged her tail and watched with hopeful eyes.

"No, I think it would be best if I do it. You're much too close to this problem for him to accept the gesture."

"I see. Then I'll have to step back and leave him alone until he asks for my help."

"Yes, that's best. I'll summon Ashton de Sille to ride out with me and we'll take Brayleigh."

"Thank you. I hope Chanson will be all right and do what's best for himself and not what he thinks we require of him."

"Have faith, Hayden, he needs some time. The good that's been done for him will not unravel with these revelations. If anything, they will be the foundation on which wisdom is sought. Trust that his affections are secure and that no blight will come to any of you. He's a wise young man, God will help him tonight. Go home to the rest of your family and let me handle it for now."

"All right," Hayden said. He walked away shuffling his feet; his characteristic grin suppressed by the upheaval in his relationship with Chanson. He prayed within himself that God's wisdom would prevail as Chanson internalized the latest revelation.

King Sainesbury and Ashton rode through Oakhollow Forest. Brayleigh raced faithfully by the king's side, her legs keeping speed with the king's horse. They saw Chanson sitting against the tree, his arms hanging over his bent knees. Ashton waited at a distance to allow the king time alone with Chanson. The king walked toward Chanson; the leaves cracked and crunched under his feet.

"Ceri may have been your birth father, but he didn't dandle you on his knee," the king said, with Brayleigh standing by his side, wagging her tail with her ears up.

"Then why am I divided today?"

"May I sit beside you, Chanson?"

Chanson nodded. Brayleigh ambled toward Chanson and knelt on her hind legs, scrutinizing his face. Her eyes danced back and forth and her eyebrows wrinkled whenever he spoke. King Sainesbury sat down on the leaves and leaned against the tree beside Chanson. He bent his legs, crossed his hands over his knees and waited for Chanson to talk.

"I am able to pen words of poetry expressing the loneliest feelings, and yet, I cannot settle my thoughts down enough to figure out why this happened and what I am to do about it."

"That will come. You've received disquieting news that will take a few days to sort out. We're all stunned by this, but Hayden is torn inside, literally anguished of heart. He loves you more than his own life and wants only the best for you."

"Yes, I know. I feel awful for pushing him away. He is the sincerest man I've ever known. I knew he was right. . . . "

"Don't worry about it, he understands. It will all work itself out. And we're here to support you in any way we can. W-we," the king choked on his words, "love you . . . we've grown fond of having you with us—as one of us," the king said, his eyes peering into Chanson's and both shimmering in a sea of tears.

"And I love all of you, you've been my home . . . what am I to do, Your Majesty? No matter what decision I make, I'm going to let people down. It seems an impossible decision to make."

"Yes, well, tonight it is just that, impossible. Time will allow you a decision you can live with. Don't be too hard on your parents or anyone whose raised you, they were humans faced with dire circumstances. Each chose love in trying to do what was best for you.

"Life isn't always about blood ties, the big moments or winning a battle, it's about the people who remained true, constant, and loving unconditionally along the journey . . . the selfless ones who lay down their lives a piece at a time each and every day."

"Like Hayden and my parents?"

"Yes. Superb examples."

"I hope to find the answers out here while in solitude."

"Would you like for me to stay with you or leave you alone with our friend Brayleigh?"

Chanson smiled and said, "I would prefer to remain here for awhile. I can't imagine going back to my home tonight. I cannot walk into the home that's been mine for eleven years, knowing I may have to walk out the door for duty's sake."

"All right, but let us hear from you; the forest can be dangerous, as you know."

"I'll stay here until my thoughts clear then I'll go home."

"Very well," the king said. "Don't worry about bringing Brayleigh back to me until after you've rested tomorrow. I think you both need a genuine friend."

"Thank you, she's been a loyal presence too. If I have to leave, it'll be hard to say goodbye."

"Well, let's not think on that right now. Try to compose your peace."

Red, orange, and golden leaves twirled in a gust of wind; each waltzing in the air. The king took notice of the autumn dance.

"This may very well be the place for you to sit and sort this out."

Chanson did not utter another word; the world slipped from him, leaving him drained of all color and sound.

The king mounted on his horse and left Chanson and Brayleigh alone under the oak tree.

Chanson wept, his body shook in grief. Confusion and unguarded feelings erupted within him. He pet Brayleigh and wailed. There were no words to comfort, no clear-cut decisions to be made. He was in the eye of a storm, hunkered down, waiting it out.

A clamor of animal noises reverberated through the air and were in disharmony with the sound of the wind blowing gently through the forest.

Chanson fell asleep as Brayleigh kept watch; her ears perking at the sounds of the darkening forest. The dew of dusk settled on their bodies.

Princess Pearlensia reappeared to help console Chanson with spiritual insight.

"Everything is going to work out, my little friend, you will soon see," Pearlensia said, hovering over Chanson as he lay slumped against the tree. "Your parents loved you very much and only kept the truth from you because they feared you would reject them when you found out the truth. It would have been best if you had been told the truth, but that has not diminished how loved you are, and by so many. Seren and Kenley wanted you to be all theirs, while keeping the promise she made to your dying mother. Few are ever loved as zealously as you, my little friend. Think on that as you wrestle with the decision.

"God brought you to Evernora because this is where you will fulfill your destiny," Pearlensia said, pressing her warm cheek against his while holding his face in her warm wings. "You do not have to leave your friends and family here if you do not wish to become a prince. Follow your heart—it knows what you should do.

"When you awake, allow your mind to reside in a quiescent state, knowing love is about to burst forth. Now, wipe away those tears and spring up. Go to the family who cherishes you, that needs you as you need them."

Brayleigh wagged her tail, gazing at Pearlensia with eyes spellbound.

"As for you, Brayleigh, you keep our little friend safe and warm tonight," Pearlensia said, wrapping her wings around them before trotting away.

Chanson awoke, exhausted and ready to go home and rest. He rose to his feet, noticing Pearlensia's essence twirling around him in the cool breeze.

"Was Princess Pearlensia here, sweet girl?" Chanson said.

Brayleigh wagged her tail and barked.

"I'll take that as a yes then!" He pet the dog's fur. "Let's go home, my friend!"

With Brayleigh by his side, they rode back to the castle. Chanson slept the rest of the night with the dog nestled beside him.

Late morning the next day

Chanson and Brayleigh were on their way back to the king's quarters when Parisina was seen promenading across the leaf-strewn lawn.

"Chanson, I'm elated to see you!" she said. "Are you well? Father told me about the letter."

They walked toward one another, Parisina's ruffles sweeping gracefully over a burst of flaming leaves. Their eyes met.

"I am better now that I've had some time to reflect," Chanson said.

"I'm happy to hear it. But I'm sure you must be disappointed in your parents for not trusting you with details concerning your childhood."

"I am, but I have made some peace."

"So, does that mean you will stay with us and not accept Princess Wynne's proposal?"

"Do you want me to stay, Lady Parisina?" he said, his eyes beholding hers. "Please, tell me you don't want me to go."

He leaned in closer to her, took her hands into his. He kissed one hand, then the other.

"Stay, Chanson, please stay with us—with me. You've been my friend since I was a little girl . . . I could not bear the pain of seeing you go. Do you remember the promise we made when we were chasing each other around Father's favorite cherry tree as frolicking children?"

"I could never forget that dulcet Spring!" Chanson said, smiling.

While gazing in each other's eyes, they drifted in memory, floating back to days of blooming innocence.

'You can't catch me, Chanson. I've no shoes; bare feet race faster!' Parisina giggled, her onyx tresses bouncing around her shoulders as she scampered across the lawn.

'Well, I'm the fastest sprinter of them all, I'll catch you!' Chanson said, kicking up his heels behind him.

They chased around the tree.

'I didn't think you'd catch me!' Parisina said.

'And now what am I to do with you?' he said.

'Chase me again, and again, and again. I like being chased by you because you're my very best friend!' she giggled, twirling around with her arms outstretched and her yellow dress fluttering in the fresh open air.

'Parisina, marry me when we grow up—please say you'll be my princess and I can be your prince.'

'I will marry you and we'll have our thrones side by side! Here, let's make our rings out of the daisies.'

'How do we make them?' Chanson said, looking down at the blossoms growing at his feet.

'We have to pick the flowers. We'll need four flowers with the stems.'

'All right, I have mine,' he said.

'And I have mine,' she smiled, clapping her hands.

'This is how we make them,' Parisina said, 'take the first flower then the other one and make a loop around the head of the first flower. Make a knot and pull. You wrap it around your finger, with the daisy flower on the top. Then tie the ends together. Are you ready to make them?'

'I'm ready!' Chanson said, proceeding to make his ring.

Their flower rings were made.

'Now we have to put on our wedding rings,' she said, her eyes sparkling.

'I'll go first, since a gentleman should. Give me your hand.'

Parisina giggled then gave Chanson her hand. He tied the two ends of the ring onto her finger. He smiled.

She repeated, tying her ring on his finger.

'We must say our vows now, Chanson.'

'What do we say?'

'You take my hand and ask me to marry you until death.'

He took her hand and said, 'Parisina, will you marry me until death?'

'I will.'

She took his hand and said, 'Chanson, will you marry me until death?'

'I will.'

'Now we're supposed to kiss, but I don't like to kiss, do you?' Parisina said.

'No. So then what should we do?'

'We could press our foreheads together and then hug,' Parisina said.

'All right.'

They took hold of each other's hands and gently pressed their foreheads together.

'Now, we should take our rings home and put them in a secret place, and not get them out until the day of our wedding,' Parisina said. 'Father gave me a pretty little box that I'll put mine in.'

'I will hide my ring too.'

Parisina lifted her hands in the air, and while looking up to the cloudy sky, twirled around in circles. Soon rain sprinkled onto her face. She squealed and took Chanson's hand and they danced in the rain until a servant came and took them inside the castle.

"Chanson, your heart is intertwined with mine now; I could never unravel them. I've grown attached to seeing your eyes gazing at me with absolute adoring—does your heart ache for me too?"

"My heart bleeds when you are not near me. The way your eyes dance when you see me tell me you love me as I love you . . . I have always loved you, Parisina. I want to kiss the breath you breathe."

Chanson took her face in his hands, his sparkling eyes gazed into her longing eyes. She wrapped her arms tightly around his waist. No force of nature could hold them back a moment longer. Their lips met and they kissed for the first time.

"So, Chanson, it appears you've made your decision!" King Sainesbury chuckled delightfully, walking up and seeing the couple unexpectedly.

Embarrassed, Chanson and Parisina refrained from kissing, putting their arms at their sides.

"I did not mean to interrupt, but I'm sure glad to see you in better spirits today."

"I have made my decision," Chanson responded, glancing lovingly at Parisina's glowing face. "I love your daughter. She has allowed me to see what's important in my life and why I cannot accept ruling in a country that would tear her heart from me. May I court your daughter? I promise to care for her as I would my own soul."

"I believe that's the best news I've heard in months! I could not be more pleased to hear you'll remain. By all means, if you love each other that intently, then enjoy one another. Stay here with us . . . you're a part of our family.

"Hayden will be most relieved by this news. You should tell him now. He's beside himself with worry, fretting like I've never known him to do."

"Where is he?" Chanson said.

"He told me this morning he was taking a little time to clear his mind. I suspect he's in the chapel."

"I'll go to him now," Chanson reassured.

"Very well. Would you like for me to take Brayleigh with me?"

"Yes. Thank you for the time I was allowed with her," Chanson said while smiling at the dog and smoothing her fur.

"As you wish. I'll leave you two," the king said, singing as he walked away with Brayleigh wagging her tail.

"My beloved Parisina, would you like to watch the sun set this evening? The crimson sky is sure to enchant our souls with its flames of grandeur."

"That would be divine."

"I'll come by your manor later this afternoon to take you on my horse and we'll ride along the beach of Kaishore. Will that please you, Love?"

"Most!" she said, wrapping her arms around his neck and kissing his cheeks exuberantly. They embraced again before Chanson left to find Hayden.

Chanson walked into the chapel and saw Hayden praying, overhearing his sorrowful expressions.

"Father God, I don't want to let him go, I don't want to lose my son," he poured.

The hand of fear tightened its grip on Hayden's throat, suffocating his prayerful mutterings. Breathing grew increasingly difficult as sorrow increased within his heart. Tears stained the stone floor as he struggled, baring his heart before the Almighty's altar.

"I'm selfish, I know, but I don't want Chanson to leave us—*to leave me . . . Please God*, have him stay—"

Chanson tiptoed to where Hayden was praying with his face to the floor.

"I'm staying," Chanson said definitively, his eyes shimmering like diamonds in the sea.

Hayden sprung to his feet, taking Chanson into his arms. They wept audibly. While folded in the embrace, Chanson choked back regret and said, "I'm so sorry, I never meant to hurt you. I love you, *Father*."

"*I love you too*, Son . . . welcome home."

"*Home*, I like the sound of that. You are right, this is my home . . . *you*—you are my home."

"How was it that you were able to be at peace with this situation?" Hayden said.

"It was hearing Parisina tell me she wanted me to stay. Her love showed me that my first duty is to my king, fulfilling my oath as a knight. I guess I needed to wrestle alone before seeing that there was no decision to be made, destiny had already done it for me."

"Chanson, you're an honorable man, I am so proud to call you my son. I know the news of your birth parents was upsetting, but I can't help but feel blessed that the hand of Providence placed you in my arms on that despairing Spring day."

"Father, I have fallen desperately in love with the king's daughter. He has granted me permission to court her. We plan to enjoy the sunset together tonight."

"Chanson, that's wonderful news. A lady is able to help us to see what's important. As for the sunset, King Sainesbury said the ambassador was coming back for you before nightfall."

"Well then, I'll leave now and speak with the man before Parisina and I ride out to the ocean. I have questions about my birth parents, perhaps he can tell me more."

"If that will settle you, then you should find out what else he knows. So, I'll see you in the morning for archery practice?"

"Yes. It's good to know I won't be missing it after all."

They hugged again and parted.

Firegate Castle
The king's throne, late afternoon

Eurig Symons returned to talk with Chanson about his decision regarding the letter. The king summoned Chanson to his throne. Upon arriving, Chanson bowed before the king.

"Sit gentlemen," the king said, indicating two chairs.

They sat down.

"I hope you're packed and ready to go," Eurig said.

"I am honored that the princess of Beauport has sought me as a potential prince, but I do not wish to accept the title. My duty is to defend this kingdom, a commitment I had already made when I was dubbed a knight."

"Well, she will be disappointed, but I understand and commend you for honoring your king as you do."

"If I may ask, did you know my parents?"

"No, but I was privy to the fact that your mother had a melodic voice and was often called upon to sing for the prince. Your father was a poet and painter, commissioned to paint tapestries for the royal family. They were devout in their faith. That is all that I know about them."

"I believe I inherited my mother's heart for music. I love the flute and find the melodies bring solace to my soul."

"I'm glad you've found healing through the years. It's been a pleasure to finally meet you and put the mystery of your whereabouts to rest. I need to be leaving now. May God's grace be with you."

"And to you."

Eurig left.

"Parisina's expecting you," the king said, jovially. "Enjoy the sunset. I believe you'll see a grand one since the sun's been shining gloriously all day. I'll see you in the morning."

"I'll have Parisina home at a reasonable hour. Have a good evening, My King."

Clarity once again flowed in the river of Chanson's soul; love perched her gentle wings upon his beating heart. With a spring in his step, Chanson left the castle and mounted Diamond Belle and was off to meet Parisina for their ride on the beach of Kaishore.

Lorlea Manor
Late afternoon

Chanson arrived to take Parisina to the beach. He got off his horse and knocked on the door of her manor.

A servant opened the door and greeted him. "She'll be down momentarily," the servant said, waking away and leaving him standing in front of the spiral staircase. After waiting for a short period of time, Parisina appeared at the top of the spiral steps. She floated toward him wearing a pink satin gown with long bell sleeves. The corset-laced dress flowed with a ribbon sash cinched above her waist. The hem swept over each step as she promenaded toward Chanson. Her waved tresses bounced elegantly at her waist.

She was a serendipitous vision who mesmerized him. Her tresses invited him to caress each lustrous strand. He reached out as if to take hold of her locks, but withdrew his hand to his side knowing it wouldn't be proper to do so. Her face and supple lips delighted him; he wished to be kissed by them . . .

"Chanson, Chanson," she whispered. He was surprised and did not realize her beauty had bewitched him. "Where were you just then?" she said, having sashayed close enough to touch him.

"I must confess, it was your luminous beauty that held me captive."

"Oh, my dearest Chanson, your words are endearing. You are divine. Have I ever told you I find your blonde curls most attractive?"

"I cannot recall, but it makes me happy to hear it now."

"I admire the way they touch your collar ruffle," she said, gazing into his eyes.

They drew closer. Chanson took her hand into his and kissed one hand then the other. He let go and took her checks into his hands, she pressed her hands against his and they kissed.

"Are you ready to leave for the beach now?" he said, caressing her cheeks with light touches.

"Yes, my Love."

Chanson took hold of her hand and led her outside to his horse.

"Let me help you up," he said taking hold of Parisina's waist and lifting her onto Diamond Belle.

Parisina positioned herself atop Diamond Belle and Chanson mounted on in front of her. She wrapped her arms around his waist. He whisked her away; her tresses flowed behind as her gown whipped in the autumn air. They rode through Oakhollow Forest and arrived at Kaishore's beach.

The sun's crimson glow illuminated the white sand to a pearly pink. Diamond Belle kicked up the sand as she galloped toward the setting sun. The blaze of color—crimson, pink, and purple—illuminated their faces as the first buds of love bloomed in their hearts. The sun gradually lowered herself for rest in the quivering ocean waters. Twilight would soon fall as the glory of the heavens opened up.

After Chanson returned Parisina to her manor, he found it difficult to leave her. He took out his flute and stood outside her window charming her with his melodies. A few moments later she pulled open her curtain and sat on her window ledge listening as he played. Their eyes were like twinkling stars; exuding radiance lit the night.

On the new horizon, Chanson would secure hearth and home with the keys of love.

He shall cover thee with his feathers,
and under his wings shalt thou trust.

Book of Psalms

The Engagement

Firegate Castle
King Sainesbury's throne
Early morning on June 7, 1423

Chanson and Parisina had often been seen sitting in the castle's gardens, holding hands while sharing sweet glances and smiles. It was no secret to any that the two were deeply in love.

Chanson was granted permission to speak with the king. He bowed reverently.

"Chanson, that smile on your face tells me you are having a jolly day. Have you come to bring me good news?"

"Yes, Your Majesty. I am happy and honored to have this time with you."

"Then tell me, what is the merry news you wish to share?"

"There's been something I have wanted to ask you. The respect I have for you has allowed me to see the need for asking your permission to marry your daughter. I love Parisina more than my own life and I do not want to live another day without her as my bride."

"Well, Chanson, I had begun to notice the love blossoming between you. And yes, you may marry my beloved Parisina. I want her to be happy, well taken care of, and I cannot imagine a young man more honorable than you!"

"Thank you, My King, for your blessing!"

"Of course. I had already granted it before today. You will be a superb husband for my precious Parisina. This truly is jolly news!"

"May I be permitted to leave, Your Majesty? I wish to propose to Parisina this afternoon, now that I've been granted your approval."

"By all means, go—make her happy!" the king said, tears forming in his kindred eyes.

Chanson penned a note and had it delivered to Parisina's manor.

My dearest Parisina,

Please indulge me with your captivating presence and meet me this afternoon in the rose garden. I have something grand to express, I can hardly contain the rapturous stanzas. The rose petals pirouetting at our feet will be a lovely place to share my heart.

Ever yours,
Chanson

Parisina arrived at the luscious rose garden. The birds chirped sweetly while perched nearby on the limbs of the evergreen. The fragrance of rose blossoms filled the jubilant, summer air.

"Chanson, I came as soon as I received your note."

"My dearest, Lady Parisina," Chanson said, taking Parisina's hands into his and kissing one, then the other. "I have loved you from the moment I first saw you—the innocent spark ignited within my heart the moment you walked up to me after my first performance at the theater. Do you remember it, and the cheesecake, how delicious the ripe strawberries were?"

"Yes, my dearest Chanson . . . and the water fountain escapade too; the sweet memories still vibrate in my heart."

They laughed.

"From that night on, I had been given a rare and special gift; the grandest friend a little girl could have ever imagined having."

Chanson let go of Parisina's hand. He took out his flute and played a melody for Parisina.

He knelt on the rose petal lawn and whispered, "My heart was once an ocean; my lonely tears drops rippled on the sea. But now you've given my heart a new melody and showed me how wonderful life is. I cannot wait a moment longer to hear you say you'll marry me and be my wife, my cherished lady."

"I have longed to hear the words. Yes, my sweet man, Yes, I will marry you!"

Chanson and Parisina's eyes meet. He cupped her cheeks in his hands and kissed her dewy pink lips. They embraced passionately.

"I'd like for us to marry right away," he said, while caressing her cheek with feathery touches. "Would you like that too, Parisina?"

"Yes," she breathed. "I don't want to live another day waking without you next to me."

"My dearest Parisina, I want to awaken each morning to your beautiful eyes."

Their lips touched again. Savoring the innocence of their affection, they pressed their lips together softly and tenderly.

"Do you think your father would approve of us getting married in a few days?" Chanson said.

"Yes, I believe so. Father only wants my happiness. I'm sure he would call on his many servants to help in the wedding preparations. My darling knight, would you continue to play for me?"

"Yes. Why don't we spread a blanket on the lawn and enjoy the rest of this day together basking in the warm summer breezes?"

"I'd like that very much."

He spread the blanket out on the lawn under a white dogwood tree. He played a memorable tune.

"Parisina, without you, I could not have known love as rich as yours. Your warm and wonderful heart are a part of me now. Today I am the happiest man alive."

"And I, the happiest woman . . . our souls will lie folded as one for all of Eternity. I love you, my dearest Chanson, I adore you so!"

They kissed again.

"My dearest Parisina, I pledge my deep abiding love to you."

As Chanson and Parisina sat slumped against the tree, they laughed, kissed, and talked for hours about the wedding, relishing in the engagement. They were lost in each other until sunset; their love was a budding Spring.

The Wedding

Firegate Castle
Late morning on June 14, 1423

King Sainesbury was about to give his lovely daughter away to one of his most favored knights, Chanson Westbrook. Never in the history of Evernora was there ever a young woman fairer than King Sainesbury's daughter, Parisina. With only one hour until she would be given in marriage, Parisina was adorned in a wedding gown with fresh water pearls and several yards of the finest blue silk available in Evernora.

Each long bell sleeve was gathered at the upper arm and secured with a white satin ribbon covered in the fresh water pearls. The gown's seven foot train swept the floor with pearls sewn along the scalloped edges. The veil was also massively covered in mother of pearl with scalloped lace framing Parisina's porcelain face. She was ready to take the hand of her handsome knight when her father came to see her one last time before the wedding ceremony.

"My dear daughter, you're glowing with love," King Sainesbury said.

"Papa, please do not cry."

"Dearest Parisina, these aren't melancholic tears. You take my breath as I stand here and see your dark curls glisten in the sunlight from the window. Oh how you do remind me of your mother, so beautiful and pure."

"Father, I am so happy you have allowed me to follow my heart and marry Chanson. I adore him so . . . I always have."

"I know you do," King Sainesbury said, tenderly brushing his hand over his daughter's cheek. "I've known for a very long time that you had sacred feelings for the young man. The first time you two met and shared that cheesecake, I knew buds of affection would blossom between you. It was the first time I'd heard Chanson laugh. I was exasperated at the time, seeing the three of you soaked at the fountain, but the memory, oh how heartwarming it is now," he chuckled.

They laughed reminiscing about the childhood memories.

"Father, I was so delighted to have the cheesecake—the new-found friendship made it all the sweeter."

"Precious Parisina, I knew early on Chanson would cherish you like no other. That's why I had to permit this marriage, God showed me that."

"Oh Papa, I do miss Mother so deeply, *especially today.*"

"I know you do. She was not only my queen, but the woman my soul loved—I will grieve for her until the sword is laid over my body. The only comfort I am afforded is that she left me with you, my precious Parisina—my daughter whose face and soul mirror the very image of her mother, my beautiful wife, the only queen my heart will ever know."

"Papa, *please*—do not cry. It breaks my heart to see you weep and still miss her so."

"I feel her presence with us," King Sainesbury said, placing his hand inside the inner pocket of his robe. "Before you marry, I must present these to you. These are your mother's jewels worn the night we were given in marriage. *Please,* allow me to put them on you."

King Sainesbury removed the hand-carved cameo choker and matching earrings from the purple satin-lined box he had kept them in since the death of his wife, Queen Chloette.

"Oh Father, they're so lovely. I shall cherish them always. One day if Chanson and I have a daughter, I'll give them to her on her wedding day."

"That would please me very much, Parisina."

"My heart is elated! In only a moment I will be with the man I love."

King Sainesbury kissed his daughter's cheek and left to join the officiating minister.

The honorary guests and the families gathered outside the doors of the church building where Parisina and Chanson would soon be married. The minstrels played flutes, bagpipes, and trumpets. The bride and groom walked side by side toward the church. With Parisina on the left side of Chanson, they faced the minister who was standing in front of the closed chapel door. Hayden Cheswick rode on horseback behind the bride and groom. He was outfitted with his sword and chosen by the groom for his skills as the best swordsman. They continued walking toward the rose-strewn marbled steps where King Sainesbury, the minister, and the rest of the wedding party waited.

Chanson and Parisina stood in front of the minister.

The minister said, “Dearly beloved, we are gathered together in the sight of God to join this man and this woman in Holy Matrimony; which is an honorable estate, instituted of God in Heaven. Therefore if any man can show just cause, why they may not lawfully wed, let him now speak, or else hereafter hold his peace.” The minister observed the faces of those assembled and saw only reassuring smiles. “Let us proceed with this union,” he said.

The minister placed the wedding rings in Chanson and Parisina’s hand. “You may exchange rings,” the minister said.

The light of love shone in their eyes.

Chanson took Parisina’s hand. He placed the ring on her finger. He kissed her cheek. Parisina took hold of Chanson’s hand and placed her ring on his finger. They smiled, held in one other’s eyes.

The minister recited the vows, “Chanson, will you take this woman to be your wedded wife, will you love her, and honor her, keep her and guard her, in health and in sickness, as a husband should a wife, and forsaking all others, keeping yourself only unto her, so long as you both shall live?”

“I will. She is mine and I am hers.”

The minister continued the vows, “Parisina, will you take this man to be your wedded husband, will you love him, and honor him, keep him and guard him, in health and in sickness, as a wife should a husband, and forsaking all others, keeping yourself only unto him, so long as you both shall live?”

“I will. He is mine and I am his.”

"Chanson you may recite your sonnet to your bride, after which you may kiss her, affirming your marriage in the lawful affection of married love."

Chanson took Parisina's hands and said:

Dear bride, my lovely bride in silken blue,
Thou art my dove, my fairest, come away;
My heart is yours to take, come follow too
Let love awake desire, dear bride alway.

Kiss me with scarlet lips, oh press to mine.
Let's seal our love, fulfill our lovelorn souls;
Unveiling Holy garden's sweeter wine
Of posies, pearls—bouquets in promise grows.

Oh darling, beauty bride in silken blue,
Your love consumes; a constant passion fire.
My heart's your home, dearest an fairest true
In seasons high an low my one desire.

Together haply wed our hearts entwine;
Forever yours, an you, forever mine.

Parisina trembled lightly, anticipating Chanson's touch. Her blue eyes dazzled as if captured by the sun. They embraced and kissed. Their cherished affections moved many to tears of elation and rapturous applause. Hayden was seen smiling proudly as he, too, welled in tears of joy. King Sainesbury brushed away a few tears of his own. The people were joyed at being a part of the grand union.

The minister prayed.

> *May the Lord God look favorably upon you and bless and keep you. May He shine His face upon you and grant you grace that you may live together in this world so as to inherit everlasting life, amen.*

The crowd cheered as the married couple made their way into the castle to begin the wedding feast.

Hayden, Landon, and King Sainesbury arrived at the wedding feast.

"Sir Chanson, I believe you've done well for yourself. Your bride is impeccable," Hayden said.

"I could not agree more. I've loved her from the moment my eyes beheld her."

"I agree with my father. Parisina is a stunning bride," Landon piped. "You deserve a good woman by your side. I like seeing your smile of contentment. You complement each other very well."

"Thank you for the generous words," Parisina said. "Look at this ring Chanson has given me. The two golden hands laced over the jewel heart is an exquisite piece. I will cherish this ring and his love for me until I breathe my last."

"And I pledge greater love for you," Chanson said. "I hope the red jasper stone is always a reminder of my undying love and commitment to you, for you are the only one my soul loves."

King Sainesbury interrupted, "Parisina, please eat. You need nourishment after declining this morning's victuals. Look, strawberry cheesecake, your favorite!" the king said with a jolly chuckle.

"Not to fret, Father, I intend to have plenty."

"You too, Chanson, eat!" King Sainesbury said. "There's plenty. The cherry juice is splendid—*please*—have all that you want!"

"Your Majesty," Hayden piped, "indeed, these are fine victuals, the finest in all of the land!"

"I'm glad to hear it! Only the most exquisite food and drink would do on this joyous occasion!" King Sainesbury said, raising a goblet of the cherry drink as a toast to his guests.

Many nobles from surrounding areas were in attendance, including a longtime friend of King Sainesbury, King Alexander Blackmore from the Kingdom of Abbystone.

"May I join in the cheer of this grand occasion?" Alexander Blackmore said, raising his goblet.

"Alexander, my old friend, so good of you to come!"

"When I received your invitation, I was so glad to hear the wonderful news and would not have missed this for anything. So, who is the young man who was able to capture your daughter's heart, or more, *yours*?"

"He is one of my knights, a conscientious man. Come, meet him," King Sainesbury said, walking toward Chanson and Parisina.

The wedded couple was seen talking with a few other nobles when the kings approached. King Sainesbury introduced Alexander to Chanson and Parisina.

"Sir Chanson, Lady Parisina, so grand to meet you," King Blackmore said, nodding reverently and taking hold of Parisina's hand and kissing it.

Chanson bowed and Parisina curtsied.

"It's good to see you too," Chanson said.

"Parisina, you have grown so much since I last saw you as a child, sitting on your father's lap. I know your father is delighted that you have turned out so lovely. You must be a fine man indeed, Sir Westbrook. I've been Roland's friend for twenty-five years now and I can tell you, he esteems you greatly."

"That I do, my friend," King Sainesbury said, glancing at Chanson's elated eyes.

"May you have a long and prosperous marriage in the blessing of our Lord and Savior," Alexander said.

"Thank you. May you also continue to be blessed," Chanson said, taking Parisina's hand and leaving to talk with other guests.

King Blackmore and King Sainesbury resumed their cordial visit.

"Alexander, how's your family?" King Sainesbury said.

"My wife and children are doing well," he said, his eyes casting downward as if troubled.

"And you, friend, have you been well since we last spoke at the tournament?"

"Well, I have been having some stomach issues, but my wife suggested I rest more. I took her advice and have been taking an afternoon nap each day and that has helped. Also my son, Rylen, has suggested I allow him the kingdom and step down. But I told him he would rule soon enough."

"I'm very sorry to hear of your ailments. You have my prayers. Please let me know how I may help. Thank you for the gifts, very generous of you. Please give my regards to your queen."

"Of course, Roland."

With those words they parted and mingled with the other guest.

King Sainesbury was known for his generous heart. Whenever there was an occasion to celebrate, he instructed his servants to prepare extra food to help nourish the poor and unfortunate in the community. Parisina's wedding feast was yet another opportunity for King Sainesbury to extend kindness beyond the doors of his castle. He sent his squires out in the community to distribute pistachios, red currants, fresh fruits, cheese, and pine nut bread to the impoverished.

The wedding feast continued into the early evening. The maidens joined hands together and sang, dancing around the wedded couple while the minstrel played the harp.

Parisina and Chanson made their way into the crowd to personally thank each guest for attending their wedding. When Parisina stepped away to bid farewell to her father, Hayden saw an opportune time to express a few sentiments to Chanson before he and Parisina left to retire to their manor.

"Chanson, you seem the most contented I've ever known you to be. I'm glad for it!" Hayden said, smiling.

"Father Hayden, I am. For so many years there had been a desperate longing within me. I begged God to fill it, but it seemed he had turned his ear away. That is, until I fell in love with Parisina. She completes me."

"You've grown into a sterling knight, and a superlative warrior of strength and integrity. Battles may prove fierce, and you may lose a few, but integrity can never be defeated. Don't ever lose sight of that precious attribute. Cling to God and Parisina's heart, always. Begin the day in His Word and let His Holy Scripture enrich your soul."

"I am thankful for your wisdom and example of integrity," Chanson said, his eyes beginning to well in tears of gratitude.

Hayden, moved by Chanson's praise, embraced him and said, "You have been like flesh and blood to me. It is I whom God has blessed. I only wish your parents, all of them, could see the young man you have become—"

"I believe they have!" King Sainesbury whispered, placing his hand on Chanson's shoulder.

Chanson and Hayden expressed a few sentiments to the King then parted for the evening.

Chanson loved Parisina more than life itself; she was his kindred soul tie. An indelible impression was left on Chanson's heart after losing his family at a vulnerable time in childhood. He loved with a sense of urgency and believed one must be willing to die for the other if love demanded it.

Musette

Firegate Castle
Early afternoon on August 1424

King Sainesbury was about to welcome his first granddaughter.

"Your Majesty, Parisina has had the baby—a little girl with a head full of dark hair like her mother!" Chanson said, beaming. "Her marble blue eyes have already captured my heart!"

"Chanson, that's delightful news!" King Sainesbury said with a huge grin. "Have you a name for the child?"

"Musette."

"Ahh, it has a melodious ring to it," the king said.

"Parisina and I are hoping she will want to play an instrument or sing when she grows."

"Well, if she has your talent, Chanson, she'll be a virtuoso before she's out of her bassinet," King Sainesbury chuckled.

"Thank you."

"No, no, Chanson—the gratitude goes to God who bestowed the gift. Only He could create your gift and bless you with this inborn talent. Speaking of the little one, when may I see my granddaughter?"

"Now," Chanson said, his eyes beaming with pride.

King Sainesbury held his baby granddaughter for the rest for the evening. To celebrate the birth, he arranged a special feast of roasted quail and turtledove served with carrots, cabbage, and plenty of cheese, apple tarts, custards, and strawberry cheesecake. Music and dance were also a part of the celebration honoring the granddaughter's arrival.

Hayden and Lady Genevie approached Chanson and Parisina as they sat admiring their newborn daughter.

"Congratulations to you both!" Hayden said. "She's a beauty! You'll have to keep a close eye on that one when she's grown into a young lady, Chanson!"

"Oh, you can count on that!" Chanson said while grinning at the placid infant swaddled in her mother's arms.

"The little bundle has already taken hold of your heart," Hayden said, chuckling. "I'm so proud of you."

"Long before Musette was born," Chanson said, "I pleaded to God for wisdom and grace in raising the child. And now that she is here, I am overwhelmed in both joy and humility. The love I feel for her and Parisina has taken me by surprise."

"It's a profound love no one can rival. As a father you want the best for your child. When they hurt, you hurt far greater. God's Word will give you wisdom in raising her."

"Thank you, Father Hayden—"

"I know Chanson's going to be an exquisite father," Parisina interrupted. "He's so tender and strong already. I can only imagine him growing even wiser and more grounded with age. He plans to begin reading the Holy Scriptures to Musette tonight. And we will kneel beside her bassinet and pray for her every night as her little eyes close and she sighs off to sleep."

"I'm happy, Lady Parisina," Hayden said. "Those early values will mean a lot as she grows."

"I couldn't have said it better!" King Sainesbury interrupted with a colossal smile on his face. "And I could not be more pleased with the man my daughter loves."

"Thank you, My King," Chanson said. "On behalf of us both we appreciate the bountiful festivities you have provided for us today. I will do my very best to be the father your granddaughter needs. I am happy that, in this moment of time, I have Lady Parisina's heart; the tender presence that completes me."

Chanson gazed at his wife with a gleam in his eyes. He put his arm around her waist.

"I'm glad to hear you say it, Chanson," King Sainesbury said. "Let the festivities continue! Please have some more food and drink. The day isn't over yet! I'll stay here with the little one if you and Parisina would like to have some more refreshments. It would do my heart good to see you folded in dance while the merrymakers play their tunes. *Please*, go on, enjoy yourselves!"

"If you insist, Father. Come, Chanson, let's mingle with a few before nightfall."

"As you wish!" Chanson said as he took the hand of his wife. They joined the others, dancing in celebration of Chanson and Parisina's daughter.

When news spread of Musette's birth, gifts of gold and silver were delivered to the castle from neighboring countries that had a strong alliance with the king. They thought it only fitting for a king who had established a reputation for being a man of valor. One of those bearing extravagant gifts was King Sainesbury's longtime friend, the king of Abbystone, Alexander Blackmore. He made a special visit to the king.

"Roland, my friend," King Blackmore said, bowing gently to King Sainesbury. They hugged, greeting one another with vivacious smiles.

"Thank you for coming. Please, sit, let's talk for a while. Alexander, the last time we spoke you were not feeling well, are you better now? Has getting extra rest helped?"

"Actually no. I have been feeling excessively weak on most days. The doctor advised me to rest and to consider turning the kingdom over to my son. My son of course insists it's time for me to do so as well, but I worry he isn't mature enough. If I may be candid, my friend?"

"Of course. You can trust me, that has never changed."

"Indeed. Well, my eldest son will succeed me to the throne, should I die soon. I fear grave repercussions if he's allowed to reign. Rylen blows up in rages toward me over some of the decisions I've made. I walk away from him after his outrageous tirades, refusing to allow my temper to escalate with him. The relationship has become strained . . . listen to me, I've poured only dreadful news since arriving. This is a joyous occasion for you. I should not talk of such contempt today. Forgive me, my friend."

"Nothing to forgive. Please go on. I want only to help."

"Very well then. As I've expressed, I'm getting older and know that the end of my rule is nearing."

"Oh . . . you may have many more years, Alexander. I believe you're discouraged seeing more lines and graying hair. I too have those times when I feel dreadful," he said, rubbing his wrinkled neck as if to prove he, too, was getting old.

"Perhaps you are right. My wife reminds me that I take it all to heart too much and our son sees the future of the kingdom from a different perspective. My queen is so kind to this old man," he chuckled.

"I believe your wife has the best solution. Pray on it and leave it with God. I'll also join you in prayer. For now, let's enjoy some more food."

"I don't mind if I do," Alexander said.

King Sainesbury and the others continued to celebrate the birth of Musettc. King Blackmore's concerns about his health failing would soon become a reality. He passed away peacefully in his sleep two days after his last visit with King Sainesbury. His son, Rylen, took the throne immediately, but he was not at all like his father. The son wreaked havoc with Alexander Blackmore's legacy, bullying his neighboring kingdoms to forfeit parts of their land.

King Sainesbury grieved, for not only the loss of a trusted confidant, but also for the mess his heir was making of the long established, peaceful kingdom. The son became known as a greedy king who used dishonest means to secure territory and to gain power. Those under his rule who disagreed with his methods or decisions were put to death for even the slightest suggestion that questioned his leadership.

His army was massive and not because Rylen Blackmore was a sought after leader, but because the people were afraid not to succumb to his demands. It wasn't long until his temper and brutal rule became known to neighboring countries. Many gave in because they feared he would carry out his threats to harm their families or reveal secrets that would cause outrageous repercussions if known.

The peace between the two kingdoms—Evernora and Abbystone—would soon be torn apart. Rylen's aggressive nature would lead him to launch a deadly rampage against his father's closest friend, King Sainesbury. Through a bloody stampede, Chanson's integrity will be tested when he loses someone vital to his well-being.

Mortality hangs in the gallows.

Fallen Knight

Firegate Castle
King Sainesbury's throne
November 18, 1424

Esmond Scott arrived at the king's quarters to warn him about an urgent matter.

"It's imperative that I speak with the king," Esmond said to the guard.

"Of course, proceed. He's on the balcony."

Esmond approached the king who was sitting with his dog by his side. He bowed.

"Esmond, why the gloomy face, my friend?"

“There’s been some rumors heard in the community that King Rylen Blackmore is planning to take your territory as his own.”

“Not if I have anything to say about it! Evernora is my country and I am entitled to be in power, not Rylen! I will not allow anyone to take away this fortress that has been ruled for years by mighty men of God. And I defy anyone who thinks they can overpower the breath of God. For it is in the Almighty’s breath these stones were built, each ancient and loyal pillar withstanding the battle scars of every generation,” the king said, gripping the arms of his chair.

“I understand, My King, but a few peasants said they saw foreign men walking around assessing the land. Perhaps they are leaping to conclusions, but they seem to think Blackmore is planning to throw you out of power. What would you like for us to do?”

“I’ve been hearing about Alexander Blackmore’s son and know that he is a devious man. Men like him are cowards and we won’t allow ourselves to fret over him or those unsubstantiated rumors. Until he actually declares war on me, I’m going to continue to rule peacefully next to him and leave him alone. I’ve not seen any indication that he’s planning such an attack.”

“All right. I’m sorry I bothered you with this news.”

“No, Esmond. Don’t ever apologize for bringing news to my attention. I suppose it won’t hurt to be extra vigilant and increase security around the castle’s exterior.”

“I’ll get on that right away!” Esmond said, exiting.

Six months later on May 14, 1425

Esmond's fears concerning the rumor that King Rylen Blackmore of Abbystone was planning to attack Evernora had come to fruition. In the early hours of

Saturday, May fourteenth, King Blackmore positioned six thousand men to descend upon the castle's exterior.

King Sainesbury and his warriors were at a grave disadvantage by the unexpected attack led by the mentally deranged king. The castle's outer gatehouse was breached by King Blackmore's men after midnight.

Hayden Cheswick barreled through to King Sainesbury's chambers, bypassing his guards.

"My King, wake up, Your Majesty, we're under attack!" Hayden said, nudging the groggy king.

"What, at this hour and by whom?" the king said frantically while gathering his clothing and armor.

"King Blackmore's men crept in and have slaughtered a great number of our soldiers. I heard the screams at the outer gatehouse and have come now to tell you of this attack."

"Go Hayden! Wake the other knights, assemble them at the inner gatehouse. Our God watches over us—stand united—strike true for our country!"

Hayden Cheswick left and followed the king's instructions, but before King Sainesbury arrived at the inner gatehouse he was taken by three of Blackmore's men.

The inner gatehouse

Hayden, Esmond, Chanson, Ashton de Sille, and nine other accomplished knights were now armed and ready for battle. The men were standing in formation, awaiting Hayden's signal. When the king failed to meet Hayden and the others, they became alarmed.

"Gentlemen," Hayden said, "we must assume our king has been captured somewhere between here and his quarters. Let's ease out cautiously and try to find him."

"The only way out is through the outer gatehouse, but how did Blackmore's men manage to break through all those traps set for our defense?" Chanson said.

"It's apparent Rylen knew the outer layout of our castle," Esmond said.

"Then we must assume the men have King Sainesbury and are planning to smuggle him out through the outer gatehouse," Ashton piped. "If we hurry and take the secret passage we may be able to rescue the king and take those cowards down!"

"For God, king, and our country, let's go!" Hayden shouted.

The men quickly made their way through the inner gatehouse's secret passages and arrived at the outer gatehouse. They stood in disbelief at the number of dead bodies strewn across the premises like bloody rags thrown on the ground.

Rylen Blackmore's army was massive; their murderous feet could be heard stampeding through King Sainesbury's fortress.

"Men, on my command, charge ahead," Hayden said.

"But we can't take them down, Sir Cheswick—we're outnumbered!" Ashton warned. "We should surrender while we're still alive."

"No! We must fight until the bloody end if that's what it takes to defend our honor and save our king!" Hayden blurted.

Esmond chanted the warrior's code.

Souls of iron, knights of steel,
Bind for life, in heart and seal.

The men repeated the chant.

"NOW, gentlemen!" Hayden commanded.

Swords flew as they counterattacked.

Hayden charged at a soldier, slicing through his chest. Another soldier thrust a lance in his path causing Hayden to fall. He parried each thrust before lashing out and stabbing the man in the chest. The man collapsed.

Three soldiers charged toward Ashton. He avoided the first sword thrust, hit the ground and rolled, avoiding the soldier. Esmond stepped in and they defeated the men. Esmond suffered a wound to his hand, but he continued to fight as more soldiers approached him and Ashton.

Meanwhile Chanson saw a soldier and charged toward him with his sword, startling him. Their eyes met in the dark, both daring the other to strike first. As the soldier drew his sword in the air, Chanson speared him in the chest. Hayden ran alongside and stabbed him again. A few of the soldiers ran away.

"Ashton, we need to fight our way through this and get to the king," Hayden said.

"Behind you, Hayden!" Chanson said, after seeing a soldier charging toward him. Hayden whirled around swiftly and sparred at the man. Chanson raced toward the man and pierced his side. He fell.

The other knights finished off a few of the oncoming soldiers. One of the knights stumbled on a dead body. That left him distracted and he was fatally wounded by an oncoming soldier.

Chaos mounted as the two sides continued to fight, wrestling with each other. The air would normally be fresh and smell of nature's wonders, but instead was a nightmarish symphony of screams and swords sparring.

Hayden and the remaining men fought feverishly. Several of King Blackmore's men surrendered. They could no longer stand behind a king who chose to bring harm on innocent men. They joined Hayden and the others in the fight against King Blackmore. The warriors were exhausted, breathless, but still searching for King Sainesbury.

"Look, King Sainesbury!" Hayden alerted.

The knights charged toward the three men who were holding their king.

With their swords drawn, and shields up, they sparred with the men, killing all but the one who had a blade at the king's throat.

"I'll kill him!" the Abbystone general said. "If you don't surrender now, your king's a dead man!"

"Don't do it!" King Sainesbury shouted. "Don't disgrace our honor by surrendering to this debauchery!"

"Then take me," Hayden pleaded, "and let my king go!"

"Very well!" the general said. He threw King Sainesbury to the ground then lunged swiftly toward Hayden with his sword. He pierced Hayden through his breastplate, penetrating his heart. The hilt of the sword broke off in the man's hand. As Hayden lay dying, the man fled, soiling the bottom of his boots with blood from the dead bodies.

Hayden was fading quickly. Chanson's sword plummeted to the ground. He ran to where Hayden lay, mortally wounded. He forced his sorrow away and placed his hand on Hayden's bleeding chest as if doing so could stop death from taking him.

Chanson whispered through the muddled words, "Father, please—please don't die, I don't know how to do this again—wake up—please . . . wake up—"

Hayden opened his eyes, a tear trickled down his cheek. He took a shallow breath and said, "Take care of Landon, he'll need you . . . let the resiliency you had when you were first orphaned help you." His heartbeat slowed under Chanson's hand. Hayden rattled, "You're stronger—you've found your place in this world, everything you need is inside you. You can do this . . .

carry on, my brave son, warrior of my heart—it's your turn now—"

His heartbeat ceased; those were Hayden's final words. His mirrored eyes set their gaze on Chanson, but Hayden was no longer there. Chanson grabbed Hayden around the neck and held him in his arms. Memories consumed him while he sat numb to the bleak world around him. He recalled Hayden first reading Scripture to him at Marblemist Chapel. His eyes welled remembering Hayden picking him up and holding him tightly to his chest after he was consumed with grief. Hayden patted his back and whispered, "I know, Chanson, I know it hurts . . . go ahead, cry and let it all out . . . "

The king knelt beside them and said, "H-he was my best knight, I've lost a friend—a brother. Why did he do it, why—" the king choked, placing the back of his hand over his sweaty brow.

Esmond placed his wounded hand on King Sainesbury's shoulder and whispered, "He loved you . . . he did it because he loved you."

"So, this is what it means to lay down your life for your friends?" the king said. He took a deep breath, then another. The king rose to his feet, took his sword in his hand, held it in the air and shouted, "This war is not over! Men, pull yourselves together and let's drive them back!"

Chanson, Ashton, Esmond, the king, the remaining knights, and some of King Blackmore's men stormed toward oncoming soldiers. The men overwhelmed several of Blackmore's soldiers. More joined Sainesbury's army.

The sun had risen, though the sky was cloudy. The warriors could see more clearly to fight. Several of the soldiers were defeated by King Sainesbury and his men. Some of Blackmore's men succumbed to panic and hid or ran away from the fight, while others thought only of home and who they left behind.

Several hours later

King Sainesbury's army had now grown with hundreds of soldiers defecting from King Blackmore's army. The ones who had not defected were seen wandering around, injured and dazed. King Sainesbury was boiling with anger when he and his men came face to face with Rylen Blackmore.

"I think it would be in your best interest to surrender, Rylen," King Sainesbury said, after seeing the king rush toward his warriors and a few hundred men with him. "You're outnumbered now. Look around you, countless men have given their lives here and for what?

"Many of these dead warriors, your men—mine—have wives and children waiting at home for their return . . . faces they'll never see again. You've lost this war and any respect you thought you had.

"How could you stain the Blackmore legacy like this? Alexander was a good man, ruling with strength, compassion, and integrity to a higher calling. None of that was ever part of your reign!" the king yelled. "Step down from the throne of your almighty self!"

"I wanted my father to love me. Be proud to call me his son, but I was only an embarrassment. I think he secretly wished I were never born! Why did he hate me?" Rylen said, as if he were a desperate child.

"You have gravely misunderstood your father! He loved you, but he saw weaknesses in your character and they have overshadowed all the virtues he tried to teach you. Your impatience, bouts of rage, and vindictive actions against your own people are precisely why he did not want you to take the throne. Choosing to take land or kingdoms by force, using any means possible to do so, is a disgrace."

"I'm a b-brave king, I've . . . n-never cowered to any," Rylen said, his lips trembling and tears welling in his eyes. "I've devotion . . . to my wife, to my country. I only wish Father could have admired *those* virtues. To have heard him say he loved me, even once, would have shored my heart to greater excellence . . . then he would have been pleased."

"I'm sorry your father did not express that love to you verbally. You consumed his heart for he only wanted God's best for your life. Alexander was deeply wounded when you did not choose wisdom and compassion. He feared for the people *and your country* in the event you rose to power. Will you now say his concerns weren't warranted?" King Sainesbury said, extending his arm out at the brutal slayings.

Rylen looked around at the bodies, considering all the brutality he unleashed. His arms laid motionless at his sides. He dropped his sword, turned toward his remaining soldiers and shouted, "Men, lower your weapons!" They slipped their weapons into their sheaths. Rylen walked away, taking a few of his soldiers with him. The war was over and now the warriors had to deal with the aftermath. The air was thick and loomed of death.

King Sainesbury and his remaining warriors returned to where Hayden lay slain. Chanson knelt beside Hayden's body; the weight of sorrow pressed in on him. The remaining knights stood nearby sniffling softly.

Ashton walked slowly to Chanson's side and said, "Chanson, I know this hurts, but we must prepare Hayden and the other men for burial. We need to tell Landon about his father. Come, *please*, let me help you."

"Yes, well, I won't tell Landon—I won't be the one—I won't rip his heart out. Our father deserves a burial fit for a king, because that's what he was, a loyal man who served and ruled his family in the royal graces of God. And now he will rest with the legends who went before him."

"Chanson, let's ready him for his send off, all right?"

"Ashton, I owe him so much . . . how do I say goodbye?"

"Moment by moment, hour by hour, day by day . . . that's how we'll all have to do it."

"Well then, I guess we'd better take the first step and get his body away from this bloody mess," Chanson said.

Ashton stepped closer to King Sainesbury. "My King," Ashton said, interrupting the king in reflective thought. "I'll leave now and gather coffins for the dead and inform the coffin maker to begin construction on more."

King Sainesbury regained his composure and said, "Very well, Ashton, and ask Seabert to bring the ritual herbs . . . and bring Hayden's coffin in a carriage."

"Of course." Ashton bowed and left.

"When Seabert gets here, and has placed the necessary preserving herbs on Hayden's body we will put him in a coffin and take him for his last ride through Oakhollow Forest," the king said, barely able to speak. "How he loved the rides . . . they made him smile. I'm going to miss that sunny smile."

The men sat on the ground, staying with Hayden's body until Seabert arrived with the preserving herbs. Meanwhile, news of Hayden's death reached his wife. Lady Genevie ran toward Hayden, her hands gripping the sides of her gown to prevent tripping over the hem.

Esmond Scott sprung to his feet, placing himself between Lady Genevie and her husband, attempting to block her view of her dead husband. He said, "There was nothing we could do . . . he surrendered his life for the king. Before we could defend him, Blackmore's general stabbed your husband."

"Did he suffer?" she said. Her face was ghostly pale and her lips quivered.

"It was quick," Esmond reassured.

She slowly walked backwards, stunned in disbelief. "I must see him, I must see my husband." She ran around in circles, forgetting to breathe, groping for something to hold onto.

"All right," Esmond said, stepping aside and allowing Lady Genevie time with her husband.

She dropped to her knees, shook all over, and said, "Hayden, *my Hayden*—Oh, my darling Hayden!" She kissed both his cheeks, then his lips, and pressed her cheek against his cold face. She screamed; the sound ruptured the blackened sky, its high pitch sending memories through her head. 'If I die defending the king, please forgive me for leaving you,' Hayden said, kissing his wife before leaving for battle. She screamed again. Her life was irrevocably changed.

The castle grounds were littered with bodies, daggers, and swords. Red, pink, and gray were the new colors of what was once a harmonious, tender terrain.

Seabert arrived with his apothecary bag. His face hung down. Disturbed by the bloodshed, but trying to step around the bloody mayhem, he bent down to Hayden's wife and said, "Lady Genevie, please, may I be allowed to put some herbs on your husband's body and prepare him for burial?"

She kissed Hayden's lips again and whispered, "Goodbye my love, goodbye my knight . . . your heroic light will live on—in our sons."

Trying to be discreet and not upset Lady Genevie further, Aston and two other knights arrived with the carriage, Hayden's coffin and his horse, Silver Belle.

Lady Genevie stepped aside while the physician put myrrh, aloe, and incense on Hayden's skin. She did not utter another word, but stood with her hands crossed in front of her, and tears pooling in her eyes. Her blue gown was stained by Hayden's blood.

Ashton pulled the broken blade out of Hayden's chest. Enraged, Chanson seized the weapon from the knight's hand. He held it at his side while walking toward the other dead bodies; his teary eyes scanned his fallen comrades. Chanson lifted his gaze to the indignant sky and cried, "You won't be forgotten . . . your death won't be in vain, our friend!" Chanson threw the bloody sword down on the body of a dead Abbystone soldier and walked solemnly toward the coffin.

The knights lifted Hayden's body and put him in the coffin. They placed his sword in his right hand alongside his body and covered his bleeding chest with his shield. The shield's edges were emblazoned with layered metal rings and decorated in a scaly texture. Its center bore his rank and emblems of victory.

It was clear Hayden's shield had withstood the test of battle. His trophies of defeating death were left behind by scores and scratches on the shield. The shield was ready for more battles and tournaments, but its master had laid his armor down for the final time.

Seabert placed white lilies on the shield and closed the lid. With eyes full of tears, each stood reverently over the coffin of their earnest friend and reflected. Rain pattered lightly, small drops collected on the coffin.

Lady Genevie dropped to the ground and wrapped her arms around the coffin. She pressed her cheek onto it and sobbed.

"My King . . . *Landon*," Esmond whispered, noticing Hayden's son had walked up and saw the coffin.

"I'll talk to him," the king said, turning toward Landon who was stilled by the shock of seeing a coffin and his mother weeping over it.

"Father," he uttered in a hushed whisper, "is it Father?" They glanced at Landon, but were unable to speak.

"*It is my father*—no—not Father!" he cried.

King Sainesbury grabbed Landon, pressed him into his chest and whispered, "Yes, it's your father—"

Landon clung to the king like a lost child, pressing his face into his breast. The king wrapped one arm around Landon and held his head with the other hand.

Lady Genevie rose to her feet and placed her hand on her son's back. He turned around and fell into his mother's arms. They embraced tightly. "We'll be all right; for Hayden, we must be," she panted.

The king paused to collect himself then said, "Gentlemen, I'll take the reigns of Silver Belle and lead us through this forlorn forest later."

The knights lifted Hayden's coffin into the carriage and left to bury the other soldiers. Lady Genevie stayed with Hayden's body and continued to grieve. She held onto his coffin, reliving memories of her husband as the world faded away.

Landon, King Sainesbury, and his men returned to Hayden's body and found Lady Genevie still clinging to her husband's coffin.

"Mother," Landon said, taking hold of Lady Genevie's shoulders, "it's time . . . would you like for me to take you home?"

"No, my sweet boy . . . " she said, wiping away her tears with her hands. She stood and continued, "You go . . . be with your father one last time." Landon and Lady Genevie's eyes meet as tears steamed down their cheeks. He kissed his mother's cheeks and joined the men who were waiting to take Hayden for his last ride.

Seabert noticed Lady Genevie's frail state and rushed to offer his assistance. "Lady Genevie," Seabert said, his eyes connecting with hers, "please allow me to escort you home."

"Thank you, Seabert," she said, taking hold of Seabert's outstretched arm. "I'd like to stay until they take him," she said, as tears continued flowing down her cheeks.

"Of course," Seabert said while placing his hand over Lady Genevie's hand that was holding onto his arm. The men secured the carriage to Hayden's horse and then mounted on their horses.

King Sainesbury and Landon led the knights into Oakhollow Forest for Hayden's farewell ride. They chanted the warrior's code as they rode away, struggling to sing the words while brushing away tears with their gauntlet-covered hands.

Souls of iron, knights of steel,
Bind for life, in heart and seal.

When Lady Genevie could no longer see her husband's coffin, Seabert escorted her back to her manor. "My husband's not coming home this time . . . my sweet Hayden's gone," she kept repeating.

Seabert sat with her in her parlor, allowing her to talk about Hayden. He then summoned a maid to stay with her during the night, instructing her to alert him if she needed anything.

He holds me as the apple of his eye and
Carries me home when I die.

The Letter

The king's quarters
Early the next morning on May 15, 1425

Esmond Scott and King Sainesbury met to discuss the aftermath of Blackmore's vicious attack.

"What will you do, My King?"

"I can only think of one man suitable to step into Hayden's place."

"His son?"

"Landon's still too young," the king said, struggling to keep his composure. "Chanson's earned a place among my knights. He's ready to serve as my second. I'll permit him the honor of Officer Knight, but Landon isn't ready to lead like his father. He'll grow into it and so that's why I'm appointing him a knight. How is Landon handling the news?"

"It's difficult. He's understandably angry and keeps expressing the unfairness of the war. He has his father's strength now; I'm confident he'll work out these feelings."

"And Chanson?"

"Taking it hard as well," Esmond said, his eyes casting downward.

"This I would expect—his soul is tender. Where is he?"

"As soon as Hayden's body was buried he left on his horse for the forest again. I expect we won't see him for a few hours."

"Very well."

"The men who took care of the bodies reported back early this morning," Esmond said. "They said there were hundreds of widows and fatherless children in the wake of this tragedy. Many have been housed with the knights and their wives, but others don't have homes or a means to take care of themselves. What are we to do with them?"

"I'll start making plans to build a large manor to house them. Go now and gather the carpenters and architects to begin working on a sizable structure for the remaining widows and children. Then prepare Landon for the knighting ceremony to take place tomorrow evening."

"As you wish, Your Majesty."

Meanwhile, Chanson remained in the forest all night slumped against an oak tree, remembering times shared with Hayden.

'Chanson,' Hayden said, 'distraction can be a good remedy to help the mind deal with loss. You have a poet's heart, given to you by the Almighty. If used properly, you could leave a lasting legacy of tenderness and strength. The balanced man is precisely that, tender and strong. The great warriors of old used to chant a knight's poem before heading out to battle.

Souls of iron, knights of steel,
Bind for life, in heart and seal.

'Wisdom is eternal. Plead for God to bless your heart with wisdom and discernment. Remember King Solomon's request to have a wise, discerning mind. You, too, can petition the Almighty to grant you heavenly wisdom. Allow the wisdom of God to saturate your soul while using the strength of youth to help mold you into a warrior with iron and heart. With God's help you will mature into an honorable and worthy man.'

Firegate Castle
King Sainesbury's quarters
Early morning on May 16, 1425

Landon's knighting ceremony was only a few hours away and no one had seen or heard from Chanson since late the day before. King Sainesbury was beginning to worry about him and how he was reacting to the death of Hayden Cheswick.

"Your Majesty, you called for me?" Esmond said, rushing in to the king's quarters after being summoned.

"Esmond, we need to locate Chanson. I want to present him Hayden's horse, Silver Belle, tonight after Landon's ceremony. Hayden had told me a long while ago that he wanted Chanson to have Silver Belle if he were to die in battle. I must honor his wishes."

"But wouldn't the horse belong to Landon? He is blood."

"No. This was his father's wish. Landon has his father's first horse and that's how he wanted it. Please find Chanson and bring him to me."

"Yes, My King," Esmond said, bowing. He left the king's chamber.

Chanson went to the only place that could help him cope with the death of his faithful mentor, a serene brook in Oakhollow Forest. He took his flute out of his bag, intending to soothe his sorrow with a favorite melody, but the clutches of grief would not allow him.

Chanson took off his leather boots, sat down on the bank and dipped his feet into the cool rolling waters. He recalled the times that Hayden had stopped to pray while sitting on the bank of the clear flowing stream. Looking into the water, Chanson saw pebbles and small fish swimming quietly. His tears flowed, falling into the water, drop by drop, forming a gentle ripple on the surface. His face became contorted, he screamed, but no sound came out; his breath was held captive by the searing sword of grief. Loss had once again taken someone cherished from Chanson's life.

"I know you loved Hayden like a father, my little friend," Princess Pearlensia whispered, appearing beside Chanson and patting his head with her wing.

"It's you! It never crossed my mind you'd come today, but I'm glad you're here," Chanson said.

"I would choose no other place to be than by your side in this hour of tremendous trial. The pain you feel will soften with time."

"Perhaps you are right, but I can't imagine my days without Father Hayden. He understood me, his devotion was with me from the moment he picked me up off that bloody ground and took me in his arms. Why, Princess Pearlensia, has God allowed one so pure and kind to be taken from us?"

"My little friend, I do not know why God allows sorrow. I am only able to affirm that Hayden has been taken from evil . . . it will not touch him ever again. I hope you will find solace knowing Hayden was a devout man of God and suffers no longer."

"Yes, that he was. He ruled his home, and his heart, with tenderness and strength. Few men I've observed were like him, well, except King Sainesbury. He and Father Hayden seemed more like brothers than a King and knight."

"You have observed correctly. King Sainesbury's soul is torn asunder by this tragedy. He will need you, your courage, your loyalty for the days ahead."

"And he will have it . . . he will have my devotion even if I must die for him as my father has."

"Soon, you must return to Firegate Castle and resume your position as knight. Do not despair, my friend, God has carried you through all your other troubles and griefs, He will do the same this time. He remains in your heart and is touched by your sorrow. Do you remember when I spoke those words at your bedside years ago?"

"I have never forgotten your words. As I've done with God's words, I have stored your pearls of wisdom deep in my heart so that I would never forget them."

"Good. My little friend I must go now. Will you be all right?"

"Yes. I am stronger now that you've been here. Will I see you again, Princess Pearlensia?"

"Oh, I cannot say for certain. But if God wills it then I know a way will be made for me to come to you. For now, be assured of this: glistening sunlight will soon overshadow this cloud of sorrow, leaving sweet memory in its place."

Princess Pearlensia wrapped her feathers around Chanson's slim frame and said, "Goodbye, my little friend . . . the Lord cradles your heart. Lay your head on his breast and let His gentle spirit soothe you."

"Goodbye, thank—"

Before he could finish his expressions, Pearlensia was gone. He searched for her, peering around the trees, glancing down the dirt path, but she had vanished.

Chanson heard a rustling of leaves. His eyes quickly took him to an ancient oak tree standing to his right. Perched gingerly on one of the green leaves was a large butterfly with multicolored wings. Brushing away his tears, he stood and walked barefoot toward it. As he drew closer, he was taken by the butterfly's brilliant appearance; he had never seen one like it. Her wings spanned the width of the oak leaf. Three sets of wings fluttered in unison, each in shades of emerald, ruby, and amethyst.

Esmond arrived and saw Chanson standing under the swaying tree. The butterfly fluttered away, startled as Esmond was getting off his horse.

"Chanson, are you all right?"

Chanson looked over at Esmond, but he said nothing. He resumed sitting on the brook's bank. As Esmond approached the distraught young man, Chanson still said nothing. It was apparent to Esmond that Chanson was suffering greatly; his face was pale and his eyes reddened from the scar of loss.

"Chanson, are you all right?"

"I've not only lost a friend and a brother, but a man who stood me on my feet and helped me through life. How do you settle that in your mind? Tell me, Esmond—how do you do that?" Chanson's eyes watered and his lips quivered. He was barely able to speak.

"You can't . . . not today . . . the blade of anguish cuts too deep. It seems unreasonable to expect you to do anything but sit here and grieve over the loss of one as significant and loyal as Hayden. Please . . . as difficult as it is, you must pull yourself together; it's what Hayden would want you to do. The king needs to see you before the ceremony."

"Well, I guess it's time I mount up like a man and not let my hero be forgotten—but I do not know how . . . a million swords have pierced my soul."

"I know it hurts. I beseech you, young friend, find that place from long ago where the sheer will of mind forced you to carry on, and use its strength now to guide you. Allow the past sorrows to get you through Hayden's death by focusing on how much you overcame to get to where you are today. You have the most resilient spirit of anyone I know. It's a blessing that God has bestowed upon you, use it to help you.

"Hayden's loss is a tragedy for all of us, and as difficult as it is, we must honor Landon now as he will join us in the brotherhood. You need to get back to the castle, we've much repair to do."

"All right," Chanson said. With a heavy sigh and a despondent air, Chanson rose. He put away his flute, slipped on his boots, and rode away with Esmond to the castle.

Firegate Castle
King Sainesbury's throne

Chanson arrived at the castle. He bowed and approached King Sainesbury.

"You wanted to see me, Your Majesty?"

"Yes, Chanson. Please sit."

"It looks serious. Have I offended you, My King?"

"Not at all. I know Hayden meant a lot to you. His death was not something even I was prepared to accept. Of all the men to serve next to me, he was the most trusted—my second. Our friendship spanned more than two decades. This kingdom has lost a valuable pillar of strength . . . its soul. Despite the heaviness we all feel today, we must persevere. Chanson, Hayden left a letter to give to you after his death."

"*A letter?*"

"Yes, right here," the king said, picking up the letter and handing it to Chanson.

"But I don't understand, Your Majesty."

"I believe his final script will clarify. *Please*, read it."

Chanson took the scrolled parchment, untied the linen string and read.

Chanson,

If you are reading these words then you know I've fallen in battle. In watching over you all these years you've been nothing but a son. It never mattered to Lady Genevie either that you were an orphan and not our blood. We took you as one of our own and hoped you'd be able to turn your unfortunate loss into a heroic legacy long after we're both gone.

The tender musician in you will want to find a tall oak tree and serenade your sorrow away, but don't do that. Keep your focus and never forget who you are. Believe in yourself while holding to the brotherhood. You weren't appointed a knight solely upon the exceptional way you played your flute and charmed the king and those in his exclusive ladies' court. All of those attributes are precisely why you have stood out among your fellow warriors. As I've said many times, if you take that sensitivity and seal it with honor and courage you will leave as a legend worth remembering centuries from now.

Landon thinks of you as a brother; I know you are aware of this. He's younger, he admires you, but you will need to look out for him; he's not as controlled in his spirit as you. He has my first initiation horse, and now I want you to have Silver Belle, provided she is survived by me and fit for battle. Remember the code of honor and live it to the best of your ability, keeping God as the fire of your heart.

I love you, my son,
Father

"When did he write these words?" Chanson said, tears welling in his eyes.

"The eve following your knighting ceremony," the king said. "He loved you as his own fresh and blood and the same can be said of me, Chanson. When you did not report back after Hayden's death, I had a good idea where you were. Every man has a potential weakness, but if he bridles it wisely it will become the essence of nobility."

"I won't disappoint you or Hayden's legacy. You have my word, Your Majesty."

"Chanson, it's that musician's soul that has allowed you to weave yourself into the very heart of this kingdom. Use it, but keep it guarded. A good warrior must know his weakness, for you can be sure your enemy will uncover it. When we are aware of our weaknesses we can then plead with the Almighty to help us overcome them.

"Humility is not a symbol of weakness, but a manifestation of a pliable character, one God can use. It's only in being honest with ourselves that we become strong men of honor. Don't allow that tender side to become tarnished by the brutality of war. Always fight for the good and know in your heart you've done well, no matter the outcome of the battle."

"Thank you for those words."

With a pleasing nod King Sainesbury said, "When we ride out tonight for Landon's initiation, I want you to take Silver Belle. It's what Hayden would want. He considered you and Landon as sons and that's how it will be from now on."

"Yes, My King."

"Very well. Leave now and prepare yourself for the ceremony and make sure the others do likewise. You're now my second in command."

"*Second*—I feel honored, I truly do, but I am not the man Hayden was. I am not worthy to step into his shoes. I dare say no one is, if I may be bold."

"Yes, I know. No one rivals his heart, his essence. He often told me he wanted to have the very soul of King David and for his wisdom to match King Solomon in the Bible. I can't imagine a better man of valor than Hayden, nor a more trusted friend, but I am confident that you, Chanson Westbrook, are the man to step into Hayden's place. He prepared you well. He knew your potential early on, we all did. He'll never be forgotten, but we must rebuild quickly."

"I understand," Chanson said. He bowed and left.

Oakhollow Forest
Evening on May 16, 1425

King Sainesbury gathered his knights to honor Landon and to bid farewell to Hayden Cheswick.

"Welcome all," King Sainesbury said, "even though our land lies in ruin, we won't allow our spirits to be defeated too. It will take us some time, but we'll rebuild and come back, a mightier fortress than before.

"Hayden Cheswick gave his life and if it had not been for his bravery, I would not be standing before you now." King Sainesbury choked back sorrow and kept speaking. "I know the battle was vicious and along with you, I, too, grieve the loss of our friend, my brother. But tonight, his legacy will live on. His son Landon will be my new knight. Chanson is now Officer Knight. From this moment on, you will take orders from him. Honor, duty, and courage are our badge no matter what we face as we carry on.

"Landon, in honor of your father, I want you to lead the traditional knights' ride tonight," Chanson said, holding the reins of Silver Belle to allow Landon and his horse ahead of him. "I know Father Hayden would want it this way . . . *Please*, after you."

"Thank you, Chanson," Landon said, his eyes misting. "Somehow it doesn't seem right for Father to be absent tonight. He told me years ago he'd like for me to serve as a knight when I was ready. It never crossed my mind I'd be called to serve because of his death. I wish he could have been a part of my ceremony today so that there would not be this gut-wrenching sorrow now. Instead, death has stolen from me the strongest, yet most tender man I have ever known."

"Landon, it grieves me too that he's not with us and missed being a part of your knighting ceremony," the king piped. "But your father *is with you tonight;* his spirit lives on in your heart. You've demonstrated great courage today by putting your grief aside and stepping into your responsibilities. The greatest test of character is how a man gets up when life has thrown him down. I know Hayden would be proud of the courage and loyalty you've shown today."

"Thank you, My King. Your words mean a great deal to me, *especially today*. I will do my utmost to live by the codes of chivalry and not allow this grief to consume me. I have Chanson's example to help me."

Chanson turned toward Landon and said, "Landon, we are brothers now, *family*. I will be here for you as you've been for me."

The young men's teary eyes connected. Chanson paused, then continued, looking thoughtfully into Landon's eyes, "We were both blessed to have been nurtured by such a loving man."

"We were," Landon said, smiling with teary eyes.

"Count me in too, Landon!" Ashton said. "Your father was one of my best friends. When I wasn't fighting or training with him, I spent time with Seabert, having supper with him and his nightingale. He's not one to upset others with his troubles, but last night when I dropped by to check on him, he was sitting with Karina and shedding tears over our lost friend. We sat for a few minutes, sharing our sorrow and exchanging uplifting stories about Hayden.

"I don't know how any of us would cope with life's problems if we didn't have each other to lean on. Both those men have been supportive friends since losing my wife and daughter in childbirth. As we struggle to move forward, let's try to focus on Hayden's generous spirit, allowing his infectious smile to remind us there is still beauty in this world."

"Thank you, Ashton," Landon said. "I believe it's almost midnight and you know how Father loved the moonlight with all its tranquility. How about we ride further in and pause for a moment of prayer near the brook where he used to sit and pray?"

"That's a fine idea! Let's go!" Ashton said.

Landon led the knights and King Sainesbury deeper into the forest with the moon's radiance guiding their way.

Evernora field
May 28, 1425

Landon and Chanson's emotions were raw after the death of Hayden. It was while on the field during jousting that Chanson worried about Landon and the impact Hayden's death was having on him. Chanson noticed Landon kicking a stump as if wanting to punish someone. He waited until the practice was over and approached him about his outward display of aggression.

"Landon, are you all right?"

"I'm upset about Father. If it had not been for Rylen Blackmore, he would be here today, practicing with us. I miss him . . . the world is cold now. My ambitions and the spark of joy I once had has died too. Father's voice is gone—his embrace, his love, and support—all gone because of one man!" Landon said, his eyes misting with tears.

"I'm not even sure I believe in fighting any more. Look at us Chanson, are we not just as evil as some of Rylen's men, leaving children without their fathers?"

"But Landon, we didn't take innocent lives like Rylen. He killed for his own power, invading without a reason for declaring war against King Sainesbury. Grief is horrible, I know I'm feeling Hayden's loss too. I miss his laughter and the way he ran beside us, pumping us to give our all. He was more than a father, he was the pillar in these fields, a pillar who can't be replaced."

Chanson scanned the brevity of the field, hearing Hayden's laughter and his upbeat spirit echoing in memory.

"There just has to be a better way than senseless wars like this!" Landon said as tears plummeted down his cheeks.

"Landon, we'll get through this . . . together, all right?"

"All right, big brother. I'm going to need you."

"I need you too, Landon. Now, let's get some food. We must try to get our appetites back so that we carry on in Father's tenacious spirit," Chanson said, putting his arm around Landon and walking back to Oakmoor manor.

The flute of solace is silenced;
Lamenting melody steals my song.

Breath of Hope

Oakmoor Manor
May 29, 1425

Lady Genevie found herself engulfed in sorrow following the death of her husband. King Sainesbury and Esmond Scott visited her after the customary days of mourning were fulfilled. They knocked on her door. Lady Genevie opened the door.

"My King, how delightful to see you. And you too, Esmond," she said, curtsying. "Has something happened to the boys?"

"No, no," the king said. "I've come to talk with you about the children who have suffered the loss of their fathers."

"Oh yes, it's a dreadful reality. I've been praying for them, seeking some way that I may help."

"Lady Genevie," King Sainesbury said, "I know of a way that you can help."

"*Please,* tell me."

"I've already begun construction on a manor to house the widows and their children. I would like for you to live on the estate and help the women with their young ones. There will of course be nurses, cooks, servants, and guards assigned to the new structure. Inside the manor I am also building a new chapel where the women and children will worship as they recover from the wounds of the war.

"One of my knights, Thomas Crane, will also help you to organize the new home and help to instill spiritual understanding and comfort in the grief-stricken mothers and their children. I want to enrich the surroundings with flowers and gardens. I'd like for you to choose them and I'll have my gardeners plant them. Perhaps the gardens will help to bring peace to their souls."

Lady Genevie was consumed with sorrow.

"Please forgive me, Lady Genevie," the king said, thoughtfully, "perhaps it's too soon. It was insensitive of me to ask you to assist these families when you yourself are suffering."

"No, no. It's not that. I am touched that Hayden's death, while cruel and senseless, allows me to be a source of understanding for the women. I believe Hayden would want me to help them. If he were here, he would not hesitate to take the little children under his wing and nurture them as he once did with our Chanson." She continued to sob, but determined to finish her thoughts. "Of course, I will help. I know that keeping busy and trying to be a source of encouragement will help to soothe my own sorrow."

King Sainesbury's eyes moistened with tears. He placed his hand cautiously on Lady Genevie's shoulder and said, "You won't be the only one to be soothed by caring for the fatherless and the widows."

"We're all going to miss his kindred presence," Esmond piped, his eyes also misting with tears.

"Thank you, My King," Lady Genevie said. "I am honored that you have selected me. I will do whatever I can for them."

"The gratitude belongs to me, Lady Genevie, for you are a lovely woman of God, one whose compassion surpasses many. I pray one day this sorrow will be lifted from you."

"Thank you, My King. I know you understand."

"If you need anything else, no matter the hour, summon me and you'll have whatever you desire."

With misty eyes, she curtsied and whispered, "Thank you again."

Esmond and King Sainesbury left and resumed their conversation in the king's quarters.

"Lady Genevie impresses me with her fervent spirit," Esmond said.

"Yes. I, too, was taken by her strength . . . her faith. I needed that today . . . "

"Are you all right?" Esmond said. "You'll rebuild, and quickly. Is that why your face has fallen just now . . . you're concerned about our remaining soldiers and how the war has affected them? Be assured, the men who defected have confirmed their loyalty and want to join your army. In no time it will be larger than before. Blaine and the knights are getting the men settled as we speak . . . they are devoted to you."

"I'm all right. I've been reflecting on Scripture, the book of Ezekiel specifically. I pray God's breath comes over our land and restores our hope too. It's all symbolic somehow . . . my dead soldiers, Alexander's, now in the valley of dead bones."

"I had not thought of it that way."

"Though I cannot say I am not bewildered by all that has happened. I will proceed, nonetheless, in the joy of the Lord. For it is only in the strength of the Almighty's power we will be able to rebuild this land, igniting the fire of hope within the hearts of our people again."

"Of course, Your Majesty. You, and only you, could stand on the threshold of such debauchery and refuse to let it squelch the fire of your reign."

"Thank you, Esmond, my trusted friend. I believe I'll retreat to my sanctuary now and allow God's Word to soothe my soul, unless there's more we need to discuss."

"No, My King. I'll leave now and check on the builders. I'll also secure the men's swords and armor, getting them ready for the ceremony."

"Very well. Your loyalty means a great deal to me, especially in the wake of what has happened."

"All your requests are being carried out. Soon, we'll all be lit with the torch of hope again," Esmond said, clasping his hands in front of him, graciously bowing and exiting the king's presence.

The king sat down in his sanctuary. He took the Bible in his hand, opening to the book of Ezekiel, and read.

The hand of the Lord was upon me, and carried me out in the spirit of the Lord, and set me down in the midst of the valley which was full of bones,

And caused me to pass by them round about: and, behold, there were very many in the open valley; and, lo, they were very dry.

And he said unto me, Son of man, can these bones live? And I answered, O Lord God, thou knowest.

Again he said unto me, Prophesy upon these bones, and say unto them, O ye dry bones, hear the word of the Lord.

Thus saith the Lord God unto these bones; Behold, I will cause breath to enter into you, and ye shall live:

And I will lay sinews upon you, and will bring up flesh upon you, and cover you with skin, and put breath in you, and ye shall live; and ye shall know that I am the Lord.

So I prophesied as I was commanded: and as I prophesied, there was a noise, and behold a shaking, and the bones came together, bone to his bone.

And when I beheld, lo, the sinews and the flesh came up upon them, and the skin covered them above: but there was no breath in them.

Then said he unto me, Prophesy unto the wind, prophesy, son of man, and say to the wind, Thus saith the Lord God; Come from the four winds, O breath, and breathe upon these slain, that they may live.

So I prophesied as he commanded me, and the breath came into them, and they lived, and stood up upon their feet, an exceeding great army.

Then he said unto me, Son of man, these bones are the whole house of Israel: behold, they say, Our bones are dried, and our hope is lost: we are cut off for our parts.

Therefore prophesy and say unto them, Thus saith the Lord God; Behold, O my people, I will open your graves, and cause you to come up out of your graves, and bring you into the land of Israel.

And ye shall know that I am the Lord, when I have opened your graves, O my people, and brought you up out of your graves,

And shall put my spirit in you, and ye shall live, and I shall place you in your own land: then shall ye know that I the Lord have spoken it, and performed it, saith the Lord.

Landon and Chanson were pillars of support for Lady Genevie. The young men were often seen escorting their mother, one on each arm, down the wide hall that led to the chapel. She found peace for her soul and comfort in reading the same scriptures her husband read. Lady Genevie lived faithful to God and cherished Hayden's memory through her two sons.

It took the king a little over a year to rebuild his kingdom. The widows and fatherless were given a home in the new estate, Larkfair Gardens, in the summer of 1427.

Rylen Blackmore was overthrown in a military revolt and later murdered by a widow whose husband was killed in the battle against King Sainesbury. The woman had disguised herself as a knight, slipping into the king's quarters while he was sleeping. When she knew he was soundly asleep on his side, she took a spear and stabbed him through the temple. The blade went through his skull and killed him immediately. The woman was found out and sent into exile. She was hailed a hero by many for releasing the people from a brutal king.

The new king, Easton Blackmore, Rylen Blackmore's youngest brother, took over his throne. Easton ruled much like his father; tempered, compassionate, and forthright. Peace once again resided in the kingdom of Abbystone. The new-found peace in Evernora would be short-lived, however.

It is often on the eve of calm waters that a storm gathers its greatest strength. A fruit seed will flourish and unleash devastating loss for King Sainesbury and those closely associated with him. The bonds of friendship and brotherly love will be tried in the furnace of affliction.

The Lord is our harbor; His light watches over us
When we must be absent one from the other.

Eternal Sleep

Firegate Castle
October 19, 1428

Evernora suffered several storms, but one was peculiar and dreadful, leaving the castle grounds in disarray with fallen tree limbs and scattered leaves. Three of the king's workers, Wells, Ward, and Morris found unusual vines of bright red berries strewn among the storm's debris. Because the berries were unusually large with black pointy leaves, the workers collected the vines of berries and brought them inside the palace to have them inspected. The men were ushered to the king's throne.

King Sainesbury was apprised of the strange berries. While the workers were discussing the berries, one of the king's advisers, Garrick Aynsley, interrupted with urgent news.

"Your Majesty, something dreadful has happened. *Please*, you must come quickly!" Garrick said, fidgety and rubbing his balding head.

"*Garrick*, what has happened? Is there a threat?" the king said.

"No, Your Majesty, but your immediate action is warranted. One of the children from the ladies' court got into some of the berries. She ate them and is now behaving strangely."

"It must have been the berries the workers recovered from the premises," the king said.

"There's more," Garrick said with grim expression, hesitant to tell the king rest of the dreadful news.

"*Garrick*, stop hesitating—tell me."

"The child, well—she's your granddaughter, Your Majesty."

"*Musette!* How did this happen?"

"Her mother had stepped away for only a little while, leaving the child in the care of one of the other ladies. She must have wandered off."

"Come with me," the king said.

Lorlea Manor

The king and Garrick entered Parisina's manor and found Musette staring at the wall.

"Father, Musette found the berries when we were outside the courts having afternoon refreshments. She had already eaten several when I noticed. She's been unresponsive to my voice since. Look at her, she appears to be dazed."

"Indeed, she does," the king said after glancing at Musette lying on her bed, limp and drowsy.

"Garrick, summon the physician quickly!" the king said. "I must resume the meeting to warn the workers about the berries. Do not tell anyone about what has happened. Keep Musette and those who know about the berries separated from the others until we know what they are and what further effects the berries will have on the child."

"Of course, My King." Garrick left to alert the doctor.

"Parisina, please do not worry, we'll find a cure. Seabert Gaines is very knowledgeable about herbs in the apothecary," King Sainesbury said as he kissed his daughter's forehead and patted her hand.

"But Father," Parisina cried, "what if the berries are poisonous and my baby dies—*Oh Papa, I won't lose my child!*"

"Let's let the doctor examine her; there's no time for delay, dear one. I must leave now so that we can find an antidote and secure those berries before further disaster!"

"Where's Chanson?" Parisina asked while collapsing in her father's arms.

"He and Landon are not in the castle, but I'll have one of the other knights to get word to him. Try to keep Musette calm. Seabert will be here any moment. He's extremely skilled—*please*—do not cry. He'll know what to do," King Sainesbury said, prying his daughter's arms from the desperate grip she had around his neck.

King Sainesbury left to inform Chanson of the unfortunate accident and to question the workers more extensively about the berries.

Garrick and the physician, Seabert Gaines, returned to Parisina and Musette. The doctor concluded Musette had suffered profound memory loss after a thorough examination was made. The doctor left the child guarded with instructions that Parisina and Musette were not to be approached by anyone until further notification. They left immediately to report his findings to the king.

King Sainesbury's guard escorted Seabert and Garrick to the king's quarters where he, Esmond Scott, and the three workers were discussing the berries.

"Seabert, how is my granddaughter?"

"It's bad. She can't remember her name nor is she able to identify her mother. Naturally she is frightened, given we're all like strangers to her now."

"Is there anything that can be done? Is there an antidote?" the king said.

"If I knew what kind of berries these were I could formulate one using herbs and plants. Until I know exactly what properties the berries possess, creating an antidote could prove difficult. Time could be a factor as well. I don't know. I can only keep Musette isolated for now."

"Do you suspect Musette will die?" the king said, choking back sorrow.

"I do not know that either, Your Majesty. Other than memory loss, crying, and appearing dazed, I can find nothing else wrong with the child. I'm afraid to use any medicinal herbs or potions for fear of what might happen, considering the unknown origin of the strange berries."

"Seabert, is it possible these berries were transported over from Ein Island?"

"Well, that possibility has certainly crossed my mind. Perhaps the gale winds struck that island the greatest. Would you like for me to join the men in searching near the coast for some clues?"

"No Seabert, you're most needed here. I'll send Chanson and Landon out. Is there anything in your apothecary bag that would help my granddaughter until you are able to formulate a cure?" King Sainesbury said, looking down at the physician's black leather bag.

"I believe it best if she go untreated until I know more. I'm terribly sorry, My King. But rest assured, I will do my best to save your granddaughter."

"Very well, Seabert. Thank you. I knew I could count on you. I am confident that if there's a medicine that will help, you will uncover it with your expansive knowledge regarding herbs and plants.

"Please take the three workers and examine them. They said they only touched the berries, but even that could prove problematic. Stay with Musette through the night. If there are any changes, report back immediately, no matter the hour."

"Of course, Your Majesty."

The doctor left with the three workers. The king continued to discuss the emerging crisis with his advisers, Esmond, Blaine, and Garrick.

"My friends, it looks like we need to put Landon and Chanson in charge of the berries; destroying them so no one else suffers the same fate as my granddaughter," the king said. "We also need to expand our search for these berries. Fruit doesn't drop from the sky; there has to be some reason why they were scattered around the castle."

"Your Majesty, allow me to go with them," Garrick piped. "This crisis will be brought to a swifter resolution if I am allowed to go."

"No, Garrick, your services are better suited here. I want you here in the event we uncover other details about these berries."

Garrick did not respond to the king's decision to not allow him to be a part of the search for the berries. He cast his amber eyes toward the window as if contemplating.

"My King, shall I send for the knights?" Blaine said.

"Yes, immediately. And be sure to not tell the others. I want to keep the situation as contained as possible. We cannot allow distraction and panic."

"Of course, Your Majesty."

Blaine left to summon Landon and Chanson. The king and his advisers resumed their discussion concerning the berries.

Landon and Chanson entered King Sainesbury's quarters.

"You sent for us, My King," Chanson said, bowing before the king.

"I'm glad you came so quickly. We have a potential new threat," the king said. "Some outlandish red berries were discovered on the premises. The grounds workers found them and brought them to me. While I was discussing the berries, news came that Musette had accidentally eaten a few of the berries. The workers appear fine, but Musette has suffered memory loss."

"Why wasn't my daughter protected?" Chanson said, his face turning red and his body tensing. He turned to leave, desiring to check on Musette, but the king cautioned him.

"Chanson, I share in your concern and she will be dealt with later. For now, however, I need you to search the entire property thoroughly for any remaining berries, stems, and branches. I want both of you to extend the search close to the shoreline. Perhaps the storm uprooted them from Ein Island. Do not touch them directly; wear gloves. As soon as the berries are collected, bring them to me. Tell no one about them."

"As you wish, My King," Chanson said. "How is Parisina? May I see her and Musette before we collect the berries?"

"I've never seen a child behave like this before, but Seabert's doing everything he can to help formulate a cure for your little girl. Yes, Chanson, you may visit her, but keep the visit brief."

Chanson arrived to where Parisina and Musette were being examined. He noticed Musette was quiet and appeared to be sleeping. As soon as Parisina saw Chanson, she threw her arms around his neck and sobbed. The wails were muffled by Chanson's neck.

"Oh Parisina, Love. It's going to be all right. Please be strong for our daughter. I must leave at once to secure the berries."

"I will try, my sweet man," Parisina said, kissing her husband's face.

Chanson let go of his distraught wife and knelt beside his daughter's bed and whispered, "I love you, my little Musette. I'll be back later." He kissed her cheek and stepped away, taking Parisina into his arms. He whispered, "Our Musette will be all right, my faith tells me God will calm her confusion and Seabert will find a cure. I must leave now—will you be all right?"

"Yes, I will trust in God to cure our baby."

"That's my brave lady, keep hope alive in your heart. I will return, but until then, allow my kiss to comfort you while I'm away," Chanson said after kissing his wife and wiping away her tears with his hand.

Oakhollow Forest

Landon and Chanson had ridden through Oakhollow Forest for over two hours before reaching Kaishore Ocean. They noticed a massive pile of branches and leaves lying on the sand with a brown boat overturned. They got off their horses to inspect the troubling scene.

"It's a Tavik ship!" Landon said. "Look, the dragon head on the front!"

"I pity whomever was sailing in this, the damage is colossal," Chanson said. "No one could have survived the storm out here. We'd better turn the ship over and inspect underneath. Maybe someone's under it."

"All right, let's lift it. Ready, Chanson?"

"Yes, let's do it!"

Chanson and Landon tilted the boat on its side and noticed a gruesome scene. They gasped in horror at the sight of a dead man.

"He's been crushed to pieces!" Landon said.

Stooping down to examine the other debris scattered near the broken body, they saw a cloth bag. Landon poured the bag's content out onto the sandy ground.

"Look, Chanson! It's the berries! We have to take these back to the king!"

"Those are the same berries my little girl ate," Chanson said in a somber tone, his eyes welling in tears. "I hope she will be all right. It's difficult to see my baby girl frightened and unable to be comforted."

"Chanson, we need to report back now—the sooner the better so that Seabert can be apprised of our findings today. We have to keep the faith that Musette will be cured."

"Yes, you are right. It will be nightfall by the time we get back if we don't leave soon."

"More importantly, we don't want to be in the forest at midnight when the wild beasts prowl around for their meals. We need to leave now or we may be their supper," Landon said, grimly.

"But first we need to bury the man's remains," Chanson said, picking up the berries with his gloved hand and putting them back into the soggy bag. "I'll secure the bag of berries on my horse and then we'll bury the unfortunate fellow."

"All right. We can use the large tree branches to dig his grave," Landon said. "A sandy grave is all this man's going to have anyway. He's far too crushed to secure on the horse and bury back on the land. Sure is a pitiful way to die."

Chanson and Landon buried the dead body and left.

Firegate Castle

Chanson and Landon returned to the castle with the bag of berries. They also collected a basket full of berries that had been strewn around the castle's premises. The guard ushered the two knights to the king's personal chamber.

"Your Majesty, the berries," Chanson said setting the bag down on the floor in front of the king. "We found a Tavik ship that had wrecked on the shore. The man sailing the boat was dead, but near his mangled body we found the bag of mysterious fruit. These are the same berries Musette ate."

"A Tavik must have smuggled them on his longship and was overturned by a strong gale," the king said.

"We drew the same conclusion," Landon said. "The berries must have scattered during the high winds and rains that came through here."

"At last we can settle this mess and apprise Seabert. I know it's difficult, Chanson, but everything will be all right. Seabert's the most knowledgeable man I've ever encountered. He'll have a solution before too long. Keep your faith, young friend."

"I will."

"Good job gentlemen! Now take a few to Seabert to examine and then destroy the rest, leaves and all."

"Understood, Your Majesty," Chanson said.

The knights left. Meanwhile, the king was alerted the three workers who had been exposed to the strange black leaves were behaving oddly. He was informed about the situation by his medical adviser.

"Your Majesty," Seabert said, "I've examined all three workers and have found something peculiar."

"Peculiar?"

"Yes. After asking Wells why he picked up the berries, knowing they could be poisonous, he responded that he did not know. Then Ward blurted out 'because I told him too!' Then Wells responded, 'That's right. I had forgotten that.' At the beginning of my conversation with the men they each gave a different tale. Ward said he saw the berries first and alerted the other two. He later switched his story after Morris piped and said it wasn't true; that he had been the first to see them and ran to tell the guard about them."

"But the guard didn't know about the berries until the workers were escorted to my quarters. Why would the men switch stories and lie?" the king said.

"Well that's the very same question I've been asking myself. I conducted some mind tests by making a few suggestions to see if they would agree to the stories they had previously shared."

"What was the response?"

"The men agreed to every scenario I presented to them even after I changed the details and presented them again. In essence, I think the berries have had an effect on their memories as well. The men can recall their names and even function in their responsibilities, but appear to be influenced by mere suggestion as evidenced by their confusion. The leaves are the real threat, Your Majesty."

"Seabert, are you saying the berry leaves have left the workers in a stupor?"

"Well, not exactly. I believe the men are not as mentally strong as they once were. To test my theory on the workers I suggested what I thought they should do next and they were ready to leave immediately and do it merely because I suggested it."

"If these berries have the potential to destroy memory and the leaves powerful enough to render a man vulnerable to suggestibility and confusion, then they pose an enormous threat, to not only this kingdom, but the world over," the king said.

"Your Majesty, I believe they have the potential to create confusion in the mind and therefore must be destroyed immediately. We can't let anyone get hold of these; the fallout could be detrimental."

"Well then, we know what we must do," the king said. "How is Musette?"

"She is able to move about and function in every way, but has no memory. It's dreadful seeing her cry out, afraid, and not even recognizing her mother."

"Do what you can for the child and keep the workers confined with the guard until I give further instructions. Thank you, Seabert. Good work."

"I think I should conduct some more tests on the men before making my final conclusion about the berries. I'd like to observe them over the next few hours and see if the effects wear off or hasten."

"Of course Seabert. Do whatever is necessary."

Seabert bowed to the king and left. With the new crises wearing on King Sainesbury's mind, he anxiously awaited news that Chanson and Landon were successful in getting rid of any traces of the threatening berries. The king apprised his three advisers of the situation.

Early the next day on October 20, 1428

King Sainesbury held another private meeting with Seabert, his advisers, and Landon and Chanson.

"Good morning gentlemen," the king said, "Seabert informs me he has news concerning the berries. I summoned all of you so that you would also be apprised of the situation. Seabert, what's the latest concerning this matter?"

"Your Majesty, I believe I've formulated an antidote to the noxious berries."

"I gathered from the distressed look on your face that Musette hasn't recovered and is still in need of an antidote?"

"Yes, My King. Drowsiness has hastened and listlessness advanced rapidly during the wee hours this morning. Her condition has not improved. Please allow me to administer the medicine as soon as possible."

"Are you certain further harm will not befall Musette if treated with the substance?"

"I cannot say with certainty, but if she is left in her current state, she may lapse into an eternal sleep."

"*Eternal sleep*—are you submitting she could die, Seabert?"

"I do not know, but if she's not helped soon, she may never regain her memory. I could use the antidote on your granddaughter with hopes it will cure this malady. If we do nothing and let the poisonous berries run their course, I fear that the Musette you once knew will cease to exist."

"You're firm about this, I see."

"Yes. With your permission, I'd like to administer the medicament in small doses at first. Perhaps only a small amount is needed to cure the ailment."

"Very well, Seabert. I want Parisina and Chanson to stay with her during the treatment. What have you concluded about the worker's conditions?"

"Their confusion hastened in the night. I observed lethargy settling in their legs. I had them stand in front of me, but even asking them to do so seemed a foreign request. It was as if they did not understand or could coordinate their bodies to do as I commanded. Ward even cried when I asked him about his children and wife. I asked him why he was crying and he said he didn't know."

"That's certainly unusual for Ward's disposition."

"What I found most disturbing, however, was that none of the men recalled ever being married or having children. Then when I told the men the names of their wives and children they agreed to having families."

"But you're not convinced they actually know what their marital status is, are you?"

"Not at all. The men appear mad with confusion. And further, their state seems to be temporary."

"*Temporary?* Seabert, please explain."

"I left the men alone for a few more hours, went back later and found that suggestibility had worn off. The men continued to believe the last suggestion regarding their lives; adamant there were no other facts to the contrary. It was as if their minds could be conditioned to believe anything suggested in the first few hours of coming in contact with the berries."

"So I would assume the men would benefit from the antidote?"

"Yes. Their pupils are enlarged, indicative of poison like Musette. The men and Musette are losing strength by the hour. They all share the symptoms, except Musette's condition is more pronounced."

"If news of these berries spreads beyond this castle, we could have a potential take down of the kingdom," the king said.

"Is there any more you can tell me?"

"No . . . it's imperative we act on the treatment right away!" Seabert said, eager to get to work on the cure.

"Keep the workers in confinement until you are able to treat them. You may leave to ready the formula."

"All right then. I'll send word after the procedure is complete," Seabert said, bowing before the king.

The king's advisers, along with Landon and Chanson, remained discussing the berries.

"I am assuming the berries were destroyed," the king said, looking at Chanson.

"No, My King," Chanson said. "We tried to burn them but they would not ignite. We used our swords to dice them into tiny pieces."

"The leaves can't be burned?" the king said while stroking his beard.

"No," Chanson said, "They have a strong vascular structure with stems as tough as leather."

"It's imperative that we destroy these berries as quickly as possible. Please leave me while I consider other options. We'll meet again tonight to discuss the situation further."

The Lord has taken hold of my right hand
His sword will defend me.

Mind Maze

Firegate Castle
King Sainesbury's quarters
Late evening on October 20, 1428

Seabert, the king's advisers, and Landon and Chanson had returned to the king's private quarters.

"I have a plan for destroying the berries," the king said.

"Since we can't burn or destroy the berries conventionally, we can mix them with molten metal and bury the ingots. We'll have to make preparations to obtain the appropriate amount of metal. It will be best to divide the berries and leaves among you. Chanson, I want you and Landon to divide a few and then give the rest to Garrick to destroy. Do not tell one another where you've buried them."

King Sainesbury, noticing that Landon appeared deep in thought said, "Landon, is something troubling you?"

"We should not destroy them, Your Majesty," Landon said. "We should instead conduct experiments and find out everything we can about the capabilities of the leaves."

"We already saw what the effects on the workers were. Why would you want to do that to other people?"

"If these leaves have the potential I think they have, then we could use them to take over other kingdoms by making their kings loyal to us."

"It sounds like you want to rule the world," the king said, becoming concerned by Landon's suggestions.

"We wouldn't be taking over these nations to enrich ourselves; we could bring an end to all wars. Imagine if we had these berries four years ago and had used them to subdue Rylen Blackmore. My father, and all the other soldiers, would not have had to die in a pointless battle. A pointless war declared by a power-hungry king."

"But we'd be destroying free will. And any man who has that much power has the potential for complete and utter destruction of not only himself, but for all of mankind."

"But look at the lives we could save. So what if a few people lose their free will? That would be a small price to pay for a society free of the brutality of war and merciless slayings. How long will it be before another war and Chanson dies leaving Musette without her father? Think of how many widows and fatherless children we would be saving. We could change the course of history.

"We could wake tomorrow and arrange a visit with a ruler of another kingdom and expose him to the leaves. In doing so, we could suggest our political views while his mind is pliable, thereby altering his mind to accept our peaceful agendas. Tomorrow the world could begin to be unified if we act on the premise that these berries can affect the mind's perceptions within the first few hours of exposure. Why would you not want that for your family and future generations?"

"I cannot believe what I'm hearing from you, Landon. I understand your concerns about the brutality of war, and I share them. I know your father died senselessly, but to suggest we manipulate our neighbors like this is not what my kingdom stands for. That would cross ethical lines and I will not stand for it!"

"Exactly what does your kingdom stand for then? Violence and wars and rumors of more wars?" Landon said, crossing his arms in front of his chest.

"My kingdom stands for generosity, compassion, civility, and as much as possible, peace with other nations. Consider the long-term implications of your plan. Even if we implemented your plan perfectly and brought peace to the world in our time, what happens after we're gone? Human nature will not have changed, so our descendants would have to continue this task. We may be able to instill our ideals in the next generation, but somewhere down the line, a future generation's ideals may end up very different from your own.

"We are dealing with the absolute power to control humanity. Eventually, it could corrupt our descendants, turning them away from your original ideals. One day, perhaps only a few generations from now, our descendants may use this power only to enrich themselves, without any compassion or care for the poor. The world will have evolved into a land ruled by their greed, all because of what was set in motion here."

"So that's it! You're willing to allow debauchery to run rampant while good people like my father continue to die? Perhaps you don't care about your offspring and future generations, but I do!" he yelled, glaring at the king. "If your ideals rule us then we're never going to have the opportunity to show the people a better way!"

"Landon, I'm sorry this has disrupted your soul, but I cannot hear any more of this absurdity. I will not allow those berries to get into the wrong hands. That's final!"

Something had ruptured within Landon; his face grew red, his khaki green eyes were ablaze, and his hands trembled. He stood, pointed his fingers at King Sainesbury and shouted, "It wasn't your father who died, it was mine . . . giving his life for you! A man who didn't deserve to die . . . he was mine and Chanson's father!"

"Landon!" the king rose to his feet and shouted, "I will not—"

"Landon," Esmond interrupted, standing and placing himself between the king and Landon, "you need to go to your quarters now and get your emotions under control. I will not allow you to speak to Our Majesty like this. He's heard your opinions and now it's time to temper your attitude and accept his decisions."

Landon shifted his attention to Chanson and said, "Don't tell me you agree with them too?"

"Landon, there's not one day that I don't wish Father were still with us," Chanson said. "We're all peace seekers here, but we have no right to disrespect our king. Come, let's talk elsewhere." Chanson stood and put his arm around Landon and they left the meeting.

Meanwhile, the king was shaken. His brow broke out in perspiration. Firm about his convictions, however, he glanced at Garrick and said, "All right, back to these berries. I want them destroyed as soon as possible, Garrick. When Landon's had time to settle his temper you go and instruct him and Chanson to rid the premises of those berries."

Garrick nodded and left. Esmond and Blaine remained with the king while Garrick approached Chanson and Landon about destroying the berries.

The King's private quarters
Late evening

Seabert returned. He approached the king.

"Seabert, did the treatment help Musette?" King Sainesbury said, raising his head and squaring his shoulders. He took a deep breath and his eyes widened.

"Yes, My King. Only one small treatment was needed to fully arouse the child. Parisina hugged my neck after Musette sat up and cried out for her mother to console her. I was relieved to observe no residual effects of the poison."

"That's jolly good news, my friend!"

"Indeed it is, Your Majesty. I knew this report would lift your spirit. I've observed the crisis has worn you down. Perhaps you will rest better now."

"I certainly will, Seabert. How many treatments do you have of the antidote?"

"There were two treatments left after the workers were also given the antidote. I did not feel the need to make more since no one else fell ill to the berries.

"I have also hypothesized these berries were likely planted from seed years ago and took root on Ein Island. The island is rather remote. Perhaps the Tavik discovered the berries and was en-route with them when the sudden storm drifted him to Kaishore's beach. It is entirely plausible too that the man was confused after handling the berries and lost his way on the ocean."

"I see," the king said, placing his fingertips together. "There will likely not be a reason for further treatment, however, the remaining antidotes need to be preserved."

"As you wish," Seabert said.

Seabert followed the king's orders and secured the last two treatments. King Sainesbury retreated to his prayer sanctuary and praised God for healing Musette and bringing a peaceful outcome. He continued in prayer and reading Scripture until he went to sleep.

King Sainesbury's quarters
Early morning on October 21, 1428

King Sainesbury held a brief meeting with his three advisers and his physician. Chanson and Landon were also summoned.

It was apparent Landon had lost a great deal of sleep. His eyes were swollen and red as he slouched in the chair. He remained silent with his hand on his cheek and his brows furrowed, avoiding eye contact with anyone. The king, believing Landon would soon come to see his wisdom in destroying the berries, did not worry about the knight's reserved disposition.

"Gentlemen," King Sainesbury said, "I want to take this time to thank each of you in helping to bring a resolution to the berry crisis. It does my heart a lot of good to know I have fine men like you to defend this kingdom.

"In celebration of this peaceful outcome," King Sainesbury continued, "let us take the rest of the day and enjoy some good food and sport."

"I cannot think of a better medicine!" Seabert said, grinning. With those words the men left to enjoy a day of recreation.

Chanson will be in the peak of success and happiness when tragedy strikes again. No one close to Chanson will be spared the fallout.

Goblet of Death

Fircgate Castle
Inner courtyard
Afternoon on October 21, 1428

King Sainesbury, Esmond Scott, Blaine Morgan, and Seabert Gaines sat on the raised platform, enjoying the pleasant afternoon and light refreshment while the other members of the court engaged in sports such as horseshoes, wrestling, tug of war, and stone throwing.

The king's food taster, Osment Aldair, appeared before King Sainesbury holding a gold goblet. He said "Your Majesty, I've cherry juice for you." The king nodded and Osment tasted the juice, clearing it for the king's safety. Osment bowed and left.

"Seabert, I'm glad you suggested I get some rest," the king sighed. "I had not realized the toll the crisis had taken on me."

"We all needed this," Seabert said, warmed by the joyful faces in the crowd and the sounds of laughter.

"Ahh, so good to see Chanson playing his flute again," Esmond piped. "Parisina and Musette have those steps to perfection with that circle dance."

"Musette bears no resemblance now to the tortured tot she was a few days ago. Fine work you've done Seabert, fine work indeed," King Sainesbury said, smiling while finishing his cherry juice.

"I'm glad my work pleases you. Seeing your granddaughter's restored health is cause for celebration enough!"

Garrick Aynsley reappeared, holding another goblet filled with cherry juice.

"Aynsley, my friend, where have you been? I haven't seen much of you today."

"No need to concern yourself, Your Majesty. I asked Osment to prepare another goblet of this delectable juice for you. *Please*, have another goblet full, it will nourish your body," Garrick pleaded, holding the gold goblet in his outstretched hand.

"Very well," the trusting king said, taking another goblet of the cherry drink and proceeding to sip it.

The festivities had gone on for the majority of the day and nightfall would soon arrive. Seabert had begun to notice that the king appeared distant. Concerned, he said, "Your Majesty, are you not well? You seem distracted."

"Ahh, don't concern yourself. I assure you, I am in fine spirits. Only tired, nothing more."

"Well, you have had quite a strain recently. May I be bold and suggest you turn in early tonight?" Seabert continued, noticing the king was yawning and beginning to look weary and pale.

"The sweet ocean waters bring great settling when I am in need of rest," Seabert said. "Perhaps you should take a ride out to the ocean in the morning and let the peaceful breezes of Kaishore soothe your weary soul, My King."

"I concur," Blaine piped, "I believe the physician's perceptions are correct. Now that this infirmity is over, why don't you take this time and rest? We'll apprise you immediately if a new threat arises."

"That's right, My King—I'll even be the first to alert you if it's needed," Garrick said, grinning.

"As you wish, gentlemen. I believe I'll retire to my private quarters now."

The king left the celebration and was not seen or heard from until the next day. Alone in his room, King Sainesbury laid down in his bed. He was asleep the moment his heavy eyelids closed. He thrashed about, dreaming.

'My dear, Chloette, you're an angelic vision tonight; motherhood suits you well. Do you think our son will want to take my place as king when I lay my sword down for the final time?'

'Oh Roland, my darling, you mustn't speak of this now. Let us enjoy the time we have together with our newborn son. Would you like to hold Ambrose before I put him back in the bassinet—Roland! Roland! What's wrong? Your face—I can't see your face—what's happening to you my dear man? My dear Roland—don't leave us! Please, Roland . . . come back—Roland—'

King Sainesbury's quarters
Late morning on October 22, 1428

Seabert Gaines rushed into King Sainesbury's quarters to alert him of a security breach.

"Guard, it's urgent that I speak with the king," Seabert said.

The guard gave Seabert permission to enter King Sainesbury's chamber. He was not prepared for what would befall next. The king's dog, Brayleigh, was heard whining as she lay beside the king on his bed.

"Your Majesty," Seabert said, gently nudging the king to arouse him, "someone has stolen the antidotes. Please awaken at once. Something is dreadfully wrong."

Despite Seabert's efforts to awaken the king, he did not respond, but continued to lay as if in a deep sleep.

Distressed that the king had not removed his robe before retiring, Seabert examined the king for symptoms of illness. He checked the pupils of his eyes; they were enlarged like those of Musette. He also took notice that the king was perspiring and his countenance chalky. Fearing the king had met a similar fate as Musette, Seabert raced to alert Esmond about the situation.

Esmond's quarters

"Esmond, I am fairly certain the king has been poisoned!" Seabert said.

"The cherry juice, Seabert! His goblet must have been laced with it!"

"Since the poisonous berries are virtually undetected, it would be reasonable to conclude that someone could have slipped it in his drink," the doctor suggested, fraught with worry lines on his forehead and around his tight eyes.

"The king was adamant that only his advisers and the two knights, Landon, and Chanson be apprised of the berries. One of our own has betrayed us!" Esmond said. "Are you able to make more of the antidote for the king?"

"It would take time to collect more of the properties needed. I could alert Chanson and have him help secure the medicine," Seabert said.

"But can we trust Chanson? Can we trust anyone, Seabert? I hate to think it, but Landon seems the most plausible consideration. He vehemently disagreed with the king, we all witnessed it. Perhaps his hostility has led him to do something drastic! But why would he do this? What would his plan be? Think, Seabert, think hard—have any of the men behaved strangely? Does someone have a secret agenda contrived against this kingdom?"

"Well, I do not know of any! Ashton de Sille has been away taking care of an urgent family matter so it cannot be him. Chanson was with me the whole time and nowhere near the feast preparations. I can't imagine Landon would soil his father's memory like this despite his strong disagreements with the king. Surely the traitor is not him! I don't know, Esmond, none of this makes sense! Whoever it was, he was devious and shrewd!"

"Seabert, perhaps it was not one of our own, but instead an intruder who made his way to the goblet!"

"But King Sainesbury has guards around this castle at all hours! The logical assertion is that whoever it was had help from inside. We were distracted, not considering the berries could be used by one of our own to harm our king."

"Seabert, since we don't know who to trust, it seems Chanson would be the preferred one to entrust with this grave crisis. We must apprise him of this serious threat immediately or we may lose our king tonight! In the meantime, I'll check with the guards and find out if they saw anything out of the ordinary."

"And the cooks . . . King Sainesbury's food tester, Esmond! Perhaps the intruder threatened one of them and they were forced to comply."

"Seabert, we can't allow anyone to know of the king's illness, given the kingdom has been compromised. You must find Chanson and tell him what has happened. May God help us all!"

"It will be done!" Seabert said, opening his apothecary bag to make sure he had the supplies needed to treat any further health crises that might arise on his way to inform Chanson.

"Oh and Seabert," Esmond said, about to walk away, "I know that you are not in favor of engaging in warfare, but a spear or sword might be needed if you were to come under attack before getting to Chanson."

"I don't know that I am able to take someone's life, Esmond. I'm a healer—healing is all that I have ever known!" Seabert turned away, reflecting in frustration.

"Seabert, my brother, we won't lose you; your knowledge of herbs is valuable to the safety of this kingdom. King Sainesbury reveres your work. He considers you an endeared friend. He would not want you to be defenseless should someone come against you unexpectedly. You must take a weapon. Perhaps you will not have to use it, but you cannot risk your life."

"Very well, Esmond, I'll arm myself with a dagger."

Esmond summoned King Sainesbury's food taster while Seabert prepared himself for potential danger.

Firegate Castle
Midday on October 22, 1428

One of King Sainesbury's guards ushered the food taster, Osment Aldair, to Esmond's quarters. The stocky plump man looked up, pushed his choppy brown hair away from his eyes and said, "Is something wrong?"

"The king has been poisoned."

Osment gasped and said, "Oh, don't tell me our king is dead!"

"He's still alive, but we don't know if he'll survive."

"Who c-c-could do that to our king?"

"We don't know. I'm questioning all of the those involved with the king's food and drink preparations."

"You don't suspect I had something to do with it do you?"

"I was just wondering if you saw anything unusual or noticed someone you didn't recognize."

"No I didn't. I tasted all of the drinks for the king— Oh, b-b-but wait, didn't Garrick serve the king another goblet of juice?"

"You're right," Esmond said, astonished. "This was actually a violation of protocol, but I guess we didn't notice it because of Garrick's position and the stress we've been under. It was Garrick who poisoned King Sainesbury!"

Before Osment could react to this shocking news, Esmond dismissed him and stormed off. He summoned

King Sainesbury's guards to find Garrick and lock him in the dungeon.

Oakhollow Forest

Garrick arranged a secret meeting with Eugen Lanstein, chief adviser to Emperor Felix Marek from the Empire of Romanague. They were deep in the forest, surrounded by a large grouping of oak trees, away from the detection of King Sainesbury and his guarded fortress.

"Are you sure no one saw you, Garrick?"

"Yes."

"Kee-ahh," a red tailed hawk screeched. The bird's powerful talon gripped the branch of a tree. They saw the hawk peering from atop the evergreen.

"Well, we are not alone after all," Eugen said with a sneer on his face. "What did you find out?"

"I've found a weak link," Garrick said, pausing.

"Go on."

"A storm brought in some strange berries that have the power to wipe out memory when eaten. But the berries' leaves are the real surprise. They will give us a way to overpower other kingdoms if we're able to smuggle a few back to Romanague."

"What are you saying, my friend?"

"Well since spying on King Sainesbury, I had not discovered any secret we could use to overthrow him until the berries blew in from the storm. Three of King Sainesbury's workers collected them, not knowing their potential danger. The king's granddaughter became ill with memory loss after accidentally ingesting a few."

Garrick further apprised Eugen of the facts concerning the danger of the berries and their leaves.

"The physician confirmed the workers did not suffer memory loss like the king's granddaughter, but were very suggestible," Garrick continued. "The physician formulated an antidote and saved the men and the little girl. One of King Sainesbury's knights thought of an ingenious plan that we can use. Since the leaves of the berries cause confusion, we can subject our enemies to the leaves and force their allegiance."

"That's a fantastical story. Are you certain of these facts?"

"Yes, I personally witnessed the granddaughter and the worker's conditions and saw first hand the berries' effects. In addition, I was in the meetings with the king's advisers, knights, and the doctor—I heard everything."

"Who else knows about this?" Eugen said.

"After the three workers resumed their duties, I killed them. They won't be talking! I've already taken care of King Sainesbury; I took the berries and laced his drink with them. If our plan goes as we desire, the king will never wake to rule again," he laughed, throwing his head back.

"Great work, Garrick. If we can manage to get these berries to the emperor then we'll use them to alter people's minds and take over other kingdoms. They can be puppets for our cause. We can then rule the world, Garrick! Imagine all men bowing to us!" Eugen envisioned himself wearing a crown of distinction; he stood before a massive crowd robed in royal eminence while being hailed in honor.

"The emperor will be most pleased hearing this news!"

"This is a day I have been waiting for too!" Garrick said with a malicious smile.

"Garrick, I assume you do not have any of the berries left for me to take back to the emperor?"

"No, it took all the berries I had to assure the king's drink was a fatal dosing, so I'll have to retrieve the other berries from one of the knights. However, I managed to take the antidotes so the king is most certainly a dead man. But I'll have to go back to get the antidote formula from the doctor. It won't be easy because he's very loyal to the king."

"Good. We should take every precaution to make sure no one can stop you. You had better go, Garrick, it won't be long until someone finds out what you've done."

"Yes, you're right, perhaps only minutes away. I'd hate to have our plan foiled when we are this close to gaining the upper-hand. Felix would have both our heads if we fail to deliver!"

"That he would!"

"Kee-ahh . . . Kee-ahh—" the red tailed hawk screeched while swooping over the men, piercing their ears with his high-pitched scream.

"That hawk's unnerving! You'd better go!" Eugen said, peering up at the perceptive bird.

Garrick left on his horse, surreptitiously slipping back into the castle without being detected.

King Sainesbury and those close to the king are about to be hurled into a catastrophic nightmare. The repercussions will change their lives, leaving them in a state of confusion and despair.

The gatehouse
Late afternoon

"Chanson, are you certain no one followed you?" Seabert said.

"Esmond's guard kept watch while I was en route to meet you here. Seabert, your pallor is ghostly—it must be serious for you to summon me to this grungy place. What has happened?"

"It's abominable, Sir Westbrook, abominable! King Sainesbury has been poisoned, his cherry juice spiked with those toxic berries. I fear it may have been a lethal amount. He's still alive, barely. His breathing is shallow and his color is waxing pale."

"The traitor will pay dearly for this!" Chanson said. "We have to save our king before it's too late!"

"And that's not all, Chanson! The remaining antidotes are missing! We've been compromised greatly."

"You must make more or this kingdom will go down without a king—we'll be vulnerable, in enemy hands!"

"I will try, but there's little time to save the king . . . that is, if I am able to formulate the potion in time."

"What do you need me to do?" Chanson said.

"I need the snowdrop plant, the buds specifically. I have the honey and other bitters needed to formulate the tonic. Once I had the formula perfected, I memorized the blend so no one could steal it with a sinister deed in mind."

"You mean a sinister deed like this one . . . ugh!" Chanson yelled, shaking his head from side to side.

"It's a deplorable action one has taken against the king! It has to be someone close among us, it has to be! Garrick may be involved, so be careful. We must act now, before King Sainesbury meets a terrible end!"

"Very well, Seabert. I know where to find the snowdrops, they are still growing deep within Oakhollow Forest. It will take me the better part of the day to retrieve the plant. I'll meet you back here a little past sunset. Will that suffice, Seabert? Does King Sainesbury have that much time?"

"I don't know how much juice was ingested. The antidote may be futile, but healing is possible as long as there is breath."

"We must try, for our king, we must! We owe it to him to remain hopeful and work quickly to help save him," Chanson said, taking a sealed note out of his leather pouch. With a forlorn face, he handed it to Seabert.

"What's this, my friend, it looks important, sealed with a wax emblem, Sir Westbrook?"

"It's a letter to my wife. I wrote it a while ago in case something happened to me. I want you to give it to her if I do not come back alive or am captured. Please, it would mean a great deal to me."

"Of course, my friend—but let's pray that it will not come to this."

Seabert placed the small parchment letter in his bag.

"Seabert, whispers of prayer will be on my lips. I must leave now, if there is to be any hope of saving King Sainesbury. We might save our friend from impending doom and spare all of humanity from this cataclysm."

"Chanson, make certain you are not followed, look over your shoulders at all times. We do not know who to trust now. The traitor who pulled this off was shrewd; look out for traps in Oakhollow Forest. The deplorable man might be right under our noses!" Seabert said.

"I will!" Chanson said firmly before leaving quickly to collect the snowdrop flowers. He mounted his horse, Diamond Belle, and rode into Oakhollow Forest.

Chanson was in Oakhollow Forest when he noticed Garrick and Landon ahead, talking under the tree tunnel. In remembering Seabert's words to not trust anyone, Chanson slipped off his horse and crawled closer to the men without being detected. Hunched near the thickets he could not believe what he was hearing.

"Do you have the berries, Landon?" Garrick said.

"Yes, here in my pouch." He gave the berries to Garrick. Landon saw the two bottles of antidote when Garrick opened his pouch to store the berries.

"How did you get the antidotes from Seabert?"

"I followed Seabert and saw him hide them in the dungeon wall. I went back later and retrieved them. When King Sainesbury's out of the way, we'll have full control to implement our plan."

"What?" Landon yelled. "What do you mean 'when King Sainesbury's out of the way?'"

Landon was nauseated when he saw blood on Garrick's clothes. "Did you stab him?" Landon said. "Is that his blood on your breast?"

"No, it's Seabert's blood. I had to stop him! Poor pathetic man; he didn't have it in him to kill! But he tried, barely grazing my side with his dagger." He laughed, holding his head high.

"You said you weren't going to harm the king or anyone! The king trusted you to defend him, not be the cause for his death! How could you do this? I only agreed to help you because I thought you believed that promoting peace among nations was worthwhile. It's why I agreed to do this even when the king did not sanction it. But bringing harm on others completely defies the ideas of unity and goodwill toward all men!" Landon yelled, clenching his jaw and grabbing his abdomen as if he had been punched in the stomach.

"But Landon, you knew King Sainesbury would never have chosen to use the berries for the good of protecting his kingdom, he's too merciful for that! We had to get him out of the way. I thought you knew that!" Garrick said, pressing his lips together and rolling his eyes.

"You tricked me! I can't betray the king like this! I must get to the king and save him, even if I am sentenced to death for what I've done!"

"No! I won't allow you to foil the plan!" Garrick said, seething with anger. He held his mouth closed and lowered his brow with a frown.

"What have you done? You've ruined us all! I've acted foolishly to trust you. No more, it ends now!" Landon shouted, pulling out his sword to slay Garrick.

Garrick laughed pridefully. He drew out his sword, but before they had a chance to strike with their blades, Chanson leaped out at the two men. He drew his sword and shouted, "STOP!"

Garrick and Landon paused.

"I can't believe my ears. We had suspected you were involved in poisoning the king, but were hoping it wasn't true. No matter what you do, Garrick, even if you wipe out the entire kingdom, you will be left with an ugly core, a shell of a man with no honor or dignity left! You were once a man of integrity, with a devoted sense of duty, but now you've become a corpse that I don't recognize! Look within—at your own hands you have poisoned your very own soul and have forsaken the promise you made to uphold the sacred virtues—loyalty—generosity—truthfulness—protecting the kingdom with your very life!" Chanson shouted, disgusted.

"And Landon—how could you betray your father like this? He didn't sow seeds of honor, mercy, and faith only to reap a harvest of ruin from his own flesh and blood. How could you—how?"

Garrick raised his sword to strike at Chanson. A fight ensued and they sparred ferociously with a strong possibility of pain or death resulting in the end. Chanson struck Garrick's wrist, slicing his hand. Garrick pierced Chanson through the upper part of his shoulder. Chanson whirled around Garrick several times attempting to throw him off balance and confuse him. When Garrick was distracted by his bloody hand, Chanson pierced him in the abdomen.

Garrick grabbed his bleeding side and said, "Soon you'll be destroyed too, Chanson! The poison's in your body now—"

"You won't get away with this act of treason against my king . . . your wicked deed will be etched upon a stone of dishonor!" Chanson said.

Chanson's head was eerily light, the world seemed to spin around him in a blur of motion. He was weak and his legs could barely carry him.

"NO—GARRICK—tell me it isn't true. Have you poisoned my brother?" Landon yelled.

Dizzy and unsteady on his feet, Chanson collapsed onto the dusty, twig-strewn path.

"Before nightfall he'll remember nothing! To the death of memory—Chanson, to the death of you and the world as you have known it! No one can save you now!"

Garrick was doubled over in pain as he tightly grasped his stomach. With the point of his sword at Garrick's neck, Landon demanded, "Surrender the antidotes or you'll die right here!"

He threw his pouch to the side. Landon went to retrieved the pouch. While unguarded, Garrick stumbled to his horse, mounted up and rode away. Landon had only a moment to make a decision, leave his dying brother where he lay or get on his horse and attempt to capture Garrick. Landon looked at Chanson as he lay poisoned and bleeding. He decided to save his brother with the antidote then chase after Garrick. Landon opened Garrick's pouch to retrieve the bottles of antidote. Horrified, he found one vial had been broken during the scuffle.

Landon rushed to Chanson's side and said tearfully, "Chanson, forgive me. I never meant for it to turn out this way. I have the last bottle of antidote. Let me save you!"

"No, I pledged I'd give my life for the king! Landon, go—*leave*—give the remaining antidote to King Sainesbury."

"I won't leave you behind like this, I can't!"

"I'll only slow you down. P-please go—" Chanson said breathily, struggling to resist the ominous effects of the berries, "and summon Esmond to search for Seabert. He may have been ambushed near the outer gatehouse. The king's life is now in your hands."

"Chanson, I'll send someone to help you. My brother, please forgive me—I allowed grief over Father's death to cloud my judgment. I thought defying the king's ideals, and implementing my own would accomplish a greater good. But I was clearly deceived and betrayed by Garrick! Hang on, Chanson, help will be here soon!"

Landon rose from Chanson's side, wiped back tears of regret and rode off quickly to administer the remaining antidote to King Sainesbury. He galloped through the eerie path, desperate to reach the king in time.

I know the Lord will fight this battle for me;
He will do so without breaking one blade of peace.

Anissia

Oakhollow Forest
Early afternoon on October 22, 1428

Chanson feared his memories were leaving him as he lay pierced by the sword. He raced toward every corner of his mind to try and take hold of the memories before they faded into obscurity. Like a desperate man reaching his hands out on a turbulent sea to prevent his drowning, Chanson fought the impending fate of his mind.

A young girl giggled.

"Who's there?" Chanson uttered while weaving in and out of consciousness.

Chanson heard the girl giggle again.

"Please, help me," he pleaded with the girl who still could not be seen.

He thrashed about trying rise to his feet, but his body failed him. Autumn breezes swept over his wounded body. A soft fluttering graced his cheek.

"Who are you? Why aren't you helping me?" he pleaded with the little girl heard skipping around the forest, kicking up leaves behind her bare feet.

Trying to focus his eyes so as to uncover the girl's identity, Chanson's heavy eyelids would not open. His vision was betraying him too.

Despite Chanson's desire to find out whose voice he was hearing, he knew that his mind was falling prey to the poison. Unable to fight against the berries' inevitable influence, Chanson's mind wafted in a dream state. He remembered his fallen hero, Hayden Cheswick.

'Chanson, believe in yourself—find a way to hold on,' Hayden said, 'Do not let Garrick break your spirit. You've been given great strength through all that you've suffered. Use that strength now to find the way out of this maze. Remember, no one can break your mind's will if you determine it so.'

Firegate Castle

Landon arrived at the castle doors, but no one was allowed in without first being questioned and searched.

He was met at the outer gatehouse by Esmond and Blaine.

"Who's blood is on your sleeve, Landon?" Esmond said, tugging at Landon's arm.

"It's Chanson's! He's been stabbed," Landon said while reaching into his vest to retrieve the curative vial. "Here, the remaining antidote, please take it to King Sainesbury."

Esmond seized the antidote and said, "Who stabbed Chanson and is he alive?"

"Chanson was struck in the shoulder with Garrick's sword. He is alive, but the poison is in his body now. Garrick's been plotting to steal the berries and use them against King Sainesbury. Chanson overheard the plot and leaped out to defend me when Garrick tried to stop me from reporting this to the king."

"Why were you there in the first place?" Esmond said, confused about the details he was hearing.

"Garrick told me he agreed with my reasoning for keeping the berries and felt we should defy the king and start a new government. He convinced me King Sainesbury would eventually see that we were right and would thank us."

"So, you went against the king's explicit orders to destroy the berries?" Esmond said, grinding his teeth and shaking his head.

"Yes, but I never thought it would end like this!" Landon said.

"Like what, exactly?" Blaine piped, stepping closer to where Landon was standing.

"When Garrick asked me to help him, I merely gave him the berries, not knowing of his intentions."

"Seabert was in charge of the antidotes," Blaine continued. "Don't tell me something has happened to him too!"

"I haven't seen Seabert today, but I fear Garrick killed him," Landon said. "Garrick said he saw Seabert hide them in the dungeon's wall. He went back later and took them and stabbed him with a dagger. I forced Garrick to surrender the antidotes before he got away."

"How could you have done this? King Sainesbury trusted you, we all did!" Blaine said, circling around and flinging his arms out in frustration.

"I'm sorry. I didn't mean for this to happen. I love Chanson like a brother!"

"Well, *your brother* may be dead now because of yours and Garrick's actions!" Blaine yelled, glaring at Landon.

"Speaking of Chanson, we need to get to him and see what can be done for him," Esmond interrupted. "Blaine, I'm going to take this treatment to the king now. I think we should put Landon under guard until we get all the details sorted."

"I concur," Blaine said.

"Landon, you had better hope and pray the king lives and Chanson is all right!" Esmond shouted.

"Blaine, see what else you can find out from Landon and then search for Chanson. Perhaps we'll find a way to save him too," Esmond said, storming off to help the king.

King Sainesbury's chambers

Esmond arrived back at the king's bedside. The king was still unresponsive. Esmond proceeded to pour the medicine in a spoon and administer it to the king, a few drops at a time.

Before sunset Blaine was escorted to the king's quarters. He observed Esmond sitting in a chair beside King Sainesbury's bed. He walked up to Esmond and whispered, "How is the king, any changes in his condition?"

"He's coming around," Esmond said, smiling and looking at the king who was shifting in his bed. Brayleigh has not moved from his side. I offered her some food, but she turned her nose away and kept whining as she's doing now."

"The king's a good man . . . I hope he pulls through this because it won't be just his family mourning his demise. That poor dog's bound for a broken heart too!"

"Blaine, any news on Chanson?"

"Esmond, I led a search into Oakhollow Forest but we did not find Chanson. Only his sword and leather pouch were left where he had been wounded."

"I wonder what could have happened to him." Esmond said.

"It's possible he crawled away and is under a tree. We searched thoroughly, but didn't find him. I hate to even suggest such a horrible notion, but it is possible a wild beast may have taken him, given the profuse blood trail leading away from where Chanson fell? We followed the trail, but it disappeared too, just like Chanson."

Blaine's face dropped as he envisioned Chanson never returning.

"I'd hate to think it too," Esmond said, "but we all know that Oakhollow Forest is dangerous when nightfall approaches and the wild animals hunt for their next prey. I pity any man who meets his end that way! Have you told Parisina the news?"

"Not yet. I'll leave now and tell her. I wish her father was able to be with her. I fear what this news will do to Lady Parisina."

"But it has to be done, Blaine. I don't think we'll be able to hold off much longer given she already suspects something has happened to Chanson. You should take

Lady Genevie with you. She may be able to offer some comfort."

"Good idea. I'll also give Chanson's pouch to her. I hope it will comfort in some way."

Blaine left to notify Parisina about the fate of her husband. Esmond stayed with the king to monitor his condition.

Lorlea Manor

Lady Genevie knocked on the door of Parisina's manor and said, "Parisina, it's Lady Genevie. Blaine Morgan is with me, may we come in to talk with you?"

Without haste Parisina opened the door. "Oh no, it's Chanson, isn't it? That's his pouch, he would have never let it out of his sight! I knew something was dreadfully wrong! Please tell me he isn't wounded!" she cried.

"Parisina, please sit, we'll be able to talk better."

"No! I don't want to sit!" Parisina screamed.

Lady Genevie, noticing that Parisina was about to crumble to the floor, led her to the settee. She held her hand to comfort her as she sat slumped next to her. Blaine took a seat across from them and said, "I'm sorry to bring disturbing news, but Garrick struck Chanson with a sword that was laced with the berry poison. We've searched the forest, but have not found Chanson. Perhaps he isn't able to call for help. It's also possible he was attacked by an animal and is dead."

"NO!" Parisina screamed, rising to her feet and pacing around the room. She covered her ears with her hands as if to erase Blaine's words from her mind. "It's not true! My heart still beats within my breast—his heart is mine and mine his—they beat as one—"

This tormenting sword will not
steal my home a second time.

The One My Soul Loves

Lorlea Manor
The sitting room
Late afternoon on October 22, 1428

Blaine Morgan delivered Chanson's pouch and informed Parisina about the possibility that her husband may have died in Oakhollow Forest.

"I'd know if Chanson had died! I must go to him—he needs me—my beloved knight needs me!" Parisina kept repeating as she paced around the room then sat and paced again, touching her head.

"Parisina, you won't be safe out there at this hour," Lady Genevie said.

"I have go to Chanson, he needs me! My father, *oh my father,* He loved Chanson like a son, this news will crush him. They both need me! I have to go now!"

Blaine piped, "I assure you the king is in good care. Esmond knows to alert you if anything changes in his condition. If it will help settle you, I'll leave now and check on him and report back as soon as I know something.

"This news has taken a tremendous toll on you, you're very pale and understandably weak. *Please*, you must try to rest now. Here, take Chanson's pouch, perhaps it will bring some comfort." Blaine said as he placed the leather pouch in Parisina's trembling hand.

Parisina pressed Chanson's pouch close to her breast and wept, whispering, "My darling Chanson, please come back to me and our little Musette . . . please my Love, come home to my heart!"

"Lady Parisina, I'll leave now and check on your father's condition. Be assured, I'll alert you of any changes, I promise. Please try to rest."

"All right, I'll lie down, but I know my Chanson is alive and I intend to find him as soon as dawn breaks," Parisina said, with a determined look on her face. "No guard will be able to hold me back from finding my beloved. Love is a force that never lets go . . . I know my Chanson is alive and waiting for me!"

"Very well, I won't stop you. I will apprise you of any news regarding Chanson's condition or the moment he is found," Blaine said, stepping away and closing the door behind him.

"Come, dear," Lady Genevie said as she reached out to help Parisina to her bed.

Lady Genevie stayed with Parisina through the night, remaining in the parlor to allow Parisina some time alone with her thoughts. She could be heard weeping softly as she lay on her bed.

With tears flowing steadily down her cheeks, Parisina opened the pouch and poured its contents out onto her mint satin gown. Her attention went immediately to a lock of hair secured with a ribbon. Her memory took her back to an unforgettable day she and Chanson had shared.

'My darling Chanson, this is beautiful, it's the most exquisite brooch I've ever seen! Thank you for this wonderful day!'

Chanson and Parisina leaned in for a kiss.

'Nothing but the best would do for my lovely wife. I could not be more pleased that you like it. I've had something weighing heavily on my mind lately.'

'Please tell me what it is. I cannot bear knowing you're in pain. Those tears welling in your tender eyes tell me it's serious.'

Parisina placed her pink gloved hand on Chanson's cheeks and wiped away his tears.

'May I snip a small lock of your hair to carry with me in my knight's pouch?'

'Chanson, my sweet, you're not worried I'll die and leave you, are you?'

'No, no, I need you with me when we are apart. Your onyx tresses are glorious. When they cascade on my pillow at night, I am comforted knowing you are beside me. That is all it is, I want a token of you near me when I am in battle.'

'Of course you may.'

Chanson took out his knife and snipped a lock of Parisina's silky hair.

'Here, cut a piece of the ribbon from the sash of my gown and use it to secure the strands,' Parisina said as she held out the pink satin ribbon.

Chanson cut a piece of ribbon from her dress and secured the strands of hair; he put it in the outer pocket of his pouch for safe keeping.

'Chanson, promise you'll never leave me here to live without you. I could not bear it if we're ever torn apart by tragedy.'

'My lovely Parisina, not even death could tear you from me,' Chanson reassured before taking his wife into his arms for a kiss.

Parisina screamed.

"Parisina, Parisina, are you all right?" Lady Genevie said after hearing Parisina wail loudly.

Parisina did not answer. Lady Genevie entered Parisina's room and saw her collapsed on her bed weeping loudly into her pillow.

"Parisina, there's still hope Chanson will be found alive. You said it earlier, your heart knows—it knows. Trust your heart, dear Parisina, trust it now."

"Oh, Lady Genevie, the strand of hair . . . he truly cherished me didn't he?"

"Oh yes—more than his own life! He's exceptional like my beloved Hayden was! Lovers like him never truly leave us. Let's wait until we know more before we conclude he has perished in the forest.

"Your husband knows how to take care of himself. Hayden and your father prepared him for the fiercest rivals. He's an exceptional warrior—trust that. Keep believing that God will save him and will bring him home. Will you do that sweet one?"

"Yes, Lady Genevie. I'll try . . . for my sweet Chanson, I'll try."

Lady Genevie left, closing the door behind her.

Parisina took out a round hand-carved box made of walnut wood; it stood on three wooden legs. She opened the small box and removed the daisy wedding ring Chanson made for her when they were children. The ring was fragile and dried with age, but still intact. She slipped it gingerly on her small finger. She sat looking at the cherished ring, reminiscing about fond memories as tears collected in her eyes.

'When we're crowned Prince and Princess of Evernora we'll need royal crowns,' Parisina said to Chanson, tilting her head and smiling.

'Where will we get them?' he said.

'By weaving forget-me-knots together. I'll make mine and you make yours. Then we can practice crowning so that we will know how to greet our court.'

'I'd like that,' Chanson said.

Parisina clapped her hands in glee. They giggled.

'Do you remember how we made the rings?' Parisina said, holding out her hand as if to remind him of how the floral ring looked on her finger.

'I think so.'

'Then that's what we have to do with the blue flowers; tie the long stems around the heads of the blossoms. Let's make them now.'

'All right.'

They tied the flowers together and their small crowns were made.

'I love you, Chanson!' she said, squeezing him.

'I love you too!'

'I now crown you Prince of Evernora,' Parisina declared, placing the floral crown on Chanson's head.

'And I crown you Princess of Evernora,' he said, placing the floral crown on her head.

They took hands and stood before all the nobles, accepting cheers of jubilation and gifts of gold laid at their royal feet. They continued holding hands and swung around in a circle, laughing and then skipping over the lawn.

Parisina placed Chanson's pouch on his pillow. She held the bag's strap in her hand and soon drifted off to sleep while still wearing the daisy ring.

Meanwhile, the king continued thrashing about in his sleep. Pearlensia appeared beside his bed.

"King Sainesbury, I am Princess Pearlensia from the Isle of Wisteria. You will soon awaken and go on a perilous journey to find your knight, but be careful, danger will come against you. Do not fear, I will go before you. A new beginning awaits you when you get to the pearl gate."

In the locket of my heart,
You remain with me.

Gardenia

Firegate Castle
King Sainesbury's chamber
Before sunset on October 22, 1428

While Esmond Scott sat praying, he noticed the king was beginning to move about. King Sainesbury gradually opened his eyes.

"Your Majesty, you're awake!" Esmond said, with an elated smile. "I'm so glad to see it!"

King Sainesbury sat up, distracted, confused, and surprised at seeing Esmond sitting in a chair next to his bed. Brayleigh inched closer to the king to inspect his face while wagging her tail. King Sainesbury pet her and said, "Gardenias—do you detect the scent of gardenia blossoms in this room?"

"Your Majesty, I don't and I don't see flowers either," Esmond said, scanning his eyes around the king's chambers.

"Why are you sitting here—what has happened to me, Esmond? I'm dreadfully weak," the king said, perturbed.

"You were poisoned, my friend. Garrick mixed the toxic berry juice in with the cherry juice you drank at the celebration feast."

"What—there has to be a mistake—Garrick wouldn't do this!"

"Oh, but he did, My King! I'm certain of these facts."

"How did he get past my taste tester and manage to pull off this evil act?" the worried king said.

"Osment Aldair was not responsible, Garrick was. He laced your drink with the berry juice instead of destroying them. We were too distracted by the recent crisis to notice how odd it was that he served you the drink."

"And all this happened without detection? Esmond, how could such treachery have taken place? Where is Seabert? I need him to work on a new batch of the antidote before we are at the mercy of our enemies."

"Well, My King—" Esmond paused, hesitant to not upset the king further with new details concerning the physician.

"What else are you not telling me?" the king said, taking a deep breath to prepare himself for more disturbing details.

"Your Majesty, Seabert's missing. I fear he may have been killed when he would not surrender the secret to the antidote. Landon betrayed you, along with Garrick. Garrick saw an opportunity to persuade Landon to side with him when he disagreed with you about destroying the berries. Garrick convinced Landon to not destroy the berries, but instead give them to him. He was unaware of Garrick's nefarious plot of using the berries and the antidote for his own gain."

Distressed by the news, King Sainesbury interrupted Esmond and said, "They must be punished! Right away!"

"Well, Your Majesty, Garrick got away and took berries with him."

"And Landon?" the king said.

"He is in confinement. He tried to redeem himself by bringing the remaining antidote back to the castle to help save you. He also expressed that Seabert was in danger. No one's seen Seabert since this morning when he met with Chanson to formulate a plan for creating more of the antidote."

"I knew I could count on you, Esmond. Please summon Chanson, it is urgent that I speak directly with him about these developments. I want him to go with us in search of Seabert; he's my best knight and I trust him."

"I can't, My King," Esmond said, glancing down in a solemn pose with his hands gently laced together in front of him.

"What's wrong? Has something happened to Chanson?"

"*He, too,* has fallen prey to the malady! Garrick stabbed him in the shoulder with his sword. The blade was smeared with the poison."

"Why do you look so grim? Go to him, give him the remaining antidote!"

"The last bottle was destroyed during the scuffle, Your Majesty. Chanson sacrificed his life for you. While he laid in his own blood, he urged Landon to spare your life and give you the remaining antidote instead."

"This cannot be! I must set this kingdom right again! Chanson has been more loyal than a thousand sons! I must find him and save him! I owe him my life, *my very life, Esmond!*"

"According to Landon, Chanson was last seen lying in Oakhollow Forest near the ancient tree tunnel, but Blaine Morgan could not find him. The forest was searched thoroughly, but neither Chanson or his horse surfaced."

"Chanson has to be out there, he has to be!" the king said.

"I've been pondering . . . I believe it's possible a wild animal drug him away. Blaine reported seeing blood stains leading away from where Chanson was wounded. The trail soon ended, however," Esmond said, voice breaking.

Esmond's words struck through the king's heart like a bolt of lightning. He fell forward on his bed. Concerned, Esmond reached over, placed his hand on the king's forearm and said, "Are you all right, My King? Is it your heart?"

Regaining his composure, the distraught king said, "I won't accept this! We must search again; he has to be out there, alone and suffering. Perhaps Chanson was able to walk away from the scene, but in his confusion, wandered too far and cannot find his way home.

"As soon as morning breaks, we will mount up the horses and search through the entire forest, leaving no stone unturned. Chanson's a fighter. If anyone is able to survive the forest alone with that festering wound, it's Chanson! So until I've seen for myself that he is dead, I will comb all ends of the earth to find him!" King Sainesbury said with as much hope as he could muster under the dire circumstances.

Blaine Morgan was ushered in by the guard.

"Your Majesty, I'm glad to see you've recovered!" Blaine said, his tawny hair tousled and hazel eyes bright with surprise. "How are you feeling?"

"My body's better, but my soul is grieved over the news Esmond shared a few minutes ago. How's my daughter?"

"Lady Parisina refuses to believe Chanson is dead," Blaine said. "Lady Genevie is with her now. A visit from you would help to settle her. She called out for you, but I concluded she needed to settle down before coming to see you. Your Majesty, none of us knew what the outcome was going to be in regard to your treatment. I feared allowing her to see you in your previous state would shatter her already fragile spirit."

"I agree," the king said, "you were wise to shield her. Until we know for certain that Chanson has perished, we must be careful how much we tell her."

"My King, I know you want to believe Chanson has survived," Blaine said. "But we all know his chances of surviving are slim, given the size of Oakhollow Forest and the wild beasts lurking in the swampy areas. The large amount of blood gives rise to the fact that he suffered greatly."

"I won't hear of it, Blaine! In the fifty-five years I've been alive, I have never known a more tenacious soul than Chanson. We should have faith he will be found, and that by the grace of God, a medicine will be formulated to save him."

"I beg your forgiveness, My King. I acted hastily in telling Parisina the tawdry details."

"I understand the reasoning that went into informing Parisina about her husband. I'll drop by her manor later and try to calm her. I'm worried about Seabert. Nightfall is now upon us and no word from him. That's not like him. We must go now and find him."

"Your Majesty, are you sure you're well enough to go to the gatehouse?" Esmond piped. "It's garish and damp in there. Not to be disrespectful, but you were nearly at death's door only a few hours ago, wouldn't this be too strenuous for you?"

"We must find my friend. If something has happened to Seabert there will be severe punishment for those who were involved in this heinous plot! We are wasting time, gentlemen, we must leave now to find Seabert. Perhaps he's merely injured and in need of medicinal care."

King Sainesbury stood and motioned for Esmond and Blaine to follow him to the lower gatehouse.

The king, Blaine, and Esmond advanced deeper into the secret passages of the gatehouse. With twists and turns they eventually made it to where Seabert was planning to meet with Chanson.

"Look gentlemen, that may be Seabert," King Sainesbury interrupted, fearing the worst after seeing a man lying on the ground ahead.

Until all ends of the earth have been upturned—the seas drained, the forests brushed through—I will remain vigilant in bringing you home.

Rose Buds of Summer

Firegate Castle
The lower gatehouse
Nightfall on October 22, 1428

As the men drew closer to the body they recognized their friend. Seabert was laying on the cold, damp ground with blood pooling around his body.

"The dagger . . . Seabert's dagger," Esmond said, wilting when he saw the blood-stained dagger lying next to Seabert's body.

"Seabert, my friend," King Sainesbury said, noticing the physician had been stabbed in the chest, but was still alive.

Seabert opened his eyes and said breathily, "You're well, My King . . . Chanson must have given you the antidote. G-Garrick, he betrayed you, he beguiled us all!" Seabert continued, gasping for air, every movement sending waves of throbbing pain through his chest and back.

"Shhh, don't try to talk Seabert. Let's get you out of this ghastly place," the king said as he put his arms under Seabert's body to try to lift him.

"No, Your Majesty, there's no time. Let me say these last words, p-please," Seabert groaned.

"As you wish my friend," King Sainesbury said as he knelt beside Seabert, taking his hand into his.

"Garrick took the vials from my bag. I stabbed him in the side, but he was too swift for me. He overpowered me and demanded I tell him the secret to the antidote. But I clenched my lips together and refused to answer. That's when h-he—stabbed—"

"Seabert, save your strength, that's not important now," the king interrupted, pressing his hand firmly on Seabert's wound to help stop the profuse bleeding.

"Please, My King," Seabert said.

"Of course, go on."

"I wish I could have killed him. I failed you."

"No Seabert, you gave your life protecting the antidote. My granddaughter now lives because of your cure—*and me*—look at me, I'm alive because of your knowledge. You're a true warrior of healing. You've been a loyal friend to me over the years. I won't forget you. I will find out who else was involved in this plot and punish them severely!"

"My King, open my bag, there's a letter, please take it out."

King Sainesbury took the crinkled parchment out of Seabert's pouch. "But it's addressed to Parisina, why?"

Struggling to breathe Seabert whispered, "In the event Chanson doesn't return home, he wanted Parisina to have it."

"I'll give it to her."

"My Truth, you are the noblest and most generous man I've ever known," Seabert uttered, beginning to choke on his blood. Determined to express his last words, he took a deep breath and continued. "Y-you have been unwavering in wisdom, patience, and kindness during your reign as king. T-to have you as a friend has been an honor, Your Majesty. Be well, live long—" Gasping, struggling to hold onto the brevity of life, Seabert continued, "Take my body to Kaishore Ocean where its sweet waters will soothe my soul, forever . . . then I'll be with my sweet girl again."

As Seabert's face faded of color, he fixed his eyes intently at something above him. He smiled. "She's coming . . . *she's coming,*" he mumbled, taking his final breath.

"Seabert, *Seabert,*" the king said in a hushed whisper, trying to banish tears from his eyes, "don't go—please . . . "

"What did he mean about seeing his girl again . . . did Seabert have a child? I thought he never married," Blaine said.

"He was referencing Karina," Esmond said in a hushed whisper, "his nightingale bird he buried in the ocean last Spring."

Observing the king's lamenting state, Esmond knelt beside the king, placed his hand on his shoulder and whispered, "Your Majesty, I'm sorry, he's gone—Seabert's gone."

"How can this be?" the king asked, "H-how can two of my finest men be gone in one day? Tell me Esmond, how can a man slay men whose hearts are guileless?"

"I do not know," Esmond said.

"Seabert had remained faithfully by my side when I needed precisely the right treatment," King Sainesbury said, holding back tears. "My son, my son . . . Seabert . . . he folded my dead son gently in his arm as if he were his own flesh and blood, cradling him close to his breast and taking him away. The respect he had for mankind was exemplary. He was the kindest, most benevolent human I have ever known."

Blaine was surprised to hear the king speak of his lost son, given he had forbade anyone to ever mention him again.

"You've suffered a terrible blow today. Please, My King, let's get out of here. We must prepare Seabert's body for burial. This place is not where you need to be after what you've been through. Please, let's leave this filthy place, now," Esmond said in a persuading tone.

"You're right. This is no place for a comrade like our brother Seabert," King Sainesbury said. "He deserves to be laid out on a bed of fresh leaves with the rose buds of summer placed on his breast, not slain on a slab of moldy clay. How he loved the ocean. We'll send him off into the waters of Kaishore, which he said brought him God's sweet peace. Yes, that's what we'll do, Esmond."

"That will be a fine farewell," Esmond said.

"Let's go," the king said as Blaine and Esmond picked up Seabert's body.

The two men carried the physician's limp body. King Sainesbury followed behind languidly, reflecting on the day he and Seabert met.

A young, slender and distinguished raven-haired man was sent an invitation to join the king for a feast to honor those chosen to rule with him in his kingdom. The invitation was sent requesting that the man accept a hired position as the king's personal physician. Esmond and Blaine were also in attendance.

'Hello, Your Majesty,' Seabert Gaines said, bowing. 'I am grateful for this invitation. I had always wanted to live near Kaishore Ocean, but being under the apprenticeship of my father's work never allowed me the opportunity . . . well, until now.'

Seabert's kind gray eyes filled with tears.

'I'm sorry to hear of your father's death; his fame was far-reaching. I hope you've considered accepting the position, Seabert. I'd like for you to move your belongings into the castle right away and live here as my personal physician. I am in need of only the best this world affords me. Having been taught by the land's most renowned doctor tells me you are most qualified, Seabert.'

'Thank you, I would be honored to serve you in whatever capacity is needed. I only ask two favors in return.'

'Say it and they will be granted!' the king said, gesturing with his hand.

'I have never been trained in warfare like my father. If I am called upon to take another life, I will not be able to set aside my disdain for the shedding of blood.'

'Of course. Let it be as you wish. Now, what other request do you desire of me?'

'She won't be a bother, I promise it. Well, except when it comes to her meals, My King,' Seabert said, placing his hand cautiously on his chin as if thinking.

'Of course, bring the child—name it, whatever your girl needs—she will have!' the king agreed.

'Well, she will need fresh worms on occasion, but a sack of fruits, seeds, and nuts should keep her singing for awhile.'

'What—of what benefit does feeding a child worms accomplish?'

'No, no, she's not a human child; she's my pet, a beautiful nightingale bird!'

'Haha, haha,' the king roared, 'a bird . . . of course!'

'Her songs used to wake people at night, that is, until Father allowed me to bring Karina inside after constructing a sizable cage.'

'Two of my knights will help you move.'

'I should also tell you, Karina gets scared and plucks out her feathers when she hears loud noises and harsh voices.'

'Seabert, I know just the place for you and Karina. I've a secluded manor nestled around a clear, flowing brook. Fairdell will supply you with the serenity you both need while providing peaceful streams to drink from.'

'Thank you! I accept your generous accommodations and will move in right away.'

In the rose buds of Eternity, I leave thy soul;
Live on forever, my friend, live on forever.

My Heart Will Wait

Lorlea Manor
Late evening on October 22, 1428

While Seabert's body was being prepared for burial, King Sainesbury went to visit Parisina.

The king approached Parisina's bedside where she laid sleeping. He stood over his daughter and revisited memories from her childhood. He recalled being in the arms of his Queen Chloette and admiring their newborn daughter. They doted over her supple complexion, and placid disposition as she lay peacefully asleep in her bassinet. King Sainesbury's eyes welled in tears; he wiped them away with his handkerchief. He took

Parisina's hand, caressed it and kissed her cheek, whispering, "My dear Parisina, I'm here, *Papa's here*."

She awoke upon hearing her father's soothing voice.

"Father, you're well! I was so worried," Parisina said, grabbing her father around the neck and sobbing.

"Yes, sweet girl, I'm better now, but my heart is heavy with the passing of Seabert and the unsettling news about Chanson. Chanson penned a letter for you, in the event he doesn't return."

"But Father, Chanson is not dead. No one believes me, but in my soul I know that he is alive! You must not give up the search for my husband. I beg you, please look one more time for him. *Please Father!*"

"As you wish, my dear. I'll gather some men and we'll look for Chanson. While I'm away I want you to rest. Will you do that for me?"

"Father promise me you will take me with you. I must go. I could not bear the waiting."

"I forbid it! It's not safe. Further, I won't lose you to illness in that marsh. And if we are to find Chanson, we may have to venture into terrain that none of us want be in."

"Will you look for him on the Kaishore beach too?"

"Wherever the search warrants," he affirmed.

"Please, Papa, let me go! I don't care about myself! Without my Chanson what difference would it all make anyway?"

Parisina glanced at her wedding ring as she reflected on the sonnet Chanson recited on their wedding day. Tears cascaded down her cheeks as she remembered her groom's eyes and the light of love mirrored in them. She sang the last two verses of his poetic expressions.

Together haply wed our hearts entwine;
Forever yours, and you, forever mine.

King Sainesbury cupped Parisina's wet cheeks into his hands and whispered, "I'm sorry this hurts you, my cherished girl, but we cannot deal with this crisis effectively if there's a lady to safeguard. And since I don't know who else is behind these treacherous actions, I cannot have you exposed to potential harm. You need to remain here where I'm sure of your safety. You are more than life to me, more precious than this entire kingdom, I won't risk anything happening to you. I'm placing more guards near your door," King Sainesbury said as he kissed his daughter's forehead and turned to leave the room.

Parisina noticed the crimson seal bearing two hearts knotted together with a ribbon. After kissing the seal, she carefully broke it from the folded parchment. Teary eyed, she unfolded the note and read.

Parisina, my treasure, my heart, my everything, the woman my soul loves,

If I do not return, always remember the promises we made when we declared our love around the cherry tree; our love knotted together on the sands of Eternity. Somewhere on the splendid shores, my heart will wait for you.

I've left two kisses on the parchment, one for our cherished Musette and the other for you, my adored wife. Press the kiss to your lips and close your eyes, never forgetting our love sealed in the soul of time. I will love you into Eternity.

I am ever and always yours, as you are mine,

Chanson

Upon reading those words, Parisina held the paper kiss to her lips, then she touched her cheek, remembering the last kiss Chanson placed upon it before leaving. Parisina laid down with Chanson's note over her breast, refusing to believe her lover was dead.

The king retreated to his chamber after sunset. He stood on his balcony looking across Scarlet's Peak and reminiscing about old memories. Chanson's cries echoed through his mind. He recalled the orphan's reluctance to surrendering the cherished locket and picking him up to console him.

Determined he was not going to accept that Chanson had died, he summoned a guard to bring Landon to his private quarters.

Landon was escorted to the king with his hands bound behind him. The guard stood nearby, reserved and stoic.

Landon dropped to his knees, bowing his head toward King Sainesbury's feet. He pleaded, "Your Majesty, I am not worthy to be in your presence after what I have done. Please believe me when I say, I never intended to hurt anyone when I defied your orders to destroy the berries. I only wanted to help create a unified world where we'll all be safe and free of bloodshed."

"Landon, seeing you shackled like a common criminal grieves me greatly. It's not something I ever expected from one so pure of heart. You have lived and conducted yourself honorably before this. How could one so upright side with the enemy to betray me?" the king said, peering into Landon's teary eyes. "Why did you defy my orders to destroy the berries?"

"Garrick came to my quarters after Chanson left and persuaded me to defy you. He told me his father also died in a senseless war and agreed we should enact my proposal to help rid the world of violence. He further expressed he had also thought of the idea, but didn't know anyone else had felt that way until I voiced it in the meeting. I told him I didn't want to betray you, but he said I wouldn't be betraying you, in the end. To help soothe my conscience he said he'd implement the plan and all I had to do was surrender the berries and leaves. I agreed to work with him, but he demanded we keep the agreement confidential.

"I only meant for the berries to be used as a means of achieving peace among nations. I had no idea Garrick was sneaking behind your back, planning to use the berries to murder you. He vehemently disagreed with you about destroying the berries, but I never thought he would actually want you dead or use the berries for his own power! I'm very sorry for what I've done; I didn't consider that my actions were a direct betrayal, until today." He sobbed profusely.

"Was anyone else involved in this heinous crime?" King Sainesbury said.

"I don't know of anyone. Garrick's last words to Chanson were, 'To the death of you and the world as you have known it!'"

"Then we can't know how far his plan has traveled or who has the poisonous fruit. Landon, by disregarding my orders to destroy the berries you have betrayed the trust I placed in you; you did not try to protect this kingdom at all costs to yourself. When we abandon integrity, compromises begin to happen and before we know it, we've not only betrayed those we love, but also our values.

"Sometimes it takes only one small step of defiance to led to a heap of ruin. Do you not see that your rebelliousness led to Chanson's injury and my poisoning? I could have died—and Chanson, who is to say what has become of him! Do you have any idea what it's like to tell a daughter her husband may be dead, and that her child may have to live without a father?" the king yelled.

Landon continued sobbing, remaining quiet in a reverential posture before the king's feet.

"Your actions have compromised the safety of this castle, and more, we're all grieved by it. Moments ago I knelt beside Seabert, who gave his life for this kingdom, and watched him take his last breath. I've lost a good friend, a loyal friend at that! How could you have been part of such wickedness?" the king said. "*How?*"

"I'm deeply sorry," Landon repented, with his face to the floor. Anguish overtook him and he could speak no longer. He prayed within himself.

> *Father, God, forgive me—brighten the darkness in my soul—please, let me once again walk beneath your Light.*

"Landon, I've known you since you were born, the actions you took against this kingdom are most certainly out of character for you. I will take this into consideration when deciding your punishment. It grieves me to my core, to my *very core,* to stand before my best friend's son and take action against him for betrayal!"

Disappointment declared war against the king's spirit.

Those words pierced Landon's heart. He crumbled at King Sainesbury's feet.

"I will take extra time in considering your punishment, out of respect for your father, but if Chanson is dead then you must know what awaits you."

The king cried, remembering Hayden's great sacrifice. He regretted being a king and facing the possibility of having to execute his best friend's son for treason.

"Yes, Your Majesty, I have behaved poorly and am deserving of death. I know that!" Landon said, looking at the king's distraught face. "I no longer deserve to be called my father's son after what I've done! I hate myself for not holding onto my honor!"

"For Hayden's sake and the sterling behavior you've had before this action, I will wait until tomorrow evening before making a decision."

"If I could redo this day, I would. I only wish I *could!* I will live whatever hours or moments I have left with remorse and angst of heart. I know I have no right to demand anything, I am at your mercy, Your Majesty, *but please*—I beg you to allow me to ride with you in the morning. I owe it to my friend, my brother, to help bring him home. I believe I've proven that I am not a threat. I made a bad judgment, but I would never hurt Chanson intentionally."

The decision weighed heavily on his mind. He turned away from Landon and deliberated, pondering more memories shared with Hayden. His vexation was softened when he recalled a day Hayden had won a tournament and was seen carrying his toddler son away on his shoulders. Landon had his arms wrapped tightly around his Papa's neck while his feet were being held by Hayden. The two walked off the field smiling and giggling.

"Very well, I'll allow it. Guard, take him!"

King Sainesbury turned his back to Landon again and sighed deeply.

"T-Thank you, My King. I am sorry for the reproach I've brought on my father's memory . . . by my own doing, I have putrefied my legacy," Landon said before being ushered away by the guard.

The king sat down on a stone bench on his balcony. He slumped forward, his arms dangling between his knees.

"Come, sweet girl. What's on your mind tonight? I noticed you didn't eat your food earlier; are you feeling all right?" the king said, noticing Brayleigh ambling toward him after being awakened from a nap on the balcony floor.

The aged dog sat down on her hind legs and wagged her tail gently, searching out the king's weary-worn face. She watched him with soft eyes. He pet her head, trying to sooth his angst-ridden soul. Tears of regret could not be staved off a moment longer, they gushed like a mighty downpour from his eyes.

"Brayleigh, why has the Lord placed this impossible decision on my shoulders tonight? How will I execute our best friend's son for treason when I promised Hayden years ago I would look after Landon if he died in battle? What man kills a mother's child?"

Please let the kisses of my soul soothe
until we are united again.

Ambrose

I will behold your face once again,
And when I do,
We will feel this pain no longer.

Firegate Castle
Before midnight on October 22, 1428

King Sainesbury checked on Parisina. He entered her sitting parlor and found Lady Genevie reading by an oil lamp. She stood and curtsied.

"How is Parisina?" the king said.

"She's asleep for now, but she's having visions."

"What do you mean by visions? Is she having night terrors? Please explain further," He furrowed his brow and sighed, pressing his hands together.

"Well, Your Majesty, she mumbled, 'I must get to the forest, he's alive, my beloved husband is alive, Pearlensia told me so!' I asked who Pearlensia was, but she did not answer, only repeating Pearlensia and Chanson's name over and over. The tortured tossing has been going on for some time now. I worry what she will do, given how confused she is."

"I had always known Parisina had a delicate heart, but I had not realized how fragile until tonight," the king continued, tears welling in his weary eyes.

"Are you all right?" Lady Genevie said, perceiving the king was staring into space and trying to hold back a floodgate of tears.

"I'm reliving the memories of the night Parisina's mother died. I might be the king, with thousands of soldiers at my command, but I'm still a tender father. I am saddened that my daughter is ripped apart by the deeds of evil men! This is a disgrace to my kingdom and a slap in the face of the Almighty.

"The news of Chanson's fall has shaken this entire kingdom. He was more than a loyal knight and the man who loved my daughter, he was like my flesh and blood. We will miss him for the rest of our days, if indeed he has perished in the forest. I've been blessed to have known great men like Hayden, Chanson, and Seabert.

"Tonight I must wipe away these tears and proceed forward like a mighty warrior. I'll ask God to do what we mere mortals cannot, but it's not easy with so much weighing on my mind. I guess because of all that has happened today, painful memories of the past have been brought to mind. I miss my wife and my son."

Lady Genevie gasped.

"I am so sorry, My King. I thought you had only one child. I did not know of another child," Lady Genevie said with soft eyes.

"Chloette and I had a little boy, but he died shortly after birth," King Sainesbury said, reflecting on the excruciating loss.

"The weather was dismal that late autumn night. High winds whipped the limbs of the evergreens, breaking their branches while the thunder roared.

"The midwife and her servants settled Chloette in the birthing chamber; our child was on the way. My knights, counselors, and members of the kingdom prayed. I was soothed by the chants heard echoing through the chapel walls. Esmond and Seabert were with me. They, too, folded on their knees in prayer as the promise of a new heir was soon to arrive.

"It was while in prayer that I was told the wonderful news. My queen had birthed a son! I rose quickly to my feet, elated our prayers had been granted favorably. The servant informed me Chloette and the baby were fairing well, and I'd get to hold my son as soon as he was bathed and swaddled.

"Esmond and Seabert shared our elation. I was humbled by the Lord's favor on my life. Soon news of my son's arrival spread throughout the castle; cheers and laughter were heard. Nobles had brought sumptuous gifts and gold in honor of our child.

"It was a night I had anticipated for months. My prayers were answered for an heir to rule my kingdom, but it was not meant to be. I was alerted immediately that something had gone dreadfully wrong after being told of my son's birth.

"Also alarmed by the news, Seabert asked if he may be permitted to go with me to see my wife. The servant led us to the birthing chamber. Seabert moved quickly in front of me, arriving at the bedside of my weeping wife. With thoughtful eyes, he asked Chloette if he would be allowed to examine our child.

"Chloette screamed, 'He's dead, my baby is dead!' She was not going to let go of our son; she held his gray body tightly upon her breast. It was clear his soul had left him; his lips were blue. I stepped closer to her, placed my hand on hers and begged her to let the physician take him.

"Seabert opened out his arms to receive our limp child, but Chloette still would not hand him over. The tenderhearted physician had the daunting task of prying our infant son out of my wife's arms. Her screams intensified and I stood helpless by my own grief.

"The doctor laid the child down in the bassinet beside Chloette's bed. He examined my son's body. After a thorough examination, Seabert concluded the infant died from having a weak heart. His pallid complexion and the swelling in his hands and ankles were telltale signs he was lacking blood flow to his organs.

"My wife screamed and thrashed about. Her cries soon ceased and the room turned desperately sullen. My wife cradled her arms as if our son were still laying in them. She chanted a prayer, over and over, repeating, 'God, save my baby, save my baby . . . '

"Seabert looked into her eyes, but she did not seem to recognize him nor was she aware of anyone being in the room. Chloette continued to pray, rocking back and forth with her arms cradled. Seabert took me aside and whispered, 'Your wife has suffered a spell. It's best to let her alone for awhile, letting the women remain with her during the night. Please allow me to take the infant and prepare him for burial.' Seabert gazed reverently at our deceased baby as he lay beside his praying mother. I nodded my head unable to speak. Esmond placed his hand on my shoulder and said nothing. Seabert then picked up my dead son, folded him gently in his arms and whisked him away from the view of others.

"I bent over my grief-stricken wife, placed my arms around her, but she did not receive me. The maids who had assembled to assist in the birth encouraged my wife to allow them to take her back to our bed chamber. She sat with an empty stare as if she had not heard us. It took four of us to carry her back to our bed; her silence broke the moment we moved her arms out of the cradled fold. She wailed in our arms while screaming, 'Don't take my baby, don't take my baby!'

"Chloette refused my comforts. I stepped away from our bed, alone, staring out the window of our morose room. The ceaseless drops of rain beating against the white glass were cruel reminders that I was not going to see my infant son grow into manhood. Knowing Chloette is holding our boy forever, is the only solace I have."

"I'm so sorry. Neither Hayden nor myself ever knew of this. What was the infant's name, if I may ask?"

"Ambrose, his name was Ambrose. A few days before his birth, my wife told me she sensed our child would be a boy so we settled on his name being Ambrose, my heir to the throne. His loss was unbearably painful—it was a tragedy of heartbreaking proportions. Neither me nor Chloette could speak of it for days to follow. She often turned her face to the wall and sobbed into the wee hours. I tried to comfort her by reaching over to touch her, but she refused my affections. We were both suffering, but unable to help each other through it. Seabert was able to calm her a few times when she was overcome with sorrow, refusing to eat and drink. Even though I knew she cherished me, it was not me she turned to for solace."

"Perhaps she sensed your hurt and was convinced she would only be compounding your sorrow if she revealed her deeper anguish."

"Your perceptions are impressive—even in her own sorrow, my wife was trying to spare me. Seabert was a man so young and yet filled with compelling wisdom. He was the first to mention this insight to me.

"One night I awoke and found my dear Chloette collapsed in the floor wailing and unable to breathe. All she would say was, 'My heart—my heart—my heart.' I had one of the guards to summon Seabert immediately while I held my queen in my arms, praying and crying with her. Her state was so critical—hysterical—I wondered if she would even live to catch another breath before Seabert had time to return. I questioned why God could take a babe of innocence from a mother's arms. I did not feel God's presence near me; it was as if He had forsaken me after our son died.

"Chloette was with child again a year later. Feeling the leaps in her womb consoled her some. Parisina kept her busy and she soon turned her attention toward her as the memory of Ambrose's death softened a little.

"Our daughter's lively spirit brought laughter once again to this kingdom. Chloette was an outstanding mother; gentle and perceptive of the heart. She was my queen . . . her spirit still guides me today. So much has happened over the past few days. I only hope I am able to rectify this mess, bringing a peaceful resolution to all of us."

"My King, it grieves me to know of Landon's part in this wicked plot. I beg your forgiveness for what my son has done. Is he not allowed one bad decision in his youth and it not discredit all the good he has done up to this day?" Lady Genevie said, her eyes misting with tears.

"Landon is remorseful and has begged my forgiveness. I know he acted for the good of the kingdom and meant no harm to me personally. I'm also aware of the manipulation Garrick used to take advantage of Landon's naivety and trick him. I will consider all the good that he has done when deciding his punishment."

"I am grateful for any mercy you extend to my son. Landon's heart is pure, I know you are aware of that. I'm his mother, I cannot suffer the same fate as your queen. Please don't execute my child."

Lady Genevie wept, falling in the floor at the hem of King Sainesbury's robe. With her hands cupped together in prayerful pose, she glanced up and cried, "I beg of you to have mercy on my son! Punish him however you wish, but *please*, do not take his life. I could not bear it if I were to awake tomorrow and find he is no longer with me.

"Please remember your friend Hayden. You know it would grieve Landon's father to know that his son's action cost him his life. Please recall all the good he has done for Chanson, whom he's loved like a brother. Hasn't he proved his loyalty to us all, My King?"

Moved by the woman's pleas for mercy, King Sainesbury bent forward and placed his hands cautiously on her shoulders, helping her to her feet. He said thoughtfully, "Lady Genevie, that's precisely why this offends me so. I feel as though I've lived a thousand lifetimes since finding out these details.

"In all my duties as king, I've never had an event to trouble me greater than this—it's sheer torment! I am not able to make a decision of this magnitude without God's guidance, and for this, I will not be in haste to decide Landon's fate. I know God's wisdom will prevail."

Tears continued to roll down Lady Genevie's cheeks.

"Please be assured, I'm touched by what you've expressed tonight. Out of respect for my dear friend Hayden, I will consider laboriously all that has been discussed before making a decision. In knowing how brutal the loss of a son is, I pray the Lord shows me a way to spare yours."

"My King, I am grateful that you have listened reverentially to all my expressions. I clearly see this has grieved and upset you deeply. Not to speak dishonorably, Your Majesty, but I don't believe I've ever seen you look so downcast as you do tonight. I, too, will pray and ask God to remove this torment from us."

"We must all leave this mess with God to handle," the king sighed.

"Chanson!" Parisina cried out.

"I must check on her," the king said. "I'll comfort and help her through this."

Lady Genevie wiped away Parisina's tears with a silk handkerchief, her delicate hands trembled as she patted her cheeks with the weaved cloth. She walked over to close Parisina's window after noticing it had been raised a couple inches.

The king knelt beside Parisina's bed, kissed her forehead and whispered, "Sweet daughter, you're going to be all right. *Please,* get some rest and calm down—getting upset like this isn't good for you."

Parisina sighed, being comforted by her father's voice. "Papa, you must find Chanson, he's very cold tonight. Follow Princess Pearlensia, she will lead you to him, *please—hurry Father—he has little breath left!"* she screamed.

"Shhh, dear one. I will do my best to bring your husband home."

King Sainesbury kissed Parisina's forehead. She rolled over and continued to mumble Pearlensia's name. He covered her exposed arms and proceeded to walk away when Lady Genevie whispered abruptly, "My King, you must see this!" she said, pointing to the window ledge. "There's a strange dust on the ledge—*please*, come see for yourself!"

The king stepped over to where Lady Genevie was referencing. He, too, saw what appeared to be powdered pearl strewn over her window ledge. Intrigued by the mysterious dusting, the king inspected Parisina's window and saw that the pearly powder also cascaded down the castle wall and onto the ground below. It was lit by the moon's glow as it lay sprinkled on the snow-covered ground.

"Lady Genevie, I can't worry about this powder now. I have to assemble my men and not wait until sunrise to search for Chanson. Please, will you stay with Parisina?"

"As you wish, My King. Please be vigilant if you must brave this unusual weather. Watch out for the ice creature."

"I will," the king said, taking a deep breath.

He that loveth pureness of heart,
for the grace of his lips the king shall be his friend.

Book of Job

The Sleeping Monster Awakens

Firegate Castle
King Sainesbury's chamber
Early morning on October 23, 1428

King Sainesbury summoned the only men who could be trusted without question. Esmond Scott and Blaine Morgan were ushered into the King's private quarters.

"We came as soon as you sent word, Your Majesty. How may we assist in the search for Chanson?" Blaine said.

"We must mount up now to search for Chanson and capture Garrick before he's able to use those berries.

Given the way the temperatures are falling, I surmise snowfall is on its way. If we are fortunate, it has already started further out and will slow Garrick's effort in escaping. In addition to the snow, his injuries should prevent him from traveling far.

"I believe Chanson is still alive, but Seabert expressed the berries would likely result in death if ingested without treatment right away. We have to assume Chanson is near death at best, in a state of confusion, and cannot find his wits to make it out. Since he hasn't returned, we have to assume he wasn't able to defy the ravages of the poison.

"Chanson is like a son to me . . . I love him like my very own soul. My daughter is sure to suffer a broken heart if Chanson has perished. How will I tell Parisina that her lover is dead? And Musette . . . what will become of her without a father?" the king said, throwing his hands in the air.

"Perhaps you are correct that Chanson will survive," Esmond reassured, "but if he does not, the Almighty will grant you the strength to cope with whatever befalls. Musette will have the nurturing soul of her grandfather to help her. You, more than anyone, understand the arduous wounds of losing a spouse. You got through it, Parisina will too . . . if that is the unfortunate outcome."

"The loss of Seabert, and now the possibility of losing Chanson, leaves me questioning my own frailty. How will I find the strength to rule as I've done before if, in the end, I find Chanson has died along with Seabert? I'm getting old, Esmond . . . it won't be long until my strength fails me too."

"Take it one day at a time like you did when your son and queen died. Remind yourself of your very own words—'To grieve one day's portion and not think about tomorrow's sorrow.' Do you remember those words, my friend?"

"Yes, thank you Esmond. You're a good friend. I think it's time I put away despairing talk and focus on finding Chanson. We can't change Seabert's fate, but perhaps we can change Chanson's."

"And let's not forget about Havís; he may reveal himself in this approaching blizzard," Blaine piped. "I pity anyone who is killed by that creature."

"Make no mistake, gentlemen, if Chanson has managed to survive the deeper thickets of Oakhollow Forest, we too may become the creature's supper in our quest to find him. I fear there's little time for our comrade and our efforts to stop this tragedy. Leave at once and summon Ashton de Sille to ride with us. I heard he got back last night. We need him on this search. His keen vision and impressive attention to details may help us find both men. Put your best armor on, and don't forget the wool blankets for the horses. We're in for a harrowing night with the freezing temperatures and a potential blizzard developing."

Esmond and Blaine left to carry out the King's orders.

"Guard," King Sainesbury said, "remove Landon's chains and bring him to me."

"Yes, Your Majesty."

While he waited for Landon, the king sought prayer to strengthen him for the harrowing night ahead.

King Sainesbury entered his private chapel. His scarlet robe swept behind him as he quickly made his way to the altar. He knelt and lifted his eyes, gazing at the crested windows. It was a full moon, evidenced by the glare shining through the white glass. King Sainesbury prayed.

Father God, I pray for strength to get through this nightmarish turn of events. Protect us through the night; let me not be consumed by the threat of peril. I plead with you to spare Chanson's life and to help me find a way to pardon Landon for his treachery.
Holy Spirit, our keeper, hold my daughter in your gentle embrace and soothe her heart.

Hallowed God, You are worthy of all honor and praise. I am nothing without your flaming torch of grace guiding my way. It is with a grateful heart that I pour out these words to you, amen.

Before leaving, King Sainesbury opened his Bible and read from the book of Psalm.

I will go in the strength of the Lord God.

The guard led Landon to the king's presence. He bowed in respect and waited for the king to speak.

"Landon, I want you to dress in your warmest clothes and armor; we're leaving in search of Chanson and Garrick. Since finding Chanson is my immediate concern, I am choosing to put the past aside for the greater good. Leave at once and I'll soon join you and the others at the stables."

"Thank you, My King. I won't fail you a second time," Landon said.

Meanwhile, Garrick continued riding through Oakhollow Forest. Snow had been falling rapidly and the temperatures dropping by the hour. Despite the rags wrapped on his wounds, he had lost an enormous amount of blood. The cold temperatures, coupled with his injuries, sent his body into shock. He fell off his horse and into the snow. Soon after, his horse ran away without him.

King Sainesbury and his men were mounted up and on their way in search of Chanson and Garrick. The weather had worsened considerably. The wind howled and snow accumulated, drifting and swirling around them.

"We've been traveling for nearly an hour, King Sainesbury, and yet, no sign of Chanson or Garrick," Esmond said. "I fear we're in for a daunting night if the snowfall hastens."

"Given the size of Oakhollow Forest, it could indeed be a treacherous night for us all," the king said. "Despite these frigid conditions, we must keep believing Chanson's still alive and that we'll find him in time."

"Even if he is found, how will he be healed without the antidote? Seabert was the only one who knew the formula," Blaine piped.

"That's a concern I have had too, but finding Chanson alive is my first objective," the king said. "My faith tells me God will spare him. How, I cannot say, but I won't give up nor will I fall into despair or disbelief. There's still hope. That's what we all must do, have faith and not let it waver in the face of this wretched storm coming our way. Trust and believe, we will find our friend and bring him home . . . we will."

"Of course, My King," Blaine concurred.

"Esmond, watch out!" Ashton yelled, "That limb is about to break and fall on you!"

Esmond veered to the right, narrowly missing the tree branch.

"You may have saved my life!" Esmond said.

"If I had not been looking so intently for a sign of Chanson, I would have missed seeing it. This wind is brutal tonight."

"And the snow's hastening with it," King Sainesbury said. "We're not even halfway into the forest and already we're in blizzard conditions. It sure is early for a storm like this one, but no matter how bad it gets, we have to keep going. Hopefully we will find Chanson before white-out conditions come upon us."

"Look gentlemen, even the moon seems to be bothered by it!" Blaine piped. "Those pitch-black clouds are worrisome. It's almost as if the moon is dying too."

"Well, it is God's world," the king said. "I believe His creation is mourning with us tonight as we grieve the loss of our friend Seabert. She, too, senses the danger that has consumed Chanson."

"I wish I had been able to help with the berries . . . perhaps Seabert would not have died." Ashton said. "I can't begin to tell you the depth of my anguish over losing my friend. He was the sort of man you could tell anything to and still have a friend at the end of the confession. If only I had been there with him after Chanson left; I could have protected him. I've now lost two of the greatest friends I've ever had. Along with Hayden and Seabert, I hope Chanson isn't the next one to die!"

"You can't blame yourself, Ashton," the king said. "None of us could have prepared for this kind of betrayal. I pray we find Chanson . . . it will be bad enough to bury Seabert, but Seabert *and* Chanson? No, I won't! We will find him alive!"

"If you ask me," Blaine said, "I believe those murky clouds are a warning that danger is ahead. I'm having a hard time being as confident as you, My King."

"Keep your eyes focused, gentlemen," King Sainesbury piped. "We can't allow our minds to invite more trouble. Remember what happened when Peter took his eyes off Jesus?"

"I recall, your Majesty," Blaine said.

"Gentlemen, we must stay alert to what's out there, even if the path ahead is darkening from this blizzard. God won't let us fall prey to this storm or a wild beast if we keep our focus on Him. Guard you hearts, gentlemen!" King Sainesbury affirmed.

"Look, there's a figure ahead lying in the snow. My King," Landon said. "It could be Garrick or Chanson!"

"Slow your horses men, nice and easy. If it's Chanson we don't want to startle him by moving too swiftly. We don't know Chanson's state of mind.

"Quietly, get off your horses and tie them to that tree," King Sainesbury said, pointing to a tall pine tree with branches twisting in the wind.

"Swords ready gentlemen, and walk to the side of the path. Esmond and Blaine, you take to the right with me and the rest of you creep along on my left."

The men divided themselves into the groups as the king had instructed.

"On my command, Landon, if that's Garrick I want you to secure him with your rope," the king said.

"Of course Your Majesty."

When Landon was a couple feet away from the man, he whispered to the king, "He's not Chanson, it's Garrick!"

"Secure him," King Sainesbury said.

Landon swiftly approached Garrick, who was unresponsive. He was bleeding profusely, shivering, and his eyes circled in darkness.

"Your Majesty, he's probably lost a lot of blood and is barely breathing," Landon said. "I believe he's in shock." Landon tied his arms behind his back with a rope from his pouch.

"Landon, check his bag, search his pockets, and secure those berries!" King Sainesbury said.

"Right here, Your Majesty, the berries," Landon said, holding up the bag.

King Sainesbury stepped in closer. He looked into Garrick's eyes and said, "Pride is the seed of destruction and now it has come for you, Garrick! I have a lot of words to describe how I'm feeling right now, but I'm going to refrain. The Lord would not want me to sink to that level!" the king continued, yelling with his sword lifted in the air.

"There was something that had bothered me about you, but I could never figure out what, until now. You were never one of us, were you?" the king said. "I say you lost the fight with Chanson . . . Hayden trained him well and now we're going to find him and bring home."

The king turned toward Landon and said, "You and Ashton secure his ankles and throw him over your horse. Let's find our friend before it's too late. We've wasted enough time here!"

The warriors resumed their search for Chanson after they secured Garrick.

Crystalhaven Lighthouse
Early morning on October 23, 1428

The heavy snow blanketed the entire region, leaving Evernora nearly crippled in heavy snow drifts. Chanson awoke not realizing he had been left in a trance while nestled inside an ancient lighthouse. Snow had fallen so feverishly, he was fully enclosed with no way out. The wound inflicted from Garrick's sword had worsened; his strength was failing. Death was imminent if he was not found soon. Slumped against the cold floor of the lighthouse, dozing in and out of consciousness, he heard a faint whisper swirling in the approaching blizzard.

'Don't give up, try hard to remember what I told you years ago, Chanson. God in Heaven knows how you suffer and it is *He* who will help you. Be brave—discover your strength—strength that will help you through.'

Though Chanson sensed a familiarity to the words echoing near the lighthouse, he could not recall that King Sainesbury uttered the words years ago. Having been exposed to brutal temperatures had also impaired Chanson's mind. He soon fell prey to a fever state with pain like that of needles of fire pricking his skin. His memory fragmenting, he could not hold onto the faces of those dearest to him. Like waves shifting to and fro on turbulent waters, Chanson could not settle enough to put the tormenting thoughts to rest.

It was about four hours before sunrise and the warriors still had not seen any trace of Chanson. Blistering cold and blizzard conditions had now made it difficult for them to find their way through the winding forest. Still, King Sainesbury and his men were not about to give up on finding Chanson.

"Your Majesty," Landon said, with concerned eyes, "we'll soon approach the most dangerous part of this forest. I believe it is imperative that we be on the lookout for wild boars or worse, the ice monster! Father rarely took me to this part of the forest and never during the winter because of the legend of Havís. The monster may rise out of the ocean any moment looking for his meal."

"Didn't you mean to say, *human meal*, Landon?" Ashton piped.

"Yes, well we'd best pray we don't find out!" Landon agreed. "According to legend, few men or beasts are able to escape the creature's momentous speed. Once his saw-like teeth get a hold, death is imminent. If we weren't in a snowstorm, we wouldn't have any worries regarding the creature's attack. Unfortunately for us tonight, the beast may soon rear his ugly head during this unexpected blizzard!"

"Even if our search leads us to the lighthouse," Ashton said, "Chanson may still be in peril. The keeper has likely abandoned the place, fearing the return of Havís. We're on this journey alone, I'm afraid."

Lightning flashed across the sky. The men gasped in fear, hunching down to avoid being struck by the turbulent sky.

"And now lightning during a snow storm—I sure hope it doesn't strike our plate armor!" Blaine continued.

"The monster is certainly not sleeping tonight!" the king affirmed. "Stay alert to any rustling out here. Let's not fail to overlook Chanson for fear of the potential threat of the monster's appearing. Listen for soft cries of help. I can't imagine our brother was able to venture much further out," the king said, thoughtfully.

"Chanson's no longer the man we once knew!" Esmond piped. "I plead the Lord's mercy if he has ventured this far into this awful forest."

"Of course," the worried king responded. "That's a reality I wish I didn't have to consider tonight! I hope our knight hasn't met his end by way of those frigid saws!"

Garrick was in and out of consciousness while riding, but as soon he heard the words 'frigid saws' he stirred with fear; soft moans and grunts escaped his mouth. He screamed, "No! Drop me here. I don't want to go to that part of the forest! For all of our sakes, don't go!"

"Shut up!" Landon shouted.

"No, no—*please* don't let me die by the ice creature's jagged swords! Kill me, kill me now! I don't want to be sawed to death by his freezing blades!" he continued to scream.

"Quiet!" the king shouted. "Landon, keep your focus on the mission at hand! I'll deal with him later. We can't fail Chanson! Further, if we're going to stay alive, it's imperative we remain alert and focused!"

"Of course, Your Majesty," Landon said.

Garrick continued to wail in fear of the ice creature's potential appearance. "PLEASE—we have to go back!"

Landon gawked at Garrick and said sternly, "If I hear another word or even as much as see a flinch from your pathetic body, I'll hurl you right in the path of the creature's icy spears as soon as he appears!"

Garrick groaned loudly and then calmed himself.

"Watch out, My King, falling limbs ahead!" Ashton shouted.

"I see them! Whoa ole boy, whoa," King Sainesbury whispered to his horse. "It looks like we're going to have to clear this path before going any further. Gentlemen, off your horses and secure them to the trees until we've made a clearing."

"But how will we get through all that brush?" Blaine said. "With the rate at which this snow is falling, we can't possibly expect our horses to wade through all of this. I don't think there's feeling left in my face and I believe my helmet has frozen to the sweat on my brow. We should turn around before it's too late! It does not appear we will find Chanson alive anyway. If he indeed has come this far, only God knows where he is or what has happened to him."

"We cannot fall to defeat, Blaine. Compose yourself," the king said. "I know fear is escalating, even I have to ward it off, but God will see us through this. Hurry men, let's clear these limbs—time is fleeting! If we make it to the lighthouse, we'll be able to take a respite before planning our next move. That is, if Chanson has not been found."

After clearing the path, they got back on their horses and braved the brutal elements once again.

"Be careful—danger ahead," a soft voice whispered through the swaying pine trees.

"Who was that?" the king snapped quickly, inspecting the area.

"My King, it sounded like a female, but how is it possible that a woman has managed to venture out in this dangerous storm?" Esmond said.

"Quiet, I hear it again!" King Sainesbury blurted.

"The creature's furiously approaching!" the female screamed again.

"And where is that scent coming from?" Ashton piped.

"I notice it too!" the king said. "It smells faintly of rose and gardenia. Perhaps we have an angel in our midst, sent to warn us. Men, on my order, brace yourselves, swords drawn, shields ready for attack. I believe we're in the creature's path."

"King Sainesbury—watch out!" the voice screamed.

"Gentlemen—NOW!" King Sainesbury shouted. "Proceed cautiously, I believe the ice creature is crouched somewhere ahead of us and waiting. When I give the order, charge ahead with every ounce of strength you've got. If we are going to survive, we must get to the lighthouse before he does! Fix your eyes on the lighthouse and don't take your eyes off its faint beam. I sense we're about to meet the beast we've been dreading. Ready, gentlemen?"

"Ready!" they piped in unison.

"NOW!" King Sainesbury shouted.

As King Sainesbury had predicted, Havís was eagerly awaiting to devour the brave warriors. The colossal creature darted forward, aiming his blades at Landon.

Landon lunged at the creature. The ice monster was wounded after several sparring moves, but not fatally. The creature came back at Landon a second time, despite being injured and missing a few of his deadly ice spears. The other knights swiftly come to his aid, and lunged their swords at the beast's jagged spikes. They broke a few more of the monster's deadly blades.

"KILL HIM!" the king shouted.

Determined to take out the monster, Landon and Ashton struck the creature's side, piercing him again, but the monster was relentless. With fire coming from his colossal red eyes, he swirled around Landon and his horse. Defenseless, Garrick fell off the horse; he was fated to die. Immediately the creature alighted upon him. Garrick screamed as Havís opened his mammoth mouth and chewed him to death.

Blaine was repulsed by seeing the man who used to be his close friend killed in a horrific way. The world seemed to spin around him as a sharp cramp crippled him and he was forced to stop riding. He heaved and vomited violently.

The king, noticing Blaine's delay, shouted "GO! The creature will be satisfied for a moment, but we are sure to be his next meal if we don't get to the lighthouse in time!"

The warriors sped away in hopes they would get to the lighthouse before the creature had time to advance. Havís soon disappeared from their view, staying behind to relish his latest catch.

Though the sun forsakes me
and the stream of sorrow floods my soul;
I shall awaken tomorrow in the beams of joy.

An Old Friend

Though the black midnight overshadows my path
I will keep my eyes on the Star of hope
Where ten thousand candles light the way home.

Crystalhaven Lighthouse
Before sunrise on October 23, 1428

Chanson awoke to a vivid halo of light encircling a beloved friend from his youth.

"Jade, is that you?" Chanson said, rubbing his eyes as if to confirm the alluring visions were indeed real and not imagined.

Jade walked closer to Chanson. He licked Chanson's face, placing his paw on his thigh. The halo of light remained around his being.

"It is you—I'd recognize those jade eyes anywhere! How good it is to have you back with me again!"

The puppy's fur was as he had remembered too; dark gray with a smooth, velvet sheen.

Chanson had clear memory of his youthful days; playing his flute under an old oak tree with Jade sitting beside him with his head resting peacefully on his thigh. He wondered how it could be that his dog had survived all those years and never advanced in years. He was lucid with memories from youth, yet still not able to recall the later days of his adulthood. Confusion once again bathed Chanson's mind as he desperately tried to make sense of the fragmented pieces still haunting him. He reasoned that if he held onto the elusive memories, one day he would be free from the muddle plaguing his mind.

He pet his childhood friend and sobbed over Jade's return. Jade tucked his head under Chanson's chin as he continued to pet him. Flashbacks of the day his parents died resurfaced.

He recalled dashing to his mother's side and the last moments shared with her. Kneeling next to his mother's bleeding body, Chanson noticed his mother was struggling to tell him something. With little breath left in her, she whispered, 'Chanson, my sweet boy, don't let that pure soul of yours become tarnished by the cruelty you've seen today. Please, dear one—take the locket from my neck. Hold onto it . . . never forget my love for you.'

Interrupting with screaming, Chanson wailed, 'Mama, I tried to save you . . . *Mama . . . Mama—*'

'If the baby survives, you will need to be strong to help take care of her . . . seek God's heart and He'll help you. Follow the light, it'll lead you home.' Chanson's mother breathed her last, succumbing to the blade's deadly piercing.

Visibly shaken and trembling, Chanson removed the engraved locket from his mother's neck. Adrenalin rushed through his body; he ran outside to search for his father and Jade. He saw the killer stabbing his father and then running away holding his bloody hand. In horror, Chanson ran to his dead father, threw himself on his chest and screamed, 'Papa, *Papa*, wake up Papa . . . *please Papa—*'

Hayden Cheswick appeared after Chanson found his father's body on the lawn, covered in blood. Hayden knelt beside the boy and said, 'Come child, let's get you to my home where you'll be safe.'

'No—I won't go!' Chanson screamed, 'I won't leave my Papa or my puppy!' He clung tighter to his father's body.

'Please, trust me.'

Hayden knelt down and pulled the screaming orphan off his father's corpse. He pressed Chanson's head into his chest to shield his eyes from the bloody mayhem before whisking him away. He mounted his horse, securing Chanson in front of him. With one arm wrapped around the boy and the other taking hold of the horse's reins, Hayden rode back to Oakmoor Manor. The orphan sobbed all the way there. He spent the night jerking in and out of sleep with disturbing flashbacks and terrifying screams.

As Chanson recounted the memories, tears welled in his eyes. Jade whimpered softly as if he, too, was touched by Chanson's sorrow.

"The limbs hang low, and oh so bare—the willow bends of fresh-snow lingering air. Seasons come and they go, but I won't give up, I won't let go!" Chanson mumbled as he drifted off to sleep with Jade lying beside him on the cold floor of the lighthouse.

Chanson awoke and found himself alone once again. He searched for Jade, but could not find him. Clinging to what life was still in him, he closed his eyes and rested, seeking to preserve his strength. The giggling girl he had heard earlier returned.

"Who's there?" he whispered, attempting to arouse enough to get a glimpse of the child's face.

Determined to find the little girl, he scanned the lighthouse, staring at the spiral staircase leading to the top. He saw the girl's long ginger curls flowing behind her in a gentle breeze. She did not reveal her face nor acknowledge she was even aware of the knight's pleas for help.

"Wait, please, don't go, come back . . . I'm hurt and need help—*PLEASE!*" Chanson cried.

The merry little girl kept giggling, pattering barefoot up the spiral steps, determined to ascend to the top of the light house. When she disappeared, Chanson turned his attention to his wound noticing that it was bleeding more profusely. He tried to get up from his slumped position on the frozen floor, but his strength was nearly gone. He closed his eyes and prayed.

Gracious God, Holy Light of my life,
hold me in your heart.

Soft flutters caressed his cheek. He heard the giggles of the cheerful little girl again. He saw her standing next to his wounded side, smiling gently. Her glistening emerald eyes comforted him, unexpectedly.

He noticed the butterfly with three pairs of wings poised on the bell sleeve of the girl's blush pink dress. He fixed his eyes on the brilliant creature, remembering its presence near the brook where he sat grieving Hayden Cheswick. He shifted his attention to the little girl's clothing, which seemed unsuitable for playing in the snow. He carefully observed she was not wearing slippers and wondered why she was not bothered by the cold beneath her bare feet.

She stood before him wearing an airy dress more suited for warm weather with pink ribbons crisscrossed around her feet and legs. Her lustrous curls swung loosely behind her with a garland of gypsophila at the crown of her head.

The girl reached out her hand, as if to help him up, but he could not gather enough strength to rise to his feet. He reached out his trembling hand, touching the girl's sleeve, verifying she was real.

"Who are you? Why do you seem so familiar, little one?" he earnestly pleaded with shallow breath succumbing to death's cold grip.

The girl did not answer.

"Please help me," he pleaded again, his arms falling helplessly to his side.

The butterfly fluttered about the girl's petite frame, each completed circle intensifying the hues of her bejeweled wings; the colors radiated with warm light. The elated little girl opened her creamy hand to the butterfly; it settled serenely in her receptive palm. She drew the butterfly to her dewy rose lips and placed a kiss on its massive wings. Tears welled in her innocent eyes. With warm breath she whispered, "Goodbye, my cherished friend."

The butterfly left her hand and hovered over Chanson's chest. The melancholy girl turned away from the knight's body as he lay on the cold floor. She walked toward the staircase again, placed one tiny foot onto the first step, paused and looked over her shoulder at the dying man and the fluttering butterfly.

The girl turned back toward the iron steps and resumed climbing the spiral staircase, intent on getting to its peak. Before she disappeared from Chanson's view, he saw a white-robed man descend to meet the little girl. His face was covered in a veil of light as he stood with an outstretched hand to the teary-eyed girl. She placed her hand into his and they ascended the staircase, disappearing from Chanson's view.

Chanson closed his eyes and saw the outstretched arms of his parents. They were waiting for him along the stream of a clear, flowing brook.

The butterfly's wings beat rapidly, gaining strength and intensifying in jeweled brilliance. The vivid wings expanded, gently fanning out, covering Chanson's body. Death lurked in the shadows of the dawn; the rains of surrender carried his soul over the surging seas.

His songs cradle me through the night.

Heart and Seal

Crystalhaven Lighthouse
October 23, 1428

King Sainesbury's daunting pursuit led him and his men to the lighthouse. Along the way they were not met with any other beasts, only a few fallen tree branches to contend with. They also found Garrick's horse; Blaine took hold of her reins and she galloped along with the warriors. It was just before sunrise when the men arrived at Crystalhaven Lighthouse.

"Look, Your Majesty," Esmond said, "the lighthouse. We made it!"

"It sure is the brightest light my weary eyes have seen!" the king said when he saw the faint light beaming in the heavy swirling snow.

"Surviving that horrendous creature has most certainly given me hope that we will find our friend still alive. I hope he's in there. Still your horses men, let's have a look around."

King Sainesbury led the men toward the lighthouse door, the hem of his long scarlet coat brushed over the tall snow drifts. With renewed hope, he held faith in his heart believing Chanson would be found alive. Before approaching the door, he noticed the opalescent powder he had seen earlier on Parisina's window ledge.

"Would you look at the way it glimmers, as if lit by the heavens," the king said. "I believe God is watching over Chanson."

"Well, you've been adamant about the importance of faith, My King. Perhaps angels are among us!" Esmond quoted.

"Indeed," the king chuckled, "indeed."

"It looks like an animal was here too!" Landon piped.

"I see. It surely does! I believe it's the same animal that trotted near my daughter's window earlier. Never mind that now, let's open this door!"

Landon quickly brushed away the snow from the door's threshold. They entered.

"Blood," Esmond said, "and lots of it! He was here, Chanson was here!"

"And frozen blood at that!" the king said with worry lines creasing between his eyes.

"Where could he have gone? Is it possible someone rescued him?" Ashton said.

"I highly doubt it since everyone knows not to get near the ocean when the ice monster is believed to be roaming about," the perplexed king said. "Our search is not over, gentlemen. We must keep traveling. Perhaps Chanson is near the water's edge."

"Your Majesty—petals of gypsophila!" Ashton said after noticing the blossoms scattered on the iced steps. "That's strange, don't you think?"

"We've had a dismal turn of events ever since we came in contact with those berries!" the king said, his brow furrowed in confusion and anger.

"I'll go further up and see if he's there," Ashton said.

As Ashton was about to ascend to the top he made a puzzling discovery. "His armor and shield are here, Your Majesty! He left them behind, but why?"

"I expect it was because of the blood sticking to his skin," Landon said, standing at the foot of the steps.

"Gypsophila—foreign powder—voices—perfume, and now Chanson's whereabouts still unknown?" Ashton continued. "What is going *on*?"

"I don't know," the king said.

"I don't think Chanson's still alive," Blaine said, looking around as if the search had already come to an end. "With these freezing temperatures and the ice monster on the hunt, we may be in for a grim discovery when we do find his body."

"The sun's beginning to peep over yonder; its rays will warm the ocean," Esmond reassured, indicating the clearing horizon.

"Surmising won't bring our injured warrior home," the king said sternly. "I believe he's still with us and it's up to us to not let our friend die. Chanson saved my life and we're going to save his! Ashton, grab Chanson's sword and armor, and let's go! I can't explain its appearing, but we are going to follow this opalescent path and see where it takes us. Follow my lead, gentlemen."

The men's faces were lit with the fire of frost when the snow finally tapered off. Even though the king was not about to accept that Chanson may have perished, his strength was failing. His arms started twitching, and his voice became hoarse with exhaustion.

"My King," Esmond said, "the powder is gone."

"Yes I know. But we're not far from the ocean's edge. I hope we find Chanson soon," the king said in a melancholy tone.

"Are you all right, My King?" Esmond continued. "Your eyelids are getting heavy . . . you're unsettled, aren't you, believing he may have drowned?"

"The idea has haunted me since leaving the lighthouse. I hate to admit it, but my faith in finding Chanson alive is beginning to wane. I don't think this aging heart of mine will survive if he has died. I can't lose another friend."

"Well then, let's keep the faith and maybe we'll see him soon," Esmond said with positive resolve.

"You mean by some twist of fate, don't you Esmond?" Blaine said. "If you ask me, I don't understand why God allowed a man as genuine as Chanson to suffer. We should assume he's dead and go back before we die in this cold. I no longer have feeling in my feet and my legs have been cramping since leaving the lighthouse. Our search has been in vain."

"Blaine, keep your despairing thoughts to yourself or turn around right now and go home! I'm not going to allow your faithless comments to stop me from finding the man who laid down his life for me! I won't turn my back on him or my faith!" the king said, gravelly.

"Of course, Your Majesty," Blaine said, stiffening his upper lip and determining to not allow panic to take over.

"My King are you all right?" Esmond interrupted, noticing the king winced, grabbing his chest and crouching in pain.

"Thank you, Esmond. I'm all right, perhaps still under the influence of those berries. Soon we'll be back in our beds, putting this nightmare behind us. I must not allow myself to fall to despair too. I won't!" King Sainesbury said, rubbing his tired red eyes and shifting his focus back to the task at hand.

The king and his men had made their way through Oakhollow Forest, and still no sign of Chanson. The snow had now eased with only flurries. King Sainesbury was determined to continue the search.

"Gentlemen, now that the wretched forest has been searched from one end to the other, we need to shift our focus to the water."

"Do you think he could have drowned in the ocean, My King?" Blaine said.

"I hate it, but we have to prepare ourselves for the possibility," the king said.

"Look, My King, to your right, I believe Chanson's lying in the snow near the ocean's edge!" Ashton said in a melancholy tone.

"Hurry!" the king shouted. "Let's see if it's him!"

I flee to the turreted tower of my Lord;
There in His Majestic fortress I am safe.

Son

Take my hand dear Lord and
bathe my soul in Siloam's fountain.

Kaishore beach
Sunrise on October 23, 1428

Chanson had been found, but a tremendous sorrow was about to overtake the men, especially the king. Ashton peered across Kaishore Ocean. He observed a puffin perched on the icy waves; her head was lowered respectfully on the water's waning ripples.

King Sainesbury jumped off his horse, stumbling as he sprinted to where Chanson's storm-ravaged body lay. Choking on tears, he knelt beside him and touched his chalky face. He whispered, "Chanson—breathe, open your eyes. We've come to take you home . . . Chanson breathe—Please breathe my son—*breathe* . . . "

Chanson did not respond. His ivory shirt was heavily soiled in frozen blood and his soft curls lay on the snow-covered ground; the flaxen strands floating on the chilly breezes.

"Look, Blaine—an unusual butterfly laying on Chanson's chest!" Ashton said, pointing to the velvet-winged butterfly that had visited Chanson earlier. "It's dead too."

"The king hasn't even noticed it," Blaine observed. "If you ask me, I'm beginning to think those berries have cursed us all. I wonder who's next or if any of us will make it home alive."

Ashton looked around and noticed the trees drooping uncharacteristically of snow-covered branches. He piped, "Have any of you noticed the drooping trees? Their trunks are leaning as if they are dying at their roots. Even the tree branches have wilted to the ground. Not one bird has chirped and not one animal has scurried since we've arrived at this beach."

The men scanned their surroundings. Their faces fell and their shoulders slumped as they stood observing the silent, melancholy world.

Blaine agreed, "It's as if those berries have cursed our world too. We are but a fleeting shadow . . . our days are nearing the end."

Esmond's attention went to King Sainesbury, who was removed from anything except trying to revive his beloved knight. The king's heart was ruled by grief.

Esmond approached the Majesty. He knelt beside him, gently placing his hand on his snow-covered coat. "I'm sorry, he's gone, my friend," he said. "We've arrived too late . . . your knight is gone."

"Not Chanson, no—not my son . . . " he whispered, tears pooling in his eyes. The king trembled; lassitude lived in his body. He pressed his tear-drenched face against Chanson's frozen cheeks and wrapped his arms around his body in a fatherly embrace. He shivered in disbelief, chanting, "My son, *my son*." While rocking back and forth he wailed, "I let you down, I let you die! It should have been you to get the last vial of medicine! If only I had come sooner, you would have lived . . . lived to take my kingdom as your own when my reign was over in this pathetic, wretched world. I'm sorry . . . I failed you, I failed you, *my son*—"

The men were surprised of the king's promised endowment to the dead knight. They looked at each other and remained quiet.

Esmond knelt beside the king whose hope had withered like grass. The adviser had seen the king's heart laid out before, raw and bare, but this time he worried about the visible strain this shock was having on him. The rain of sorrow squelched the fire of royalty; the kingdom's pillars fell like shattered glass breaking on foundations of stone.

The warriors circled Chanson's body. They closed their eyes and prayed while stifling tears.

> *Spirit, empower us with your infinite flame and burn away this sorrow from our souls . . .*

Engulfed in grief, none of the men noticed Princess Pearlensia had arrived, lowering her wings and standing close by. Her lithe, compelling figure trotted toward the circle. "I have petals in my land that may heal your friend," she said.

Taken by Pearlensia's voice, the men opened their eyes from meditation and saw her poised nearby.

"Hello warriors, I am Pearlensia, Princess from the Isle of Wisteria. I have come to help you," she whispered, her lashes sweeping gracefully over her arresting eyes and her essence covering the snow around her.

The king rose to his feet, glared into Pearlensia's eyes and said, "So you're the reason for the jeweled dust that led us here, only to discover our friend dead?"

"Yes, King Sainesbury. Allow me to help you get home."

"'*Get home!*'" the king said, raising his voice. "How is it you are able to make that promise? Leave me! I want nothing to do with you or your promises!"

Pearlensia was troubled by the king's sorrow and by that of Chanson's friends. She was moved to tears; the stream rippled down her gardenia-scented cheeks. The empathetic drops glistened like diamonds bathed in sunlight. "Please, let me take him to the Isle of Wisteria and I will bathe his body in the petals. God's earth holds many secrets to healing. If he is dead as you say, then what harm would befall taking the loyal warrior to my kingdom?"

"Winter is upon us!" the king said. "Healing petals don't grow in the frozen earth and still, you try to tell me otherwise?"

"Winter does not occur in the Isle of Wisteria, only zephyrs of Spring and Summer caress the fertile land. I beseech you warriors to remember the prophet Samuel whom the Lord helped defeat the Philistines. The Bible records that Samuel took a stone, and set it between Mizpeh and Shen, and called the name of it Ebenezer, saying, 'Hitherto hath the Lord helped us.' Please have faith like that of Samuel and allow me to show you God's power to help Chanson."

"My King," Esmond said, placing his hand on the king's shoulder, "as we've all seen thus far, nothing has been normal since those berries came into our lives. There's no doubt in my mind that Chanson's dead, but I guess it can't hurt to let her try to heal him. Her knowledge of Scripture is compelling; perhaps we could be wrong about Chanson's current state."

"I do recall Seabert alluding to the Isle of Wisteria as having rare petals of healing," the king said. "Nothing was mentioned about the land. I had assumed it was a passing comment and dismissed its validity at the time. Perhaps you are correct, Esmond. Very well, I will allow it."

"I'll speak on your behalf, My King," Esmond said.

"All right," the king said, falling to his knees beside Chanson's body. He removed his gloves and took hold of the knight's cold hand, caressing it gently. His eyes filled with tears. He prayed silently for the Lord's healing and to grant him an heir to the throne. He, too, felt the weight of his years and his time on earth were closing in.

"The Majesty has granted your request," Esmond said, turning toward Pearlensia. "But I warn you, if any further harm is brought upon my king, you will—"

"You have my promise!" Princess Pearlensia interrupted. "The knight has little time; we must be on our way!"

Pearlensia trotted to where the king knelt praying over Chanson's body. "King Sainesbury, may I take him now?"

Consumed with sorrow, the king could not speak, only nodded his head, granting Pearlensia permission to take Chanson. He let go of Chanson's hand. The king stood with his hands crossed in front of him. His legs trembled.

The warriors rushed to the king's side, each standing beside their king. Pearlensia opened her warm wings and folded Chanson into her ineffable breast. After securing his limp arms she whispered, "King Sainesbury, I will lead you. Mount up your horses and follow me."

The men mounted their horses. The stress and lack of rest were weakening the King as each moment passed. Still, he paused and prayed for strength to follow through on Pearlensia's request.

With power in her legs, Pearlensia led the warriors to her kingdom. She sped away swiftly and at a speed none of the horses had risen to before. The breath of God had given the horses power beyond earthly reach.

Love is an unquenchable fire:
No sword can maim it
No water can quench it
No flood can drown it
No possession can replace it;
The world can never contain love.

Sonnet of Wisteria

Oh fairest flame of Heaven's sun so bright,
Your sweetly Spring has sprung; soft petals sway.
They kiss the morning breeze on blooms delight;
Gardenia's cords of three inspire today.

Oh fairest mane of pearl from realms above,
When summer's sun has set and leaves behind;
Ah softly whisper wisdom's song of love,
And take my hand in thine, oh keep entwined!

Oh Holy fire, autumn's twilight fades soon,
Let ancient days enlighten secrets lore,
With comfort words concealing tears that loom;
Since time and sun remember Spring no more.

Oh breath of Heaven's wings have come to free;
Eternal summer—Father calls for me!

The Isle of Wisteria

In mere moments Pearlensia, Chanson, and the others had ridden over heavy snow drifts arriving at a gold-paved bridge. Under the glassy gold was the beautiful Rose of Sharon blooming. They glanced down, captivated by the lush blossoms growing beneath the scrolled bridge. Pearlensia galloped onto the bridge, following it until they came to a rose-adorned garden with a gate overlaid with pearl. Tall statuesque roses were seen; each unprecedented velveteen petal perfect with rich color.

"My faithful friends, the Isle of Wisteria will comfort and heal you from all that you have suffered. God has blessed this land and now I share its beauty with you. I believe when we demonstrate exemplary faith, Our God rewards it. Through the pearl-bejeweled gate lies a blissful place to restore your hope, if only you will believe as I do," Pearlensia continued, sprightly batting her sweeping lashes.

"Go ahead, King Sainesbury, step down and open the gate and see for yourself what lies behind it."

The men got off their horses and placed their feet firmly on the golden step leading to the gate.

King Sainesbury unlatched the hook from the jeweled gate. A light breeze swung open the door. He stood on the threshold of a world he had never seen before with fields arrayed in incandescent flowers and glossy-leafed trees. The warriors examined their leather-laced feet, as if to confirm they were standing on a luscious spring path with no snow in sight. A white dove, cooing a melody, serenaded their ears.

"Welcome to the Isle of Wisteria, my friends. I assure you it is real. Go ahead, touch the emerald earth at your feet; allow each tender blade of grass to pass through your curious hands," Pearlensia said to the king as he stooped down to run his hand across the satin grass at his feet.

"How is it we have missed seeing this world . . . a world untouched by time and the changing of seasons?" the king said.

"I cannot say," Pearlensia said. "For as long as I can recall this has been my home."

"Your Majesty," Esmond piped, "perhaps it's because there was not a reason before now."

"Perhaps this is, *indeed,* where Seabert's father collected those rare potions," the king said.

"Yes, my friends," Pearlensia said, "Michael Gaines, Seabert's father, did visit my land. It was when he was a young man, seeking petals to use in a healing balm for his mother."

"And was the treatment successful?" the king said.

"It was. I instructed him to pray for God's healing and to rub the balmy petals on the inflamed wound."

"If Seabert believed this land held blossoms that could cure, then I must as well! Proceed with the petal treatment, Princess Pearlensia!" the king said robustly.

The men glanced at the unicorn, observing Chanson's lifeless body still draping in her wings, held tightly against her breast. Though the warriors questioned whether Chanson was still alive, they chose to embrace Pearlensia's insight.

King Sainesbury's faith convinced him he must put his human frailty aside and trust God to heal his beloved knight. For the first time since finding Chanson, the king's spirit lifted with the hope Chanson would survive.

Princess Pearlensia placed Chanson's body on the warm grass and said, "Wait here my friends, and I will return with the petals from the wisteria tree."

"Very well," the king said, taking a deep breath as if to prepare himself for what would arise from trusting the princess.

Pearlensia trotted to the pink wisteria and plucked off several petals. She folded the petals close to her breast and lifted her gaze toward the heavens.

"What is she doing, My King?" Landon piped, his eyes still swollen from sorrow.

"I believe she is praying as I pray now in my heart."

"I've never known a unicorn to pray," Ashton said.

"And neither have I," Blaine piped. "I find it amusing that many a human fails to bow their head, and yet, here we stand witnessing an animal respecting the Almighty! How would we ever explain this to our wives, let alone to anyone else?"

"They would certainly believe we had suffered a spell from coming in contact with those berries," Esmond piped.

"Oh look, she's coming back toward us," the king said. "Quiet all. Let's see for ourselves if those petals can indeed restore Chanson's body."

Princess Pearlensia hovered over Chanson. She dropped the petals on his chest, and with her wings, rubbed the blossoms into the gaping wound. The pearly essence from her wings settled on his skin and clothing. She gazed toward the sky, with her wings bowed to the earth, and prayed again. Her prayerful mutterings could not be heard by the men, but her faith impressed them. They were beginning to see there was more to this unicorn than they had previously thought.

While still in prayerful uttering, the warriors noticed Chanson's fingers beginning to move and the wound closing until there was no longer an injury. His eyelids twitched and he opened his eyes.

"He's alive! My son's alive!" the king cried, tears of joy rolling down his chafed cheeks.

Pearlensia set her sparkling eyes on Chanson. Her breast lit up with light as if touched by sunlight.

Chanson's cheeks ripened with color. He sat up. His smile burst forth and his eyes were lucent as jewels. Chanson glanced up and saw Pearlensia standing stately over him. The powder essence swirled around her being, encapsulating her in a bewitching light. He locked eyes with Pearlensia as though communicating with each other. Time ceased, they were stilled in thought.

Chanson sprung to his feet and said, "Where am I? I've never known peace like this before . . . I'm alive! All my memories . . . they are coming back to me. Garrick Aynsley—he stabbed me, the wound—" he continued, checking his shoulder, "it's gone, no scar left in its place. I've been healed! I cannot recall ever feeling more vibrant than I do this very moment . . . alive—I'm alive!" he continued, jumping around on the dark satin grass.

The warrior's eyes and mouths opened wide, astonished at seeing Chanson rise to life.

The king sprinted toward Chanson. He placed his arms around him, squeezing him tightly, and wept, thrilled his fervid knight was very much alive.

King Sainesbury cried, "Chanson, indeed you are alive! Oh, how my heart soars now in seeing health restored in your body! I know all about the plot to overthrow my kingdom, but you stopped it, my friend—my endeared one—you have saved us all. I am honored, touched to the depths of my soul, for the ardent sacrifice you have made for me, for all housed in the fortress of my rule.

"It will be yours one day, the entire kingdom yours, for you are as close to my heart as my own flesh and blood. You embody the son I was never meant to see mature into a man. My own son, Ambrose, died before he could ever walk or talk."

"He is the loss you were referencing when I was first orphaned . . . " Chanson said, weeping.

"I could not speak of it then. I wanted to tell you, but the words would not come. Chanson, it's true, an excruciating reality twenty-four years ago. I have spent *my entire life since* grieving for the son who was taken so cruelly from me. My soul had been pierced with a sword of fire. But I stand now, broken by tragedy and convinced that all along God knew this moment would come to me. You are my God-given son, the orphan who bravely rose out of the ash of loss to become the heir to my throne. *I love you.*"

"My King—my father—I love you too," Chanson said. "I only wanted you to be proud of me. When you first took hold of my small hand as a freshly orphaned child, I clung to something about you I recognize in my own father. It was the Holy Spirit living in him who gave me hope and soothed my despairing wound. Hayden, he was as you are to me now, a man whom I admire and call Father, my cherished family. I will go to my grave honoring your legacy and the virtues you have fought so boldly to protect."

"Well, you did put one foot in the grave, Chanson!" the king sighed, embracing again.

Chanson turned toward Pearlensia and said, "Princess Pearlensia, your devotion is truly endless. Thank you for perceiving my breath. I could hear your words, but I could not rise up to confirm there was breath in me. If it had not been for your faith, I would have died."

"I was sent again to help you as I was when you were a young child and needed me. Do you remember when I visited you in your room during your fragile childhood? I reassured that your pain would ease and you would once again feel happy."

"Yes and every word was true! The Cheswicks loved me deeply, but losing Hayden has been one of the worst blades to pierce my heart! He was a fine knight and a devoted man of God. He deserved so much more of the goods this life could have given to him. King Sainesbury wanted him to serve until he was a very old man. He was struck down far too soon; I miss him every day."

"When a righteous man dies," Pearlensia continued. "it is a blessing because he has been spared from evil. Chanson, you must keep the faith and continue to fight for the good while following the light. One day it will lead you to a magnificent place where there will be no more wars, pain or rose-covered caskets.

"I know you are confused about all the events unfolding here, but you must trust these were given to you as a door back to your life as a father, husband, and the king's valuable knight," Pearlensia softly reassured, her sweeping lashes blinking slowly.

The king and his men's faces were etched in wonder at what they had witnessed. The king turned toward Pearlensia and said, "So, why didn't God heal Chanson when he was first wounded? Why allow him and our faithful friend, Seabert, this cruel hardship? If God loves us as He claims in the Word, then why is it necessary for Him to hurt us like this?"

"I cannot presume to know God's thoughts nor am I able to search Him out. But my faith tells me Jehovah allows the testing of one's faith to give us the choice of choosing to honor or dishonor Him in the face of great adversity. He wants the soul to choose His love and blessings, not be forced to do so. I believe God knew you would use His strength and wisdom to overcome the fiery trials leading you here today.

"It is in these difficult valleys God prepares the heart for the next season of life. My faith tells me this new season will not be free of turmoil and disappointment either. It will, however, bring refreshing times and new blessings while unfolding deeper revelations about your life. Do you believe your prayers were being heard, every one of them answered?"

"Yes, indeed they have! I am humbled the Lord cares so deeply for me," the king said, having a change of heart toward Pearlensia.

"Chanson," the king continued, "it appears you and Pearlensia were friends long before today! Why didn't you ever tell us she had appeared in your youth?"

"I wasn't sure any of you would believe me. I guess I wanted it to be something shared with only my mother since she believed in unicorns."

"Well, perhaps I would have thought you were imagining her. Children often do have active imaginations. I'm overjoyed knowing that Pearlensia was a source of comfort to you."

"I detect gardenia scent," Ashton said, glancing at Pearlensia and examining the flowers in her mane. "It's coming from you, Princess!"

"I've sensed it before," the king piped. "Pearlensia, did you visit me when I was laying afflicted with the poison?"

"Yes, my friend. I placed my cheek on your forehead, to help soothe your troubled mind. God allowed the medicine to heal you so that not only you, but your friend Esmond, could witness the power of prayer."

Esmond piped, "My faith was strengthened when I saw my king open his eyes, and my faith has increased in fervor by all the mysteries unfolding since."

"I believe we can all agree there is more to our world than what earthly vision is able to perceive," Pearlensia said.

"Well, there's no question about that!" the king said, glancing at Chanson who was still examining his healed shoulder.

"I don't know how any of this is possible, but Princess Pearlensia, you've made my heart swell," King Sainesbury continued, his eyes red and moist from the happiness of his reunion with Chanson. "It's a splendid day, a splendid day indeed to have my knight back with me."

"I concur," Esmond piped. "I've been a believer since I was a young lad, but now I've a longing no earthly joy will ever satisfy again."

"And for me too," Blaine agreed. "No disrespect intended, but I feared we were going to freeze to death before ever finding Chanson, or worse, meet our end by way of the creature's teeth."

"My faith has been strengthened as well," Ashton said, peering at the sky's blue light of dawn. "I'm going to need it when we return and I have to bid farewell to my friend, Seabert."

"*Come*, my friends, let me share my kingdom with you before you return to Evernora," Pearlensia said. "Drink in my blossoms and rest your minds on the floral meadows for awhile."

The warriors, along with King Sainesbury, stood admiring the welcome scene. The harrowing fight for their lives and the sorrow incurred in their search for Chanson was soothed away.

"In this sacred world stands the blooming wisteria, a blissful symbol of new life," Pearlensia said. "Take in her sweet fragrance, my friends."

They took deep breaths and allowed the scent to permeate their senses, keeping their gaze on the wisteria's arching branches.

"Allow her selfless branches to embrace your hearts, erasing all sorrow and pain from your memory. The tree's blossoms have graced you with this beginning. Let her intertwining trunk remind you of love's immortality."

The warriors stood mesmerized by the inspiring scene.

Princess Pearlensia extended her feathered wings and said, "Go in, enjoy and leave when you are ready." She trotted back to her castle, Perldore, a turreted white pearled structure reaching far into the sky. She waved with her wing, batting her lustrous lashes, and ascended the castle's scrolled, spiraled steps. She disappeared from their view.

"I feel as if my soul is floating with no sense of urgency or trouble . . . indescribable," Chanson said, looking onto a budding meadow as far as the eye could reach.

"It is a splendid place indeed, Chanson," the king said, "let me look at you again. My, my, it's a grand day to have you standing by my side once again, restored . . . you're even more vibrant than before."

"Your Majesty, Father, I, too, am in awe of this moment with you, well, with all of you," Chanson said, gazing at all his brothers of faith.

The men engaged with smiles.

"I say we immerse ourselves here for awhile like the princess advised," Esmond said, proceeding to walk further into the Isle of Wisteria.

"Indeed, Esmond, let us!" the king said. "Ahh, how beautiful it is! I'm beginning to get very sleepy, gentlemen," the king said. "I believe I'll lie down on the grass and rest my eyes before we go home. Why don't you do the same. Rest, sweet rest is what we all need now, not drinking in blossoms."

"As you wish, My King," Esmond said.

"I concur," Blaine piped. "For I, too, am drowsy."

"We'll explore the princess's kingdom later," Ashton piped.

The King and the warriors were spent; they collapsed on the breezy meadows and were fast asleep within moments.

Zephyr's Song

God's thoughts immeasurable
When He remembers me;
Like grains of sand
On celestial seas.

I'm held in His heart
Engraved on stone;
Ever on His mind
Rarest jewels ever known.

I'm set before His face
Dandled on His knee;
He wipes away my tears
Forever healing me.

I'm carried on his shoulders
Above all concerns.
I'm His and He's mine;
His sealing Spirit affirms.

The Majesty rules my heart
Promising castles fair;
Refines with swords of fire
Crowning me over there.

Zephyr's Chords of Love

Heaven now holds your rose bud of promise;
Your cherished child blossoms with God.

Sunbeams danced in their eyes as they walked in the Elysian meadow.

"The sun seems brighter in Wisteria," Chanson said. "Just look at the grass, even it glistens with sunlight."

"Indeed, Chanson," the king said. "I noticed the petals on the wisteria were of a satin I'd never seen."

"Do any of you hear a dog barking?" Ashton piped.

Chanson cast his eyes further ahead and said, "It's Jade! He's looking at me and wagging his tail like he used to do—he recognizes me!"

"Of course he does, Chanson. He's been waiting to see you!" Princess Pearlensia beamed.

"Look at his swift legs, determined to come to me! His eyes are focused on me like they were when he ran to me on my family's lawn. He does remember me, *he does!* He's coming toward us—my old friend Jade is alive!"

Jade continued skittering across the floral meadow, barking the whole way with his eyes intent on getting to Chanson. His frisky body landed rambunctiously into Chanson's arms. Chanson laughed jovially while Jade licked his face all over, wagging his tail exuberantly.

Chanson pet his puppy; a long winding path had led to this momentous occasion. Chanson's heart exploded with tears of laughter. He held the puppy in the air, like a father cherishing a giggling child. Smiling in his playful eyes, Chanson said, "Jade, what a welcome surprise you are! I'm so happy to see you, my gentle friend. I knew you'd come back to me, I only wish it had not been this long. I never stopped looking for you—ever—and now you're finally home . . . in my arms!" Chanson pressed Jade onto his chest while the puppy continued to lick his neck and face with excitement.

"Oh, it is a delightful moment to behold," Pearlensia said, giggling, "a euphoric moment God has allowed us!"

While holding Jade affectionately in his arms, Chanson's eyes settled on a small child playing in a field of lilac. He recognized her and said, "Look, she's the little girl I saw at the lighthouse! She's skipping in the blossoms trying to catch butterflies! Do you see her, Your Majesty?"

"Indeed, she's thrilled and frolicking without a worry of any kind," the king chuckled.

"The gypsophila blossom found at the lighthouse must have fallen out of her hair," Ashton piped.

They all peered across the field of lilacs, enchanted by the girl's boundless energy.

"Princess Pearlensia, is she an angel?" Chanson said.

"My little friend, she is Anissia, your baby sister who you never met. And yes, God sent her to comfort you," Pearlensia said, her eyelashes sweeping over her eyes.

"That's why she seemed so familiar! It was Anissia who giggled in the forest?"

"Ahh, yes."

"Why did Anissia cry after releasing the butterfly from her hand?"

"Chanson, her work was made complete through the friendship with the butterfly. When she was able to let go of the butterfly, an angel met her on the steps of the lighthouse. His presence was there to lead her back to Heaven."

"So, that's why we found the dead butterfly laying on Chanson," Ashton piped.

"Yes, my friend."

"I felt as though she had been a part of me somewhere in my life," Chanson said. "But I did not know to trust what I was envisioning while in my weakened state. So it was her!"

"God will manifest Himself in creatures we identify with. I believe that is why He placed the butterfly on the oak leaf when you were grieving Hayden's death. He hoped you would come to recognize His compassionate and abiding heart beating gently in the butterfly's transcendent wings."

Chanson peered into the meadow and saw a couple smiling at him. The woman blew him a kiss.

"Pearlensia, who are they?" Chanson said.

"Your birth parents!"

"They both have blonde hair like mine!"

"Yes, and we see where those welcoming pecan brown eyes came from."

"My eyes do favor my father's and I have my mother's blonde curls."

"Chanson, I was with your mother before she took her last breath," Pearlensia said. "Seren did not know I was there, only your birth mother. Before she was ready to go, she asked me to retrieve a letter that had been left behind in her house. She pleaded with me to give it to you after you had grown and settled. The expressions of her heart were written after you were born. I promised her I would give you the letter when it was best to do so. The angel then carried her soul to God's gentle breast. The time for you to have this is now."

The parchment appeared. It was laying against Pearlensia's breast, her wing pressing it in place. Her warm light shone through the delicate paper. "Please, my friend, take the letter and read it after I leave."

Chanson took hold of the folded letter that was tied with a white ribbon. He set his teary gaze on the note, caressing the words *My Beloved One* written on the outside. He wondered what the letter would reveal.

"Pearlensia, I know that I was not alone at the lighthouse," Chanson said. "I was healed and comforted by the heart of God, of this I am certain. What I've experienced over the last few hours has lifted my soul closer to the Lord's heart. I have seen and been a part of a mystery that transcends my earthly life—I understand now."

"Jade was sent to comfort you and to provide a passage for unlocking your mind," Pearlensia said. "God never intended for His creation to belong solely to you, but instead to teach us more about His mysterious ways.

As a young, wounded child, God was able to mold you for His plans. Often we lose our childlike innocence when life crushes and people disappoint. The heart can then grow cold, callused by loss and betrayals, thereby closing itself from experiencing the ultimate compassion and joy of God. But you have kept the resilient spirit God instilled in your soul and it has made all the difference."

"Pearlensia, will you be returning if I need you again?" Chanson said.

"My dear friend, you need not concern yourself with what lies ahead," Pearlensia reassured, placing her wing around Chanson's shoulder. "*Trust*, that as God has been there for all your past troubles, He will be with you through all future problems. I believe you will see me again. As you have seen, nothing is impossible with God."

"I've read it many times in the Bible," King Sainesbury piped. "But it wasn't until this moment that I truly grasped its full impact."

Pearlensia smiled, looking with approving eyes at the faces of her friends being comforted by the Spring floral kingdom.

Karina, the nightingale, was heard trilling.

"Purr-purr-purr-purr-purr-purr-purrrr-chee-chee-purr-purr-purr-purrrr-cheeei-cheeei . . . "

"Look, My King, it's Seabert!" Landon said.

"Where?" thc king said.

"He's standing on top of the mountain that overlooks the kingdom. The nightingale is perched on his shoulder, singing," Landon continued.

Seabert waved, smiling. An ethereal glow encapsulated his being.

"I see him! He and Karina are together again!" King Sainesbury said, smiling as tears collected in his eyes.

"Would you look at her mouth, wide and expressive, trilling those melodies!" Blaine said. "Seabert sure looks peaceful."

"I'm glad to see it," Ashton piped. "Seabert loved the bird like a child. I'm going to miss our friendship and the way he smiled when Karina sang."

"We will all miss his gentle presence," the king said.

They waved back at the kind humanitarian.

"Look, it's Hayden," Chanson said, "he's near the huge forest of redbud trees. There must be hundreds of them! How is this possible, Pearlensia?"

"Did I not promise a glimpse of renewed hope if you believed?"

"Yes, but I never expected this . . . to see Hayden—look, Landon, Father is very much alive riding a horse."

"I can hardly believe my eyes," Landon said. "That's Lydie, Father's first horse, given to him by Grandfather. He told me often how he loved to ride her through the forest after sunrise. I was not born when the mare died, but Father's eyes were misty whenever he spoke of her. Chanson, the mare is from Diamond Belle's lineage. Grandfather raised the destrier until he passed away. Father loved those horses."

"His smile is warm," Chanson said, "even from here, I see his eyes glistening in the sun. Landon, I could not imagine a more fitting place for Father than that sanctuary of radiance.

"I am saddened Diamond Belle is not with me. I don't know what happened to her. Was she ever found in Oakhollow Forest?"

"No, not even a trace," Landon said. "Father would also be disheartened if he knew she was missing."

They continued to admire the mare's appearance. Lydie's mane, adorned with white calla lily and yellow acacia blossoms, suffused their souls with wonder.

"Look, Landon, your puppy!" Chanson said. "Dulcie is in the prairie fields."

"She loves cantering through the daisies with white gypsophila dancing gracefully at her paws," Pearlensia said.

"If only I could go to my father now and tell him one more time I love him . . . " Landon said.

"As you see, your father does live on," Pearlensia said. "He knows you love him and is aware you are here, look again and see for yourself. He is waving to you. Do you see him smiling?"

"He does know I'm here!" Landon waved back. Tears flowed as they exchanged warm smiles.

"Princess Pearlensia, *why can't I go to him now?*"

"You may! Now go to your cherished father while there is still time!"

Hayden waited beside the redbud trees with his arms opened wide for Landon to return to them. The soft wrinkles lining Hayden's eyes were cherished and familiar to Landon. He leaped into his father's arms. They embraced tightly, kissing each other's cheeks.

"Father, I'm crushed in spirit over my recent actions," Landon said, his teary eyes setting their gaze on his father's receiving face. "You must know that I betrayed King Sainesbury and brought tremendous suffering upon my brother."

"Don't trouble your spirit a moment longer, Son. I love you, nothing will change that. There was never a question about your motives; they were coming from a golden heart. What is important is that you have been strengthened by the experience. Your humility is beautiful in the eyes of our wonderful Counselor."

Landon smiled through the tears, clinging to every word Hayden spoke.

"Spiritual birth is painful, but I know you've matured because of it. You're much wiser now and that blesses me and honors God."

"My heart is overjoyed by being here with you, Father; I don't deserve a place in Heaven after what I've done."

"You are God's child, He would never turn you away, no matter what you've done. God has compassion on the contrite of heart; He forgives any transgression when the soul has made a change and resolves to do what's right. In Heaven there will be no record of your sins, so don't hold onto something that even God has chosen to forget."

"Thank you for the words, Father. I love you so!"

"And I love you," Hayden said, embracing his son.

Pearlensia continued with the others, gazing into the spring-like paradise.

"How beautiful it is to see a father and son reunited," the king said as he stood with his hands behind his back.

"King Sainesbury," Pearlensia said, raising her wing toward a sunny hillside with birds chirping, "who do you see?"

"*Chloette—ahhh,* my dearest Chloette," the king said, smiling. He reached out, longing to touch his queen.

"Ambrose is an exquisite child," Pearlensia continued, "a vision of serenity as he lies folded in the cradle of your wife's arms."

"She's fetching, a-and so h-happy," King Sainesbury whispered, his eyes moistening with warm emotion. "She hasn't aged at all and her hair's not streaked with silver like mine. Look at the halo of light around her, her dark tresses shine like strands of glass! Oh, how I would love to be in her embrace and hold Ambrose, the son whose heart I never felt beating upon my breast. Chloette's truly a vision of virtue as she smiles at our son."

"Go, King Sainesbury, be with your family again, even if it is an evanescent reunion," Pearlensia said.

King Sainesbury leaped in the meadow, his coat brushing swiftly over white jasmine petals. Chloette glanced and saw her husband sprinting toward her as if time were fleeting. The momentum of his feet competed with his hastening heartbeat. Chloette rose to her feet and with her baby in her arms, met her husband. Tears of elation flowed between them. They embraced, kissing each other's faces all over.

"I've missed you so—" the king said, caressing his queen's alabaster cheeks.

"I know, my dear Roland, I know. Here, hold your son," she said, placing Ambrose in the arms of his father.

The king's countenance was bright and his cheeks pink as his misty eyes settled on his azure blue-eyed child. Ambrose smiled affectionately as if he recognized his father. King Sainesbury took hold of the baby's tiny fingers and kissed each one. He then pressed the baby's hand to his cheek and wailed, admiring his son. Not for a moment did the child take his placid eyes off his father's face. The king said, "At last my son, at last I am able to feel your vibrant heart beating against mine. How marvelous it is and how splendid you are . . . truly a magnificent creation."

The king's tears poured onto the baby's soft skin as he and his son bonded. Pearlensia and the others stood admiring the king's reunion.

"I've known the king for many years," Esmond said. "This is the first time I've seen him truly happy since his wife's death. Oh, he lets out bellowing laughter from time to time, but this is pure ecstasy. Will this not leave a lasting impression upon us all?"

"Yes, it will, Esmond," Ashton said. "Perhaps his heart will heal now that he has had one more moment with his family."

"Even the white jasmine rejoice in their celebration; each petal dancing delightfully around them as the king coos to the tender babe," Pearlensia said, batting her eyes and tilting her head toward the king.

"Chanson," Ashton interrupted, "Hayden's inviting you to join him and Landon, look—his arms are outstretched for you."

Chanson set his gaze on Hayden's smile and noticed Landon in one arm and the other arm opened for him. He gestured with his hand for Chanson to come to him. Hayden's face was lit with the fire of love. His cheeks were luminous and lifted with an infectious smile; a smile they had all missed.

"Go to him, Chanson," Pearlensia affirmed, "allow your soul nourishment in the arms of your devoted father."

Chanson and Hayden's eyes met, their smiles were kissed by the sun of Eternity. He ran toward Hayden, his feet caressing the warm earth while carrying Jade in his arms. Hayden wrapped both Landon and Chanson to his breast, kissing their wet cheeks. They had been allowed one more embrace, one more time to behold the face of their legendary father after wishing for it for so long.

"Father, my Father," Chanson said, "I have cried countless times, missing you . . . we both have."

"Yes, Papa," Landon affirmed, "I never got over the cruelty of how you died . . . I was angry when you left me and I hated the man who killed you," Landon cried.

"I know," Hayden said, embracing his sons tightly. "My sons, my endeared sons, look at my bare chest, no wound, not even a scar . . . I'm healed and I'm still with you."

They stood back and examined Hayden's chest after he lifted his tunic exposing his smooth blemish free skin.

"Let us cry no longer, for we are together now," Hayden said. "Promise me you'll be happy and put this grief from you."

"We will Papa, we will!" Landon said.

"Have I not told you both that death does not separate the pure of heart?"

"Yes, Father," Chanson said. Landon nodded and smiled.

"I'm proud of you both. The happiness I have now as I hold you close to me, far exceeds the momentary trials I endured. Ahh, let me look at you again."

Chanson and Landon stood back again as their father's eyes took in their essences. His eyes welled in tears and he said, "My sons, I can hardly believe it myself, both of you with me." Hayden grabbed his sons again. They stood immersed in a serendipitous embrace.

Ashton, Esmond, Blaine, and Pearlensia were delighted in witnessing the kindred love displayed as they continued to take in the reunion of a father with his children.

"Ahh, this makes all that we've gone through easier to bear," Ashton said, his eyes misting in tears of elation.

"Indeed, Ashton," Esmond said, his eyes also sharing in the father and son affection. "If we had a glimpse of what awaits us after our trials, we'd be inclined to bear them more patiently while holding steadfastly to hope."

"A few hours ago," Blaine said, "I could not have imagined a God this generous to us. I won't look at life from the same perspective as I have done before today."

"Beloved friends, I am delighted to have you here with me on my island," Pearlensia said. With lucid eyes Pearlensia glanced at the majestic scene and continued, "Dear ones, I must return to my castle, Perldore."

The warriors glanced across the Isle of Wisteria and observed the ornate white structure.

"The other side of Eternity awaits where the rose bud blooms forever," Pearlensia said. "It is there you will behold God's face in a halo of resplendent glory—a light that mortal man cannot look upon and live. You will join your loved ones on the shores of home, where the breath of God embraces those who loved and honored

Him. Each of you will live in the Creator's celestial castle; having your own ivory palace while wearing crowns of grace.

"Live the remainder of your earthly days in the light and it will carry you home to the circle of love, where a beautiful forever awaits. Be well, happy, embracing, forgiving, and extending mercy to all you encounter as you resume your life in the ordered steps of our Lord."

"Stay as long as you wish. Ashton, a reunion awaits you too, under the willow tree," Pearlensia continued, extending her wing to the brook with a wispy branch delighting Ashton's youthful wife and baby girl.

Without saying a word, Ashton dashed to his family, his swift feet barely touching the petals and blades of grass beneath them.

Esmond was also compelled to remain longer on the Isle of Wisteria, having seen the aged faces of his parents and beloved grandfather. As Esmond's parents saw their son walking toward them they cheered and ran to meet him. Esmond and his family walked arm in arm across a field of blue viola, laughing and reminiscing about old times.

"Blaine, you did not think God would let you leave today without blessing your faith too, did you?" Pearlensia said, peering into his eyes intently.

"I've been such a doubting man; I didn't expect God's blessing like what the others have received. I'm unworthy of such honor."

"Oh, but that is not God's way. We all doubt at times and even on our most devout days, we still cannot measure our faith against the Son of God. We can, however, determine to grow and accept His goodness whether we feel worthy or not."

As soon as Pearlensia uttered those words, Blaine was taken by the hand of the Father surrogate who had mentored him in youth after being rejected by his family. The two sat on a marble bench and talked, strengthening the bonds of friendship and faith.

Seabert joined King Sainesbury and his family. "My King," Seabert said, peering at Ambrose lying in his father's arms, "it brings me great delight to see you with your son once again!"

"Seabert my friend, I can hardly believe I'm here with my family and now you! Look at you, healed and fairing better than you have in years."

"And I feel youthful. Actually, I've never felt more alive and at peace."

They locked eyes, both misting with tears of joy.

"I'm happy to see you again, Seabert. How dreadful it was the day we lost you. But alas, here we all are—united by faith—enjoying life together once again."

Soon the others reunited with Seabert, embracing friendship once again. Pearlensia galloped into the impressive land she had shown them; her laughter was heard echoing over the clear blue skies. As they stood watching her fade from view, they saw Jade and Chanson skipping toward the sunset, where his adoptive parents and sister sat enjoying a late day picnic. Their eyes moistened with tears of delight. The warriors were left with an unquenchable desire for a life of spiritual fulfillment.

Within moments a gentle breeze brushed over Chanson and the others, closing the pearl gate to the Isle of Wisteria. The gold bridge disappeared with it. Chanson and the others found themselves standing in heavy fallen snow once again. Diamond Belle was standing to the side, healthy, unharmed without a blemish of any kind.

"What happened to us?" Blaine said.

"It appears we fell asleep . . . or did we?" Ashton said, yawning.

“Were we dreaming?” Esmond said. “I was with my parents and Grandfather again. I also remember seeing Seabert, Hayden, Jade, and you, My King, embracing your wife and son. It doesn’t feel like a dream; I know I was in a Spring world with the unicorn. ”

“Well, it sure seemed real to me,” the king said. He touched his cheeks; they were moist. “Chloette’s kisses are still on my cheeks and the scent of jasmine fills the air.”

“Your Majesty,” Ashton piped, “white jasmine petals are lying on the snow . . . look down!”

The king glanced at his feet and saw the soft petals strewn around him, proving he had been with his wife and son. He touched his cheek again to affirm Chloette’s wet kiss and beamed. “It was not a dream . . . we were given a glimpse of Eternity. Though fleeting, my spirit has been revived by the precious moments I was allowed with my son and queen.”

“I smell roses too,” Ashton said, “a rose bush must be near.”

The warriors scanned their surroundings. Chanson saw his horse standing beside an evergreen tree.

“Not only is there a rose blossom near, but Diamond Belle is here with us too,” Chanson said.

Chanson raced toward his horse.

“Diamond Belle, my girl! I thought I’d lost you!” Chanson said, cupping her head into his hands and kissing it. “The letter!” Chanson continued, noticing the parchment laying on Diamond Belle’s saddle. A velvet rose had been placed on the letter. “Princess Pearlensia left it for me. This is like the roses she wore in her mane. I recall her telling me about them, and of my birth mother, moments ago.”

“Aren’t you going to read it then?” King Sainesbury said, observing Chanson holding the letter securely in his hand as he had once held the locket.

"I am nervous to open it."

"Afraid it'll tear open an old scar?" the king said.

"Perhaps so. Or could it be after reading, I'd have nothing left to anticipate or hold to after leaving here today?"

"Possibly. It's understandable that you could feel that way. You could wait and read it after getting home."

"No, I know this is the time. I trust Princess Pearlensia's wisdom."

"Very well," the king said.

They stepped away, allowing Chanson privacy to read his mother's letter.

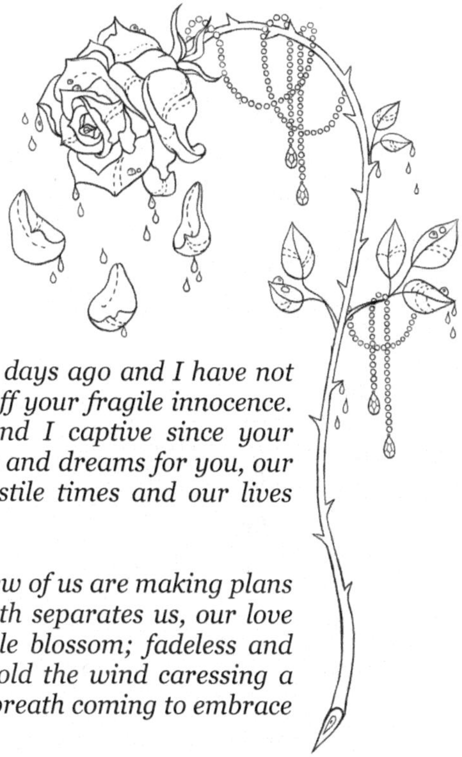

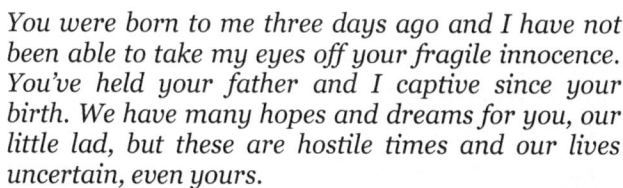

My treasured Elgan,
Precious soul from God;
Cherished son to my heart,

You were born to me three days ago and I have not been able to take my eyes off your fragile innocence. You've held your father and I captive since your birth. We have many hopes and dreams for you, our little lad, but these are hostile times and our lives uncertain, even yours.

There's an uprising and a few of us are making plans to flee the city. Even if death separates us, our love for you is as the immortelle blossom; fadeless and everlasting. When you behold the wind caressing a field of poppies, it'll be our breath coming to embrace and hold you in our hearts.

May the dawn bring you bright new days unfolding in wellsprings of joy and inspiration. May the evening gather around you, securing your heart in sheltering peace. May the fire of love rekindle your spirit with strength and hope.

I love you,
Your Mother, Tesni

After reading the letter, Chanson secured it with the ribbon and put it in his pocket.

"Are you all right, Chanson?" the king said, noticing his face turned forlorn.

"Yes. I'm ready to go home. I can hardly wait to see the beautiful faces of my wife and daughter again—our cheeks are sure to be wet with tears when we are reunited! I hope they are all right. I won't be assured of that until I have Parisina and Musette in my arms again."

Chanson mounted on his horse.

"Look, Princess Pearlensia's opalescent powder on the ground. She must have left it to help lead us back to the castle!" Esmond said.

"That's not all, friends—a red cardinal is poised on that limb," the king piped, pointing to an ancient oak tree with its limbs weighed down by heavy snow.

"It's a male bird!" Landon said. "Only the males have a deep red sheen. My father and I saw a red cardinal a few days after my dog died. He said he believed God was manifesting Himself to us that day. Father had a way of making me feel valuable and loved; I don't know how I could have betrayed love."

Landon set his misty eyes on the salient bird and wept. The king and the others stood nearby with teary eyes, touched by the sorrow erupting deep within Landon's soul. Even nature wept as evidenced by the soft sound of the treetops swaying in the whispering wind.

"I've been so wrong, my friends, *terribly wrong,*" Landon said. "Chanson, I am so sorry for what I did to you and to My King. Will you forgive me?"

"Already done. We are brothers, *family*, that has never changed," Chanson reassured.

"I forgive you too, Landon," the king said. "Your change of heart tells me you've learned a valuable lesson."

"Landon, no one here holds this against you any longer," Blaine said, " you must forgive yourself."

"That's right Landon," Ashton said, "none of us could stand before God if He kept a record of our wrongs."

"I'm so glad to hear it," Landon said.

"Your father was the most gracious, loving man I'd ever known," the king reassured, placing his gloved hand on Landon's shoulder. "His love and admiration for nature and mankind is why he'll never be forgotten today, *or ever*.

"As to the wrongs you've committed, Landon, I believe we should all take to heart the wisdom Princess Pearlensia has shared and begin anew. What's important is that we complete our work here on earth so that we will live forever when the swords of our warfare are placed over our mortal bodies."

"Thank you, My King," Landon said, resolved and bowing.

The king smiled, took hold of his horse's reins and said merrily, "It's time to celebrate Chanson's return. I think laughter and good food is what we all need!"

"I'm ready—let's go home!" Chanson said.

"After you, Chanson—lead us out!" the king said.

As the men were about to charge back to the castle, they witnessed another unexpected mystery. The sun increased with intensity and lit the emerald forest, illuminating the trees, evergreens, and dappling on all the animals stirring about. The limbs swayed with a susurrous rustle, drowsy and dreamy.

"My King, look, the trees have all lined along our path—their leaves returning as if Spring has arrived, and yet, the earth beneath our feet is still covered with snow. Have you ever seen trees do that?" Blaine said, his eyes scanning the faces of his comrades glowing in brilliant light.

"I have not," the king said, awe-struck. "I've seen many a tree sway in the breezes of Spring, and their fresh leaves shimmering in the Summer, but never in a line clapping their branches!"

"And look, Your Majesty," Ashton said, "white rose buds . . . the petals are opening before our eyes!"

"Amazing expressions of our God," the king said. "I've never seen that flower growing in the forest before. I've admired roses as far back as my youth when Father planted them for Mother. These blossoms have eluded even my sight; striking and lit with brilliance by their budding center. This old heart of mine is impressed."

"And my heart too," Chanson said. "The chords of our dear Lord's spirit beat vibrantly within me. All that I've seen, heard, and experienced over these past few hours couldn't be captured with quill and rhyme. I've been changed by the tapestries the Creator has painted."

Chanson's eyes welled in tears as did all the warriors', marveled by God's handiwork.

"We've all been changed by God's love," Ashton said.

"Gentlemen, the magnificent breath of God is in our midst, of this I am certain! And now His protection will see us home. I'm ready to go!" the king said.

The warriors proceeded ahead, the tree's crowns cheering them all the way through Oakhollow Forest. The events King Sainesbury and the others experienced in Oakhollow Forest and the Isle of Wisteria remained with them, closing the wounds of the past while igniting a stronger bond of love between them. They lived the rest of their lives choosing to remain in the circle of God's light.

The End

Praise for *The King's Son*

The King's Son is a masterpiece; a page turner that will leave readers spellbound. The protagonist, Chanson Westbrook, is beset by many obstacles, plots, and twists but he rises above them all in this outstanding adventure set in the 1400's. Excellent writing by Teresa Ann Winton! All of her books are wonderful, but this one surpasses them all!

—Reva Vandenboss
Battle Creek, Michigan

I was hooked from the first chapter until the last while reading this latest gem by Teresa Ann Winton. She hypnotized me with the plots, twists, turns, and emotionally driven scenes. I sobbed and wiped away tears, becoming more and more engrossed in this powerful story of love, loss, and spiritual awakening. The novel's ending was moving and beautifully written. It's the kind of ending you long to find as a reader; rewarding and enriching. The final moments of *The King's Son* left me sad not wanting to leave Evernora or the beautiful people who lived there. I wished for a world like the Isle of Wisteria; where I could go and recapture moments with my father. If a land like Evernora existed today, I'd be the first to move there and make it my new home.

—Laurie Norton
Johnson City, Tennessee

Teresa Ann Winton has written a beautiful story of love and faith. *The King's Son* had me spellbound from the moment I started reading; I laughed and I cried. Chanson Westbrook lost all those he loved, but through it all he maintained his faith and love for God. His new family and friends helped him to overcome obstacles while loving and encouraging him to succeed. I am rating this book with 5 stars!

—Debbie Miller
Avid reader of medieval books
Johnson City, Tennessee

Acknowledgments

First and foremost, I'd like to thank God, my Father, for His tender mercies and love. I thank Him for giving me the power of His spirit who has enabled me to persevere through loss and hardship. I praise Him for sculpting beauty and blessings in my life and the reassurance of His Eternal love.

Also an appreciation goes to Ian, for your insight and the endless revisions you helped critique. The journey to making this book structurally stronger with realistic characters and dialogue could not have happened without your conceptual editing. Your keen eye for detail helped me to banish plot holes and purple pose before they were published for the entire world to read. Mom thanks you! Even though my name appears as the author, this beautiful story and the significant contributions you made are yours too!

Thank you, my family and friends who believed in me when I was tired, discouraged, and struggling through writer's block. Your unfailing kindness and generosity inspired me to finish this book despite all the setbacks.

Thank you, Valentina, for the beautiful and original work you've done on the illustrations and cover of my book. Communicating what I wanted was so easy given your enormous talent and gift of lyrical drawing. You're not only a professional whose creations take my breath away, but also a kindred spirit!

Thank you, my wonderful fans for buying my books and remaining loyal readers through the highs and lows of my writing career.

It is my hope that as *The King's Son* is read, inspiration will flourish on the pages, leaving an impression on the heart. May we all strive to live as legends of spirituality, love, and hope.

About The Author

Raised in Kentucky and taken from her parents at age eight, Teresa Ann Winton was placed in foster care for the duration of her childhood until she went to Florida College. She continued her education at Western Kentucky University where she studied early childhood education. Teresa has also studied fashion tailoring, interior design, ballet, nutrition, and homeopathic medicines.

Her first published book, *Pieces of the Pearl*, chronicles her life as a foster child, where she gives a candid view into her life as a vulnerable and abandoned child. In spite of the abuse, poverty, and neglect, she persevered through the devastation, refusing to succumb to despair.

Teresa has used her past as insight to help inspire and encourage others who have survived backgrounds similar to her own. She has counseled and helped several teen girls, specifically becoming an appointed mentor for one of those she has helped.

Additionally, Teresa has also published *Tears in the Lilies*, *Two Tears of a Heart*, *Impressions of Eternal Love*, and poetry at Crossway Publications.

Teresa Ann Winton can be contacted on Facebook or Twitter (@GibsonGirlPoet):

Facebook

Twitter

www.ingramcontent.com/pod-product-compliance
Lightning Source LLC
Chambersburg PA
CBHW071737110726
47908CB00006B/1615
9781734462708